THE DONOVANS
Volume 3

A.C. Arthur

AN ARTISTRY PUBLISHING BOOK

Cover Art by Octopi Covers

Interior format by The Killion Group
http://thekilliongroupinc.com

WRAPPED
IN A
DONOVAN

A.C. Arthur

DEAR READER,

So now you know the history between Roslyn Ausby and two of the Senior Donovans. You also know about her son, Dane, and his hatred for the Donovans. I would like to take this moment to tell you something else…this book ends with a cliffhanger.

As I stated in the previous Donovan series book, my plan for the duration of this series is to delve deeper into the heart of this family, the six brothers that set out to continue the legacy their father and grandfather began. The Senior Donovans are about to face their past and deal with the consequences that may jeopardize their future. While, the current generation of Donovans continue to find love, they'll also discover that things and people they thought they knew, might not be who and what they believed.

Please know that I am not trying to get over on anyone, most definitely not my loyal and supportive readers. I am giving advanced notice that the upcoming Donovan books (*Embraced by A Donovan, Wrapped in A Donovan, In The Arms of A Donovan, Falling For A Donovan, & Destiny of A Donovan*) will be interconnected by an ongoing plot line. Am I doing this to insure you buy the next five books? No. I'm doing this because I want to show just how decisions that were thought to be made for the best of everyone involved in the past, sometimes come back to haunt them again in the future. I want to take my time in exploring the effects of these decisions on the entire family, not just one or two of the Seniors and maybe a couple of the children and I do not feel that this can be done in one book. So for those of you who do not like cliffhangers—I'll apologize now. For others who want to find out how the Donovans really came to be who and what they are now, stay tuned it's going to be a bumpy, but exciting ride!

As always, happy reading
AC

NOTE: This book is #12 in a series. While it may not be necessary to read each book that has come before this one, it is recommended that HEART OF A DONOVAN and EMBRACED BY A DONOVAN be read before reading this book, as there is a continuing plot in each of these stories.

PROLOGUE

Sunday
38 Years Ago
Las Vegas, Nevada

"Well, looks like we're stuck at the airport for the night," Bernard Donovan said, dropping his carry-on bag down beside the barstool he then slid onto.

Beside him, the woman with the long, curly hair signaled to the bartender for another drink. He'd been watching her from across the bar twenty minutes ago, before they'd both gotten up and went to gate number 5 with the intention of boarding their plane. He was returning to Seattle after visiting with his brothers, Henry, Everette, Al, Reggie and Bruce. Henry was getting married in six weeks and they were all going to be his groomsmen, so they'd met in Las Vegas where the wedding was taking place to get fitted for their tuxedos and to plan the massive bachelor party they were going to throw for him.

Bernard was booked on the ten thirty flight to Seattle where he had business meetings scheduled. His marketing firm was just getting off the ground and he had back-to-back meetings scheduled with an up and coming internet and coffee house chain tomorrow at noon. The ten thirty flight had been postponed to five in the morning. So it looked like he'd be staying at the hotel across the street from the airport instead of traveling all the way back to Henry's house. The woman from earlier, the one with the curvy and attractive body, was also back in the bar.

"Looks that way," she replied, sparing him a quick glance before going into her purse to pull out the money for her drink, he suspected.

"I'll get this round," he said, touching a hand to her wrist to still her movements.

When she didn't pull quickly away, but looked over to him again, Bernard figured he had a shot. She had a pretty face, a little heavy on the make-up, but he could work with that. Besides, he wasn't looking for anything beyond the drinks, or maybe a shared room for the night.

"Why? You don't think I can pay for my own drinks?" she asked, the right side of her mouth tilting into a smile.

Her hair draped down, covering just part of her face, but it looked soft and her voice was sexy, like those he'd heard during the private parties some of his friends held back in Seattle. Bernard considered himself a virile man, with needs and desires that he knew his name and bank account had contributed to. His brothers thought he was a bit too free in his exploits with women, that at twenty years old and having just graduated from college, and starting his own business, he should be calming down a bit more. Bernard begged to differ. To him, his life was just getting started, the life he wanted to lead, and not the one anybody had laid out for him. Hence the reason he hadn't gone to work at Donovan Oilwell in Houston or at the branch Henry had started up in Vegas. He did not want to be like his brothers, or his father and uncle before him. Bernard wanted to be his own man, smart, rich, happy and on his own terms.

It just so happened that women played heavily into that equation.

"I'm sure you can pay for whatever it is you want," he told her. "But I'm also certain that I'd like to buy you a drink and maybe move over there to that booth to get to know you a little better."

She'd tilted her head, staring at him for a few seconds. Sizing him up, Bernard thought. He'd considered poking out his chest a little more—he'd been working out but his body had always been more on the beefy side than the toned build Henry and Al possessed. None of that matter because he also had the dark chocolate complexion of his father and the wavy black hair and brown "bedroom" eyes from his mother. His clothes were expensive—jeans, a button down navy blue shirt, black jacket and suede tie-ups. After all, image was everything, as his father had always said.

"You know what?" she'd replied after a few seconds more. "I think that sounds like a wonderful idea."

Two hours later Bernard was lying on his back and she was riding him hard and fast. Her hair fell over her shoulders, curls dancing over her high breasts as he reached up to tweak her dark nipples. She moved like she was on a mission, to pull every drop of release from him as fast as she could. He didn't bother to tell her that he was known for his longevity, just figured he'd let her go as long as she could before he finally brought it home for the both of them.

They'd come over to the hotel, going into the room the airline had booked in his name after two more drinks and a plate of hot wings. As soon as the elevator doors had closed she'd been on him, pressing him back against the wall, cupping his dick in one hand, reaching up to place the other to the back of his neck before bringing his mouth down to hers. In the room, he'd barely gotten the door closed and locked before she was pushing his jacket off his shoulders. Game for whatever, Bernard began unbuttoning his shirt.

"Take that off," he said nodding to the red dress she'd been wearing.

She stepped out of her heels slowly, keeping her gaze on him as she reached behind to unzip her dress. When the material fell to the floor Bernard was unbuckling his belt, staring at her small waist, the curve of her hips and breasts that just about fell out of the lacy excuse for a bra she wore. After taking off his shoes he'd been about to push his pants down when he reached for his wallet, dug inside and pulled out a condom. She was there in seconds, standing in front of him as he'd sat on the side of the bed, taking the condom packet slowly from his fingers.

"Let me do this for you," she told him.

He heard her ripping the package open as he removed his jeans and boxers, then returned to the bed, wrapping an arm around her waist and pulling her between his legs. She'd stepped up to him with a sexy sway of her hips, moaning when he kissed her navel. He reached up and grabbed her tits. In the next seconds she'd pushed him back on the bed, taking his mouth in a scorching hot kiss as she straddled him. Bernard grabbed the heavy globes of her ass, squeezing and moaning with delight as she slid her core down over his rigid length.

And then she rode.

And he moaned and swore and loved every second of the deep, hot thrusts. She was wet and eager and he was feeling his buzz after three vodkas on the rocks, four if he included the one he'd had before the plane had been delayed. When she'd dropped down over him, her hair tickling his face, he'd figured she'd run out of steam.

"I got you," he'd told her, grabbing her by the waist and turning her over, lifting her legs before diving back into her waiting heat.

It was his time to ride and he'd done so until his body had trembled with his release, her thighs shaking with hers.

Afterwards, Bernard had gone into the bathroom alone to clean himself up. Now sated and still buzzed, he was ready to get some sleep. Going back out into the room he set his watch to wake him up at three-thirty so they could get back over to the airport in time to wait for their flight. Then he fell face first on the bed, sleep quickly claiming him.

"Good morning, Bernard," she said from the chair where she sat fully dressed across from the bed.

He'd just rolled over, his watch in his hand as he'd just stopped the alarm and was contemplating if he had a few more minutes to lay there while his head continued to throb.

Bernard turned to her, his eyes cracking open, the sight of her coming slowly into view. He hadn't told her his name. In fact, they hadn't exchanged any of the typical information a man and a woman probably should before having sex.

Yet she knew. He frowned then, not just because of the name thing, but because her long, curly hair was gone. It had been replaced by a shorter cut, lying flat against her head in an auburn color. Her make-up was much lighter than before, he could easily see that with the light from the lamp on the nightstand glaring down at them. Bernard sat up in bed, staring at her more closely then.

"Ah, I see it's all coming back to you," she said, a big grin spreading slowly across her face. "Not the fun we had just a few hours ago in this bed, but well before that. Like three years ago, that's the last time we saw each other." She nodded and chuckled a little. "Yeah, you definitely remember now."

"Roslyn Ausby," Bernard said with a sickening clench to his gut. "You gold-digging bitch!"

CHAPTER 1

Present Day
Miami, Florida

"This is not what I expected," Savian Donovan said with a frown, his hands hastily moving to unbutton his shirt.

"You mean you didn't expect to be attracted to a full-figured woman with brains and beauty to match?" Jenise Langley asked, as she stood staring at him, wearing only her nightgown.

It was black satin, hugging her heavy breasts then flaring out past her full hips and thighs. She was right in that she was full-figured, Savian thought as he lay his shirt on the back of one of the two armchairs she had at the foot of her queen sized bed. Yet that wasn't how he'd thought of her these past weeks. Actually, it had been more like three months since he'd begun sleeping with Jenise, his attorney.

The first time had happened only hours after he'd met her. He'd left her office in the high-rise building on Brickell Avenue, not at all sure she was the right attorney to handle the case between his older brother Parker and his now fiancé Adriana Bennett. That had been an identity theft and libel case. Now, Jenise was handling a murder case. Only then, Savian hadn't known he would need representation.

All he'd known was that there was something about this woman that had rubbed him the wrong way. As Savian wasn't the most sociable of Reginald and Carolyn's children—or a good majority of the Donovan family as a whole—he would have normally taken that slight alarm as his second nature and ignored it just the same. But hours later, after he'd left her office and returned to his own to try and get some work done, she'd still been on his mind.

When he'd leaned back in his office chair, closing his eyes and squeezing the bridge of his nose, he hadn't felt relief. Instead it had been more like concern because the second his eyes had closed a vision of her sitting behind her desk in that prim and proper, yet sexy as hell black business suit, formulated in his mind. For the duration of the work day he'd tried to convince himself he was simply tired and that maybe a couple hours of weights and cardio in his home gym, a hot shower and a bottle of wine would make things better.

He'd never even gotten that far.

Savian had pulled up in front of that office building with those turquoise colored windows for the second time in one day. He'd gotten out of his car and took the elevator up to her office. It was well after six in the evening but something told him she would still be there. She was, but her secretary was just leaving for the day.

"I can make an appointment for you for tomorrow, Mr. Donovan," the tall, slim woman with the too-short skirt had advised.

"It's alright, Gwen," Jenise said as she'd approached from the hallway where her office was. "I'll talk to Mr. Donovan and I'll see you in the morning."

She'd smiled at her secretary, a wide and totally sincere smile that showed lots of teeth and lifted her already high cheekbones. The action made her look different. Enough so that Savian frowned.

"Did you come here to scowl at me one more time, Mr. Donovan? Wasn't sitting across from me for forty minutes looking as if you'd rather jump off the roof of this building enough?" she'd asked once her secretary had gone through the glass office doors and they stood alone in the lobby.

"I don't know why I'm here," he'd replied and hated hearing the words.

Savian always knew what he was doing. He always knew what he wanted and how to get it. There was never a time in his entire life that he'd been unsure, or uncertain, or even confused. Never...until now.

"If it's not about your brother's case, then it's pointless. We obviously do not like each other and—" she'd been saying.

Savian did not want to hear anymore. He did not want to stand there with the strange and unknown feelings hanging over him like a dark cloud. In that instant he'd decided what he wanted and he'd taken the steps to close the distance between them so he could get it. With one arm going around her waist, he'd pulled her to him just as her words had drifted off. For what seemed like endless seconds he looked into her dark brown eyes, waiting for an answer, a reply, a rebuff, something to stop what he knew was about to happen. It never came.

Instead, his lips touched hers. Her mouth opened instantly. His tongue slipped inside. Her arms went around his neck. His tongue slid sinuously over hers. His other hand went to the nape of her neck. And before either one of them could think better of their actions, Jenise's back was up against the lobby wall, and Savian had unzipped his pants. He quickly sheathed his throbbing shaft, pushed up her skirt and thrust his thick erection deep inside of her.

As crazy as it was totally satisfying, that had been the beginning of the hottest and most delectable sex Savian had experienced in all his years. That, he told himself repeatedly, was why he kept coming back.

"I don't see a full-figured woman," he'd told her when he was completely naked and his mind was once again in the here and now.

"Oh really?" she'd asked with an arch of her brow as she moved to lay across the white comforter on her bed. "Then what do you see, Savian? What do you see on the nights you come to my apartment and enter my bedroom?"

He licked his lips and let his gaze run the length of her five foot, eight-inch tall frame. It had never occurred to him to lie, that just wasn't in his nature. What he said to women and what he did with them would always be in truth and with full disclosure. Savian did not operate any other way.

"I see my pleasure," he told her simply.

Savian knew the moment he lay on that bed with her that everything that was going on in his real world—the Donovan name appearing on every tabloid, gossip news show and local news broadcasts, the murder investigation, and whatever the hell was going on between his father and uncles—would disappear. There would be nothing but her, nothing but their combined pleasure and that's what he wanted most. That's what kept him coming back.

He climbed onto the bed, lying directly across from her, propping himself up on an elbow.

"I need that pleasure, Jenise," he whispered hoarsely. "I need it right now."

She'd smiled at him then. Not that happy smile that lit up her dark eyes and almost made Savian want to smile at whatever it was in response. No, this was that sexy half smile, the one that promised him everything and then some. It was the one he dreamed about and longed to see throughout the long work hours of the day.

He'd moved closer to her then, touching his palm to one full breast and squeezing lightly. He loved the feel of her in his hands, the heaviness of each globe, coupled with the softness of her skin. With quick movements he pushed the thin lacy cups of material away from her breasts and palmed her again. She arched her back to give him better access and Savian ducked his head down to lick one dark puckered nipple.

Jenise held his head tightly to her bosom, an action Savian adored. With her soft flesh surrounding his face, he inhaled the sweet scent of the soap she used, opening his mouth wider to gorge on her tender flesh. She didn't whisper his name, but moaned with the pleasure she received from his ministrations. They didn't talk much during sex, both of them too engrossed in the simple bliss of the act, Savian supposed.

With that in mind he reluctantly tore his mouth away from her generous breasts and shifted positions so that she was now lying on her stomach and he was straddling her. Today had been a particularly stressful day with the latest headlines and his cousin Dion calling an emergency meeting first thing tomorrow morning. Savian knew that he needed to unwind tonight. That's why he'd left the office an hour early, sending Jenise a text message that he was on his way. Savian had known without a doubt that she'd be right here waiting for him, like a savior.

He ripped the nightgown away from her body, resigning himself to having to replace it later. Beneath him she'd made a sound but he was certain it wasn't in dispute to his actions. Her fingers gripped the comforter and her head turned to the side. For endless moments Savian stared down at Jenise's back, to the tattoo she had going down her spine. Each time he saw it, Savian was compelled to touch it, thinking long and hard on what it said and how close to his own way of thinking it was.

Alis Volat Propriis written in a swirling script font and surrounded on each end by a spread winged red robin. It was Latin for 'she who flies with her own wings'. Savian's fingers tingled as he grazed over the first robin, then slid gently down to touch the second. Jenise moaned. She always did. He enjoyed that sound, much more than he figured he should have.

Averting his hands and attention to the plump globes of her ass, Savian rubbed and squeezed until his erection grew harder and more painful. With a whispered curse, he moved back a bit until he could reach his pants that he'd thrown over the side of the chair. He wasn't a fan of the way she had her furniture set up in here, but had to thank the heavens the chair and his pants were so convenient because he didn't think he could wait another moment before sinking inside of her.

Seconds after he was sheathed Savian was between Jenise's legs, loving the softness of her thick thighs, recalling how it felt to have them tightly tucked around him as he worked himself inside deeper. He lifted her hips from the bed, spreading her until he could watch the tender folds of her vagina open and then positioned himself right there. On a ragged moan from him and a blissful sigh from her, Savian pressed into her until he was buried to the hilt.

Jenise clutched the sheets even tighter as he began to move. Savian let his head fall back, eyes closed, his fingers gripping her by the waist as he pumped in and out. This was everything Savian needed to remain calm in the disastrous situation he found himself in. With each stroke he let go of a little more stress, relaxing into the damp warmth of her body.

The sound of his groin slapping rhythmically against the generous globes of her ass filled his ears and had tendrils of pleasure sliding down his spine. This felt so good. Here, inside of her felt so sublime, it almost felt…right.

Savian opened his eyes in that moment, hoping to get rid of that thought with a blast of reality. He was riding her from behind, a position he'd grown to favor with her because it gave him deeper access and because he enjoyed watching her ass as he took her. He was so completely inside of her now, enjoying how wet and eager for him she always was. She gave him so much and yet, at the same time, they both gave so little.

This was okay because there was nothing deep here, nothing beyond these moments of pure physical pleasure. He needed this release and so did she. While he was certain they both had pasts, that had shaped the adults they eventually became, he never offered any details of his and neither did Jenise. It was the first bit of equal footing Savian had discovered about them, all they concerned themselves with was the here and now.

For him, Jenise was the lawyer that was being paid to clear his name and the woman that was fulfilling a sexual need. Savian had no idea specifically what he was doing for her, besides the pleasure, and he refused to think beyond that point. It was simpler that way and would make for a cleaner break when the time came. It was what they both wanted, what they'd silently agreed upon. It was the way things had to be.

Things were getting out of hand.

Jenise knew it and still she closed her eyes again and let the feel of Savian so thick and hard and fully inside of her, take over. On impulse, she'd pulled away from him turning over and spreading her legs once again in welcome. She'd wanted to see him tonight. With her eyes wide open she saw his slight pause and then sighed with glee as he held his shaft at the base and guided his length to her waiting center once more. It felt so good when he began stroking in and out of her that she'd lifted her hands to cup her own breasts, loving the multiple spikes of pleasure shooting throughout her body.

The feel of him pushing her hands away from her breasts, his body leaning in closer so that while one of his hands took over kneading the now sensitive mounds, his mouth could minister to the other. He touched and kissed her breasts like he adored them.

It was two-fold, she thought as her hands went to the back of his head, holding him in place as she arched her back.

Jenise was no stranger to good sex. She'd had lovers before and she knew how to give herself pleasure when need be. This wasn't new. Well, on one hand it was. She'd never had an affair with a client, had never let that thought enter her mind. Long ago she'd sworn against such tricky situations that could end up disastrously, as they had before. She'd been so intent on that goal that no one, not one single man that she'd met in the eight years she'd been practicing law, the last one here in Miami, had even remotely appealed to her, on any personal level. Every date, every sex partner had been in a totally different career than her, and of the same mindset that the relationship was casual and could end at any time.

That was the way she preferred to operate. It was the way things had to be in her mind, to keep the last shreds of her sanity she had in place. This plan had worked for her, until three months ago, when Savian Donovan had walked into her office.

He'd looked at her as if there was nothing from her head to her toes that he liked or approved of. That was the first time she'd seen him. When he'd shown up in her office again, later that same day, she'd been surprised to see him. She'd been even more surprised about how that visit had ended.

They'd had sex in the lobby of her law firm—the only branch of Langley Law in Miami. The firm she was solely in charge of on a trial basis, against her parents' wishes. She was just a woman after all and while it was commendable that she'd been the first Langley daughter to follow her father and grandfather into the field of law, the belief was still that she'd continue to work at the main branch of their firm in Chicago until she was married. Once she found the perfect husband, there would be no time for work. Children would come next because continuing the Langley bloodline was of utmost importance. It was the only thing her parents had ever really expected of her and her younger sister Morgan.

"You'll both marry well," Marianne Langley had told her daughters when they were teenagers. "You'll make your father and me very proud."

Jenise wanted them to be proud of her for graduating cum laude and receiving a BA in Sociology from the University of Chicago. While they were at it, they could also manage to feel some semblance of pride in the fact that she'd also graduated in the top five percent of her class at the University of Chicago Law School. She wanted them to acknowledge that she was just as good a lawyer as the men in their family and that she was doing the right thing by expanding the firm that her grandparents' started on the heels of the Civil Rights Movement.

At the same time Jenise understood that approval might never come. She also knew that with or without it she planned to continue on, to create her own legacy if need be. To do that she had to remain focused, and not get caught up the way she had before. Caught up and almost destroyed.

When Savian's clever mouth moved down her torso, kissing her navel, as he'd pulled out of her and now stroked her clit until her thighs convulsed, she cried out in ecstasy. The foggy sense of floating through an abyss of pleasure comforted her and muddled the painful thoughts of her past so that they mixed with those of her reality. In seconds, her entire body was shaking, her fingers gripping the comforter once more as her release ripped through every pore of her body.

Her eyes were still closed but she knew he was watching her, knew he liked to watch her when she came. She'd looked at him one time, saw how intensely dark his eyes became. When she'd first met Savian and Parker Donovan she'd immediately noted the differences between these brothers. Parker was of a darker complexion and had an athletic build that wore his designer suits well. He was also the more laid back brother, the one who smiled and charmed. While Savian's complexion was lighter, like perfect caramel, his build was broader, his suit custom-cut and made to accentuate how totally fine he was. Their eyes were startling but Jenise had recognized immediately that Parker's were lighter and brasher against his dark skin. Savian's on the other hand, while still green but filled with darker brown and gray flecks that made him look more ominous and to her chagrin, sexier, gave him a steadier, more intense look. When he watched her come, his eyes grew even darker, his mouth partially open, and body perfectly still.

At six feet, three and a half inches tall, he always looked down at her when they stood. Lying down, his sculpted body—thanks to the hours she now knew he spent working out—lay perfectly aligned with hers, flanking her with a sense of strength and power she'd never experienced before. Not that she needed to feel anyone's strength or power, because she had enough of her own. Still, she had to admit she liked it. She liked it a lot.

He was, once again, turning her over, rubbing his hands over her ass as she came up on her knees and again arched her back. Even though she'd desperately wanted to see him take his pleasure this time, Jenise knew that Savian liked taking her from behind. He always ran his fingers up and down her spine, pressing his palm at the base of her back to see if he could get her to arch a little more. She also sensed that he liked looking at her tattoo, even though he never said a word about it since the first time he'd asked, "What's this for?"

Apparently, he'd already known what it said and while she'd been a little surprised at that fact, Jenise had replied honestly, "It means I do what I want, not what is expected or demanded of me. My life. My choice."

Savian had nodded his response as if he understood, even though he'd never said those words exactly.

She sighed when his fingers brushed slowly down her spine while his thick, hot length, poked persistently at her bottom. He found his target in no time, finally sinking into her waiting heat. Jenise could think of nothing else at this point—only the way he expertly stroked her, pulling out and then sinking in once more. It was a delicious sensation that rippled through her body like a fine wine after a long day's work. No, it was so much better than that, so much more addicting.

That's precisely what Jenise was afraid had been happening. She was becoming addicted to Savian Donovan.

He stilled over her at that moment. His fingers gripping her waist tightly. His moan came next, long and slow, as if the sound itself omitted some sort of relief. Very much needed and coveted relief, at that. Jenise's eyes were wide open at this point, her gaze fixated on her headboard since she couldn't see him. That was most likely his plan, she'd thought long ago, because this was how their sexual escapades always ended. No matter which position they started in, or the others they enjoyed throughout the session, it always ended this way. Savian would find his release from behind her. He would then pull slowly out of her and offer to help her to the bathroom.

There were no shared showers. No holding or cuddling. No words of endearment or promises of a next time.

Jenise knew the drill, and after a few seconds when she felt him moving off the bed, she moved as well. When she stood she was on the opposite side of her bed, looking up just in time to see Savian's gloriously naked body standing at the chair where he'd dropped his clothes.

"You can have the bathroom first," she offered this time, but knew he would decline.

"I'll just use the guest one out here," he said, dropping his clothes over his arm and ready to turn and walk out of the room.

"That's fine," she said. "I'll be out in a moment."

She moved a little faster than normal, wanting to get away from him sooner than she ever had before. Once she was in her bathroom with the door closed securely behind her, Jenise leaned against it. She closed her eyes and cursed softly.

She didn't want to get away from Savian. What she really wanted was to lay in her bed curled in his arms and ask him how his day went. He was stressed, she could see it the moment he walked into her apartment. Then again, that had been Savian's look since the first day he met her. Still, she knew the ongoing murder investigation was weighing heavily on him. It was her job, as his attorney, to assure him that she would take care of his legal troubles, and she was confident that she could. But there was more. In the past weeks she'd seen the worry in his eyes, the heaviness of his shoulders each time they were together. That was the real reason he was here tonight.

It was the reason every night he showed up.

She was his release, his safe haven so to speak. Jenise knew that and at first she hadn't minded at all. As she preferred, Savian was good at the "friends with benefits" theme. He didn't ask questions, didn't give any unnecessary information and didn't intrude. He requested her time, at the very least, hours in advance and whenever—which in the past weeks had grown even less frequently—she needed to reschedule or cancel, he'd been understanding. Their arrangement had been perfect.

It *had* been.

"I need to get going," he'd said after a soft knock on the bathroom door.

Jenise had jerked away from the door for fear he'd somehow known she'd been standing there thinking about him and what she might be beginning to feel.

"Ah, oh okay," she said grabbing her robe from the hook and hurriedly slipping it on. She opened the door to see him standing right there, completely dressed and ready to leave.

"Early meeting tomorrow," he said, with his brow furrowed, his lips in a thin straight line.

"Is it something I can help with?" she asked, then immediately regretted the question as it went against every nuance of their arrangement. "I mean, is it about the case? Do you need me to speak with your family to give them an update on where the investigation is now?"

Circling back to their professional relationship, the one with the only true commitment, Jenise tied the belt at her waist tightly.

"No," he replied immediately. "I can handle my family on my own."

He could handle everything on his own, Jenise thought. He always did.

"That's good," she said with a curt nod.

They stood there for a few silent moments, the room still heavy with the scent of their sex—or was that her? Yes, she thought. She could still smell him on her skin and if she closed her eyes she would feel his hands and his mouth on her, just as it was so devilishly good only minutes before.

"It's time for me to leave," he announced, although he did not move.

Jenise cleared her throat and her mind of those pointless thoughts. There were never two times in one night, or one visit. Only one very potent and exceptionally pleasing encounter and then they went their separate ways. Every time.

"Yes," she said, more quietly than she realized. "It is."

Savian still did not move. In fact, he stood just a few feet away from her for so long Jenise had to fight the urge to close the space between them and initiate another interlude herself. That wasn't what Savian wanted. It wasn't what they'd silently agreed upon. And so, with her mind still reeling with traitorous thoughts, she said, "Good night."

Another few seconds and Savian was nodding. The light and perfectly barbered beard almost hiding that muscle that twitched on the left side of his jaw. She'd seen that before and had wanted to reach out and touch it, to possibly rub that bit of tension away. This time she thrust her hands into the pockets of her robe and gave him the smallest smile she could muster.

"Good night, Jenise," Savian said finally, before turning and leaving her standing there.

He knew his way out. He would flip the latch on her door knob to lock it before closing and walking down the hall to the elevator. From there he would ride down to the garage where he'd parked his car two levels up. Jenise had no idea if Savian knew anyone else in this building, but since the first time that she'd invited him to come here, he'd insisted on parking on another floor so as to hopefully not be seen leaving her apartment or even coming from the floor where her apartment was located. It wouldn't do for the press to find out about them sleeping together. Not the press, or his friends, or his family.

She was Savian Donovan's secret. And he was hers.

Three months ago that had made perfect sense to her.

Now…her phone rang, thankfully jerking her away from those thoughts.

"Hello?" Jenise said into the phone after retrieving it from her nightstand.

"Well, hello," her mother, Marianne Langley, replied. "It's so nice to hear my daughter's voice after so many weeks."

Jenise closed her eyes and took a deep breath, trying to recalibrate her patience. This was always a required act when speaking to her mother, or her father, or one of her older brothers. It was only those calls received or made to her younger sister Morgan that had the relaxed and familiar tone that should be had with family.

"Hi, mom," was her response. She opened her eyes and moved to take a seat in the chair opposite the one where Savian's clothes had been.

In fact, she looked away from that chair altogether.

"And that's all I get is a 'hi mom'. This is exactly why you shouldn't have moved so far away from home. You're losing all your manners down there."

Marianne Langley spoke in the crisp tone she thought would keep her daughters in line. Only Jenise and Morgan had always been the insubordinate ones in their family. They'd been bucking against their parents' strict rules and regimens for them ever since they learned to talk. There was no sense in stopping now, Jenise thought with another sigh.

"How are you, mom? How's dad? And Gramps and Nana?" she continued, without addressing her mother's sarcasm.

"Your grandparents are in Italy. Emma finally convinced Victor they didn't need him hanging around the firm looking to find something wrong. Your father has been running that firm expertly for too many years to count now and your brothers are holding their own there as well. Langley Law is thriving just as it always has been."

All of this was said with pride and enthusiasm because Langley Law Chicago and Bradford Langley were the sun, the moon, and everything in between to Marianne.

"Langley Law Miami is also doing well," Jenise said because she knew her mother would never ask. "Referrals are bringing in more clients. I may have to hire an associate in the next few months to help with the litigation workload, although I try to settle as many of those as I can. Some of the larger malpractice claims are going to take more of my time and attention. And I have a couple of criminal cases that may go to trial."

Her gaze had wandered back to that chair, then to the door where Savian had walked through. She shook her head.

"I knew Wade should have been the one to go down there," her mother said. "I tried to tell your father."

"And I told both of you that I wanted this opportunity to manage the firm on my own. I don't need Wade to come down here. I'll hire associates, just like Dad does at the Chicago firm. That's what managing partners do," Jenise snapped.

"Well, it shouldn't be all your responsibility. That's all I'm saying. All that working takes too much of your time. When's the last time you've been out on a date? I haven't heard anything about a man in your life."

No, Jenise thought. Nobody had.

"That's not important," she said, her mind begging to differ with that comment.

"It is important," Marianne argued. "A woman your age should be happily married and having children by now. The clock keeps on ticking regardless of how many cases there are to be tried."

"I'm only thirty, not sixty, mom," Jenise countered. "Besides, there is more to life for a woman than finding a man and having his babies."

That shut Marianne up as surely as if Jenise had hung the phone up on her instead. Then, came that wave of guilt that never failed to assail Jenise when she'd done what she felt like she had to with her mother.

"I know it's what worked for you, mom. I just think I was made to be different," Jenise added in a much more amiable tone.

"You strive to be contrary, you always have. And it's rubbed off on your sister. No matter how I've tried to give you two the best of everything, and to teach you all that I know, you insist on going in the opposite direction."

"Did it ever occur to you that it might be the direction we're meant to go in? I mean, not everyone is created the same," she continued the same old argument with her mother.

It was pointless, Jenise knew. Marianne had been born and bred to be a wife and mother. Her mother had taught her just as Marianne tried to teach her daughters. It was her only goal in life and she'd achieved it in spades by marrying into one of Chicago's most affluent black families. Now, Marianne hoped to make the same advantageous love connections for her daughters, if only they would cooperate.

"You need a man to take care of you so you don't work yourself to the bone."

"I need to stand on my own two feet and to know without a doubt that I can take care of myself. That is more important to me than any husband or baby."

"It does not keep you warm at night," Marianne rebutted.

"And neither does dad because you're in bed most nights before he returns from work."

The silence fell like a gavel in a courtroom and Jenise instantly regretted her words.

"Look, mom, I love you for all that you've done for me and I appreciate your care and efforts. I'm just saying that this is the life I want to lead right now and I'd really appreciate it if you could find a way to respect that."

"I don't like it," Marianne said finally.

"I know," Jenise agreed.

"Your father wants to talk to you about work. Call him sometime tomorrow so he doesn't continue to worry," her mother said after that, her tone indicating she was finished discussing the disappointment of Jenise's life goals for the moment.

"I will."

"Get some rest," Marianne continued. "You sound tired and irritable. You probably have bags under your eyes too. Boil some tea bags and put them on before you go to sleep. Are you eating healthy? Did you get the juicer I sent to you last week?"

Jenise took another deep breath and slowly exhaled. Marianne's other big disappointment in her oldest daughter was that she was overweight.

"I did get the juicer but have absolutely no appetite for pureed vegetables and/or fruit. But you'll be happy to know that I received a clean bill of health at my last physical," Jenise reported.

"Oh that's good. What was your weight? Has it gone down?" Marianne asked in a much brighter tone.

"It's exactly the same," Jenise replied thinking of the lovely sage green dress she'd purchased just after her doctor's appointment in celebration of that fact.

When she'd entered law school Jenise had been a size twenty. By the time she'd graduated she'd gone up to a size twenty-four, causing her mother much worry. But in the years since then and after claiming her own peace and developing an appreciation for herself that she never had before, she was able to come down to a size eighteen. That's where she'd been for the last three years and Jenise had discovered it was where she was the happiest. She loved herself, her life and her size and didn't care who didn't.

"I'm fine, mom. I know what to eat and I know what I like. There's no need for you to worry." Even though she knew Marianne would, especially since she was convinced that Jenise's size had something to do with why she wasn't getting a good man to offer a proposal.

That thought had Jenise wondering once more about what she was doing with Savian and how smart it was to continue. Savian Donovan was not going to ask her to marry him. Hell, Jenise didn't want to marry Savian Donovan. The sex was good and she wouldn't mind spending a night or two with him, or having a real conversation with him for that matter, but marriage? Hell no, that wasn't on either of their agendas and she was glad of that fact.

After a few more familiar exchanges with her mother, Jenise finally managed to get her off the phone. Then it was time for her shower and afterwards she went to her home office prepared to work for an hour or so before she went to bed. Of course, the shower and work were both designed to keep her mind from circling back to where it seemed determined to go tonight. But when she opened her email box to a message from the detective assigned to the Giovanni Morelli case, she couldn't help but whisper his name once more, "Savian."

Her heart sank as she read the message knowing that this new development was going to be a hard blow to the man she was still trying to convince herself she wasn't falling for.

CHAPTER 2

Savian was first to arrive at the meeting, as always. This wasn't the standing status meeting that was on every family member that worked for Donovan Multimedia Corporation's calendar, the last Thursday of every month. No, this was a special meeting called by Dion, and Savian had a feeling he knew exactly what it was in reference to. Another reason, besides his normal studious manner, that Savian made sure he was here before anyone else.

He walked over to one of the leather conference chairs that surrounded the ten foot long cherry oak table. Before taking his seat, Savian turned to look out the tinted windows of the Excalibur building. They were darkly tinted to ward off the intense rays of southern sunlight, and so no one could see inside. Yet, Savian could certainly see out to the city he'd grown up in. Taking a deep breath and then releasing it, he watched as the world continued to go on, as it always did, no matter what was going on in his life. That had been the one piece of solace he'd taken even when the times were rough—which, for Savian Omar Donovan, they had on so many occasions.

He didn't like to think about those times, nor did he wish to dwell on the fact that he was the cause of this special meeting. Savian would much rather focus on more pertinent business, such as the success of their family business. That had always been the highlight of Savian's life, knowing that one day he would be a complete part of what his father and uncles had started before him. While he had been blessed enough to be born into the Donovan family legacy, Savian had known early on that he would have to work just as hard as anyone else to create and maintain his place within the reputable family business. He'd had a pretty shaky start early on in life, but he liked to think that he'd grown into his own here at the company. He was proud of that fact, if nothing else.

The Donovan Multimedia Corporation was founded by two of the senior Donovans, Bruce and Reginald. Bruce's sons, Dion and Sean, worked primarily in the print division, where Dion was editor in chief and Sean was managing editor of *Infinity* Magazine, a steadily growing African American publication focusing on up and coming African American businesses, entertainers and the overall movers and shakers in their community. Jaydon Donovan, Parker's ex-wife, used to be the director of Donovan Management Network, which employed over one hundred literary, sports and talent agents. She'd resigned a few months before and they had yet to name a permanent replacement for her.

Donovan Network Television was Savian and Parker's domain, but their younger sister, Regan had recently begun to work double-duty. She continued to oversee the fashion and entertainment segments at *Infinity*, while branching into the television network with the fashion reality show her and Camille, a renowned fashion designer and their cousin, Adam's wife, had produced. Gavin Lucas, a local chef and Regan's boyfriend, now had two shows on the network that Parker produced. Regan had also begun working on Gavin's shows as they'd rapidly soared in popularity.

As for Savian, he preferred to stay out of the spotlight. He always had. Still, he had a knack for organizing and managing, as reflected by the master's degree he'd acquired from Florida State University. It had been his choice not to travel too far from home to attend one of the three Ivy League schools he'd been accepted to. His father hadn't understood, but his mother—the one who had always seemed to know him better than anyone else—had championed his choice. Now, at the tender age of thirty, he'd successfully created the entrepreneur and business spotlights at *Infinity* Magazine, while lending his business savvy to the growth and management of the television station where he'd just begun to take on the executive producing role in the news and documentary shows DNT presented. This was where

Savian belonged, in his hometown, close to his family, contributing to the legacy that was the upstanding Donovan name.

Until a couple months ago when he'd been named the top person of interest in the murder of Giovanni Morelli, the director of the number one rated show on DNT.

"Despite what you think, Savian, the early bird does not always get the worm," Regan said jovially as she entered the conference room.

Savian turned to see his younger sister's slim frame walking towards the table where she placed her cup of heavily sugared coffee no doubt, notepad and pen. With a sleek and fashionable style all of her own, Savian was not surprised to see that Regan's hair had changed since he'd seen her just two days ago. It was honey blonde today, falling in bouncy curls down the center of her back. Her make-up was flawless, highlighting her expression-filled eyes and wide and ready smile. She wore black skinny slacks, a white button front blouse and a black and white blazer held together in the front by a gold chain. Her black pumps had sky-high heels, the way he knew Regan preferred so that her normal five feet six inches was pushed easily to five feet eleven and brought her just about eye level with most of the men in this building. Regan loved to remind everyone that she was on the same level as they were, regardless of their sex.

"Maybe not," he replied with a shrug and more than a pinch of pride brimming inside at seeing how well his sister had grown up. "But it always gets me a few moments of silence before you arrive."

She cut him a quick and searing gaze that had Savian chuckling. If there were anyone in this family that could get him to smile when it was the absolute last thing he wanted to do, it was Regan.

"Well, that's over, so sit yourself down and tell me what you plan to get mom for Christmas." Regan tapped her hand on the table signaling him to sit.

She always did act as if she was the oldest of their parents' three children. Still Savian pulled out the chair he'd already set his briefcase beside, and took a seat.

"Christmas is more than six weeks away, Regan. Why on earth are you thinking about shopping now? Oh, I forgot, you're always thinking about shopping." The last was said with an inward chuckle because Savian knew it would get his sister rolling on the necessity of going out and buying things.

He supposed it had worked out well for Regan that their family was very well off financially, or she would have had a hard time keeping up with all the things she liked to buy. And honestly, Savian was glad to see that her favorite pastime had developed into a flourishing career for Regan. She was really at the top of her game in the fashion industry. It was no wonder she'd made those shows that focused on Camille's clothing line such a hit.

"First of all, shopping is an art. You'd know that if you spent some time actually planning the things you wear instead of relying on that tailor you pay a fortune to," she snapped back, then took a sip of her coffee.

"Mr. Franques is a genius. He makes the best suits and when he doesn't have something that he's made, he orders the best. There's no need for me to go shopping, when he knows my style so well."

"You might be the only one I know with a sixty-five year old stylist still working out of the same store-front after forty-five years. But I'll admit, he doesn't do a half bad job dressing you," Regan replied with a nod and an arch of her brows as she looked at what he was wearing today.

Savian didn't bother to look down. He knew the navy blue suit with double button, notched lapel jacket and vest combo looked well on him—Mr. Franques and his assistant/girlfriend Ms. Meg had said so the first time he'd tried it on. Savian liked to work out so his frame was bulkier than most businessmen that Mr. Franques dressed, but Ms. Meg was always on point in making sure that he did not get the metro and slim fit suits that were all the rage with young men now. His clothes had a fuller, yet still stylish fit. After all, as she always said with a twinkle in her eyes, "You are a Donovan."

"Anyway, she's having Christmas dinner at her house this year. Aunt Janean is doing Thanksgiving. So the plans for the holiday season are already under way, regardless of what your calendar says. Now, I have a list of some things I know she likes and hasn't had a chance to purchase for herself." Regan talked as she flipped open her tablet. "I'll email the list to you and Parker right now. We can all use it and just let each other know when we've bought something, so we won't buy the same thing."

"Leave it to you to organize a shopping list for everyone," Savian said, opening his own MacBook and pulling up the latest statistics for the studio and the magazine. A part of him was hoping this meeting was to actually discuss business.

"Good morning," Dion said as he walked into the room, touching Regan on the shoulder when he passed her and giving Savian a nod.

Parker and Sean came in next taking their seats at the table and greeting everyone. The door had been closed only a few moments before Regan said, "Where's Lyra and Tate? I thought they were coming too."

Lyra Donovan was Dion's wife and a very popular photographer. She'd trained professionally in L.A. but came back to Miami a few years ago to work at Infinity. In the time since she and Dion had been married, she'd also opened her own private studio. Tate and Sean had a beautiful daughter named Briana who kept them both on their toes when Tate wasn't taping her relationship advice show or writing the 'Ask Jenny" relationship column for *Infinity*. Savian had adored them both and watched with only mild curiosity now at the way they'd seemed to transform his cousins.

"Lyra wasn't feeling well," Dion said while taking off his suit jacket and hanging it on the back of his chair.

"And Tate's working double time to get all the episodes of the show pre-taped before the holidays. We're going to visit her family the day after Thanksgiving and will be gone for almost two weeks. Then by the time we come back it'll be Christmas. I hear Aunt Carolyn's hosting this year so we know there's going to be lots of food. And between her and my mom, Briana's going to have more toys than Santa's factory," Sean added.

"Oh that little minx has already given me a list of things she wants for Christmas," Parker added with a chuckle. "And just to forewarn you, Adriana and I plan to buy each and every item she requested. Especially the noisy ones."

Everyone laughed at Sean's immediate frown and for a moment Savian felt content. He was with his family—cousins and siblings that he'd grown up with. They'd stayed at each other's houses, gone on vacations together, got into trouble together. They were as close as he knew he ever would be to anyone else in his life. And he was letting them all down.

His jaw clenched at the thought and he said, "So, do we want to go over the current sales numbers first?"

"Ah, actually," Dion replied, his voice going somber, all semblance of the smile he'd had just moments before disappearing. "I called this meeting because I thought there was something a little more pressing we needed to discuss. Something that I knew we would want to keep just between us."

Savian sat back in his seat, his hands falling from his laptop as he inwardly sighed.

"Sean and I were very concerned about the break-in at our parents' home a few months ago," Dion started.

Parker was already shaking his head. "I don't think we can call them break-ins in the traditional sense. The incident at your parents' house and the one at our parents' house were cowardly attacks. A burglar would have simply gone inside, taken what they wanted and then left. This jackass broke all the windows and then sent that bullshit email message."

Regan was immediately alarmed. "Wait, I thought we still didn't know who sent the email. Has there been a new development?"

Savian would have sighed with relief if the reason they weren't talking about his personal situation wasn't that they were talking about the attack on his parents, aunt and uncle, instead. His frown was already in place as he recalled the night that he and Parker had received the call from the security company stating their parents' house alarm was going off. He'd arrived at Reginald and Carolyn's, house located in the Coastal Accolade's area of Biscayne Bay, as quickly as he could only to find that his mother was home alone and that all the windows on the first floor of the house had been broken, but nobody had ever entered the home.

Not an hour after this happened, Sean had received a similar call from his parents' security company, informing him that the

Big House—what the family had come to call Aunt Janean and Uncle Bruce's house in Key Biscayne—had all its windows on the first floor broken out as well. Worried about their mothers' safety because both Reginald and Bruce were out of town when all of this was going on, Savian had stayed at the Big House with his mother and aunt, while two police cars remained parked outside.

Then, there'd been an email message sent to every member of the Donovan family. It read:

People living in glass houses shouldn't throw stones. Glass breaks. Stones hurt. And what goes around, comes back around.

"That's why I called this meeting," Dion continued. "Now, when Sam Desdune was here, we were also dealing with the sexting scandal that somebody attempted to pull on Parker and Adriana."

Savian didn't need to look across the table at his brother to know he was still pretty pissed off about that situation. Photoshopped pictures and sexy text messages were said to have been sent between Parker and Adriana, had made it to the front page of the tabloids. Quick and thorough investigating by the Connecticut office of D&D Investigations—Sam Desdune, his sister Bree and their cousin Bailey—had proven that both Parker and Adriana's cell phones had been hacked. Giovanni had turned out to be the hacker that initiated that course of events.

As for the incidents at their parents' homes and the email message they all had received, there had been no new developments in that regard. But Savian had been working on getting to the bottom of that situation as well.

Now, it seemed, Dion had too.

"As you know, Trent was out of the country with Tia when all this was going on. That's why Sam and Bailey were the ones to help out. But the moment Trent came home, he called me. He used a remote hook up to all of our home computers, because that's where we received the messages, and came up with an IP address for the sender. He's run that address through every system he has and keeps coming up with locations throughout the world," Dion told them.

"They scrambled the signal the moment they hit send," Savian spoke up. "You're never going to pinpoint a location and if you do, it's probably going to be to some coffee house or internet café where there were probably more than a dozen people at the time. And, even if we trace the computer, it doesn't mean we'll get the person that sent it."

"Thanks for the positivity," Regan quipped.

Savian shrugged. "Just because we can't trace the message doesn't mean there's no problem. I'm very aware of that fact, Regan."

"We're all very aware of that fact," Sean interjected. "That's why we need to work together on this."

Dion nodded. "He's right and you know Trent, he's determined to get to the bottom of this before anything else happens."

"So, wait," Regan said, leaning forward in her seat and looking around at her brothers and cousins. "We're still thinking that something else might happen? Something like what? Does this mean we're going to keep all the extra security we've had for the past few months?"

"I don't know that we're at that point yet," Parker said reaching out to touch his sister's hand. "But just like Sam and I discussed when he was here, this is definitely personal."

Sean nodded. "Yes, somebody has something against us."

"Jealousy is nothing new toward our family," Savian said, remembering all too well the things he'd personally had to deal with from others that had been jealous of him and the Donovan name.

"But this seems like more, don't you agree?" Dion asked him.

It was Savian's turn to nod this time and to agree wholeheartedly with his cousin. "This person definitely has a vendetta against us. The question is why."

"No," Dion told them. "The new question is if the vendetta is against us." He motioned between himself and everyone else in the room. "Or them?"

"Them being?" Regan asked.

"The Seniors," Parker said, still holding her hand. "He's saying that since the attacks were at our parents' homes that, maybe it's someone they pissed off.

"Right. And unfortunately, I'm not convinced that they're finished," Dion added.

Regan sat back in her chair, her facial expression—as usual—clearly depicting exactly what she was feeling.

"Don't worry, we're going to get to the bottom of this," Parker reassured her.

"We certainly are and then we're going to—" Savian was saying before the door to the conference room opened.

"She said it was an emergency," Venora, the receptionist on this floor of the office said from the doorway. When she stepped to the side Savian's gaze immediately met Jenise's.

He was the first to stand as he watched her walk in wearing a skirt suit a few shades of blue lighter than his, black pumps and carrying her briefcase.

"I'm very sorry to interrupt," she said. "But I've been calling you all morning."

All eyes went immediately to Savian who wished he could disappear in this very second. This was a private meeting. To have a female interrupt it and say that she'd been trying to get in touch with him looked like he was involved in some type of lover's quarrel, something that went along with Parker, or even Dion's personality, more than it did Savian's. To say he was uncomfortable with the situation was a definite understatement. Still, he pulled his jacket together, buttoning it as he walked towards Jenise.

"This is a private meeting," he said as he came closer to her, getting a quick whiff of her perfume. "We can talk later in my office."

She was shaking her head before he finished his sentence. "You don't understand. When I began calling you over an hour ago, we had time. Now, we do not."

"What are you talking about?" Savian asked realizing in that moment that Jenise was not looking at him the way she usually did.

She glanced to look around him to the others and then back to Savian before sighing. Reluctantly, she said, "I told them you would be at the police station by ten this morning to turn yourself in. If you're not there they'll come down here and arrest you in front of everyone."

Regan was by Savian's side in seconds. "Arrest him? For what?"

Jenise looked directly at Savian. "For the murder of Giovanni Morelli."

Another block and they would be there, Jenise thought as she comfortably gripped the steering wheel of her cherry red Mustang convertible. While today was a beautifully sunny morning and a comfortable sixty-eight degrees, the top and all the windows were up, air conditioning running on low. Beside her, seat-belted and sitting rather stiffly was Savian Donovan. A man about to be arrested and processed for murder, and the man Jenise had spent the night dreaming about.

"We'll enter through the back loading dock. I've already spoken to Detective Rubin and let him know that we're on our way. The press may still be out there even though Rubin said he'd do what he could to hold them back," she said, keeping her eyes on the road.

"It won't matter what he does. They'll know I'm there and it'll be all over the television and in the papers within the next hour," he said solemnly.

He'd looked genuinely surprised at her announcement just about twenty minutes ago. Jenise wished that could have gone differently, but Savian hadn't answered any of her calls or text messages. She'd asked his secretary several times to go into the meeting and interrupt him but the woman had staunchly refused. If Jenise had been a relative or even a real girlfriend, instead of a tawdry little secret, she would have been able to simply give her name and whatever she asked would have undoubtedly been done. She shook her head at those thoughts because they weren't doing her or Savian any good at the moment.

"You're probably right, but we don't have to give them any more access to you than is absolutely necessary," she said as she drove closer to the station.

"We'll go in through the back door and take you right back to Detective Rubin's office. There, he'll read you your rights and tell you what you're charged with. Then you'll go to processing. I won't be able to go back there with you but I'll be working on getting you a quick and private hearing in front of the commissioner regarding bail," she informed him.

"I don't want my family paying," he said adamantly.

The tone of his voice had changed so drastically Jenise looked over to see that he was staring intently at her.

"I'll give you a check or authorize direct payment from my account but I do not want my family posting my bail."

Savian Donovan was a proud man. He worked hard and very rarely reaped any of the rewards from his work. He was humble and discreet. She'd realized these things in the months that she'd known him. What she hadn't really understood until right this moment was how much he loved and respected his family. The Donovans were a wealthy family. So much so, Jenise was certain that Savian's parents had created trust funds for each of their children when they were younger. Savian had probably never touched his, preferring to make his own money, which he was definitely doing at DNT. His payments to her were made from his personal account so she shouldn't have been surprised that he'd want the same for his bail.

"You don't have a prior record," she said taking her eyes off him so she could turn into the back parking lot of the police station. "But you have the means to disappear before trial so the prosecutor will undoubtedly ask for a no bail status. I'll rebut with your lack of a criminal record, family and community connections. In the end they're going to go with something high and will most likely ask you to surrender your passport."

"It's at my apartment," he told her as the car slowed.

"That's fine. We'll get that to them tomorrow. As for the money, it'll have to be ten percent and they may ask for cash," Jenise said as she cut the engine and dropped her keys into her purse.

"I have cash in my safe deposit box. Here's the key. " He talked while he was pulling out his wallet and his cell phone.

The key came to her first and she tried not to look as shocked as she felt. Jenise and Savian had gone from stand-offish business associates to lovers in a matter of hours. In the past few months whatever they now were had remained a closely guarded secret. Now, he was giving her something as personal as the key to his safe deposit box. She wasn't sure how to take that but eventually chalked it up to the severity of the current situation.

"It's going to be alright, Savian. While they came up with something to get an arrest warrant from the judge, their case is still very thin and very circumstantial," Jenise told him.

She didn't like how solemn and serious he was, even though it wasn't totally different from his normal personality. It was still hard for her to see him this way, and even more difficult to accept that in a few minutes he would be handcuffed and led away. She didn't want to think about that, let alone accept the fact that she would have to stand there and watch helplessly while it happened.

He sat back in the seat, still holding his cell phone as he stared straight ahead. "They have a surveillance tape of me leaving Giovanni's house and a letter on my letterhead giving him an ultimatum about the show and Adriana. I'd say they're building their case."

"That's because you're not the lawyer," she snapped. "We have yet to have that tape reviewed by our own expert. You said you went to see Giovanni days before the night he was killed. And just because that letter is on your letterhead, it doesn't mean you wrote it."

He nodded. "You're right. I didn't ki—"

"Stop!" she said immediately, holding up a hand to make her point. "Only answer the questions I ask you. Nothing else. And don't say a word to anyone when I'm not there. Not one word."

Savian looked over to her then and Jenise had to resist the urge to extend her hand and touch his cheek. His beard was low cut and dark, a stark contrast to his lighter complexion. His jaw was set, eyes staring at her fiercely, as if he were barely restraining his true emotions at this moment. Jenise knew exactly how that felt.

His lips snapped shut and Jenise grabbed her briefcase and opened her car door to get out. Across the parking lot, at the entrance where they'd come in had been a circle of reporters and cameramen, obviously hoping to catch Savian should he come in this way. Fortunately, they hadn't expected him to arrive in a red Mustang. Score one for Jenise.

Now that they'd spotted him, they began to run across the parking lot. Jenise had just enough time to turn around before Savian was grabbing her by the arm and hurrying them to the side door that had been pushed open for them by an officer. They made it inside before the reporters could reach them and were hustled through a long narrow hallway by another officer. Savian never released his hold on her.

Not until they walked into the dour-looking detective's office. Wilbert Rubin had been with the police department for more than twenty years. Jenise had done her research the minute Savian had told her he was a suspect. Rubin was a tall man with a wiry build and thinning gray hair. He stood from his creaking old desk chair the moment they walked in.

"Thanks for coming down," he said in a dry tone.

"Let's just get this over with," Jenise replied. "I want a copy of the surveillance tape and that letter before I leave here today."

"We're gonna check the letter for his prints once we get them," Rubin said as he came all the way around the desk to stand beside Savian.

"Fine. Just be sure that I get a copy of the results." Her stomach had become very jittery all of a sudden and Jenise gripped the strap of her briefcase to keep from shaking.

Rubin nodded towards her and then turned his attention to Savian.

"Savian Donovan," he began, pulling handcuffs from the back of his pants. "You are under arrest for the murder of Giovanni Morelli."

She'd never felt this way before. Not in all her years of representing criminal clients and having to be in police stations, correctional facilities and courtrooms with them, or any time before. Jenise walked slowly attempting to steady her breathing as she moved down the hallway towards the meeting room where one of the officer's had told her the Donovan family was waiting. She had to go in there, it was her job. That didn't mean she really wanted to. Sure, she'd been thinking a lot about Savian's family and the type of people they were, but this wasn't how she'd envisioned meeting them.

Yet, this was the situation at hand. So she said a silent prayer for her own strength as she turned the knob and walked into the room. The first thing she noticed was that there were too many people in this small room. Jenise immediately felt warm, closed in and nervous.

"Hello," she managed to say as she closed the door behind her.

"Everyone, this is Jenise Langley. She's Savian's lawyer," Regan Donovan said.

The tall pretty woman had immediately come to stand beside Jenise, as if they'd known each other much longer than a couple of hours.

"Jenise, these are my parents, Reginald and Carolyn Donovan," Regan continued, pointing to a lovely woman who had been sitting in a chair, but now stood, offering Jenise a cordial smile. The man gave her a nod, his jaw set in a serious line that was very similar to the way Savian had looked.

"My Aunt Janean and Uncle Bruce," Regan announced the next stately-looking couple.

"You remember Dion, Sean and Parker. And of course, Adriana, although she wasn't there with us this morning at the meeting. But she's here now. This is also Gavin. He's with me," Regan finished.

Jenise couldn't help it, she turned to the woman and grabbed her hand.

"Thanks for the introductions," she told Regan. "It's going to be okay. He's going to come home today."

Regan let out a whoosh of breath, her shoulders visibly relaxing as Gavin came over to wrap his arms around her. They were all tense, Jenise had realized during the introductions, so there was no need for her to feel like she was the only one. Worry over Savian was their common link here, she just needed to focus on that and forget the rest. The part that was probably just a wish in her mind anyway.

"Can you tell us what's going on?" Reginald spoke up next. "Last we heard Savian was a person of interest. That was months ago. Then we get a call today that he's being arrested."

Jenise looked to Savian's parents and wanted to hug them both for standing there attempting to look so brave. This wasn't an easy place to be, she knew that and knowing that your son or loved one was behind bars was even more difficult to swallow.

"One of the first things the police did after Giovanni Morelli's body was found was to subpoena the surveillance tapes from the security company that had installed them at his house. Savian was seen on one of those tapes leaving Morelli's house the night he was killed," Jenise told them.

"That's not possible," Parker interjected. "Savian was at the party with us. When we arrived he was already there. What time was that? Around eight-thirty or something like that. And after Giovanni attacked Adriana at the party he was arrested and taken to the police station," he said looking over to Adriana who was nodding her agreement.

"You're correct about that," Jenise told Parker. "The problem is your story only gives Savian an alibi for the night of the party. Morelli was killed hours after he was released from jail the next night, between eleven and eleven-thirty," Jenise continued. "Still, all the tape confirms is that Savian was at Morelli's house. From what I was originally told there was no time stamp on the video, just the markings on the outside of the case that indicated it was the day of the murder. That's why they didn't immediately arrest Savian, because there was still nothing affirmatively connecting him to Morelli's death. Last night I received a message from the detective that they now have a letter on Savian's letterhead, with Savian's name typed as the sender to Morelli. The letter supposedly threatened Morelli's job and his life if he didn't back off of Adriana."

"What?" Adriana gasped.

Parker was shaking his head. "No. Savian would never do that. He'd never write a letter like that. It's doesn't even sound like him."

"No, he's right." Dion said. "That's something Parker or I might say face-to-face to the guy, but not Savian. He's not the violent type."

"He's the exact opposite, my son," Carolyn said quietly. "He never wanted any bother out of anyone. He never looks to physically hurt someone."

There was something odd about what Carolyn Donovan just said. Jenise picked up on it immediately but just as quickly brushed it off. "Good," she replied. "Then we'll need to gather as much evidence to support Savian's honest, upstanding and non-violent personality as possible."

The room went quiet after that.

"I'm going to get a copy of the surveillance video and have my expert look at it. If there's a possibility that it was edited in any way, we'll know about it. Same for the letter. I told them I want to see the finger print report as soon as it's ready and I want a copy of the letter for my own records. What we need to do now is focus on showing the court that Savian is a good man and not a murderer. I'll do the rest."

Carolyn walked over to Jenise at that point, taking both her hands. "I know you'll be able to save my son. I know it."

Jenise was a confident attorney. She knew her stuff and she knew how to present it all in court to her client's advantage. There were holes in the prosecutor's case but since the Donovans were a high-profiled family and Morelli had been a reputable director, they were receiving pressure to close this case. She knew that drill.

What Jenise didn't understand was why each time she'd looked into Carolyn Donovan's eyes she'd felt an instant pang of guilt? It was as if she were somehow being dishonest. It was silly, she knew. Savian was her client so he was really the only person she had to remain on the up and up with. Not his family. Still, standing here, holding hands with his mother and seeing the tears well in her eyes, had Jenise's chest swelling and her own tears threatening fall.

Dammit. This wasn't supposed to be personal. It was work.

It was always work.

Until now.

Until Savian Donovan.

CHAPTER 3

Savian hadn't been this angry in a very long time. He'd sat—even if for only an hour and a half—in that jail cell with his elbows resting on his thighs, his fists tightly clenched and his brow furrowed. There wasn't one part of this situation that was good or even acceptable in any way. He was too old and had too much going for him to be in this predicament. The fact that the situation was a bunch of BS also irritated the hell out of him.

Yes, he had gone to see that bastard Giovanni Morelli the day after the All Access event. The man had not only tried to ruin his brother's reputation and attacked Adriana, but he was still attempting to sue the company they'd all worked so hard to build. Savian had gone to see him to try and talk some sense into him, and because he'd wanted to learn more about the claim that Giovanni had made that night at the party—the one about someone paying him to knock Parker and Adriana down a notch. That statement had something clicking in Savian's mind, after he'd rushed Parker and Adriana out of the hotel. He'd thought about it all night long until he'd heard that Morelli had been released on bail. Savian immediately decided to drive to the small house the guy was leasing in Coconut Grove later that Sunday evening.

"What the hell are you doing here?" Giovanni had asked when he'd answered the door.

He'd looked like he'd slept under the jail instead of in it, but Savian hadn't an ounce of pity for the bastard. In fact he hadn't even offered an answer, but instead had pushed his way inside Morelli's house.

"You can't just come in here and do whatever you want!" Morelli had yelled, slamming the door after Savian had come in. "You damn Donovans don't own everything and everyone! Somebody's going to bring you to your knees and I'm going to be glad to see it!"

Savian had snapped then. Before he could stop himself he'd crossed the short distance between them and grabbed the front of Morelli's shirt. The guy smelled like stale cigarettes and liquor as Savian slammed his back against the wall so hard the pictures that had been hanging there shook.

"You're gonna tell me who the hell hired you to attack my family right now!" he yelled into Morelli's face. "Were you responsible for the break-in at my parents' house? Who's paying you? I want a name, now!"

Morelli had only laughed at him.

"You think I'm gonna tell you anything? I don't work for you anymore and even if I did I wouldn't—"

Savian had punched him then. He hadn't planned on getting physical with this guy. He'd only come here with questions that needed answers, but Morelli wasn't cooperating. Being knocked to the floor hadn't made him anymore cooperative.

"He's too powerful for even you to stop him with your bad temper. He's going to get each and every one of you high and mighty Donovans, and I can't wait to see you all fall. I can't wait," Morelli was saying when Savian finally decided that it was best he left.

His fists had been clenching at his sides while Morelli talked and it had taken every ounce of restraint in his body to keep from punching that idiot in the face again and again. He'd yanked open that door and walked fast to get to his truck. Once inside he simply sat there, his hands wrapped securely around the steering wheel. Every muscle in his body had been tense, his temples throbbing as the anger moved through him like a blustering storm. He'd wanted to hurt Morelli because the man was trying to hurt his family. He'd wanted to see Morelli on his knees in pain because he realized he'd messed with the wrong person. It reminded Savian of when he was in high school.

Dropping his head Savian remembered the night he'd last seen Morelli, just as clearly as he'd recalled the rainy afternoon more than ten years ago. That was the last time he'd felt that way. It was the last time he'd wanted to inflict as much bodily harm as he possibly could and damn the consequences.

But he had not killed Giovanni Morelli.

He wasn't a murderer.

Flexing his fingers out in front of him, Savian told himself that over and over again. He was not capable of taking another human life. He simply was not. And yet, there had been another time when he had caused physical damage, so much that he'd been arrested and charged with assault.

Jenise didn't know that and neither did Adriana, Tate, or the people he worked with. What had happened in high school was a family secret that Savian was certain only the Donovans that lived here in Miami knew about.

Taking a deep breath Savian sat up. He dragged a hand down his face and tried to focus on how he could clear his name. There was a call he needed to make, someone he needed desperately to speak to before this went any further. From the night he'd heard his name announced on the evening news about being a person of interest, Savian had known this moment would come. He'd hoped, of course, that something would be revealed by that time. That whoever had paid Morelli to come after them would be identified and caught and this would all be over. It hadn't worked out that way, so now he'd have to come up with another plan.

"You made bail," the portly officer announced as he unlocked the cell. "I don't guess that was much of a surprise. That lawyer of yours is something else too, marching in here and making demands. She's a spitfire."

Savian hadn't even realized he'd cleared the space between them, but he was in the officer's face quickly, clenching his teeth to keep his words at bay as the officer simply raised a brow and chuckled at him.

"Rich boys like you can't handle it in here long. Makes you start thinking crazy, doesn't it?" he asked.

Savian continued to seethe, but again, did not speak.

"Well let me give you a warning, keep your anger in check and pay that lawyer any amount of money you can because if she can't get you cleared of the charges, I'm gonna personally make sure your ass is up for grabs when you get over to the penitentiary," he said with a smirk.

Another officer had showed up then, pushing the first one aside and letting Savian walk out of the cell. He'd escorted Savian out to the waiting area where Jenise and Parker were waiting.

His brother approached him first, clapping his hands on Savian's shoulders as he stood in front of him.

"You okay?" Parker asked.

Savian nodded in reply.

"We're gonna get them, you hear me? We're going to find out who's behind this and we're going to bury their asses. They're not going to get away with trying to frame a Donovan," Parker stated in a tone that did not allow for any argument.

Not that Savian intended to argue his brother's statement. "Right," Savian said. "You're absolutely right."

"There's press everywhere," Jenise added as she joined them. "They were all over your parents and the rest of the family when they left."

"My truck's still at the office," Savian stated. "Parker can drive me back there to get it."

"I don't think that's a good idea," Parker said. "They're probably camping out at Excalibur too. We should get you somewhere private at least for a couple of hours until they come up with something else to run on tonight's news broadcast."

"I'm not running from these pricks. They want to report on what's going on, fine, report it. But I won't go into hiding like I'm guilty," Savian argued.

"No, not like you're guilty," Parker replied. "But like you're smart. They're looking to catch you saying something, or doing something. Anything, Savian and they're going to hang you for it. You've got to think smarter than them. I'm not saying hide out, I'm just saying to take careful steps. Get somewhere and clear your mind for a few hours. You know you don't want reporters in your face right now."

Parker was right and by the way he was looking at Savian, he knew how close his brother was to the breaking point as well.

"I hear you," Savian said, releasing a breath he hadn't realized he'd been holding.

"I can take him back to my place for a while. No reporters will be there," Jenise said.

"I think they're going to remember your bright red Mustang from this point on," he told her.

She nodded. "You're right, but they're not going to follow us out of the parking lot. They're going to think they're the smart ones and head to either your office or your apartment building."

"They may even go to the station," Parker suggested. "But she's right, they won't think about her place. Text me her address when you get there just so I'll know where you are and we can meet up later at mom's. You know she's cooking and wants to see your face before this day is over. We almost had to have the cops escort her out of the building because she didn't want to leave without knowing you were safe."

"He's right. She waited until I came back with the bail money and watched me go to the cashier's office to post it before she would leave," Jenise said with a tentative smile.

Today, she'd met his parents, his siblings and his cousins. This was not supposed to happen and now he wasn't sure how he felt about knowing that it had. Hell, he was still grappling with being arrested for murder, everything else should be taking a second seat, but as he looked at her, he wondered.

"Fine. But I'm going to need my truck," he told Parker.

"I've got the spare key," Parker said. "You text me Jenise's address and Regan and I will bring your truck over there and park it, so when you're ready to leave you'll have it."

Savian nodded. He moved first because he was beyond ready to get out of this place. "Let's go then," he told them and walked out of the waiting area.

Ten minutes later he was back in the passenger seat of Jenise's car. The police had cleared the back parking lot of reporters, but as soon as they drove out onto the streets, cameras flashed, while men and women with microphones in hand and an exposé in their minds, rushed towards the car. Jenise didn't hesitate, but stepped hard on the gas until the engine purred and the car jolted quickly forward. The quickly moving car sent the bravest of the reporters rushing back for fear of being hit. Savian couldn't help but chuckle as they pulled away.

"You had them believing you were going to hit them," he said.

"I was," she replied with a shrug. "They shouldn't be in the street."

For the first time in he didn't know how long, Savian laughed out loud.

"Pardon the boxes, I just had them delivered from storage this morning," Jenise said as she let Savian into her apartment.

"Are you moving?" he asked immediately.

"No," she replied as she stepped down the two steps into the sunken living room of her apartment. "They're my Christmas decorations."

"Oh man, not you too," Savian groaned.

He'd moved further into the living room, dropping the suit jacket he'd been carrying in his hand onto the end of the love seat.

"Regan and Parker were just talking about Christmas lists and gifts this morning. It's only the first week of November," he continued.

If his laughter in the car had surprised—and yet pleased—Jenise, watching him walk comfortably over to one of her boxes and open it up made her want to smile herself. She remained calm however, because this was Savian after all. He'd had a very trying day and probably didn't know what he was doing or saying at this point.

"I love Christmas," she replied. "Waiting until November to start my decorating is like pulling teeth every year. I can't wait to get started."

"You don't even have children and you're decorating," Savian was saying as he stared down at a box of crystal ornaments he was holding.

"Christmas isn't only about children. It's about the magic and the feeling of this time of year. It's a peaceful and happy feeling and I just love it," she said, stopping herself finally because she thought she might be gushing just a little bit.

Savian was looking at her as if she might grow antlers or a white beard and start shouting "ho, ho, ho".

"What? I'm sure your family celebrated Christmas and probably in just as big a way as mine. Your mother and Regan were talking about the dinner menu while we waited at the station. Regan brought it up. I think she wanted to keep your mother's mind on something cheerful." Jenise talked while she moved, going into the connecting dining room to sit her briefcase in a chair and removed her jacket.

She took her cell phone out of her purse and put it on the charger she kept in the living room. There was one in her office and another in her bedroom because she always had to stay connected, as her mother would complain. When she came back into the living room it was to find that Savian had continued to go through one of the boxes of decorations.

"Did you make these?" he asked while holding up two paper ornaments covered with puffy cotton balls and bright red and green glitter.

"I certainly did," she replied with pride and moved closer to take them from his hands. "When I was in the third grade. I made an entire set of twenty four, so my mother has some, my aunt and my grandmother. I kept a few for myself for when I had my own tree to decorate."

"You kept these all that time when it would have been just as simple to buy ornaments," he said more as a statement than a question. "Did you make some for your sisters and brothers?"

Jenise walked over to the bar to fix them a drink. She knew she needed one and even though Savian wouldn't admit it, he could probably use some liquid relaxation as well. They weren't discussing his case right now, which was a good thing. She had some thoughts about strategy as well as some pressing questions, but nothing she was ready to discuss with him. For the time he was here she would keep him relaxed and stress-free because that's what he needed, even if he would never admit it.

"Wade is the oldest," she began as she took two glasses from the shelf and set them on the bar. "He used to be a terrible agitator so I wouldn't have thought of making him anything. Now, he's a playboy bachelor and wouldn't be caught dead with homemade ornaments on his store-bought and pre-decorated tree."

She poured them both glasses of wine as she continued.

"Tucker used to be obsessed by basketball so if I wasn't making a hoop or a ball, he definitely didn't want it. And Morgan, she's younger than I am, was just starting first grade and was making her own paste-filled knick-knacks to clutter mom's table with."

"Are they all lawyers working at your family's firm?" he asked when she returned to where he was still standing by the love seat and the boxes and offered him the drink.

After he took the glass and was sipping the wine, Jenise nodded. "Yes. We're all attorneys, to my parents' dismay."

His brow arched. "They didn't want you to follow in their footsteps?"

"Oh no, my mother's not an attorney. She met and married my father the year she graduated from high school, which worked out well since Bradford Langley would not hear of his wife having a career other than being a wife and mother."

Savian sipped his wine again and shrugged. "I guess you could say that's a full-time job. I know my mother used to say that when we were growing up."

Jenise felt like a total idiot. Of course Carolyn Donovan would have stayed home to raise her children and take care of her husband. From what she'd seen of the woman Jenise liked her. The way the woman's children and husband surrounded her like a fortress to be reckoned with was probably only a fraction of the love and dedication they had towards her.

"It's great if that's what you were meant to be, but just because I happened to have been born female, doesn't mean it's etched in stone that I have to marry and have children to be complete," she said a little too vehemently.

She took a quick sip of her wine to hide that fact.

"I agree," he said after a few moments. "You should have the right to decide who and what you want to be. Everyone should."

He'd set his glass on the floor and continued on with the boxes as if he were really interested in seeing everything that was inside of them. For someone who didn't seem too thrilled about Christmas, he certainly was adamant about this.

"What about you? How did you and your siblings get along? Tell me some of the things you used to do for Christmas," she said, sitting on the edge of the chair and looking over to where he stood.

Savian pulled out a clump of lights and began to unravel them.

"Parker was always the fun one. He could figure out something to entertain him and every other kid in the neighborhood at the drop of a dime. He played basketball in school, too, and was pretty popular with the girls as well." He pulled a strand free, placing it in a neat pile on the floor behind him. "Regan, she's been shopping since the day she was born. She loved Christmas but I swear it didn't matter, that girl was always getting new stuff all year long."

"But you didn't like to play and you didn't like Christmas. So, what were you like the child Scrooge?" she asked before swallowing her last bit of wine.

His head snapped up then and Jenise wondered if she'd said the wrong thing once more. She didn't make any effort to take it back, just leaned forward to set her glass on the coffee table while she waited for his response.

"I just didn't like a lot of fuss," he replied finally and dropped another single strand of lights into a separate pile. "I wasn't mean or rude, just kept to myself."

"Even though everyone in your house was playing and having fun, you kept to yourself," she remarked because she could actually picture him doing this.

"It wasn't easy," he said, working the next strands apart. "Dion and Sean would come over all the time, and when Lyra moved in with them, she would come too. Regan loved that she finally had a girl to play with. Together they were all noisy and persistent and I usually ended up playing with them anyway."

"Did you enjoy those times?"

Savian didn't answer. He'd finished with the lights just as his cell phone buzzed. He was frowning when he looked at her again. "Regan says they parked my truck in one of the guest spots on the first level of the garage."

Jenise only nodded her response because she'd been enjoying their conversation and didn't want the fact that his vehicle was now here for his use, to bring that to an end. She was both shocked and elated when he asked, "What's your favorite Christmas memory?"

Jenise ran her palms over the tapered sides of her hair, then down the front of her blouse while she thought about his question and the fact that he had not answered the one she'd posed before he'd received that text.

"It's not a memory yet," she told him honestly. "I've always wanted to see the tree lighting at Rockefeller Center."

He looked perplexed. "So why haven't you just gone to New York to see it? It's not like you can't afford a plane ticket or can't get the time off from work."

"No," Jenise said quietly. "That's not the reason why I haven't done it yet."

She didn't want to think about the reason and wanted to kick herself for even mentioning it in the first place.

"Give me that," she said, coming to a stand and reaching her hand out in front of Savian.

He looked down at what he'd just pulled from the box then back to her before handing it over. She took the sprig in hand, looking down as she rubbed her fingers over the green leaves.

"Do you know about the magic of mistletoe, Savian?" she asked taking a step closer to him.

"I don't believe in magic," was his immediate response.

She rubbed her fingers over the soft red ribbon tied at the end of the bundle. "Oh but you should, Savian. You see throughout history mistletoe was reported to bestow life and fertility. It was also said to be an aphrodisiac." She chuckled at that and chanced a glance at Savian. His eyes had grown just a bit darker until they looked almost totally brown. Funny how they could change so quickly and so drastically just because…she was holding that mistletoe.

"It's no wonder that eventually, around the 19th century Victorian era, I do believe, that kissing under the mistletoe became a time honored tradition. At Christmastime a ball of mistletoe tied with ribbons just like this one, would be hung. With all their strict rules and practices during that time, it was said that no unmarried girl could refuse a kiss if she stood under the mistletoe. Each time the girl was kissed, the boy would pluck one of the mistletoe berries until there was no more, and then the ball would be taken down until the next year. If the girl wasn't kissed before the ball was taken down, she wasn't expected to be married the following year. The kiss was a promise or symbol of marriage or admiration. When in truth, it was just a kiss. But that magic, that mystical moment when that unmarried girl was waiting expectantly for that kiss, that's the mistletoe magic. I love that feeling so much that I always hang this same sprig of mistletoe every year."

Jenise stopped talking at that moment. She hadn't moved but Savian did, until he was standing directly in front of her. Her fingers still rubbed over the ribbon, the fake white berries of the mistletoe still intact.

"You hang it each year so that men will come to your place and kiss you. Do you hope they will marry you too?" Savian asked.

His words were spoken so softly, yet his facial features were so stern and serious. If Jenise didn't already know him the way she did, she would have had no clue that he was aroused at this very moment. She wasn't certain what did it—the tight fit of the wrap blouse she wore, the talk of their childhood, or was it actually the mistletoe? It didn't matter, the sexual tension was there and it was rising, just the way it always did between them.

"No," she replied. "It's not marriage I hope for, Savian. I'm not that much of a dreamer."

"But you do believe in magic?"

"I do," she admitted and on instinct lifted her arm up as high as she could. Thankfully she was still wearing her four-inch heeled platform pumps so her reach extended easily above Savian's head.

"You should try it once," she told him as she leaned in closer. "Try a kiss under the mistletoe and see just how magical it is."

He shook his head. "I'm not an unmarried girl looking to find out who admires or wants to marry me."

"Neither am I," she told him. "Let's just say, I want a kiss."

There was no movement and Jenise was not surprised. If Savian Donovan had kissed her three times in the three months she'd been sleeping with him that would be a record. It happened so infrequently that Jenise had never bothered to count. In fact, she'd never wanted to kiss him as badly as she did right now.

He still did not move, only continued to stare at her as if he were trying to figure something out. Jenise knew there was nothing to figure out or analyze, not this time. This time she was simply going to take what she wanted. She was going to reach for that mistletoe magic even though Thanksgiving had yet to arrive.

With her free hand she grasped the back of Savian's neck, pulling him down so that her lips could touch his slowly at first, but then with more pressure. She let her lips stay still over his, watching as he blinked and she did the same. He was so resistant and so damned sexy and she wanted more. The thought slammed into her like an actual physical blow. And she kissed him harder.

She parted her lips and let her tongue meet his to stroke slowly. When he still didn't move, she sucked his bottom lip into her mouth, pressing her body up against his. He jerked instantly, as if she were fire and he were ice. Jenise continued, licking her tongue over his top lip, then pressing against the seam once more, all while her gaze stayed trained on his. His eyes were so dark there was no color visible, his body so rigid she should have been instantly turned off, rebuffed and pissed the hell off. Yet, just when she was about to pull away and spend the rest of the day berating herself for being so stupid for even thinking that she could get under this guy's skin, he moved.

His arms slipped around her waist, pulling her even closer to him and his mouth opened. Their tongues clashed in a terrifically hot and exciting duel as he hungrily accepted her kiss.

The magical mistletoe kiss.

Jenise almost dropped that damn mistletoe to the floor when she wrapped her arms around him, leaning fully into the kiss now. He returned the favor, sucking her lip deep into his mouth and her thighs trembled. Her eyes had closed with the fevered passion spreading through her so she had no idea what color his eyes were now and didn't really give a damn. All she knew, all she wanted to know, was how perfect and delectable this kiss was, how it made her want…no, need this man inside her at this very moment.

Savian, however, had a totally different reaction.

He pulled away from her as quickly as he'd gone into the impulsive embrace. Taking steps away he continued to put distance between them until he was grabbing his jacket off the chair.

"I've got to go," was all he said as he walked to the door and let himself out.

Jenise didn't say a thing. She couldn't.

She did, however, toss that stupid mistletoe across the room, not giving a damn where it landed.

CHAPTER 4

This was familiar.

It was stability and safety and every comfort Savian had ever experienced. He'd used the side entrance, just off the garden his mother loved as much as she did her children. There were eight foot stucco walls here and continuing in the Spanish revival style of the home, antique teak gates that had recently been fitted with new locks and links to the top-of-the-line alarm system. Savian had used this entrance as a way of checking the security of his parents' home.

He used the specially designed key with its uniquely coded magnetic strip, to access the door and listened intently for the faint beeping that said his access code had been accepted by the twenty-four hour security monitoring. His shoes were silent on the red terracotta tile as he moved through his mother's rendition of a Spanish courtyard. Carolyn liked to sit out here in the mornings before the humidity became too much to bare and enjoy her first cup of coffee. It was a large space made to feel quaint and welcoming by the quatrefoil shaped fountain and koi pond at its center. The variety of plants situated in huge planters and climbing up the wall added color and ambiance.

As he approached the French doors that would lead him into the family room section of the house, Savian paused. It was just a little after seven in the evening and he'd felt as if he'd run across the country and back. His muscles ached and his temples throbbed. He felt like every minute concern that had plagued him in the last few months had crashed down over his head. He'd walked into that police station, was handcuffed, sat in that jail cell and then been released. There was no doubt his pictures—

ones he'd voluntarily posed for, ones that had been sneakily obtained and, of course, the mug shot—were plastered all over the television, probably gaining more ratings than DNT's top show. The world was talking about him, judging and condemning him when all they really knew was his name and how much money he had. They had no idea who he really was inside, none whatsoever.

Using the keypad on the side wall, Savian punched in yet another access code and entered the house. Immediately upon closing that door he inhaled deeply and exhaled slowly. Closing his eyes he repeated that action, letting the savory scents of whatever his mother had prepared for dinner sift through his senses. This too was familiar and welcoming. His mother loved to cook and for as long as Savian could remember each time he entered this house it had been to the appetizing aroma of some delectable meal. Tonight, he thought with a relieved sigh, it was meatloaf, mashed potatoes and corn—his favorite.

Each one of them had a favorite meal that Carolyn prepared especially for her children in times of celebration and, in Savian's case, disappointment. She'd cooked this same meal on a similar night long ago. He fought like hell to keep that memory at bay, to walk through the room full of family photos and thoughts of happier times, and not be overtaken by the eerie repeat of events.

"Hey, son," his father's voice sounded through all the noise and recriminations sounding in Savian's head.

"Hi, dad," he replied and turned to face the man that had raised him to be much stronger than he was acting.

Reginald Donovan stood at exactly six feet tall, dressed in khaki pants and a dark blue lightweight sweater. One hand was tucked in his front pocket as he stood, his dark brown eyes resting solemnly on his middle child. He'd grown grayer— Savian noticed immediately—at the sides of his short cropped hair, with the top still holding on to its majority black hue. Even his eyebrows were peppered with gray now, giving him a very distinguished look.

"Come on back. Parker couldn't make it. But, your mother has dinner ready for you," Reginald said.

Savian nodded. "Sorry, I'm a little late."

He'd taken a long shower when he'd arrived at his apartment after the two-hour long ride he'd taken down through South Beach and back. Around and around this city that he called home, he'd driven in a thwarted attempt to clear his mind. When he'd finally arrived at his apartment building it was to find a couple of reporters still hanging out. Savian had parked his truck a block away, instead of driving up to the building and using the garage as he normally did. He'd walked down to the building, using his condo key to enter through the poolside doors and then slipped into the building through a private entrance.

"Nonsense," Reginald said putting a hand on his son's shoulder when Savian had walked up to him. "Carolyn would have held this meal for hours waiting on you."

His father smiled as he squeezed Savian's shoulder as a show of affection and support. Savian looked to the man that had taught him everything and managed a small smile. "She's the best."

Reginald nodded. "Yes, sir. That, she definitely is."

"So you probably shouldn't keep lying to her," he replied without any thought to whether or not now was the right time.

"What did you just say?" was Reginald's reply.

"Why did you and Uncle Bruce really go to Houston this summer? The night of the break-ins mom and Aunt Janean were here alone. You both should have been here." Savian was probably wrong as hell for having the audacity to stand here and question his father just hours after he'd been released from jail on a first degree murder charge, but hell, Savian figured if the rest of his life was falling apart, he'd might as well jump right into this other mess that he, his siblings and cousins had been skating around.

"I already told you Al had some papers for us to sign from the estate," Reginald answered. His hand had already fallen from his son's shoulder.

"Grandpa died ten years ago. His estate was equally divided between you and your brothers, everything from his shares in Donovan Oilwell to the cash he had in all seven of his bank accounts and the three houses that were eventually sold. Split evenly between the six of you. So what could have come up now that made you and Uncle Bruce run down to Houston the way you did?"

"Savian," Reginald said. "You've been through a lot today. I know it feels like we've all been through a lot these past few months. But there's no need for you to keep poking at something that I've already explained to you."

His father was right about one thing, he had explained this to Savian when he'd asked him weeks ago. Only that explanation had never set well with him. He didn't believe his father and that made Savian sadder than anything else that had happened to him today.

"What did you think about that email? Why do you think it was sent to every member of the family, young and old?" he asked.

"You calling me old, son?" Reginald teased, his lips tilting into a nervous smile.

"We're tracing the sender," Savian told him. "We're going to find out who sent that message and why."

Reginald sobered immediately.

"Some things are better left alone, Savian," he told him.

Savian shook his head. "I don't think so."

"Well," Reginald said with a shake of his head. "Take it from someone whose 'older', leave it alone."

How he'd managed to get through that dinner with both his parents when one of them had just royally pissed him off, Savian had no idea. That wasn't totally accurate, he knew why he'd let his father's last comment to him drop and moved on into dinner with a smile on his face. He'd done it to appease his mother.

Reginald had done the same, acting as if he wasn't upset by Savian's questioning and engaging in talk of the upcoming holidays and family throughout dinner. They both loved Carolyn more than anything and would not risk upsetting her, which by the time Savian had arrived home, had answered one of his questions that his father did not.

Reginald lied to his wife because he loved her and there was something that he obviously wanted to protect her from. On any other day, in any other circumstance, Savian might be cool with that. Hell, he might even respect his father for putting his mother first and shielding her from harm because that's what a husband was supposed to do for his wife. This time, however, Savian wasn't so sure what his father was doing was right, because whatever he was attempting to protect her from was determined to come to light. That determination was evidenced in the windows of the house being broken, not only at their house, but at Uncle Bruce's as well. No, Savian thought as he sat in his dark living room and pulled out his cell phone, something definitely wasn't right.

"Hi," he said into the phone after dialing the number. "I know it's late but I needed to see if you've found anything."

"No. Not yet," Devlin Bonner replied in his gruff voice.

Devlin "Death" Bonner was a retired Navy SEAL. He was also Trent's closest friend and a trained killer, hence his self-explanatory nickname. Savian had met Devlin for the first time almost two years ago when Briana had been kidnapped. He'd seen the man in action again last year at their family reunion in Sansonique when a serial killer was loose on the island. Now, Savian needed Devlin's help.

"Dion's got Trent on the case of the emails but I'd like you to switch gears a bit," Savian said.

"You still want me to work separate from Trent?" Devlin asked.

Savian knew that Devlin didn't like keeping their conversations away from Trent, but this is the way he wanted it. He couldn't exactly explain the feeling he had, but he knew that whatever was going on would be a delicate situation, one he'd like a heads up on before it came crashing down over his entire family.

"I'm not going to keep the secret forever," he assured Devlin. "This is just the way I want to handle this for now, especially considering what I'm about to ask you to do."

Devlin was quiet for a few seconds. "Just know that I'm not going to lie to Trent. If he comes to me about this investigation, I'm telling him all I know."

"I know you will," Savian said, respecting the man's loyalty and dedication to his cousin and wishing that he felt the same from his own father. "I need you to investigate my father, Reginald Donovan."

Devlin did not reply.

"Run a background check on him, Albert, Henry, Bernard, Everette and Bruce Donovan."

The names almost stuck in his throat as he spoke. Savian had closed his eyes as he said them because somehow it felt like a betrayal. He assured himself that he wasn't being disloyal to his family. No, having them investigated probably wasn't the best show of dedication and support to them. Still, in his heart Savian knew this was the course to take.

"I want a full report on each of them from the time they were in high school up until now. Send the information to me on that secure email we set up," he continued.

"You sure you want to do this, man?" Devlin asked.

Devlin was a loner, Savian knew. The guy had no family and no relationships to tie him down to any one place or any one person. Trent had told them Devlin felt like that was safer in his line of work. Of course, Regan, Lyra and Tate all thought it was more of a protective stance for himself and his own emotions. Whatever the reason, Savian knew that Trent and their family were really the only personal connections Devlin Bonner had and he hated using that to his advantage.

"I have to find out what's going on and I'm convinced my father and uncle are hiding something. So the only way to find out what that may be is to do the background check."

"What about the others? You want to drag all of them into this too?" Devlin continued with his interrogation.

Savian nodded and then pinched the bridge of his nose. "They're all involved," he said emphatically. "First my father and Uncle Bruce fly to Houston to meet with Uncle Al. Then they use one of the conference rooms at the office for three hours a couple weeks after the All Access event for a conference call. Uncle Everette flew in for that meeting, but did not visit my mother or my aunt at their homes. I only found out he was here because Venora, the receptionist, mentioned how she'd enjoyed meeting my uncle when I'd run into her later that day. Something's going on," he said with a sigh. "Something is definitely going on."

Devlin had agreed with Savian's request and promised to get back to him by the end of the next week Now, all Savian had to do was sit back and wait, he thought as he disconnected the call and dropped his cell phone on the couch beside him. He had no idea how long he'd sat in the dark living room, staring towards the electronic blinds that were on a timer to close over the floor to ceiling windows. No matter how high up his condo was, he never wanted to chance someone looking in on him. Savian valued his privacy, which only made the fact that reporters might still be camped out in front of his building even more irritating.

He had to find a way to clear his name, he thought with a heavy sigh. Jenise was a competent attorney, of that Savian was sure, but he was the one bringing the blemish on the Donovan name. Now, he scrubbed his hands over his face again because thinking of the charges against him made him think of Jenise and of that kiss they'd shared.

Kissing was not part of Savian's forte. While he considered himself to be a very generous lover, to those which he decided to sleep with, the kisses had been few and far between. The act was too intimate, too promising and he'd shied away from it for much longer than he could remember.

Yet, this afternoon, he'd kissed Jenise. Under the mistletoe, no less.

Savian had to shake his head at that. How silly was it to be kissing under mistletoe in early November with a woman he did not have a crush on, nor did he plan to marry? Now, Savian frowned because he had no business remembering the story of mistletoe magic that she'd told him. And he definitely should not be able to sit here with his eyes closed and recall the touch of her lips against his, the persistent warmth of her tongue as she'd probed and insisted on his participation.

His body warmed with the thought, his erection growing instantly. On a curse, Savian got up from the chair and headed up the stairs to his bedroom. He did switch on the lights this time, only long enough to strip off his clothes and put them in his closet. His normal routine before going to bed would be to check the daily ratings of the network and watch the celebrity news to make sure none of their stars were in the spotlight this week. The idea of turning on the television or his laptop and seeing his own name splashed all over the place was unappealing. So it was to bed he planned to go. Tomorrow was Saturday and he'd decided he would not go into the office even for a few hours as he normally did, but that he would spend the day going over every interaction he'd ever had with Giovanni Morelli one more time, and then he would wait to hear back from Devlin.

He needed to get some sleep first, to clear his mind and regain his focus. He hadn't anticipated thoughts of Jenise still plaguing him in his sleep.

Jenise was kissing him again, her lips so soft upon his, her tongue so damn warm and enticing. His hand gripped the back of her head, rubbing along the soft strands of short tapered hair, while the other palmed her ass. As he kneaded the plump mound, his dick grew harder, poking steadily against her center. She was straddling him and as she pulled her mouth away from his, she smiled.

Savian liked to see her smile. He liked how her eyes grew brighter with the action and small dimples appeared in each of her cheeks.

"I want you, Savian," she whispered. "I want all of you, right now."

With those words she angled herself over his length, putting a hand between them to grip his erection and place the head right at her waiting center. As she lowered herself onto his shaft Savian held his breath. It felt too good to breathe and possibly interrupt the action. Inch by inch she sucked him into her, lowering until her cheeks were now on his thighs, his dick buried deep inside of her.

"Watch me as I take you," she said and began to ride.

His breath came in quick pants as she moved and Savian gripped her hips, loving the sight of her heavy breasts bouncing with her ministrations. When she tilted her head back and lifted her hips until the tip of his dick was all that remained ensconced in her heat, he gasped. His eyes remained fixed on her smooth skin, the line of her neck, and the dark circle of her nipples. Her lips were parted slightly as she breathed heavily, circling her hips over him. He couldn't see all of her face and he wanted to, so he said her name, beckoning her to, "Look at me."

When she did, Savian felt warmth spreading throughout his entire body. He moved his hips with hers, their gazes locked as they worked to drive each other to that delicious precipice. She fell first, her mouth opening wider as she gasped when her thighs began to quiver. Savian watched as her eyes clouded when the pleasure was too much for her to bear. He didn't know what to say, could only feel the enticing shivers of pleasure trickling down his spine and when his own release came… The alarm clock on Savian's nightstand blared and he shot straight up in his bed, dick still hard and sunlight peeking through the blinds.

CHAPTER 5

Jenise slammed the phone down, dropping her head between her hands as she sat in her home office. With a ragged sigh she felt like she hadn't moved in hours and she hadn't achieved much either.

After Savian had left yesterday afternoon she hadn't felt much like doing anything with her Christmas decorations so she'd walked away from those boxes. She hadn't even picked up the mistletoe she'd thrown on the floor. Instead, she'd decided it was best to focus on work and so she'd gathered her briefcase, a whole bottle of Moscato and headed into her office. She'd gone through the timeline of events that Savian had given her the night of Morelli's murder more times than she was willing to count.

It had been the Sunday after DNT's All Access event. Savian had been out late after all that had happened at the event with Parker & Adriana. Morelli had been arrested that night after assaulting Adriana. Savian had spent the early morning hours watching the news for any information on Morelli's arrest. These facts did not help in the motive department.

At nine-forty five in the morning, Savian left his condo and headed to the Southern Sunrise Baptist Church where his parents attended every Sunday. The garage attendant verified that, along with the time stamp on the tape pulled from the building's security cameras. There'd been a family gathering immediately following the church service, which had lasted a little longer than usual due to some sort of anniversary celebration. This was corroborated by an actual church program which Jenise had tucked into her file, along with statements from a couple of members from the congregation. Bruce and Janean Donovan confirmed Savian's presence at their house. There was also a receipt that Savian had given her for the gas he'd purchased on his way home from his family dinner at six-thirty that evening. This time the doorman at Savian's condo building verified his arrival home at seven fifteen. From that point on, Savian had been alone at his condo.

"I worked on a few reports, answered some emails and then needed a snack," he'd told her during their first meeting all those weeks ago.

"My aunt had prepared a feast but my cousins and I spent most of the afternoon strategizing about what, if any, damage control we would have to do on Monday as a result of what happened at the party. I don't care for too much fast food on a daily basis, so I use a service that does grocery shopping for me. I cooked myself a vegetable omelet and watched the NBA finals, still irritated that the Heat hadn't made it this year. After that, I went to bed. Alone," he'd emphasized.

As much as Jenise did not want to think of Savian with another woman at this very moment, three months ago, on that Tuesday night, she wished he had been with someone. It would have made proving his innocence that much easier.

At some point she'd finished that bottle of wine alone with a Caesar salad she'd had in her refrigerator. She'd read case law and thought about strategy for hours before finally finding her way to bed. Only to wake up, shower, dress in yoga pants and a t-shirt that had seen better days and head right back into her office.

She was expecting the results from that video tape examination sometime today. There was a tech guy in the area named Jules that she'd worked with on a couple of cases and had grown to trust. He was fast and meticulous, and he testified well. That made him worth all the money she paid him. The detective had replied to her email late last night—apparently she hadn't been the only one burning the midnight oil. She wondered briefly if Rubin had been sipping on anything in particular while he'd worked as well. That bottle of Moscato had given her a pleasant little buzz by the time she'd made it into bed, and Jenise suspected the libation had been the reason for her soundless night's sleep.

This morning she was going over case law again, trying to find any loopholes in Miami law that would help Savian's case, if the video tape turned out to be authentic and his fingerprints were found on that letterhead. Reading about the law and applying it to her client's cases was what Jenise lived for and she'd been working away for hours before she frowned at the sound of her doorbell.

She left her office wondering who could be paying her a visit at almost noon on a Saturday. It had crossed her mind to order herself a pizza for lunch, but she was positive she hadn't done that yet and as good as the Pie Palace, just two blocks away from her apartment building was, they couldn't possibly have read her mind.

Jenise didn't think she'd ever been as shocked as she was when she opened the door to see Savian standing there. He had two big shopping bags on one arm and—bless everything about this man—a pizza box in the other. Maybe he was a mind reader.

"Hi, I ah…I wasn't expecting to see you today," she said, just realizing what she was wearing. Or rather what she wasn't wearing.

Her face was clear of any make-up or products, but for the light sheen of Vaseline she'd swiped over her lips after she'd brushed her teeth more than three hours ago. She'd taken off her hair scarf, but hadn't bothered to comb her hair so she suspected the tapered parts in back and around the sides were flat as usual and probably looked passable. As for the top portion of her hair which was longer, that had most likely taken on the spiked look she normally had in the morning before her grooming ritual. Then there were her clothes…

"I hope I haven't disturbed you," he said. "I was hungry and wanted pizza. I didn't want to eat it alone."

While she looked a hot mess, Savian looked—and oh her absolute goodness, smelled—terrific. He wore dark jeans and a blue and white striped button front shirt. His dark hair and light beard were perfectly shaped-up and looked—as it always did— as if he had his own personal barber that followed him around town. Then there was his scent, like heaven, she thought as she continued to stare at him. It was Michael Kors. She'd recognized the scent on a man one day at the mall and had taken the chance on asking him the name of the fragrance. Funny how Jenise hadn't hesitated to tap that stranger on the shoulder and ask him that question, but had never even considered asking Savian himself.

"Is it that hard to decide whether or not to let me in?" he asked.

"Oh, no," she said feeling like a goof for standing there staring at the man when he'd obviously come bearing the gift of food. "I'm sorry, come on in."

"I forgot to get drinks so I hope you have something that will go with this large pizza with everything, no anchovies, and extra cheese," Savian was saying as he walked through the living room to the small dining room. He appeared to be right at home at her place.

"I have Sprite and bottled water," she told him because the Moscato was long gone.

"I'll take the water," he yelled as she was already headed into the kitchen.

She grabbed water bottles for both of them, then paused to sneak a peek at herself in the reflective side of the toaster. She grinned to make sure nothing was stuck in her teeth, then ran her fingers through the top of her hair, thanking the heavens for having the good sense to keep a short convenient cut. Her sister and mother swore by their long tresses but they spent way too much time at the beauty salon which was not one of Jenise's favorite past times.

As she returned to the dining room, it was to see Savian holding a box out in front of him. The windows in her apartment weren't large, but they were big enough for her to see some of the Miami skyline and a slip of the beach. She loved natural light so there were no curtains and the afternoon sun seemed to glow extra bright around Savian, giving him the appearance of some type of god as he stood there.

"What's that?" she asked because the box was gift wrapped and tied with a huge red bow.

"It's a replacement," he said when she was putting the water bottles down. "I ripped your other one."

Jenise didn't know what he was talking about until she'd taken the box from him and slipped off that pretty red bow. She gasped when she saw what was beneath multiple layers of tissue paper. Sitting the box on the table, she took out the new nightgown. It was black, all lace at the halter top and chiffon from the waist down. Underneath was the wispy black G-string.

"Ah," she said and then cleared her throat. "This wasn't…I mean, the gown you ripped didn't look like this one."

"I know," he said, reaching across the table to grab a bottle of the water she'd brought in. "I like this one better."

"Oh," she replied as she watched him open the water and take a generous gulp. "Okay, then. Well, thank you."

She didn't know what else to say. Why had he come over unannounced and why did he buy her this? It wasn't like Savian at all.

"I know this is probably rude, but can we eat now? I've been in and out of stores all morning and I'm starved," he said, pulling out a chair and sitting down.

"Sure. No problem. Thank you for bringing lunch. I was just getting ready to order pizza. It's like you must have read my mind," she said taking a seat also and accepting the paper plate he'd pulled out of a bag and handed to her.

"Glad I could be of service," he said with a small smile.

Yes, that's exactly what it was, a smile. Jenise had never seen Savian smile. Sure, he had a sexy little grin he'd give her whenever she held his thick length in her hands and stroked, but that was all she'd been privy too. She liked his smile. A lot.

"I'm glad you could, too," she told him.

They ate in silence for a few moments. The pizza was delicious, but Jenise was more curious about the man sitting across from her and this mysterious visit.

"I brought you more decorations," he said after taking a bite of his second slice. "It didn't look like you had enough in those boxes to cover both rooms of this apartment. I figured you would want to have decorations in this window too, since you never close the curtains. Lights probably," he added with a shrug. "I picked up some of that lighted garland. I've seen that in windows or it might be nice draped over this archway."

"What?" Jenise asked, unable to even think about reaching for her second slice. "You bought Christmas decorations? But you said it was too early to decorate."

He nodded while he finished chewing. "It is. But since you're ready, you might as well have everything you need."

And he'd gone out to buy what she needed. Jenise didn't know how to respond to that. They continued to eat in silence because she wasn't sure what to say or how to take what was happening. Savian had never just showed up at her place without calling or texting and when he came over, there were only moments before they were getting naked. He'd been here for almost twenty-five minutes now, and they were still sitting at her dining room table, fully clothed, and more awkward now than that first day they'd had sex in her office.

"I like Christmas music, too," she said abruptly after he'd finished his second slice. "Now that, I do not have to wait until November to enjoy it."

Jenise moved from her seat, going into the living room to pick up the remote that controlled the multi-DVD player on the stand just below her television. There were already six of her favorite holiday CDs inserted as she'd been listening to them often these past few weeks.

"I usually take a break from the music around January, but by the time summer rolls around I'm ready to hear it again. So I never put these away," she'd continued talking and smiled as the first track on the *A Motown Christmas* CD began to play.

When she thought she would turn around and see him frowning at her from the dining room, she was quickly mistaken. Savian had also moved from the table, so that he was now unpacking the other shopping bag he'd brought in with him.

"I'm not totally adverse to some holiday music," he was saying, his back facing her as he moved.

His shoulders were broad, his back as muscled and fantastic to look at as the rest of him. She'd known immediately that he worked out a lot, even without him mentioning it in the months since they'd known each other. She'd at first assumed he had a platinum membership to some upscale gym that he visited at least once a day. When he'd told her he only used his personal home gym because he didn't want people staring at him when he worked out, Jenise had received her first glimpse into the private and almost reclusive man that he was.

"My mother and my aunt rotate holidays at their house so that we're all together for each one. When we were little, we actually used to spend the night at Aunt Janean's on Christmas Eve so that all of the kids could wake up together. It was the same when it was my mother's turn to host," he continued to talk while emptying the bag.

"Wow, your family is really close," she said, folding her arms over her chest as she watched him move.

Why did he look so good doing something as simple as taking boxes and lights out of a bag? Even his clothes were normal jeans and a shirt, yet, the combo looked beyond inviting on him.

"There are a lot more of us," he was saying as he moved from where he'd put the new items on the couch, back to the boxes he'd been going through yesterday.

Today, he went straight for the tree.

"We're scattered across the states now, but we have an annual family reunion where we try to get everyone together. It's kind of hard sometimes as most of us have very busy schedules," he finished.

"But you like being with all of your family. You enjoy that sense of togetherness when you can because your life is normally so solitary." She stopped then because she hadn't realized she was voicing her assessment aloud.

When he turned to look at her, his brow furrowed in that way he did when she knew he was thinking something, but didn't intend to say what, she let her arms fall to her sides.

"This is a seven foot tree," she said crossing the room to where he stood, his hands still on the tall box. "One of the reasons I chose this apartment, even though the view is not all that I desired, was because of the high ceilings. When I decorate my tree I'm always thinking of the White House Christmas tree," she said, pulling the tape back from the box.

She was partially relieved when Savian stopped staring at her and reached over to finish removing the tape and flipped back the flaps on the box.

"You have very grand Christmas décor ideas," he quipped.

She chuckled. "You only live once."

"Yes," he said casting a glance her way. "You do."

The next hour was spent with Savian insisting that he knew how to assemble the tree, without the directions, and Jenise frowning knowingly at him when he inevitably did it wrong.

"Don't you dare say it," he'd warned when he'd taken the tree completely apart and snatched the neatly folded instructions she'd dropped to the bottom of his box, per his request.

"Say what?" she'd asked, attempting to hold back her smile.

"'I told you so'," he replied, mimicking a high-pitched sing-songy voice.

She couldn't hold it back then, she laughed out loud and received an amused gaze from him. When he went back to assembling the tree, this time going step-by-step with the directions, Jenise was feeling so comfortable and so lighthearted that she began opening the new boxes of ornaments he'd bought and singing along with the music playing throughout the room. Eventually, she lost track of time, as she usually did when she was decorating, and when she turned back to look at Savian, he had the tree completely assembled and the lights on it were now twinkling gleefully.

Her singing stopped in that moment and she clapped her hands. "I love it when the lights go on. It looks so pretty."

"You want to leave it like that?" he asked, taking a step back from the tree and staring at it with her.

"Oh no," she answered with a shake of her head. "It needs all the other pretty things you bought, plus my usual dressings. It's going to be beautiful this year."

Because he was helping her. She'd been smart enough not to say that part aloud.

Jenise hung the first bulb, a crystal clear one with a color Santa figurine inside. It was delicate and pretty and most likely very expensive. She would remember forever that Savian had bought it for her. In no time, her singing began again as she moved around the tree adding bulbs and ornaments throughout. Savian had joined her in the decorating and a few times they bumped into each other in passing. She'd smile and keep singing and he'd shake his head as if her were thoroughly amused with her. Then, when Jenise thought this man could not possibly shock her again today, he did.

Savian began singing. They were on the Boyz II Men *Christmas Interpretations* CD now and one of her favorite tracks had just begun to play—"Who Would Have Thought". His voice was so smooth and melodic as he sang every word while moving about the tree. There was something in her hand but she couldn't remember what. She should have been doing something, helping him perhaps, but she wasn't. Instead she stood there watching him, listening to him, falling hard for him.

He came around to the front of the tree where she was standing at that moment, placing the bulb he'd been holding in his hand on a branch, when he looked over to see her staring at him. He'd continued to sing, again to her surprise, while his gaze held hers. Jenise knew the words to this song. She knew what they meant and how sweet and romantic they always sounded whenever she heard them. Today, all of that was magnified because they were in Savian's voice.

Her heart slammed against her chest, her hands began to shake and she licked her lips slowly, not sure what to say. The only words she could think of were the ones she heard him singing, the words about falling in love on Christmas day. She sang them quietly, her not as melodic voice, mixing with his. The lights flickering on the tree brought out the intense brown and gold flecks in his eyes as he reached across to take the bulb out of her still shaking hand. He hung it on a branch without missing a word to the song and then he took her hands in his.

It was like a movie scene, one Jenise wanted to watch over and over again. Savian Donovan with his fine and complicated self, standing in front of her beautiful seven foot tall Christmas tree, singing a Boyz II Men song with her. She let her fingers twine with his as he took a step closer to her and when the song finally finished, when she thought her heart was going to hop, skip and jump right out of her chest, Savian leaned forward and kissed her.

Jenise welcomed the kiss like a breath of fresh air, wrapping her arms quickly around his neck and pulling him closer. His arms went around her waist, hands flattening on her back. He moved slowly, his tongue gliding with languid precision over hers as if he were savoring every single stroke. She cupped the back of his head, loving the warmth that spread from her palms, up her arms and throughout her torso. Wrapped in Savian's strong arms Jenise admitted to herself, with a heartfelt sigh, that she felt safe and cherished.

When his hands moved lower to squeeze her ass, she moaned, pressing closer to him and loving the feel of his hard body against hers. Another song was playing but try as she might, Jenise had no clue what it was. All she could think about was Savian's intoxicating scent, this delicious kiss and the feel of his strong hands moving lower. She gasped when he lifted her up, wrapping her legs around his waist in a motion so smooth and seemingly practiced she blinked in surprise as she looked down at him.

He didn't speak, but then again, he didn't need to. That look on his face said it all. Savian took the few steps toward the sofa and with one hand, knocked every box, strand of lighted garland, plastic wrapping and whatever else was there, to the floor. He lay Jenise down as gently as if she were one of those crystal ornaments he'd purchased for her. She stared up at him without speaking as his fingers moved slowly over the buttons of his shirt. When he stripped it away, and pulled the stark white t-shirt over his head, she exhaled slowly. His body was so finely sculpted almost like a bodybuilder and she could never get enough of looking at it. From the bulging biceps, to the contoured pectorals, down to the way his torso tapered to a slim waist and washboard abs. She was simply mesmerized. So much so that he'd taken off all of his clothes and she was still lying there staring hungrily at him.

When she grabbed the hem of her shirt and was about to pull it up and over her head, Savian pushed her hands away.

"I've got this," he said, his voice deeper than usual and sexy as hell.

Jenise let her hands fall to her sides and lay still as he undressed her in a torturously slow manner. His fingers just barely brushed over her full and now highly sensitive breasts after he'd removed the shirt and her bra. And when she'd lifted her hips to aid him in pulling down her yoga pants, those same fingers scraped along the crevice of her behind, sending spears of pleasure straight to her core. But it was after she was completely naked, the way he touched both his palms to her thighs, parting them slowly, that Jenise knew she'd lost the battle.

He was staring down at her with such a tender look on his face, Jenise wanted to lift her hands and touch him. She remained still when his fingers slipped to the insides of her thighs, rubbing her skin softly before moving upward to her waiting center. With those same fingers he parted her plump and now damp folds slowly, making a different sound of appreciation than she'd ever heard before. He flattened a thumb over her clit and rubbed slowly. Jenise sucked in a breath, her fingers grasping the pillows of the sofa beneath her as she closed her eyes to the sweet sensations rippling through her body. For endless moments he simply touched her, with one finger and then another, stroking along the length of her moistness, delving quickly inside her center before pulling out just as fast. She was circling her hips, trying to lift upward, to engage a deeper probe from him, begging for release without opening her mouth.

"I've got to," she heard him whisper before he was moving over her.

She opened her eyes then, just in time to see his head dip between her legs. In seconds his tongue was on her tender flesh and Jenise cried out in ecstasy. Savian held her legs open wide, his fingers digging into her thighs as he pushed her back further into the sofa. She was open and waiting for him like a feast and his mouth was working hungrily over her. Her head thrashed back and forth without any thought to how crazy her hair was going to look when they were done. All she could focus on now was the pleasure, the deep and pounding waves of pleasure at the feel of his tongue on her flesh. And when that tongue speared inside of her, Jenise thought she would explode right then and there. Instead she cupped her own breasts, squeezing her nipples until they stung from the assault.

He was gorging on her, the sounds coming much louder than the music that was playing and driving Jenise's desire up higher and higher. She wanted him so desperately right now, needing him to come between her legs and thrust deep and hard inside. At the same time she didn't want him to stop, as evidenced by the way she grabbed the back of his head, holding him in place. He suckled and licked for what seemed like an infinite amount of pleasure-filled time, so that when he abruptly pulled back, Jenise was instantly aware and missed the contact like an addict would their fix.

Her gaze immediately went to his hand as it gripped his thick, rigid length, stroking hard from its base to the tip as he licked his lips and continued to stare down at her. Acting on pure instinct, and remembering this part from their many trysts before, Jenise moved until she could grab his pants from the floor and dug into his back pocket for his wallet. She wasn't being nosy and didn't even look at what was there when she opened it, only felt through the side opening for the condom packet she knew would be there.

Their gazes met as she sat up on the sofa and reached for him. Without a word he moved closer to her, letting his hands fall to his side when she wrapped her fingers around his length. Again, going solely on what her body wanted, Jenise leaned in quickly to drag her tongue over the bulbous head of his penis. He moaned loud, bringing his hands up instantly to clasp the back of her head. Jenise had never done this before, never met anyone that she'd been moved to try it on. Truth be told, she hadn't even thought about it with Savian in the three months that they'd been lovers. Yet today, right here in this moment, she wanted to taste him, to feel his warm length sliding along her tongue the way it did in and out of her center.

She opened her mouth wider this time, letting his shaft slide inside her mouth slowly as he pushed forward. Closing her lips around him she began to suck, spurred on by the sounds he was making and marveling in how intensely she desired more of him now. Moments later when he pulled out of her there was a popping sound and then his simple instructions to "Put it on."

She did as he requested, smoothing the condom down his length and had just looked up at him when he touched her shoulders, pushing her back on the sofa. He was over her in seconds, spreading her legs wide once again, this time tucking one onto the back of the sofa and letting the other dangle off the side. Then he was inside, working his rigid shaft in and out of her wet center until she was whispering his name. Jenise loved that he was on top of her, that she could look up and see the intense expressions on his face—the way he bit his bottom lip in concentration, or looked to her for confirmation. She lifted a hand to touch his cheek once, when he'd leaned in to kiss her breast. He'd pulled back quickly then, as if he'd been burned and went completely still.

Jenise wasn't sure what to say or do. The touch had been very intimate, she knew, and she'd never done it before. But today was the day of "first times" for them, or so she'd thought. She'd been feeling differently around him since the moment she saw him standing in the doorway, her instincts had her following those differences and enjoying them one by one.

Savian, on the other hand, obviously had other ideas.

He pulled out of her slowly, and then moved off the sofa. Then he touched her in a way that was familiar, and that told her exactly what he wanted now. Jenise obliged, turning around so that her palms were flat on the sofa and she was bent over, ready for his taking. It came quickly. Savian moved behind her, thrusting inside her so fast she'd gasped. He'd proceeded to pump quickly then, like he was in a race with himself. It felt so good and then it felt so wrong. Jenise could do nothing but ride it out, accepting the delicious release as it tore through her body and was still shaking when, seconds later Savian's ripped through him.

What the hell was he doing?

Savian shook his head as quickly and roughly as that release that had just soared through his body. He still held on to her hips while his erection jerked inside her one more time. With his eyes closed tightly he tried to remain perfectly still, to not disturb this moment because he knew that's when the questions would come.

Jenise normally did not ask questions. She'd always accepted what they had without any arguments or comments. That was one of the things Savian enjoyed most about being with her.

But today was different.

There was no doubt about that. He'd known it the moment he woke up, chest heaving, and dick so hard he probably could have used it as a weapon. She'd been on his mind so much in the next hour that instead of heading into his home gym as he usually did first when he awoke in the morning, he'd taken a quick shower and then gone out, to the mall no less. Savian hated the mall.

Hell, he had a private tailor and a grocery service on retainer, which proved he was not the shopping type. And yet, he'd quickly found himself moving in and out of stores, carefully selecting items that he thought Jenise would like.

She had enjoyed the ornaments and the lunch and the fact that he was there. He'd seen it in her eyes as they'd sat at that table eating. A part of him had warned that he should get up and leave then, but he did not. The next thing he knew they were decorating the tree and then she was singing, and he was singing, and then…

This wasn't what he'd had planned. He hadn't known that the urge to taste her would be so overwhelming that he would push back all his reservations about such an intimate act and go for it with her regardless. Nor had he been prepared for her to reciprocate. The thought of her mouth on him made him tingle all over. He'd hurried into the sex because that was easy, it was familiar to both of them, and at this point it was expected. Only that hadn't gone as planned either. He'd looked down at her as he stroked and this time she'd been looking back at him.

It was different. Her look and his feelings.

The thought had Savian cursing as he finally pulled out of her slowly. She stood immediately and he turned away from her, not wanting to face her and the questions she might have. For that matter, he didn't even want to face his own questions and wished they'd stop running rapidly through his mind.

"I'm going to take a shower," she said from somewhere behind him. "Join me."

It wasn't a question and even if it was, Savian wouldn't have known how to answer. He did not shower with women, but by the time he'd gathered enough courage to turn around and tell her that, she was already gone.

He'd cursed then, dragging a hand over his face as he stood naked in her living room, the Chipmunks happily singing Christmas songs in the background.

The lights were still twinkling on the tree and ornaments and stuff were now tossed on the floor. He should just gather his clothes, put them on and walk out that front door. She would understand, it was their unspoken agreement after all. No strings. No attachments. No intimacies. He'd thought she was on that same page with him. Today, however, it seemed that maybe Jenise had turned a page.

Or had he?

Savian had just grabbed his shirt and was reaching for his pants when he heard the water from the shower turn on. Crap! He couldn't just walk out, not without saying something to her. He didn't know what to say, but he knew it had to be something. He owed her that much. So it was with heavy steps that he made his way back to her bedroom, his clothes clutched under his arm. The plan was to tell her he had to go, that he'd stayed too long or something like that. She would look up at him with understanding and he'd promise to call her later. He'd never done that before.

When he walked into the bathroom, Jenise was just stepping into the stall. She looked over her shoulder at him and smiled, leaving the door cracked as she eased beneath the spray of water. Crap, again! He dropped his clothes to the floor, and quickly discarded the condom. Then, he moved toward the shower stall knowing this was a mistake. Correction, *knowing* and hating how big a mistake this would inevitably turn out to be.

She'd turned to him immediately when he stepped inside the now steam-filled stall and began rubbing her lather filled hands over his chest.

"The soap smells girly, but you'll be alright," she said with a smile. "You'll be fresh and clean."

Savian didn't want to be fresh and clean. Well, he did, but not here and not now. Still, as she continued to touch him, her hands moving over his skin along with the soap and water, he felt a familiar stirring. He wanted her again.

Clenching his teeth he grasped her shoulders until she stilled. When she looked up at him, Savian couldn't figure out what to say. So instead, he lowered his forehead to hers and simply admitted, "I don't know how to do this."

"Me neither," was her reply. "But I'm thinking that it might be nice if we learned together."

Savian had no idea if it would be nice or not, what he did know was that at this exact moment, he couldn't stop it. He picked up the soap and lathered it in his hands, then began washing her the way she'd washed him. By the time they'd finished touching each other, Savian had her facing the wall in the shower stall, his hands parting the generous globes of her ass once more so that he could slip his length deep inside her waiting heat.

He stroked and she moaned. He hissed with the pleasure that soared through his body. She whispered his name and he lowered his head to rest on her shoulder wondering what the hell he was doing and how this would end. Because, if there was one thing he knew for sure, it was that the end was inevitable. That was another reason he'd never wanted to start anything in the first place. Another damned good reason.

CHAPTER 6

Two weeks later.

Gwen had already called back to announce her, so Jenise shouldn't have been surprised when Adriana tapped on her office door before coming in.

In truth, she wasn't actually surprised, but more intrigued. Adriana Bennett was a supermodel, turned actress and a stunning natural beauty. Take today, for instance, Jenise could tell as Adriana approached her desk, that the woman wore very little make-up. Still, she was flawless with her burnished gold complexion, golden brown eyes and long professionally highlighted hair. She was dressed simply enough in black slim pants, a black and white blouse and a simple black jacket. Black pumps and the large black Prada bag she held in one hand topped off the casual, yet sophisticated outfit. Then there was her smile, big, gorgeous and also sincere.

Jenise smiled back as she greeted her. "Hello, Adriana. It's nice to see you again."

She hadn't seen any of Savian's family since that day at the police station a couple of weeks ago. They had, however, been in the news more times than Jenise could count. A few days ago she'd actually felt bad for the family because there'd been an hour-long special on television. The documentary went back to Rowan and Charleston Donovan, the brothers who started the Donovan Oilwell Company, seventy years ago with a piece of land they'd inherited from their employer. In the years that followed, the Donovans' offspring had branched out, spreading their success throughout the states and dabbling into different industries such as casinos, media, real estate and Jenise's favorite—law. To say they were an African American success story born and bred, was an understatement.

While her family wasn't as big as the Donovans, Jenise had watched the episode feeling a sense of kinship, as her great-grandfather, Charles Milford Langley, had attended the Howard University School of Law alongside Thurgood Marshall in 1930. After graduation he'd assisted in preparing for the litigation of hundreds of segregation cases, before his untimely death in 1954. Her grandfather, Victor, had followed in his father's footsteps, but instead had attended the University of Maryland School of Law—the same school that had turned Thurgood Marshall away for being black, and that Marshall successfully sued in 1933. After marching with Dr. Martin Luther King, Jr. and working on several civil rights cases for a firm in Atlanta, Victor moved his family to the West Side of Chicago and in 1970 opened the first Langley Law firm. Now retired, her grandparents lived in Hyde Park and her father ran the firm.

"Hi," Adriana replied, bringing Jenise and her thoughts back to the present. "I was in the neighborhood and decided to stop by."

Jenise smiled and nodded her head. "No, problem. You can stop by any time," she told her even though she sensed that Adriana had a specific reason for coming to see her today.

"So how are things going?" Jenise asked, deciding she'd rather get to the heart of the matter—without being rude—as soon as possible. She was scheduled to meet with clients this afternoon, to go over discovery in a huge malpractice case and she wanted to be prepared for their arrival.

Adriana had taken a seat in one of the guest chairs across from Jenise's desk. She crossed her long legs and set her purse in the other chair to her right. Now, her hands were folded in her lap as her gaze met Jenise's.

"I was just wondering how Savian's case was going," she said as casually as if she was stating the time of day.

The only problem with the way Adriana was acting and talking, was that Jenise prided herself on having good insight into people. This was a skill she'd developed over time because she was determined to never be fooled again. At any rate, as she sat back, letting her hands rest on the arms of the chair, she continued to assess Adriana Bennett. Just a few months ago this woman had come into her office for the first time, angry that someone was attempting to destroy all of her hard work. At first, Jenise hadn't been certain that Parker and Adriana were more than just the "passing fling" the tabloids dubbed them, but in the months since she'd seen them photographed together, and then a couple of weeks ago when Adriana had dropped everything and come running to be by Parker's side at the police station, she'd changed her stance. This was a woman in love.

Jenise didn't know whether to pity or admire her.

"I'm still waiting for a report on the surveillance tape, but the letter came back clean. Savian's prints were nowhere on it. And even after they obtained a warrant to go through his work and home computers, there was no record of him having typed or saved that letter," she said.

"That's fantastic," Adriana said, expelling a sigh of relief. "I know the family has been really worried about whether or not that evidence would stick."

"They have a pretty good motive, but if this surveillance video doesn't hit a homerun, they'll have to dismiss the charges. Or at least I'm going to flood them with motions until they dismiss the charges," she added with a grin.

"Does it normally take this long to get the results back on the video?" Adriana asked. "I'm sorry, I'm not very familiar with murder cases or how you go about investigating them."

Jenise nodded. "It's not something people normally learn about as a hobby. But the answer is no, it shouldn't take this long. My guy was in an automobile accident the day after I had the tape delivered to his office. He broke his leg and had to have surgery. I just spoke with him this morning, however. He's off the pain meds but still bedridden, so he's going to have a colleague look at the tape either today or tomorrow. We'll have an answer soon."

"Good," Adriana said with yet, another sigh. "That would be great if the family could hear that this would all be over before Thanksgiving. There would be such a festive atmosphere at the big dinner."

"They're having a big dinner on Thursday?" Jenise asked. "I guess they would. They seem like such a close family."

"Oh, they are. My parents and my brothers are even flying in for the weekend. Does your family do a big celebration? I know they're all in Chicago right?"

Again, Jenise nodded. She'd been trying really hard not to think about the tension-filled dinner that her mother would host. Her brothers and her grandparents would come, and talk would eventually circle around to the firm and the latest cases. That's when Marianne would no doubt begin her comments about how ridiculous she thought it was for Jenise to have moved to Miami. No matter how she'd tried to convince herself that this might not happen, the odds seemed stacked against her, and Jenise had called her parents over the weekend to say that she wouldn't be able to come home for the holiday. She hadn't been the least bit disappointed about making that announcement, even though it meant she would have dinner alone in her apartment. Actually, she'd been toying with the idea of going out to a restaurant but figured that might just make her look a little more lonely and pathetic.

"That sounds nice," Jenise replied, trying desperately not to sound as jealous as she actually felt.

She would have been elated if her mother had suggested the family come here to spend Thanksgiving with her.

"They were here a few months back, but that was a very tense time," Adriana continued. "So I'm hoping everyone can be more relaxed this go round. If Savian is cleared of all charges by then, I know the Donovans will feel a lot better," she said.

"Well, that's just three days away, but I'm hopeful for that as well. In fact, I've already drafted my motion to dismiss. All I need now are the final facts that will force the prosecutor's hand." Jenise figured it was better to talk about work, than family, because that was making her way too sad.

She had hoped that would also appease Adriana and the woman would then bid her goodbyes and leave Jenise's office. Not that she had anything against Adriana, because she didn't. It was just that she did not need to be reminded of the fact that she would spend Thanksgiving alone—albeit by choice—because of her family and their narrow-minded thinking. But also, because she was having a secret affair with her client.

Adriana, however, continued to stare at Jenise, as if there were something else on her mind. Jenise was just about to ask her what that was, when Adriana cleared her throat and sat up taller in the chair.

"Is it really as easy as you make it seem?" she asked, with a tilt of her head.

Jenise didn't know what to say because she wasn't certain what Adriana meant. Was she speaking about being an attorney? Or what she thought the outcome of this case in particular would be?

"I mean, from the moment I met you, you've seemed to have it all together. You're confident and smart and don't take any crap, as evidenced by the way you immediately dealt with Savian when he was trying to question your credentials? I'm just asking because I've met so many women in the business and then being around my mother and my sister—both of which I think are very strong-minded women—I'm still in awe of how you handle yourself with such ease and embolden finesse.

Again, Jenise was speechless. Her sister would be amazed since Morgan had always said Jenise was the mouthpiece for the Langley sisters. Sitting here and not quickly responding also blew all types of holes into the complimentary declaration Adriana had just made about her.

Jenise cleared her throat, to give herself more time to think of how she wanted to respond to this different and somewhat baffling question. Adriana Bennett had been a model since she was seventeen years old—Jenise had looked into the woman's background when she took her on as a client because the last thing she needed in the midst of litigation, was surprises. In the years following, Adriana had suffered from bulimia and/or some form of binge eating, as she recollected. Now, she was an actress as well as being engaged to Parker Donovan. Talk about body image, appearance and stress, this woman had to be carrying tons of doubts and concerns in her mind at this very moment. With that in mind, Jenise knew exactly how to respond to Adriana's question.

"I believe the answer is that I really have no other choice," she told her with a slight shrug. "When people meet you, the first thing they look for is a weakness. For me, it's usually my weight. They immediately expect, that because I'm not what society believes should be your average sized female, I should be timid and embarrassed. Sometimes they actually look at me in pity, wondering how and why I would allow myself to get to this size. The moment I show them that I know exactly who I am, what I want, and what BS I won't stand for, they get their act together."

Everyone except her mother.

Adriana continued to stare at Jenise intently, as if she were sharing the secret of life with her instead of her own philosophy on idiotic human beings.

"Does it always work for you? I mean, do they really stop thinking those negative thoughts about you after you set them straight?"

Jenise shook her head and waved a hand. "I don't really care if it does or not. As long as they know what not to say to me. I'm sure you've heard this before, but I'll say it again, it's not important what other people think about you, Adriana. What's important is how you feel about yourself? If you can love you, just the way you are—at one hundred and thirty pounds tops, with your pretty mix of Brazilian and African American skin tone and longer than forever legs—then you don't need anyone else's approval."

Adriana had actually blushed at the compliment, before admitting, "You're a very attractive woman, too."

Jenise smiled. "And don't I know it," she said with a laugh. "Because you know what? If I don't believe I'm sexy, how can I expect anyone else to believe it?"

"Savian believes you're sexy," Adriana said abruptly. "I mean, I can tell by the way he looks at you that he's really interested. It wasn't that clear the first day we met you, because he'd been acting strange. But I've seen him so many times since then and I can see whenever Parker mentions your name the way he changes. It's a subtle change because you know how Savian is, but it's there. I know it's definitely there."

Jenise knew exactly how she wanted to reply to this comment with—with a resounding 'Yes!' to be followed by a big grin and a fist pump. There was no doubt that Savian was interested in her. He was interested enough to have been at her house every night for the last two weeks. They'd finished putting up the Christmas decorations and had gone through her holiday music and movie collection one night. For someone who had thought it was too early to get ready for Christmas, Savian had jumped in with both feet. One night, after sex and a shower, they'd lounged on her bed while she shopped online for Wade and Tucker's Christmas gift. Savian had offered a good deal of insight into buying for men and she'd been so stoked at having him stay longer after their sex, that she'd ordered exactly what he'd suggested.

Savian had extended his time spent at her house, however, there was still no cuddling after sex and no overnights, which meant he was still keeping his distance. In the last couple of days, however, Jenise had been thinking long and hard about whether or not she wanted that distance to be closed for good. She'd been wondering whether or not it was time that she and Savian became something more than friends with benefits.

"He's an attractive man," she told Adriana, because there was no way she was going to lay all that had just crossed her mind on this woman. "I'm really hoping that we'll be able to get this mess cleared up so he can move on with his life."

That was a basic enough statement and should work to get her out of this uncomfortable conversation. To magnify the fact that she was finished with this discussion, Jenise pushed back from her desk and stood. "So you can deliver the news to the family that I am working hard to get these charges dismissed as soon as I possibly can."

Adriana stood too. She reached over and grabbed her bag and was just putting it on her shoulder when a smile spread across her face.

"You should come over for Thanksgiving dinner," she said to Jenise. "It's at four o'clock at Bruce and Janean's house. Here I'll give you the address."

Adriana was digging into her purse while Jenise was shaking her head.

"No. I cannot come to their house uninvited," Jenise said quickly.

"But you were invited," Adriana replied looking over at her as if Jenise had possibly thought she was speaking another language. "I just invited you."

"But you don't live there. I mean, I know you're engaged to Parker, but that's not even his parents' house," Jenise continued.

Adriana was shaking her head now, as she came around Jenise's desk. "Where's your phone? Grab it, save this address and then take my number in case you get lost. Their house is all the way toward the peak of the inlet, so it can get tricky when you're driving down. Or maybe Parker and I can pick you up."

"No!" Jenise raised her voice this time and Adriana's head snapped up. "I mean, I'm not sure this is such a good idea. I don't really know the Donovans. I'm just Savian's attorney."

Adriana raised a brow then and Jenise realized at that moment what this entire visit had been about in the first place.

"We both know that's not entirely true," Adriana said.

"What are you talking about?"

"I'm talking about the fact that Parker told me you did not hesitate to say you would take Savian to your apartment after he'd been released from custody. A hotel might have been more appropriate for your 'client'," Adriana spoke with a lift of her brows. "And Savian has been leaving work around the same time every evening for the past two weeks—since you took him back to your apartment. Now, we're not snooping or anything, so it's not like we followed him and know for a fact that he's been hurrying home to see you, but I have it on pretty good authority that on at least one occasion he ordered dinner while he was at work and had it sent to your address. I'm not going to divulge how I found that out, for fear of what Savian might try to do to his sister. But anyway, you're coming to Thanksgiving dinner and it's going to be a wonderful day. Trust me."

Adriana finished all that off with a smile as she slipped the phone that Jenise had picked up in a defensive effort, from her fingers. She immediately began typing in the address to Bruce and Janean Donovan's house, where it appeared Jenise would be spending Thanksgiving.

"So how long have you and Jenise Langley been sleeping together?"

Savian slipped both hands into the front pockets of his slacks. He stood, in front of the window in his office, staring out at the fading sunlight. It was the night before Thanksgiving when most people would be home with their family preparing for tomorrow's festivities. Most people, such as husbands or boyfriends who were dedicated to family and to making memories for that family. Both of which, Savian was not.

Unfortunately, his solitude had been interrupted with a voice. A knowing voice that was way too comfortable saying any and everything he wanted to Savian.

"I'm not sure how this is any of your business, but I won't waste time by denying it," Savian replied without turning to face his brother.

"And I won't ask if you think that's a wise decision," Parker said. "I know you don't do anything without giving it complete and careful consideration."

"It's not unlike any other interaction I've had with a woman," Savian told him, the words leaving an unusually bitter taste in his mouth. He frowned, something he'd been doing more of lately.

Just as he'd been seeing Jenise more. Two weeks, fourteen days, and on each one he'd seen her. He'd spent a good part of today trying to figure out the significance of that fact.

Parker continued, as he obviously had a point to starting this conversation.

"Only this one is your lawyer. I won't ask you if you think that's a good idea, because I know you. If it's not a good idea, you don't do it," his brother stated. "What I am going to ask is have you considered—thoroughly considered—what will happen if this falls apart before your case goes to trial. Or, how about this scenario, what happens when the press gets wind of you and her sleeping together? Isn't there some type of ethics violation there? Would she be disbarred? Would the case be compromised? In short, will this dalliance destroy both of you in the end?"

On the outside Parker gave the appearance of being a carefree and jovial man. He was deceptively smart when it came to business and knew the television industry better than anyone Savian had yet to encounter. For years Parker and Dion had been dubbed the playboy Donovans of Miami, leaving a string of broken hearts in their wake. Even after Parker's divorce, he'd seamlessly picked up the torch and continued to carry that playboy reputation straight to the tabloids and all the entertainment news stations. Now, Dion was married and Parker was engaged. For that matter, Sean was also married with a daughter and even Regan was involved in a committed relationship. He was the only one alone, which had never been a problem for him before. These were things that had been on his mind the last few days, creating even more stress for him.

"It's just sex," Savian told Parker.

He turned to see his brother sitting casually in one of the leather chairs across from his desk. Sometime during the busy work day Parker would have removed his suit jacket, tossing it over the back of the couch he had in his office. Savian did not have a couch in his office. This was a place to work, not relax. Which was evidenced by the tightness throughout his shoulders and the persistent throbbing at his temples.

Parker was laughing. His head tossed back, hands coming up, only to slap down on his thighs as the guffaws continued. Savian moved to the side of his desk, sitting on its edge as he stared with blatant irritation at his brother.

"Glad I could amuse you," he said. "Now, I'm sure Adriana's waiting for you at home."

"You can't put me out," Parker said through the short breaths he managed to take in between the laughter. "I work here too, remember."

"Then maybe you should get back to work," Savian replied blandly.

"I always thought you were the smartest of the three of us," Parker commented, when it seemed he'd finally regained his composure. "But that has got to be the dumbest thing I've ever heard you say."

"What? That it's just sex?" Savian frowned. "I'm not the relationship type, you know that. And just because the rest of you used to take that stance but now have been otherwise dissuaded, has absolutely nothing to do with me. I know what I'm capable of and what I can afford to allow into my life. A girlfriend or a wife is not on that list."

"They usually aren't, little brother," Parker said, more serious this time, even with that twinkle of laughter still in his eyes.

"Here's how I see this playing out," he continued, to Savian's chagrin. "You're either going to fall in love with that woman, or she's going to fall in love with you. The reason I know this for a fact is because I know you."

Savian shook his head. "That's not possible if you're even entertaining these thoughts. I'm not serious about Jenise Langley. She's my attorney and my current lover, that's all."

"She's a tenacious and intelligent professional woman," Parker pointed out. "She's not one of those gold-diggers or opportunists that you've always thought would come after us. She doesn't need the Donovan money or status, because she has her own. She's smart and pretty enough to know that she can get another man and doesn't have to settle for your ridiculous limitations, unless she wants to. So my guess is, she'll entertain your no strings attached motto until she's ready for something else, and when she's ready she's going to give you an ultimatum."

"I don't reply well to ultimatums," Savian quickly remarked.

Parker nodded. "I know you usually don't, but then you're not usually faced with a woman like this."

"You don't know anything about her."

"I know she went against her entire family to come down here and open a law firm in a city where she doesn't know anyone. That doesn't sound like a person that's going to allow you, someone of no blood relation, to dictate to her what she can and cannot have," Parker stated firmly. "So, mark my words, when she's ready to change the rules in this game you're playing, she will. And you'll either go with the changes or you'll go home alone. That, my brother, as much as I love and care for your well-being, is something I cannot wait to see unfold."

"Because you have a sick sense of humor," Savian replied.

He slipped off the side of the desk and walked around to his chair. Sitting down, he pulled his keyboard closer and began to close the documents he'd had open. "Now, if you don't have anything else to speak to me about, I have work to do."

Parker stood, a smile spreading across his face. "You mean you have to hurry out of here so you can get to Jenise's apartment. Yes, I know about that," he said when Savian's head had snapped up in surprise.

"We all know," Parker continued. "At least Regan, Dion, Sean and I know."

"How?" Savian asked through gritted teeth.

"Come on, man, you know better than that. The same way you all knew something was going on between Adriana and me. We're family and we were all taught to look out for one another. That's what we do, Savian. As for you, well, we're all keeping an extra close eye on you and what you're doing since somebody out there is clearly trying to set you up to take the fall for this murder."

Savian could only stare at Parker. He couldn't argue that logic because he'd done it so many times himself. When Sabine Ravenell had been hounding Dion and Sean about buying *Infinity*, Parker, Savian and Regan had watched those brothers and the women in their lives like hawks. As Gavin made his play for Regan, Savian had been on that island, in the midst of a serial killer on the hunt, keeping a close eye on his sister and her tumultuous journey into love. And just a few months ago, when it was his brother, someone who had been closer to him, than if they'd been born twins, Savian had known every step Parker took, every hour of every day. So yes, to say that the cousins were committed to looking out for each other was a vast understatement.

"I'm fine," was all Savian could say in response. "I know what I'm doing."

Parker shook his head as he turned and began to walk away. "That's what we all say, little brother, right before we take that fall."

The door to his office opened, Parker walked through, giving Savian one more knowing glance and a smile before adding, "See you at Aunt Janean's tomorrow. And tell Jenise I said I hope she has a Happy Thanksgiving."

When the door closed behind him, Savian frowned.

He was not falling for Jenise Langley. She was not going to give him any type of ultimatum because they were both on the same page. And, the best point of this all was that Savian was just fine going home alone. He was content with having dinner in his office or in the living room in front of the TV, tuned to the news channels, by himself. All his life he'd preferred to be alone—for as much as a person in a family like the Donovans could. Nothing had changed.

Absolutely nothing.

He continued to tell himself that as he left the office for the day and drove to Jenise's apartment, again.

CHAPTER 7

The first thing Jenise heard when she walked through the door was laughter. Even from a distance it was loud and boisterous and solicited an immediate smile.

"We're a rowdy bunch, especially when it's so close to being time to eat," Tate Donovan said.

Jenise had seen her on television before. She was the host of a relationship advice show and she also wrote a column wherein she answered letters from the lovelorn in need of guidance. Jenise had thought it must be stressful and possibly unrewarding to continuously offer advice that may or may not be followed, or may or may not work. Still, Tate was a pretty woman with her caramel complexion and wide, expression-filled eyes. She wore dark jeans with a fuchsia tank top and a dark blue fringed cardigan. Today, she looked happy when she'd opened the door and welcomed Jenise inside. Happy and, of course, in love. It was clear in the bright spark in her eyes, the wide genuine smile and the almost blinding sparkle of that huge diamond ring on her left hand.

"I'm sorry I'm late. I had a hard time finding the house," Jenise stated as Tate motioned for her to remove jacket.

That had been another thing that had made her late. She'd changed her outfit three times. The final product was black ponte leggings, knee length leather boots and a white tassel sleeve hi-lo blouse. She'd kept her jewelry to a minimum with a simple silver choker and the charm bracelet Morgan had given her last Christmas. When she was finally satisfied with how she looked, Jenise had headed out the door. She'd gotten all the way down to the lobby of her building when she noticed it had begun to rain.

Back upstairs she went to grab her lightweight black jacket. On the elevator she turned quickly to speak to another tenant in the building and her large hoop earring touched the side of her face. For a moment she contemplated changing them as she hadn't wanted to appear too garish at her first Donovan family function, but she'd decided against it. Or rather, a glance at her watch changed her mind.

Now, she was here at just a couple minutes after four and feeling every bit as nervous as she had the day she'd been sworn in as an attorney.

"Oh, you should have called, one of the guys would have come out to meet you," Tate said.

"I guess I could have called, Adriana. She'd mentioned that it was difficult to find the house," Jenise was saying as she looked around at said house.

From the outside it looked like a mini-palace, straight out of a magazine. Jenise did not claim to know a lot about real estate or architecture. What she knew for certain was that this was a grand house, built in an old Miami style with grandeur and beauty obviously at its core. She'd parked her car in the long winding driveway, then followed the stone path around to the side entrance of the house, which also faced a long and very inviting pool and palm trees.

"You could have called any of us," Tate told her as she'd begun to walk just a few steps ahead of her. "I'll just put your jacket in here."

They were standing in a long foyer with gleaming marble floors and Tate moved to a set of doors that Jenise assumed was a closet.

"Adriana's the only one I know. Besides, Savian, I mean." Jenise tried not to fidget with the strap of her purse. She also attempted not to stare at the large paintings on the walls. They were beautiful abstract pieces with a muted color pallet of grays, pale pinks and white, that seemed to match perfectly with the stark white walls and the gray marbling in the floors.

"Don't stare at things that amaze you. People will think you're not used to having anything." Jenise could almost hear her mother's reproachful voice saying as if Marianne were standing there right beside her.

"And before you leave today we'll all have to exchange numbers," Tate continued. "Now let's get inside before they come looking for us. Ms. Janean does not like her food to get cold."

Tate had doubled back to lace her arm through Jenise's. "Adriana only told the women you were coming, so we saved you a seat. But don't worry, this is the first holiday the Bennetts have shared with us and Bree brought the triplets, so there'll be plenty of distractions from the 'you and Savian subject'."

They were already walking into the dining room by the time Tate finished that sentence, so if Jenise wanted to say something about the 'you and Savian subject' she didn't have a chance.

The table stretched from one end of the room to the other, with a satin table cloth that matched the champagne colored walls. Tapered candles graced a path down the center of the table with small bowls of fresh flowers placed throughout. At the mid-point of the table was a large floral arrangement boasting the same orange, brown and burgundy flowers on a much larger scale. There were crystal glasses, sparkling china plates, gleaming cutlery and bowls of different food items. At one end of the table was a huge roasted turkey that looked straight out of a cooking magazine, while at the other end was a whole ham, that was running a close second to turkey for best appetizing. She'd been too nervous to eat breakfast this morning and now, Jenise prayed her stomach wouldn't growl.

"Everyone, this is Jenise," Tate said and the noise that was a number of different conversations going on at one time ceased immediately.

She'd stood in courtrooms, faced skeptical jurors and even had a knock, down, drag out debate with her brother Tucker over which was the best NFL team when she was fifteen years old. On none of those occasions had Jenise ever felt as weary of being in the spotlight as she did now.

"Jenise, this is," Tate said, starting at one end of the table and calling off names. "Mr. Bruce and Ms. Janean, who you've already met. Sean and our lovely Briana who thinks she's going to sit in her daddy's lap and eat her meal today. But she is going to be sadly mistaken."

Jenise smiled at the pretty little girl who was currently giving her mother an adorable, yet obvious, 'you wanna bet' look.

"You already know Parker and Adriana and you've met Dion. This is Lyra, Dion's wife," Tate said as Adriana waved happily at Jenise.

Lyra smiled and Dion nodded his head in acknowledgment, before looking across the table. Jenise didn't have time to follow his gaze because Tate was rattling off more names.

"This is Marvin and Beatriz Bennett, Adriana's parents. Alex is Adriana's older brother and beside him is Monica Lakefield. She runs the Lakefield Galleries in New York. Rico is also Adriana's brother."

More smiles and nods.

"On the other side of the table are Mr. Reginald and Ms. Carolyn. You've met Regan and Gavin. This is Adriana's other brother, Renny. He's a sculptor and has some great pieces. If you like art, Lyra and I were thinking of taking a trip to New York after the first of the year to visit Lakefield Galleries. They have some of Renny's pieces on exhibit, but I don't know if they'll still be there in January," Tate informed her.

"There'll be a new exhibit in January," the very handsome Renny, replied with a smile.

"I like art a lot," Jenise offered, her voice deceptively strong.

"Then you should definitely visit the gallery," Monica added. "Just let me know when you ladies plan to come up and I'll make arrangements for a personal tour."

"That sounds great," Jenise replied, even though she was certain she would not be taking any girls' trip with anyone in this room. She wasn't their family or friend, after all.

"We're starving here, Tate," Parker said with an exaggerated whine that earned him a smack on the arm from Adriana.

"Okay, we're almost done. This is Bree, she's Renny's wife and a private investigator. She's also a superwoman because over there in that playpen are three of the most adorable babies you ever want to see. And she had them all in one day." Tate started clapping and every woman in that room, besides Jenise, of course, joined her in a round of applause. Bree smiled, but then turned a little in her seat to give herself a pat on the back.

"You already know Savian. And your seat is right there," Tate finished.

'Right there' meant right beside Savian who looked as if he'd come face-to-face with a long lost enemy as he gazed at her. His brow had immediately furrowed, his lips going into a thin line.

"It's nice to meet everyone," Jenise said because there was no way she could turn around and walk out of this house. "Sorry I'm late. I don't want to hold things up any longer, so I'll just get over here and take my seat."

She talked as she walked, hanging her purse on the back of the chair before sitting and scooting herself closer to the table. She made sure not to touch Savian, not even by accident, and she didn't look over at him.

"Say the blessing, Bruce," Janean said and her husband dutifully began to pray.

Jenise bowed her head silently adding a sincere 'Lord, please give me the strength to get through this day' to the otherwise gracious and heartfelt prayer.

The food was delicious, even though Jenise tried to be sure not to eat too much. Not at all concerned about her waistline, she was more attune to the fact that throughout the course of the meal, all eyes at this table eventually turned to her. They were curious about who she was and why she was here. She could understand the latter because she'd asked herself all morning as she'd sat in her living room with her laptop and the parade on television which she'd barely paid any attention to, wondering why she was even entertaining the idea of attending. This wasn't her family and they weren't going to be. If she'd ever considered differently, Savian had made sure to hammer that fact home last night.

He'd arrived at her apartment later than usual. She'd come to expect him between seven and eight in the evenings and thus made sure to leave her office no later than six so that she'd be there when he arrived. Actually, Jenise had begun to enjoy waiting for Savian to arrive. If he did not send word to her some time during the day that he was taking care of dinner, she would make the plans—always in her apartment. Her mother would be ecstatic to hear that Jenise had found a type of enjoyment to planning a meal for Savian. She liked seeing the look on his face when she selected a wine that he approved of, or a dessert that made him smile. That dessert would be warm apple pie and Vanilla Bean ice cream. They'd even changed how their evenings ended, with a shower this time, a long and sensual shower that would serve as the best type of nightcap for Jenise because once Savian left she would fall into her bed and a blissful night's sleep.

"I've always prided myself on being an independent woman," she'd said last night as they'd stood beneath the warm spray of water. "But there's definitely something to be said for having someone wash your back."

"There's definitely something to be said when someone has a backside, such as yours," Savian had replied.

He'd been dragging the soapy cloth over the base of her back at that moment, and then moved down to her bottom. He always took such care there, moving slowly, kneading her cheeks hungrily before slipping the cloth between her crevice in that way that was one part necessity and a larger part need. That need never seemed to subside between them. Instead, in the months they'd been together, it had increased.

"You like it back there, don't you?" she'd asked without intending to. However, much they'd changed in the past couple of weeks, their sexual trysts still ended in the same way.

"I lov…," he'd begun then stopped abruptly. "Oh yes, I enjoy it back here and I believe you enjoy it too."

He'd moved only slightly so that the water was now sluicing over her back, washing the soap away. While it did, she heard the cloth fall to the floor of the stall and felt Savian's hand grip her breast from the side. She turned to look at him at that moment and asked, "Will it always be this way? Dinner, sex, shower, good night?"

This, Jenise thought as she stared at him, she had meant to say because she wanted to know. For days she'd been wondering what if…what if she asked him to stay all night. What if they had breakfast one morning instead of dinner at night? What if they actually went out to a restaurant rather than staying inside?

Savian hadn't answered immediately, his fingers toying with her hardened nipple, the other rubbing lazily over the curve of her ass. He did look at her, with those ever changing eyes. He was thinking of his response, considering, she hoped. It was when his response finally came that Jenise felt that hope wither and die.

"There's no need to change what's working so well," he said.

Twenty minutes later Savian was gone and Jenise had climbed into her bed, this time not falling asleep as quickly, not feeling as content as she had before.

Now, on Thanksgiving Day, as she sat beside him enjoying everything from the macaroni and cheese to the buttered dinner rolls, Savian was the only one that did not look at her. In fact, he hadn't acknowledged her in any way, his silence punctuating his words from last night with a great big exclamation. No matter what scenarios Jenise played in her mind, she knew that Savian had been true about his words. He had no intention of changing anything about what they were. She knew that now it was up to her to figure out if that was something she could continue to live with.

"I met your sister, Morgan," Bree was saying.

Her words pulled Jenise from her distressing thoughts and she lifted her napkin to wipe her mouth before replying.

"Oh really?" she asked, wondering how Morgan's path would have crossed with a private investigator from Connecticut.

"Yes," Bree said with a nod of her head.

During the meal the triplets had awakened. Bree had immediately excused herself from the table to get them. Renny had started to move, but had been waved back into his seat when Beatriz, his mother, followed Bree over to the playpen. Carolyn had quickly stood also, making her way over to pick up the last waking baby, the little boy. Jenise remembered hearing throughout the earlier conversations that his name was Daniel. Now all three women were seated at the table once more with a baby cradled in their arms.

"My sister Lynn is married to Brice Wellington. Lynn first met Morgan at the yearly holiday party the Wellingtons have at their house. I believe she said Morgan's grandfather had worked a very important civil rights case with Brice's grandfather. Anyway, since we're family now, the Wellingtons invited us to this year's party which they held a lot earlier because Mr. and Mrs. Wellington are heading out for a Mediterranean cruise, and then I believe they plan to spend the rest of the year traveling through Europe. Morgan was at the party. She's a beautiful girl," Bree finished just as the little girl in her arms cooed.

Jenise loved the sound the baby made, just as much as she adored the way Bree had looked down at her daughter in response. The love was so clear in Bree's eyes.

"Ah, yes," Jenise replied. "Our family does have close ties to the Wellingtons. I'm glad Morgan could make the party. She usually doesn't travel much."

"She did mention that," Bree told her. "I reminded her that it's a shame for a pretty young single woman to spend all her time working."

"That's so true," Carolyn added as she lifted the little girl she held up to her shoulder, rubbing her hand over the baby's back. "Life shouldn't be all about work."

"You sound like my mother," was Jenise's immediate response. She regretted it the moment it was out.

"Really? How so?" Carolyn asked before Jenise could figure out a way to smooth that comment over.

Now, she was just going to have to work her way through yet another uncomfortable situation. Clearing her throat, she looked down the table to where Carolyn sat and said, "My parents didn't want me or Morgan to become attorneys. They thought it would be too much work for us."

She, of course, left out the part where her mother wanted her married and having children instead, because she didn't think that—in light of sitting at this table with all these married, or soon-to-be-married couples, with and without children—was going to go over too well.

Carolyn nodded. "It's a mother's job to protect her children," she said. "I think that everyone should endeavor to have a full life. One where things such as careers and reaching goals should be taken in increments."

"That is so true," Janean added. "Balance is what it's all about. When my boys were young I tried to spend as much time at the school as possible, while still taking care of the house and the bills. I swear, for as much as Bruce can keep track of every detail at the office, when he came home he didn't remember to do anything but eat and sleep."

There was a chorus of chuckles and agreeing nods after that statement.

"I know exactly what you mean," Beatriz chimed in. "Marvin is the same way. Knows everything about that job and couldn't tell you when the last time we had to have the plumbing serviced. And let's not get started on the children. He might have missed their graduations if I hadn't taped notes on his bathroom mirror to remind him."

More chuckles and more agreeing.

"Now, wait a minute," Reginald spoke up. "That's not fair. We take care of business and we make the money."

"You also make the babies that we take care of and the messes that we clean," Carolyn said to her husband just before sweetly kissing that baby on the cheek.

"I don't know what any of you are talking about, Tate gets up at the strangest hours to go into her office and write. If she's not answering letters, she's reading them to see who will be the next guest on her show. The last time Briana had a stomach ache, I was the one in her room, lying on that little princess bed beside her, rubbing her tummy until she fell asleep," Sean said, matter-of-factly.

Dion immediately chimed in with, "And Lyra stays in that darkroom so long some nights I regret having it included in the plans for the house."

"So what you're really saying is that men can dish it out, but they can't take it," Tate spoke up. "You can work long hours and on weekends when a deadline is looming, but I'm supposed to keep my job to a nine to five schedule."

Sean began shaking his head immediately. "Not what I'm saying at all."

"That's what it sounds like you're trying to say," Regan interjected.

Bree nodded. "That's what I heard, too."

Renny shook his head, but wisely remained silent.

"We don't have that problem because Alex works just as much as I do," Monica spoke up from the other side of the table.

"But that's because you don't have any children," Tate said. "Just wait until there's a little one in the picture and he has to do something with the baby while you're working. Then you'll be hearing a different song from him."

"A little one? How about three little ones?" Bree asked, pointing at all three of her children. "I'm juggling them and my cases from work. Luckily my brother is my boss so I can mostly work from home now."

"And when I'm not at the gallery or in my studio, I'm right there, taking my turn at feedings, baths, and cuddling," Renny added this time.

That was followed by a few 'awws' as he leaned over to touch the baby girl that Bree was holding on the chin. He'd smiled down at her and the little girl had replied with a huge grin.

Jenise's head was swimming with all the comments and opinions. She was glad that it had taken the heat off her, but was also surprised to hear how the wives and husbands in this family felt. It wasn't totally different from the views in her family, but not nearly as stringent. The Donovans and Bennetts seemed to take these things all in stride, the men not denying their actions, while each of the women were proud of what they did—whether in the household or the workplace—and there were no recriminations for either.

She'd just taken another drink from her glass when there was another comment, this one leaving everyone at the table silent.

"Dion and I are going to have a baby," Lyra said loudly.

Bruce looked to his son in question, while Janean's smile spread slowly.

"The miscarriage was so hard for all of us, so when I found out I was pregnant again, Dion and I thought it was best to wait until I was through the first trimester before we told anyone, " Lyra continued as Dion took her hand in his. "We're due in early April."

Regan began laughing at that moment which was a shock to everyone and immediately took the stares and smiles from Dion and Lyra, changing them to questioning glances at her. Even Jenise wondered why the woman would laugh at a time like this. Savian had told her that Bruce and Janean had informally adopted Lyra when she was ten years old, because Lyra's mother had a drug addiction. So Lyra and Regan had grown up together.

They were like sisters. Which made Regan's reaction to the announcement all the more puzzling, until Regan finally spoke.

"We've known each other too long," Regan finally said to Lyra. Tears had begun forming in her eyes and Regan swiped fingers beneath them in an attempt to keep her make-up intact.

"I swear since we met we've both been in competition with each other about one thing or another. I just never thought, that we would compete for delivery dates," Regan said.

"What...are you...saying?" Lyra asked.

Gavin leaned over then, draping an arm over Regan's shoulders as he said, "We're pregnant, too. Due in late April."

"Oh my goodness! Oh my! Oh my!" Carolyn began shaking her head. "A grandbaby? I'm having a grandbaby!"

"Me too!" Janean exclaimed. "I mean, I'm having another grandbaby! Oh this is fabulous, just fabulous. So much to be thankful for today. Happy Thanksgiving to us all!"

Kisses and hugs, handshakes and smiles, all punctuated the end of the official meal, but the fellowship portion of this day had clearly begun and Jenise wondered briefly if it weren't time for her to leave. Savian had moved from his seat, going around to shake Dion and Gavin's hands. He hugged Lyra, kissing her on the cheek. When it came to his sister, Savian hugged her tightly, whispering something in her ear that made Regan laugh. She whispered something back to him that had taken the happy look from his face, replacing it with a slight frown. Savian looked up to find Jenise staring at him. The frown deepened and he walked out of the room.

Yes, Jenise thought. It was definitely time for her to go.

"Leaving so soon?"

Jenise paused, then continued to slowly slip her arms into her jacket. She'd slipped out of the dining room while everyone seemed to be talking to someone else. Between all the congratulatory hugs and kisses and crying babies, she'd thought the timing was perfect for her to ease out of there. Clearly, she'd thought wrong.

"I'm waiting on some reports and I'd rather be home when they come in so I can get right to work on them," she replied to Carolyn as she turned around to face her.

"Because you'd rather be the woman that works and takes care of herself, instead of the woman that stays home and cares for a family?"

Jenise wasn't sure how Carolyn had been able to hit the nail directly on the head with her, but she wasn't going to insult the woman by standing there and attempting to deny the truth in what she'd just said to her face.

"No ma'am, I'd rather be the type of woman that decides what I'll make of my life and when," was Jenise's reply. She'd tried to make it sound as cordial and respectful as she could, even though she knew Carolyn might still take offense.

"You do know that you two are doing a terrible job hiding whatever is going on between you," Carolyn continued as she folded her arms over her chest.

This woman was class and beauty all wrapped in one. She wore a smart-looking pant suit, in a lovely shade of burnt orange. Her hair, cut just beneath her ears, was neat and styled, her make-up minimal but enough to bring out her mature beauty. She wore gold studs at her ears and a gold choker around her neck. And when she smiled, it was all-knowing. A fact that made Jenise just a little nervous.

"I'm not hiding anything," she said because she couldn't speak for Savian. Or rather, she wouldn't speak for him, especially since he was deep into trying to hide what was between them.

"Look Jenise, you strike me as a very smart woman. I knew that the first time I met you, that's why I trusted you with my son's future immediately. I have every confidence in the fact that you will work out his legal troubles in a satisfactory manner."

Jenise nodded and was just about to thank Carolyn, when the woman held up a hand to halt her words.

"What I also felt the moment I met you was something much more than a professional commitment. It was in your tone when you talked about finding the evidence to clear him. You don't believe he killed anyone, and not just because that's your job as his attorney. You don't believe it because you know exactly what type of man he is. And you like that type of man. You like it a lot," she finished.

Jenise readjusted her purse on her shoulder as she looked directly at the woman.

"Mrs. Donovan, I certainly do not mean to offend you in any way, but whatever is going on between Savian and I—which I believe you may be totally off base on—is our business."

"No, dear. I don't think so. What I know is my son. I know how he thinks it's better to keep to himself. He's always been that way and I've always prayed for the day when a woman would come along and remove those blinders from his eyes. When you walked into that room at the police station, I knew that woman was you."

"You're wrong," Jenise insisted. "I don't need a man to define me. I know exactly who I am and what I want out of life without a man being in the equation," Jenise admitted before snapping her lips shut.

Carolyn only nodded as she reached out to take one of Jenise's hands.

"Well, then, since you know all that, I'm sure you'll know when a man comes along that will compliment you and your independence in every way. And when you realize that, I'll bet— since you're so smart and know exactly what you want and need—that you'll know just how to convince that man that he's not only everything that you've never wished for, but so much more."

"As a matter of fact," Carolyn continued to talk when Jenise had opened her mouth to reply, then quickly shut it again. "Since we are entering the Christmas season, I'm sure you'll notice when that Christmas magic takes hold and starts to work all on its own, without any help or hindrance from you or anyone else."

"Now," she said stepping closer to Jenise and surprising her when she kissed her on the cheek. "You go on home and get your work done. It was lovely having you for dinner tonight. You're always welcome in this family."

"Thank you, Mrs. Donovan," was all Jenise managed to say.

She waved a hand at her. "Nonsense, you call me Ms. Carolyn. We're family now."

No, Jenise thought as she walked out of that beautiful house, leaving that friendly and loving family behind, she wasn't one of them. She never would be because that's not what Savian wanted. And to be perfectly fair, it wasn't what she'd wanted, not at first. Now, she simply had no idea what she wanted, or needed for that matter.

The really sad part was that just like Ms. Carolyn, Jenise had always believed in Christmas magic. She'd sworn by it and her mistletoe. That, however, was before she'd met Savian Donovan.

CHAPTER 8

Savian stood at Jenise's front door, unwilling to lift his hand to knock and unable to dismiss the fact that there was a reason for him being here.

About an hour ago, as he'd just finished his workout and was about to step into the shower, she'd sent him a text message.

New development in the case. You should come over tonight.

A part of him had thought it was just her way of getting him over there. Couldn't she have simply called to tell him whatever had happened? Wouldn't that have been the professional way to handle things? He'd put the phone back on his dresser and headed into the shower. As the water fell in stinging hot pelts against his skin, he thought of how much he did not want to go to Jenise's apartment.

He hadn't been at her apartment since Wednesday night and he hadn't seen or spoken to her since Thanksgiving Day when she'd surprised him at his aunt and uncle's house. Savian hadn't known how to react when she'd appeared unannounced at their family holiday meal. So he hadn't said a word to her and then he'd compounded that by not calling, texting or going to see her in the last two days. He'd told himself that it was the right thing to do because things had changed and he didn't want them to. It was his right to pull back if he wanted to, even if for just a couple of days.

His conversation with Parker the afternoon before Thanksgiving continued to replay in Savian's mind, just as it had when he'd looked up to see Jenise walking into his aunt's dining room. Catching Parker's unmistakable look of triumph from across the table had only made matters worse, and Savian's mood had quickly gone from thankful to agitated. He'd stayed in that state of mind for the duration of the holiday weekend and for the first time, in he didn't know how long, he was thankful that Donovan Media's corporate offices were closed until Monday.

He'd finished his shower and stepped out with the absolute intention of ignoring Jenise's text message. By the time he'd dried off and walked back into his bedroom, he'd changed his mind and picked up his phone. He was going to reply to her text asking that she say whatever she had to say via another text or call him, as he thought she should have done in the first place. A string of curses tumbled from his lips as he began to type…

I'll be there in twenty minutes.

He continued to curse and grumble as he'd dressed, grabbed his keys and headed out. During the ride to her apartment, Savian turned on the radio in the truck in the hopes of drowning out how surprisingly comfortable it felt to have Jenise sitting at that table beside him sharing a Thanksgiving meal. It had, of course been a new feeling, but still, it had also been good. That thought really pissed him off and he hurriedly turned up the volume on the radio before realizing what was actually playing on the station.

Johnny Gill's "Give Love On Christmas Day" filled the interior of the truck and Savian couldn't help but frown once more. This song had played several times while he was at Jenise's place in the past two weeks. She loved to sing along with it as she did most of the holiday songs she listened to. Savian knew the words to this one as well, but instead of singing, he liked watching her move around her apartment while she did. There was something different about her facial expression when she was singing. It was almost as if she were wishing for this same type of love in her life. That was silly, Savian told himself that every time the thought entered his mind, but still, the look on her face was the same each time.

He did not change the station, although he was certain he really did not want to hear Christmas music as he drove through the city at almost ten o'clock on a Sunday night. It would have been better if he'd stayed home, he knew that but still kept driving, until he'd finally arrived.

Now, as he continued to stand at her door, he wasn't sure what to do next. Knock or walk away. Turn around and go home and text her that he couldn't make it. Go inside and act as if he were still the same and that nothing had changed between them. He was conflicted and so he just stood still. Until she opened the door and asked, "Where you planning to stand there all night?"

Again, Savian frowned, then stopped because his facial muscles were beginning to ache from constantly being flexed that way.

"Sorry. I was thinking about something," he said as he moved past her to step inside.

She was closing the door as she talked. "Then I apologize for interrupting you. But there's something I think you need to see."

Jenise walked past him, going straight through the dimly lit living room and back toward her home office. Savian followed without saying a word.

Her home office was very different from the one in the Brickell Avenue office building. The walls were a very pale blue, the furniture—a desk, two book shelves and a file cabinet—were all light gray. On top of the shelves were fat white vases with tall wispy white flowers that he presumed were artificial. Her chairs were white and very dainty looking as he moved toward one across from her desk and prepared to take a seat.

"Come around here so you can see this," she told him before he'd made himself comfortable.

She was leaning over her desk, slipping a disc into her hard drive and waiting for it to play on the screen.

"Jules' colleague, his name is Kwame. He just sent me this video a little over an hour ago. I've saved it to a disc so I'll have it in the file."

She stood back as she talked and Savian stared at the computer screen instead of asking her who the hell Jules and Kwame were. The picture came up but it was dark, so he moved closer to the desk. She was now barely two feet away from him and already he could feel his body reacting to her proximity. He grit his teeth but kept his facial features calm.

A full moon, the roof of a house, the grass, and the garage appeared on the screen.

"There are cameras wired to do a panoramic scan of the house on an hourly basis. This service costs more but Kwame says lots of celebrities opt for it," Jenise told him as they both continued to watch the screen.

As soon as the front door came into view, Savian knew they were looking at Morelli's house. He folded his arms over his chest, holding his breath as he waited to see himself walking out the front door. Only, when the camera's focus stayed on the front of the house, Savian noticed his truck was not in the driveway where he knew he'd parked it when he pulled up there that night.

"See the time and date stamp right there in the corner," Jenise said pointing to the bottom left hand portion of the screen.

Savian looked closer. It was there, in blurry white letters, in a font too small to be of the best quality, but he could still see it: **Sunday 7.26 11:45pm**

He looked to Jenise then and she gave him a nod before saying, "Keep watching."

Savian did as she said, until he saw that front door open and the woman step out into the night air. His arms immediately fell to his sides, his mouth falling open slightly as he looked at a woman he'd known for years leaving Giovanni Morelli's house during the timeframe that the coroner had placed his time of death.

"That's—" he started to say before Jenise interrupted.

She was nodding her head. "I thought so. It's Jaydon Donovan isn't it?"

Savian turned to her. "Is this authentic? Can you personally vouch for this Kwame person and his work? Where did this come from?"

"Whoa," she said holding up a hand. "One question at a time, and after you finish watching."

He looked back at the screen to see that Jaydon had climbed into a black truck with tinted windows. Jaydon drove a cobalt blue Porsche 911 Tagra. She didn't like to drive SUV's as she'd told Savian when he'd purchased his new one earlier this year. So he wasn't surprised at all to see her open the passenger side door and get inside. He was, however, shocked as hell to see the New York license plate on the front of the truck.

"We need to find out who else was in that truck? And we need to find Jaydon," he was saying as Jenise leaned over and stopped the video.

"No," she said slowly. "What we need to do first is get the charges against you dropped. Kwame also examined the video that the police department had. It was missing the date and time stamp. He pulled some strings and was able to obtain all the tapes from that day, start to finish and he sent me the correct video."

Savian had already turned away from the desk. He'd begun pacing the little space of her office trying to figure out what possible reason Jaydon would have had to kill Giovanni.

"Why didn't you tell me you went to see Morelli the night he was killed, Savian?"

He spun around at her question, seeing her standing at her desk, her hands on the back of her chair as she stared pointedly at him.

"You told me to only answer the questions you asked," Savian replied. "You never asked me if I'd gone to his house that night."

She looked at him as if he'd said something wrong, but Savian couldn't figure out what it was. In fact, he was having a hard time thinking about anything but seeing Jaydon, still dressed in the gown that she'd worn to the All Access event, leaving Morelli's house.

"That's you telling me as your attorney, Savian. Why didn't you tell me as your... I mean, why couldn't you trust me enough to just say..." Jenise's voice trailed off as she shook her head.

"Say what? 'Hey, I know I'm paying you a lot to defend me, but they're right, I did go to Morelli's house that night.' If I had said that to you, would you have believed I didn't kill him?" he asked her.

"It's not my job to believe in your guilt or innocence. My job is to disprove the prosecutor's case against you and sometimes Savian, it's better that the attorney doesn't know every single detail. It makes it a lot easier to handle the case."

He was nodding then, as if to say that he knew he'd been right in not telling her, but when she continued to speak, he started to feel like an ass all over again.

"But as the woman sharing a bed with you, at some point you could have confided in me, don't you think?"

Savian clenched his fists at his sides. He shook his head and wondered what to say next. He didn't know. What should he tell her? What would make any sort of difference at this point? Nothing, he thought with a sigh.

"Look, I didn't tell you. Right or wrong I didn't say those words to you. But that's neither here nor there at the moment. These videos clear me of the charges, right? The one you have of me is properly time-stamped so they know that I left long before Giovanni was killed."

"Yes," she said after a brief pause. "You're right. The videos clear your name and I'll be at the prosecutor's office first thing tomorrow morning pleading that case."

"Good," he said before he turned and started to walk out of her office. "I've gotta go," he told her.

Savian had continued to walk toward the door when he realized he hadn't heard her reply. He stopped then and turned back to see her still standing next to that chair.

"Thank you," he said. "Thank you very much for all your hard work."

She nodded. "It's my job as an attorney," was her reply.

"Do I need to go to the prosecutor's office with you tomorrow?" he asked.

"No," she replied.

"Fine. Then I'll just call you to make sure everything goes alright."

"No," she said again. "I'll get a message to you to let you know when it's done."

Savian didn't like the sound of her voice, but he didn't know how to change it. In fact, the warmth and needing that had begun as he'd stood next to her had not subsided. It had grown noticeably stronger and he was now resisting the urge to go to her and to do what, he had no idea. This wasn't a feeling he was used to, and he didn't like it at all.

"Good. Then I'll wait to hear from you," Savian said and then moved as fast as he could to get the hell out of there before he did or said the wrong thing. Again.

"Where did Jaydon go?" Savian asked Parker an hour later when he sat in his brother's partially furnished living room.

Parker and Adriana had purchased a house just outside of the Key Biscayne area where their parents lived. Adriana was taking her time selecting just the right pieces for each room, some of which were very odd looking antiques, but Savian had the good sense not to comment on that. Right now, he was sitting in a chair that looked just as dainty as the ones that were in Jenise's home office. Only these were darker and looked ten times older.

"I don't know," Parker answered with a shake of his head. "Dammit!" he yelled, jumping out of a matching old chair so fast it wobbled behind him but did not fall.

"I can't believe this!" Parker continued.

"Neither can I," Savian added. "But I saw her Parker. It was Jaydon and she was leaving Giovanni's house. She climbed into a big black SUV. She wasn't driving so there was someone else with her. Do you know of anybody that she was involved with?"

Parker had walked across the room. He'd stopped at Savian's question and spun around. "How the hell should I know? Just a few weeks before she quit, she was trying to get back with me. I don't know what the hell was going through her mind."

"Right," Savian said thinking about Parker's words. "She quit. Now why would she quit a job that she was so good at?"

"Because she had something better lined up," Parker added walking towards Savian again.

"Something at another agency? Or possibly with a bigger and more successful agent?"

"No," Parker said shaking his head. "She would want to be the boss. She's been running her own show at DNM for too long to go and work under someone else. That's what I thought in the moments after she walked away from me at the event. I figured she was probably going to start her own agency and I'd have to keep a close watch on DNM to make sure she wasn't stealing our clients. But then everything went haywire and I let it drop. I didn't think about Jaydon again until...I just didn't think about her."

"She was gone and that was good for you and Adriana. And now, as it turns out it was good for DNM," Savian said.

Parker ran a hand down the back of his head. "I don't see her killing anybody," he told Savian. "She's not usually vindictive, that's why I wasn't totally buying that she was involved in leaking those pictures of me and Adriana. Jaydon's more the type to simply deal with the problem immediately, instead of letting it marinate and then striking. You take a swing at her and she swings back, then she walks away the victor."

"Except with you, the second time around," Savian continued. "Think about it, man. She wants you back, you say no. You start seeing Adriana and then you let her know that it's serious and that if she doesn't like it she can walk. You took the first swing, she took the second by getting Giovanni to put those pictures out there. He cracks at the party and starts talking about bringing you and Adriana down a notch, she has to silence him before he implicates her."

"No," Parker said again. "She's not a killer. And she certainly wouldn't kill over me. I think it's whoever was in that truck with her."

"The person in the truck never went into the house, only Jaydon did," Savian quietly pointed out.

"So she killed Giovanni and then she was going to let you take the fall," Adriana said as she stepped into the room. "That bitch!"

"Baby," Parker said immediately going to stand in front of Adriana who was dressed in her robe and fluffy slippers. "I told you to stay upstairs and that I'd fill you in when I came up."

"You weren't going to tell me this, Parker. Not all of it," she said, then moved around him to come stand in front of Savian.

"We need to find her and find out why she did this," Adriana told him.

Savian had stood then, catching the slight shake of his brother's head as he warned him not to discuss this with his fiancé. It was cool, he would respect Parker's need to protect her from this messy situation. In that moment his brother reminded him of their father and whatever he was so intent on protecting their mother from.

"Don't worry," Savian told Adriana. "I'm going to look into finding her."

In addition to seeing the make and model of the SUV Jaydon had driven off in, Savian had also seen the New York license plate. He planned to have that traced at the first opportunity. For now, it was late and his mind was whirling with the things that had happened in the last couple of hours. He needed to go home and regroup.

"I'll talk to you tomorrow," he said to Parker as he continued moving towards the door.

"I want to know as soon as Jenise has things settled with the prosecutor," Parker said following behind him.

Savian nodded. "You'll know the moment I know."

"I'll meet you in your office," Parker told him after Savian had opened the door.

"Right," he replied, because he'd expected nothing less. Dion and Sean would most likely be there too as they all discussed what it meant now that Jaydon was involved with the murder, instead of him. "I'll be in early."

"So will I," Parker told him.

"Goodnight, Adriana. Don't worry about this, we're going to take care of it," Savian told his soon-to-be sister-in-law as he noted the worry already forming in her eyes.

"I know you will," Adriana said, leaning into Parker as he'd wrapped an arm around her shoulders. "Jenise did a great job. We all owe her a lot."

Savian gave her a stilted smile before he turned to walk down the driveway to where he'd parked. Jenise had done a good job. It was what he'd paid her for, but Savian wasn't blind enough not to see that it had been much more. He may not have wanted to openly admit that to Adriana and Parker, but he knew.

Dammit, he knew.

⁕

"Rubin's going to have to do better with his investigating," Manuel Cruz commented.

Jenise was at the State Attorney's office by eleven a.m. on Monday morning. She'd been sitting here with Manuel, watching as he viewed the videos and her motion to dismiss, for the last forty-five minutes.

"These videos definitely shoot holes in his case," he continued, leaning forward to rest his elbows on his desk.

"So do we need to schedule a time to argue the motion in front of a judge, or would you like to respond right now?" she asked him.

Manuel smiled, his slightly crooked teeth a bright contrast to his raven black hair. He was a tall, slim man, in his mid-thirties she surmised. He'd been a prosecutor for three years after working in a private law practice for a couple years right out of law school. She'd done her research on him, just as she suspected he had on her. Lawyers loved to do their research.

"Tenacious and beautiful," was his response. "I'm scared of you, Ms. Langley."

"No need to be," Jenise replied. "It's simple. My client could not have committed the murder if he was seen leaving the house three hours before said murder occurred. And you have proof of another person being at the house closer to the time of the murder. Two, other people, I might add."

"Do you know who the driver of the SUV is?" Manuel asked.

Jenise shook her head. "No, I don't. But the woman was Jaydon Donovan."

"Your client's ex-sister-in-law," he continued with an arch of his brow.

"Yes. She apparently resigned from her position at Donovan Management Network the night of the murder. She attended the same event that Giovanni and the Donovan family did. I'm sure Savian and Parker would be able to give statements to that effect, but only after the charges are dismissed against my client," Jenise told him.

Manuel chuckled and drummed his fingers on his desk blotter. Jenise had given him a copy of the disc with the entire twenty-four hours of footage. She'd also given him a copy of the fingerprint analysis report that confirmed Savian's prints weren't found on the letter that Detective Rubin had used to obtain the arrest warrant for Savian. She'd already stopped at the clerk's office and filed her motion, so the only thing she waited for now, was Manuel's decision.

"I'll dismiss the charges," he said after a few more moments. "But I want to talk to the Donovans. All of them because something's definitely going on at their company if people are resigning and killing co-workers."

Jenise agreed, but she wasn't about to tell him that. "I'd be happy to coordinate those meetings. Have your secretary call my office once your order of dismissal has been filed and we'll get moving on that."

She was already standing up, reaching for her briefcase as she spoke.

"It was certainly a pleasure seeing you again," Manuel said as he too stood, coming around his desk quickly.

He was in front of her before Jenise could make her way to the door. "Same here," she said with a smile. "Much nicer meeting you here than in the courtroom."

He smiled at that remark.

"Thanks, Manuel. I'll be in touch when you've taken care of all the paperwork." She made a move toward the door.

Manuel stepped with her, blocking her departure.

"I was thinking that it might be nice if the next time I see you it were in a more casual setting. Like maybe dinner and dancing. You look like you enjoy dancing," he said.

Jenise wasn't sure if his remark had come as a result of the four-inch heeled natural colored slingbacks she was wearing with her peach colored full-skirted dress and beige jacket, or if that was simply his pick-up line of choice. She wasn't impressed by either.

"Actually, I think it's best if we keep things between us on a professional level," she replied with a cordial smile.

This time when she moved toward the door and Manuel did not act as if he were going to let her pass, Jenise raised a brow.

"Why is that? Because I'm not a Donovan?" he asked, saying the name with an exaggerated tone that irritated her instantly.

"I'm not really into names," was her response.

"Right, I see. So you don't want to go out with the lowly state prosecutor, because you'd rather sneak around with a client that's accused of murder."

"He didn't kill anyone," Jenise replied before she thought better of saying anything. Manuel gave her a knowing look, but Jenise didn't give a damn.

"Let's be clear, counselor," she said with as much agitation as she was feeling at this very moment. "I wouldn't go out with you if I'd been celibate for the last year. Petty and jealous men that are prone to believing everything they see or hear from the tabloids, don't interest me at all. Now, as I said before, I'll wait to receive my copy of the order of dismissal. If you want to speak with my clients, then call my secretary."

She pushed past him this time until she made it to the door and exited his office. She didn't breathe easily until she was safe behind the wheel of her car. Then she let her forehead fall forward onto the steering wheel and sighed heavily. So much for nobody knowing about her ethical slip-up. Not only had every member of Savian's family figured out they were sleeping together, but apparently the prosecutor had as well.

The really funny thing about everyone now knowing about her and Savian, was that it came at a time when she was beginning to think that whatever they'd been doing together was over.

Savian had come and gone so quickly last night she hadn't a moment to process the entire conversation. To be honest, she hadn't wanted to process it. Savian had lied to her. No, that wasn't totally true. He'd done what she asked, when really she'd wanted him to do what was right. Why hadn't he told her about going to Morelli's that night? Not as his attorney, but as his girlfriend, or at the very least his trusted lover. Because she wasn't either, had been the startlingly clear answer. She was nothing more to Savian than his attorney, and his sex partner.

Three months ago that title worked just fine for Jenise. She had no idea when that had changed for her and really she was a bit disappointed that she was going back on what had been the safest route for her to deal with relationships with men in a very long time. After what happened in law school, she hadn't wanted to worry about trusting someone to be loyal and committed to her. She enjoyed sex and the occasional company of a man on a casual basis, so she'd adopted the friends with benefits lifestyle and to her way of thinking had perfected it to suit her needs. Then Savian came along and whether he'd wanted to or not, he'd shattered everything she thought she'd wanted.

Damn him.

Because he didn't want the same thing. Friends with benefits was still working for him, or maybe it wasn't since he'd given her the silent treatment all weekend. Jenise just wasn't sure what was going on between them and really, she was tired of thinking about it, at least for today. Right now all she owed Savian Donovan was the good news she'd just obtained. With that thought in mind she reached into her jacket pocket and pulled out her cell phone. This was so unprofessional, but hell, she was on a roll in that department so why stop now.

She typed in these simple words: **Prosecutor will dismiss the charges. Will let you know when everything is final.**

Hitting send, Jenise tossed the phone over to her passenger seat and then grabbed her keys to start the car. She needed to celebrate and for her that meant shopping. She headed to the mall and vowed not to give Savian or their so-called relationship another thought. At least for the rest of the day.

CHAPTER 9

It was almost five o'clock, thank the heavens. Jenise could not wait to be finished with the work day. She'd had one emergent issue after another, including a difficult insurance company that refused to pay her clients what they deserved as a result of the hospital's obvious negligence. The one highlight of the day had been when she'd received, via fax, the signed and date-stamped order dismissing the charges against Savian. She'd scanned the document immediately and sent it to his private email account, feeling a sense of relief and triumph after it was done.

He was no longer charged with murder and while it would probably take a few days for the press to really back off in that regard, she knew it would be a weight lifted from his parents' shoulders as well. That made her think of Ms. Carolyn and the conversation they'd shared before Jenise had left their Thanksgiving dinner celebration. The woman really believed that Jenise was the right woman for Savian. For a moment, Jenise had believed the same thing. That moment had since come and gone.

With an exasperated sigh, Jenise began putting papers into their coordinating files in an attempt to clean off her desk. If there was one thing she hated, it was coming into work in the morning to see a junky desk. It made her feel like she wasn't accomplishing anything. This way, with everything all nice and tidy, even if she did still have a million loose ends to tie up on at least ten cases, her desk would give the impression that she was on top of everything.

She'd just stacked the last of the files on the corner of her desk where Gwen would come in to take them to be re-filed, when the phone buzzed.

"Yes?" she called through the intercom to Gwen.

"Ah, there's a driver standing out here. He says he's come to pick you up," the secretary said skeptically.

"I didn't call for a driver," Jenise replied. "My car's in the garage."

"That's what I thought, but he sure is standing his fine self, right here at my desk, giving me a seriously professional look as he waits for you to come out."

Normally Jenise would have smiled at Gwen's reference to the man's looks. Gwen was known to flirt outrageously. Funny how Gwen never made any comments about Savian. It was even stranger that Jenise hadn't thought of that until this very moment.

"I'll be out in five minutes," she told her and then stood to finish tidying her office.

She'd worked at her conference table earlier today so there were papers and pens over there. She picked all of them up, putting them where they belonged. Then she circled back to her desk to turn off her computer and grab her briefcase and purse. She wasn't taking any work home with her tonight because she planned to warm up the delicious beef stew she had left over from last night and enjoy both versions of *Miracle on 34th Street* before going to bed. Jenise was almost to the door of her office when another sound stopped her. She looked back towards her desk and frowned at her cell phone still sitting there, plugged into the charger where she'd placed it after lunch.

Jenise crossed the room once more, on feet that were tired from breaking in the new knee-length gray suede boots she'd purchased on her impromptu celebratory shopping spree two days ago. She grabbed the phone and the charger and was about to stuff them both in her purse when she remembered it had just chimed. Taking a quick look at the screen she saw that she had a text message. It was from Savian and it simply said: **Thank you**.

He was finally replying to her sending that dismissal order to him. She was just about to smile, then she remembered this was the first time she'd heard from him since he'd all but run out of her apartment Sunday night when she showed him the new videos. With a sigh, Jenise dropped the phone and charger into her bag and headed once more for the door. Tonight was all about her and the holidays. She was determined that Christmas

was going to go much better than Thanksgiving had, and that
would start with putting thoughts of Savian Donovan out of her
mind once and for all.

On her way down the hall, she could hear Gwen talking to this
so-called driver. The man had a deep voice that probably went
along with his 'fine self' as Gwen had put it. Now, that did make
Jenise smile. Gwen had no shame in her game when it came to
men. She was on the hunt for one and she was bound and
determined to find him. Jenise was shaking her head with that
thought as she made her way into the lobby of her office.

"Hello," she said interrupting the man who was currently
leaning over the front mantel of Gwen's desk.

"Oh, ah, good afternoon," he said, immediately straightening
so that he stood tall and at full attention.

She had to admit that he was fine with his clean shaven face
and deep mocha toned skin. That didn't mean she was getting
into a car with him.

"I believe you may have come to the wrong address," Jenise
told him. "I did not call any car service."

"My instructions are clear, Ms. Langley," he told her as he
reached into the inside pocket of his black jacket and pulled out a
slip of paper.

Jenise stepped closer to him and took the paper. She read it,
but couldn't believe what she was reading.

"Who would instruct you to come here and pick me up?" she
asked, still skeptical.

"All I can tell you is that if we do not hurry, we will be late,"
he said. "Oh and I almost forgot, these are for you."

He turned around and picked up a large bouquet of flowers,
handing them to Jenise. Gwen squealed. "They're so beautiful!"

Jenise smiled because they were, but that did not stop her
curiosity from brimming. Who in the world would send her
flowers and a car service? Oh, no she thought as she began
opening the card that had been tucked inside the bouquet. It had
better not be Manuel Cruz. She'd told that fool, in no uncertain
terms, that she was definitely not interested in him. Now, she
figured she'd have to really make her position known by going to
his boss and telling him the guy was beginning to harass her. But
no, as she read the card she realized it wasn't Manuel.

Come with me if you really want to see the magic of Christmas. SD

No, her mind screamed. This wasn't Savian's doing. He did not do romantic gestures such as flowers or surprises. Well, okay, he had done surprises when he'd bought her that nightgown and those Christmas decorations and showed up at her apartment unannounced. But that was before whatever had happened to spook him and whatever had changed her mind about what she wanted from him. They'd both decided to go in a different direction these last couple of days. So what was this and why now?

"Ma'am, we have to get going. I'm on a pretty tight timeline and I need to get you to the designated location," the sexy driver said.

Jenise looked up at him slowly as if she weren't really understanding his words because she was too busy trying to wrap her mind around all of this. "Where's the destination?" she asked him.

"My instructions were to pick you up and drive. Not talk," he said.

Jenise frowned at that. "Well, you've been talking to my secretary."

When Gwen chuckled and the driver looked chastised enough, Jenise decided she would simply go with the flow. It was probably just dinner to thank her for getting the charges dismissed, she thought, recalling the text message she'd received from him just moments ago. Yes, that's what this was, a simple thank you dinner. It wasn't what she had planned for the evening, but she could go along with it.

"Fine," she told him. "Let's go. Gwen, be sure to check the answering machine before you leave because I'm certain you weren't taking any calls while he was here."

Gwen didn't even feign innocence, but instead picked up that phone to punch in the code to retrieve the voice mail with a brilliant smile on her face as she nodded goodbye to the sexy driver. Jenise shook her head. "Goodnight, Gwen."

"Goodnight, Jenise," Gwen said, even though that tone was certainly directed at the driver who had just bumped into the glass door because he'd been staring back at Gwen, also smiling.

With a shake of her head and a pep in her step, Jenise followed the driver out to the elevator, where once inside, she lifted the bouquet up to her nose and inhaled deeply. They were colorful and fragrant and absolutely gorgeous. They were also the first flowers she'd ever received from a man.

Jenise stepped onto the private jet.

Yes, a private jet.

She'd never been on a private jet before and wow, she could not believe she was on one now.

Her steps were muted as she walked across the plush ivory colored carpet. To her left was a leather couch in a shade that made her think of freshly churned butter. To her right, were two deep cushioned white leather chairs with swivel bottoms, and a marble-top table in between. Further ahead was another swivel chair and a wrap-around leather couch positioned right across from a large screened television. If she would have continued to walk forward she would have entered another room, but his voice stopped her.

"Did you like the flowers?"

Jenise turned, her purse slipping off her shoulder and almost hitting the floor she'd moved so fast. "Yes. Yes, I did," she replied.

The driver had already taken the flowers and her briefcase, along with a black duffle bag from the trunk of the shiny black Lincoln Town car they'd traveled in and brought them onto the plane. She wasn't sure where he'd put them, but she had watched him bring them inside as he'd boarded ahead of her.

"Good. I wasn't sure what type of flowers you liked but when I told the florist about your love of Christmas, she said she had the perfect idea. She'll be happy to hear they went over well," Savian said.

He looked almost too large for this space. This was no small jet and there was clearly no expense spared in the décor, but Savian, he was definitely the eye-piece here. Dressed in all black—slacks, button front shirt and leather jacket—his skin tone looked almost golden, eyes a simmering pool of green-gray mix, hair as dark as his clothes. Even fully dressed his muscled physique was obvious, the strength and swagger he exuded totally breathtaking.

"You didn't have to do any of this," Jenise told him. "I just did my job."

He gave a little nod as he removed his jacket, laying it on one of the swivel chairs and walked toward her. He reached to take her purse—which she was now holding tightly in front of her—and sat that on the marble table.

"I wanted to do this for you," he replied. "And you just wait, there's more."

Jenise wasn't certain what 'more' entailed, but for the moment she was content with the brilliant smile Savian had given her and the warmth that spread instantly throughout her body when he'd taken her by the hand and led her to the wrap-around couch where they took their seats.

The driver, who Savian introduced as Pierce was also the pilot. His bright white teeth had gleamed against his darker skin tone as he'd extended a hand to Jenise and she shook it. "Just sit back and relax, Ms. Langley. We'll have a smooth ride and we'll be there in no time," he said to her before disappearing into another room on the jet.

"Where will we be in no time?" she asked Savian.

"It's a surprise," had been his immediate response as he reached for a remote control and turned the television on.

"I don't like surprises," she said, with more of a pout than she'd intended.

"Come on," he said, giving her a playful nudge with his elbow. "Just relax and go with the flow."

Jenise could not believe that Savian was saying those words to her. In the months that she'd known him she'd never seen this man truly relaxed. His mind always seemed full of something that may or may not have been pleasurable. Truth be told, she hadn't thought he was capable of doing something this spontaneous. The flowers, the driver, the jet, it all seemed so out of character for Savian. Still, Jenise could do as he asked, mostly because she loved how it felt to be sitting here with him in this private space, alone. It seemed as if this were their private space and at this moment she didn't feel like there was anyone, or any issue, here between them. That is, except for Burl Ives as he appeared in the form of a vest-wearing snowman on the large television screen.

"You want to watch *Rudolph The Red Nosed Reindeer*?" she looked over to him and asked.

"Yeah," he replied with a nod. "Rudolph and I have a lot in common. We've always been on the outside looking in."

His words broke her heart and Jenise acted on instinct when she reached over and laced her fingers with his.

"Rudolph has always been my favorite of the reindeer. He's unique and he saves Christmas. The ultimate hero," she said as she snuggled closer to him.

"I don't know about all that, but his shiny nose is kind of cool," Savian replied in a light tone.

They watched Rudolph and *Frosty the Snowman* and *'Twas The Night Before Christmas*. Jenise was in the perfect mood at that point because she loved watching the old cartoons from her childhood, almost as much as she loved sitting with Savian sharing commentary about said cartoons. Savian had admitted that he'd also watched these cartoons when he was little, although he never shared how much he enjoyed them with anyone in his family. Jenise didn't know why Savian was so reserved and had wondered a time or two if there had been some incident from his past that made him this way. If that were true, he was more like her than she'd ever imagined.

Today, however, Jenise felt as if Savian had opened up and shared little things, like how he thought Frosty had the best friends in the world because they didn't leave him when he needed them most. That sentiment had melted her heart, just like being in that greenhouse had quickly melted Frosty. So there was nothing else that could have made this moment better—well, a piping hot bowl of her beef stew since she hadn't eaten anything since the cheese and crackers she'd indulged in for lunch, at least five hours earlier, would do the trick.

"We're here," Savian announced and nodded toward the small circular windows along the wall of the jet.

Jenise sat forward on the couch so that she could see out as well. They appeared to be landing.

"Where is here?" she asked realizing with a start that she actually had no idea where she was.

She'd climbed into that car without knowing where Pierce was taking her. When they'd arrived at the airport, she'd begun to wonder. The jet had taken her breath away, along with the man that joined her for the ride. But to be perfectly honest, she'd been so engrossed in the holiday movies and the man once again, that she hadn't stopped to think that the jet was actually in the air.

"Here," Savian said while rubbing his thumb over the back of her hand, "is where the magic begins."

Savian held her hand while they rode in back of the limousine. He hadn't been able to stop touching her since he'd seen her standing aboard the jet, looking around as if she were in absolute awe. When she'd turned her gaze on him that awe had turned to simple delight, reaching inside him with a flood of light that filled every dark crevice of his soul. It had been an amazing few minutes as he'd stood there looking at her.

The dress she wore was black and very form-fitting, accentuating every divine curve of her body. Her scarf was a whimsical choice, filled with light gray and black swirls and shocking red elephants. It was bold and distinct and matched her personality perfectly. The boots, however, were the best part of the outfit. They were long, stretching up her legs to rest just above her knee and Savian found himself wanting to trace his hand up that length and further to see what he could find.

At that moment he was glad he'd had the forethought to make a stop at the mall this afternoon. There'd been a flurry of activities for him after he'd received that faxed copy of the dismissal. A myriad of emotions had coursed through him as well. There was obvious relief, touched with a bit of wonder and amazement that it could have happened to him in the first place. He'd worked so hard on his temper over the years and had felt that he'd finally reached a safe place in his life. Giovanni Morelli had pushed him back to a place where he had not wanted to go and that act alone had almost cost him his freedom.

That was over now. He had been cleared of the murder charges and now they were looking for Jaydon to see exactly how she fit into this situation. There wasn't a whole lot Savian could do about the search at the moment and he'd accepted that fact, mainly because there'd been something else on his mind. On Sunday night when he'd left Jenise's house and went straight to Parker's, he'd realized something. He liked the thought of having a woman standing beside him the way Adriana had immediately come to stand beside his brother. She'd made him think of Jenise, of how she'd taken his case the night he'd showed up at her apartment without any questions. While they'd already had sex at least a half dozen times by that point, watching the way she supported him on an entirely different level had begun to amaze him. It wasn't something he'd planned, nor would have ever predicted. Even now, he wasn't sure where it was leading.

What he'd known for certain this afternoon was that he'd wanted to do something special for her. He wanted to thank her for helping him and to give her what he'd known she wanted—a bit of Christmas magic. So the planning and the phone calls and yes, the dreaded shopping, had begun.

"Here," he said leaning across the seat and pulling a bag towards them. "You're going to need this."

She'd been looking out the windows, a bit quieter than he'd expected her to be once she realized they were in New York. Yet, she smiled when he handed her the bag.

"You're really outdoing yourself today, Savian," she said before digging a hand into the bag.

The coat was black—which he thought had been a great call considering her ensemble—three quartered wool with three huge black buttons and a wide belt. The clerk said it would look great on her and Savian had trusted those words. The smile that quickly spread across her face said she thought so as well.

"Did you think of everything?" she asked as she moved around, putting the coat on.

"I tried," he said with a shrug just as the car was coming to a stop.

When the door opened, their new driver helped Jenise out and Savian followed. He took her hand once more and led her into Del Frisco's Grille. After giving the host his name they were walked past the amazing bar and wood burning oven to the private area he'd reserved for them.

"Dinner in New York," Jenise said after removing her coat and taking a seat. "I love this idea!"

Savian could only smile because she had no clue what else he had in store for her tonight. "I think you're going to love the food as well. I had the opportunity to dine here a few years ago and I've never forgotten the service or the taste."

"Were you here with a woman?" she asked and the look on her face said the question shocked her as much as it did him.

The waiter arrived then and they ordered—cheesesteak eggrolls with sweet and spicy chili sauce, a steakhouse salad for her, and the shaved prime steak sandwich for him. They both ordered the signature sweet Hawaiian pineapple infused vodka cocktail. Savian took a swallow from the glass of water that had been put in front of them before the waiter had taken their order and then he sat back in his seat and looked at her.

"No. I did not bring a woman here," he replied to her question. "As you probably guessed I don't do the dating scene in the traditional sense."

She took a sip of her water as well, as if they both needed some type of libation—no matter how subtle—to have this conversation.

"I think you could probably say the same for me," she said with a tentative smile.

"I was born into this family, with this name, I didn't chose it," Savian admitted and felt just a bit of relief at finally saying that aloud.

"It's a good family," Jenise replied. "Your parents are so loving and supportive and so are your siblings. It was amazing watching all of you together on Thanksgiving."

Savian agreed. The Donovans were an amazing bunch. "I was totally shocked to see you walk into that dining room. Why didn't you tell me you were coming?"

"I don't know," she answered with a shrug. "Adriana stopped by my office earlier that week and invited me. I declined at first, but for a pretty, wispy woman, she's quite pushy."

Jenise smiled and Savian did too, agreeing about Adriana.

"She can be deceiving upon first glance," he said. "She has more spunk than one would anticipate."

"For the record," she told him, "I haven't taken a guy home to meet my family in years, so I know how awkward that must have made you feel."

He was quiet a moment as he realized that he knew absolutely nothing about Jenise's past relationships. He hadn't thought he wanted to at first. Now, he thought seriously, he did.

"I've never taken anyone home to meet my family. I've never had a girlfriend or a desire to make that type of connection."

There, he'd said it and now he would sit back and see how that made her feel.

"Well, aren't we a pair," was her reply as she chuckled and took another sip from her water.

Their cocktails arrived and Jenise abandoned the water to now sip from the fruity drink instead. The quick light in her eyes as she swallowed and took a second sip told him she liked it. He liked that. He also liked how pretty she looked with her hair curled at the top and silky smooth on the sides.

In the next few minutes their appetizers arrived and they began the usual dinner chit-chat.

"These are fantastic," she said after her first bite of the cheesesteak eggrolls. "I'm usually not into spicy sauces, but this is really good. Either that or I'm really hungry."

Savian chuckled. "No. I think they're very good too." Just as he thought she was the most honest and downright attractive woman he'd ever met.

While he'd never wanted a girlfriend that did not make Savian a stranger to women. Only, the women that he'd been with had never laughed as easily as Jenise. They never looked as naturally pretty as she did when she was doing something as simple as putting an eggroll into her mouth. He didn't know why this was the first time he'd noticed all that and to tell the truth he was still trying to figure out what it meant.

Their entrees were quickly devoured as they both admitted to not eating since early afternoon.

"My mom would have a fit if she heard me admit that. She swears that skipping meals slows the metabolism," Jenise said.

Savian nodded. "She's right, but unfortunately it cannot be helped some times."

"I know, business has been building at a steady pace. I'm really thinking about hiring an associate in the new year," she told him as she cut through her salad.

"You should. The whole idea is to grow the firm, to get the Langley Law name spread across the U.S. You can't do that on your own."

"Wow," she said looking over at him. "I don't think you and I have ever talked about our work before."

"We haven't," Savian admitted. "It must be that magic I keep telling you about."

She laughed out loud then, covering her mouth momentarily when she thought it may have been too loud. It wasn't, Savian thought. It was just right.

"I can't believe I'm selling you on that magic. That is so cool," she remarked.

"Yes," Savian added before the last swallow of his cocktail. "That is so cool."

She was so cool and so enticing and addictive. There was a tightness in his chest at that moment and he cleared his throat in an attempt to play it off. She was doing something to him, but it wasn't really magic, he swore. It couldn't be.

CHAPTER 10

"Oh my. Oh my. My goodness, Savian. It's beautiful!" Jenise exclaimed when the lights on the tree at Rockefeller Center were illuminated.

The temperature had dropped since they'd first arrived in the city and now as the breeze blew, Jenise shivered. As a native of Chicago this air should have been easy to deal with, but she had to admit she'd quickly become accustomed to the warmer climate in Miami. Snuggling into her coat, her smile brightened as Savian slipped an arm around her shoulders.

"Maybe we should have watched from the terrace," he told her, but she immediately shook her head.

"No, this is it right here. This is the magic of Christmas. Can't you feel it in the air?"

"I feel a very chilly breeze in the air," was his quick response.

She playfully nudged him as holiday music played and people crowded around. "It's everywhere, the tree is just the biggest symbol. But look around at their faces. Everyone is smiling because they feel the magic too. I love it, love it, love it!" she exclaimed and clapped her hands together.

"I wasn't certain at first, but I think you really like seeing this," he remarked and she giggled like a little girl once more.

"We should walk out this way," he told her. "Traffic was pretty bad and we were running a little late, but Pierce said we should definitely enter through 5th Avenue to get the full effect, whatever that means."

"Okay, let's go then," she said eagerly, grabbing him by the hand.

They hustled through the crowd, Savian holding tight to her hand and leading the way. One time she tripped and almost fell and he was right there, a hand going around her waist to make sure her footing was solid. Jenise couldn't help it, she'd gone up on her tiptoes and kissed him loudly on the lips, smiling as she pulled away.

"Look," she said immediately afterwards. "I can see my breath."

She opened her mouth slightly and watched the frost circle in the air as if she'd been smoking a cigarette. As a child, she'd gotten such a kick out of doing that on wintery Chicago days. Savian, having been born and raised in Miami, probably didn't know that joy. He shocked her when he mimicked her motions and they both looked as if they'd been smoking while standing amidst all those people. Jenise was so giddy in that moment, her smile couldn't have been half as bright as she felt.

After walking around the huge ice skating rink and traveling a bit further, they finally came upon the horn blowing angels.

"Oh my," Jenise had said, her gaze going from one golden-lit angel to the other. She was in awe of the festive beauty, her heart full from the magic.

"This is pretty amazing," Savian admitted.

"It's very amazing," she whispered, stepping closer to the display and closing her eyes as "Jingle Bells" played through the air.

When Savian came up behind her, wrapping his arms around her and pulling her back against him, she began to hum along with the music. She lifted her hands up to touch his arms, as if to signify that he was real and they were actually here at Rockefeller Center for the tree lighting, as she'd always wanted to be. She shivered again, but this time it wasn't because she was cold, it was more because at this moment, she was so very happy.

"Let's get you back to some heat," he said leaning in close to whisper in her ear.

"Oh no, I don't want to go back home yet," she immediately began to protest.

"Not home," he told her. "Not tonight."

He'd taken her hand again and walked while he called for the car on his cell phone. They'd only traveled another block or so—

which in New York felt like an average of three Miami blocks—before they were once again sliding into the backseat of the limo. Once they were settled, Savian wrapped his arm around her again and she immediately cuddled against him.

If someone had told her on yesterday that this was how she'd be spending her evening, she would have called them a big fat liar! Yet, from the moment she'd stepped onto that jet she'd felt nothing but excitement and cheer, just like a child on Christmas morning. She owed all of that to Savian. After a few moments she wondered if he were as confused by that fact as she was.

The limo came to a stop and Savian stepped out first, extending his hand to her. She happily put her hand in his and stepped out onto the sidewalk.

"Are you serious?" she asked the moment she looked directly in front of them.

"It's too late for us to go back to Miami tonight. We'd fall asleep on the jet and then have to get off and drive to our respective apartments," he said with a nonchalant shrug. "I don't feel like doing all that. Do you?"

"No," she immediately replied. "No. Not at all."

The driver walked behind them with that same black duffle bag that Jenise had watched Pierce take onto the jet and another one that matched. Savian held her hand as they walked through the iron and glass doors of The Chatwal Hotel. They were in the elevator when Savian backed her up to the wall and stood still in front of her.

"Thank you for getting those charges dropped," he said in that solemn and serious tone of his.

She hadn't seen or heard this Savian in the hours they'd been together and Jenise worried a little at his appearance now.

"I just did my job, Savian. That's all," she told him as he was shaking his head.

"That's not all," he said in an almost whisper. "I didn't know how much I was actually worried about going to jail for a crime I didn't commit, until it wasn't a factor anymore. There's just so much going on right now and I'm not used to being the one in the spotlight. I just didn't think—"

"You didn't think you were going to be convicted because you were innocent. There's nothing wrong with that," she told him.

"Except that I'm sure there are a number of innocent men and women sitting in jail right at this moment," he replied. "No. I have to give thanks. I have to be grateful because things could have gone much differently."

He took a deep breath then and reached a hand up to brush away a curl, that was probably out of place from all that wind blowing outside, from her forehead.

"I like your hair," he said then, his fingers still touching the short strands. "I don't think I've ever told you all the things I like about you. But I do, I like your hair."

Jenise couldn't believe it, this man had seen her naked numerous times. He'd brought her just as many orgasms and had heard her not-too-fantastic singing, and yet those four words had made her blush. "Thank you," she said. "Thank for those kind words and for all of this. You'll never know how much they've both meant to me."

The elevator doors opened and Savian led her out and towards what she knew was going to be a suite. However, once they were inside she saw it was so much more. She'd immediately taken off her coat and moved deeper into the room to where there was a winding staircase.

"Where does this lead?" she asked, turning to see Savian removing his jacket.

"Rooftop terrace," was his response.

"I'm going up," was her instant reply as she began taking the stairs.

From behind, she could hear him chuckle, then as she turned on the spiral part of the stairs she looked down to see him following her.

It was a large space, the crisp air smacking against her face as she turned in a complete circle to experience it all. Going to the railing she asked, "What street is this? Oh, wait its 44th right? This is a magnificent view."

He came to stand right beside her at that point, his hands thrust into his pockets. "Yes, it is. I can't believe you've wanted to come here so badly and have never done so until now."

It felt as if the sky had opened up and dumped a torrential rainstorm on them right at this moment. Jenise's happy mood almost immediately evaporated. Refusing to let those old memories steal her joy, she tried to shake it off.

"The time just never seemed to be right," she replied, keeping her focus straight ahead, on the lights on all the buildings and the cars passing on the street below.

"Christmas comes at the same time every year," he said.

Yes it did, Jenise thought. Just as her memories of the last time she'd been in New York came each time she'd considered returning. Earlier this evening when Pierce had come out of the cockpit and announced they'd arrived safely in New York, she'd felt a few moments of apprehension, but there was nothing she could do about it. It wasn't as if she could simply stay on the jet and declare she was staying there until Pierce took her back to Miami. No, she'd had to adjust, just as she had back then. That's how life worked, Jenise knew that.

"From time to time, you'll be thrown curveballs," her grandfather had told her when the family found out about the worst mistake of Jenise's life. "You can either catch that ball and throw it right back, or you can duck and hide like you didn't see it in the first place. Langleys don't duck and hide."

So she hadn't. Or at least she didn't think she had. She'd just refused to go back to New York again. Until now.

"I haven't been to New York in years," she said out loud, as if testing how that admission would sound.

She hadn't been back here since that one awful day almost seven years ago.

"Do you want to tell me why?" he asked casually, as if her response had no bearing on him whatsoever.

She wondered if that were true. Her past was her business, just as Savian's past was his. Up until now neither of them had inquired about what had happened in their lives before they met. It was one of their unspoken agreements.

Jenise was tired of those unspoken agreements. She wanted to know where she stood with Savian, and if tonight's events were going to change what they'd originally been. Knowing that she felt this way and admitting now—even if only to herself—that she definitely wanted something more with this man, meant she had to be honest. It was what she would want in return. She was chilly, but she refused to wrap her arms around herself, refused to use that as some type of shield. There was no hiding here, no ducking and running as her grandfather had said.

"During my last year of law school I was involved with one of my professors. I know, that's cliché, right?" she asked with a little chuckle.

Savian did not respond.

Jenise took a deep breath, expelling it slowly, this time not enjoying the frosty smoke as she had before.

"His name was Wesley Boyer," she began after clearing her throat. "I adored him and so did my family. My mother was ecstatic when I'd actually mentioned that I could see myself marrying Wes."

Jenise thought he'd stiffened at her words, but the wind was blowing, so he could have just been cold.

"It was Labor Day weekend when Morgan and I decided to make an impromptu shopping trip before both of us headed back to school. We had so many bags and we'd just come from this great chocolate place. You know, I still cannot remember the name of that place but I remember that I'd just finished a piece of dark chocolate and was still licking my lips and laughing when I saw a cab pull up to the curb and Wes stepped out. At first I was thinking 'oh my goodness how sweet of him to fly to New York to join me here' and I was about to say that to Morgan, but then I realized I hadn't told him I was coming to New York. That's when I saw Wes holding out a hand. In seconds, a woman had put her hand in his and stepped out of the cab as well."

Jenise shook her head as the memory moved through her mind like a bad movie on replay.

"I didn't even realize it but I'd stopped walking and Morgan had to turn back to see what was wrong with me. She called my name but I didn't respond. I couldn't hear anything, I could only see. When the woman was on the curb standing right in front of Wes, he pulled her to him and kissed her. I knew before I blinked that it wasn't a friendly kiss. And before I could think of a wiser course to take, I was walking across the street to approach him. I used to be very impulsive back then," she stated and then shrugged.

She did not look over to see if Savian was watching her or what his reaction to what she'd said was. She just took another breath and kept going.

"I said, 'hello, my name is Jenise and I'm the woman that Wes was in bed with last night.' Morgan had gasped and grabbed my arm in an attempt to pull me away, while Wes rubbed his fingers over his forehead. He always did that when he was worried about something. The woman, I didn't even know her name then, she went so pale I thought she might faint right there on the street. I let Morgan pull me away then because nobody had said anything in response to my introduction and in those ensuing moments I felt like the biggest idiot in the world. We immediately returned to Chicago and I refused to take any of Wes's calls after that. It was over. That quickly and that simply."

"Nothing like that is simple," Savian said quietly and Jenise smiled at his words.

"You're absolutely right about that."

There were a few moments of chilly silence as Jenise gathered her thoughts. This was the hardest part. Sure, Wes had been an ass for cheating and leading her on. He was a conniving bastard for living two lives and she'd been doing a damn good job of upholding her vow to hate him forever for doing all of the above. But this, what happened to the woman had never settled right with Jenise. Even now it caused her pause.

"Her name was Katherine. She'd called me a couple of times but I didn't know that was her number then and I'd stopped listening to my voicemail messages because I didn't want it to be Wes still trying to contact me. It was two weeks after New York and I was trying my best to forget and move on. Katherine sent me an email message next. She used my school email account. She wanted to meet with me. I didn't want to see her so I didn't respond at first. But then I wanted to feel like I was a bigger person, like I could deal with this like a mature adult. So I agreed to meet her at the apartment that Wes kept in Chicago."

Wesley Boyer also owned a condo in Manhattan, the one he shared with his wife Katherine Willoughby Boyer.

"When I pulled up to the apartment building that afternoon there were police cars everywhere and an ambulance was just pulling up. I tried to get into the building but the cops would not let me in. I dialed the cell number Katherine had told me was hers, from those calls that I'd ignored. I did not get an answer. And then, because my heart was about to thump right out of my chest, I called Wes. He was distraught when he answered, yelling that Katherine had killed herself, right there in his bed. In the bed that I'd told Katherine I'd shared with him."

Except for the sounds from the street, there was silence. Jenise wanted at that moment to hear some holiday music. Maybe Alvin and the Chipmunks because their voices always seemed to cheer her up. She wanted to look up toward the sky and see a sprig of mistletoe hanging down so that she could smile and think about the magic once more. She did not want to feel the sting of tears in her eyes, a result of the pain and disgrace that would never totally die within her.

"Katherine committed suicide because her husband of thirteen years had been sleeping with his student for the better part of the last year. I was the other woman and I'd caused this person I didn't even know so much pain and heartache that she'd felt she had no other recourse but to kill herself. It was the worst moment of my life."

"It was not your fault," Savian replied instantly. "It was his responsibility to love and cherish his wife. His duty to be faithful to her. You had nothing to do with that and if you had not started a relationship with him, it would have been another girl. He did what he wanted to do, so the repercussions of that act are on him."

Jenise chuckled at his words even though she was certain that wasn't the response he'd expected. Still, she laughed and laughed because she couldn't remember how many times she'd told herself that very same thing. She also did not want those tears to fall, not again, not this time. It was over and done with and it wasn't her fault, so why was she even thinking of crying for that young life that had been lost.

She was surprised when Savian turned and reached for her. Ten minutes ago she would have gone instantly into his arms. Now, however, with the memory of Wes and Katherine between them, she couldn't.

"Look," she said, trying to regain her composure. "I'm over this. Really, I am. You asked why I wouldn't come to New York and that's why. It started here and I felt like coming back would make me relive it all over again."

"I'm sorry for bringing you here."

She shook her head quickly. "No. Please, don't be sorry. I'm not sorry you brought me here tonight, Savian. This was beautiful. The flowers, jet, dinner, and that tree, they were all wonderful. This is what I'll remember about New York from now on. You've given me a whole new memory."

She didn't even realize she'd been backing up, not until Savian reached out and caught her before she stumbled toward the door leading to the penthouse. He'd grabbed her arms with such ease and pulled her to him with a gentleness she'd never known he possessed. When he wrapped his arms around her, holding her head firmly against his chest Jenise whimpered. He smelled so good and felt even better.

"You're my new memory," she told him again. "Thank you for being my new memory."

"Come downstairs," Savian said while holding her in his arms. "I have something else for you."

She let out a breath and her arms tightened around him as if she were hesitant to let him go. Savian liked that feeling much more than he figured he should have.

"There's more than what I've already seen?" she asked incredulously.

He smiled. "Yes, just a little something else and then you can go to sleep. I'm sure you're exhausted from working all day and then traveling. I wish they would have had the tree lighting on a Saturday."

"It stays lit for weeks," she told him as she finally decided to pull away enough so that they could begin walking towards the door. "We could have come at any time."

"No," he said. "I wanted you to see it the first time it was lit this season."

She looked up at him and smiled. "That was very sweet of you, Savian. I cannot begin to thank you enough."

"Then don't," he said. "We've both thanked each other enough. Now it's time we just move on."

Her smile had brightened and Savian got the impression those words may have meant more to her than he'd intended. Or had they been right on point? He was trying valiantly to mask the contradicting emotions that had been swirling through him all day. Her admission made that much harder than he'd ever anticipated because now he knew the reason why she hadn't questioned their arrangement from the beginning. Sure, Savian was used to sleeping with women and not making any other commitments to them, but those women had been nothing like Jenise. As far as he knew they hadn't come from solid families, or had focused career goals. They weren't as intelligent and seemingly fearless as Jenise was. And they certainly never appealed to him the way this woman did.

Wesley Boyer was an asshole and if there ever came a day when the two of them were face-to-face, Savian was sure he'd beat the hell out of him. It was that simple. His fists even clenched as he thought about it.

"Close your eyes," he told Jenise when he knew thoughts of doing physical harm to someone were about to overtake him.

She did as he asked while standing beside him. Earlier tonight she'd been brimming with excitement and he'd enjoyed every second of watching her. Her smile had been so genuine and so bright. He never would have thought that anything bad had happened to her while she'd been in this state before, when it would have been so easy for her to fall headlong back into the bad memories. He'd really liked being with her and watching her enjoyment, so much so that he'd begun thinking of other things to do once they returned to Miami to keep her looking and feeling this way. That was as far ahead as Savian had ever thought about any woman before.

He held tight to Jenise's hand and led her slowly into the bedroom portion of the suite, determined to remain focused on the here and now for the duration of this trip. Once they were standing in front of the bed, he turned so that he was now facing her. His intention had been to tell her to open her eyes and then move out of the way so she could see the last thing he had planned for her tonight. But as he stood there, Savian found himself looking down at her. Lifting his hand he trailed a finger along the line of her jaw, down the side of her neck to where her pulse jumped at his touch. Before he could question what his intention was and if he should follow his gut or not, Savian was cupping her face in his hands, tilting her upward to receive his kiss.

The tender touch of his lips against hers rocked something soul deep inside of him and it took every ounce of his strength not to actually shiver in response. He kissed her softly once more, loving the easy way that she moved into the embrace. Touching his tongue slowly to hers had them both sighing and sinking slowly into what was undoubtedly the sweetest kiss ever. He felt intoxicated as he opened his mouth wider, taking more of her and feeling warmth completely filling his body. It wasn't the normal rise of desire he felt when he was around Jenise, but something much deeper and when she wrapped her arms around him Savian feared he was sinking and would eventually be unable to break free.

Jolted by that sensation he pulled away from the kiss, covering his discomfort with a stilted chuckle. "I don't think I was supposed to do that first," he said.

"What? Why?" she asked, her voice husky as she licked her tongue over her lips.

He couldn't speak, not at this moment, so he just moved out of the way and waited.

"You...are...amazing," she said slowly, the sound of her smile evident in her tone.

"Not really," he said. "It was just a phone call."

She was shaking her head as she moved around the bed touching one of the many sprigs of mistletoe that hung along the length of the leather headboard.

"A phone call that you didn't have to make," she told him as she inhaled deeply. "And it's fresh. Don't you just love that scent? I'm never going to fall asleep here."

He'd moved from where he was standing trying like hell to stay focused and to stay on course. He hadn't thought this through. How was he going to sleep in this bed with her all night when he'd never slept in a bed with a woman before? And why would he even put himself in this position? For once in his life, Savian did not have the answers and he couldn't stand there and try to figure them out. He wouldn't, not tonight.

"I'm hoping you won't focus too much on trying to sleep," he told her as his hands slipped slowly around her waist.

She turned immediately in his embrace. "I don't think I will. Not if I'm wrapped in your arms all night."

He undid the belt at her waist and let it fall to the floor. She undid the buttons on his shirt. He grabbed the hem of her dress, pulling it up and over her head. She pushed the shirt from his arms and then removed his t-shirt. Palming her heavy breasts as they all but spilled over the black bra she wore, Savian groaned and then reached behind her to unhook said bra, watching in awe as it fell away leaving her totally free. And absolutely gorgeous. His hands were on her breasts again, kneading and squeezing them tightly.

She unbuckled his belt, slipped the button free and unzipped his pants. Pushing them past his hips until they fell to the floor, she grabbed his burgeoning length in one hand and mimicked the motion of his hands on her breasts. He groaned loudly because the spikes of pleasure that shot up his spine felt like an explosion and he almost trembled again.

His hands moved down her torso, loving the feel of her soft pliant skin as he did. She wore opaque tights that he would have never thought of as sexy before, but seeing them covering her voluptuous ass and thighs right now was driving him mad with desire. He pushed them down, hating that he'd have to remove those sexy as hell boots to get them completely off. She released her hold on his erection and leaned into him for support as he unzipped each boot and removed them. Her panties went next, the wisp of black silk that he knew he'd remember for all the days of his life, and then she was naked.

Totally. Completely. Naked.

And beautiful.

Every curve, each rise and swell of her body was sexier than he could have ever imagined a woman being and for the life of him he didn't know how he was going to wait another second without being buried deep inside of her. Oh, he thought with a slow smile spreading across his face, he didn't have to wait.

Jenise was already moving, lowering herself until she could untie the laces of his shoes and slip them off his feet. She finished taking his pants off and then reached up to grab the ban of his boxer briefs. Her movements were slow here as she stared at his now free arousal, a look of pure delight on her face. That look had Savian touching her cheek softly, whispering her name because she now filled his mind so completely.

"Get on the bed," he told her. "Lay back and open for me."

Her heated gaze met his and held as she moved slowly to do what he requested. The comforter on this bed was a dark burgundy and Jenise's lighter toned skin was enticing against it. She lay on her back and spread her legs wide until he could see the moist lips of her center unfolding for him. The sight had him clenching his teeth, his mouth watering with desire. He was moving immediately, touching his hands to the soft skin of her thighs as he went in closer, mouth already open, tongue extended to taste.

She was like heaven, and sunshine, and bliss all rolled into one as he licked along the hood of her clit. Her hands went immediately to the back of his head, guiding and holding him where she wanted him to be. He stayed right there, enjoying the jolt of her body beneath him as he flicked his tongue quickly over that hardened nub again and again. Slipping a finger inside of her, feeling her warmth immediately suck him inside had Savian moaning right along with her. He worked his finger in and out of her as his tongue continued to stroke over her clit. Her grip had tightened on his head as her hips began to thrust upward, pumping his face. When she shivered and tensed beneath him, Savian sighed loudly and rose above her to position himself.

The first stroke of his rigid erection into her pulsating center was soul-shattering. He'd braced himself with his palms flat on the bed, the muscles in his arms tensing, and he held completely still. His eyes were closed as he stayed there, just like that for endless moments.

"Look at me, Savian," he heard her whisper. "Open your eyes and look at me, please."

He did so slowly and was immediately captured by the welcoming and accepting look she was giving him. She held his gaze as she began to move beneath him, pumping slowly, pulling his length in and out of her. He was dazed and confused and totally captured, until all he could do was match her movements.

A slow and steady rhythm built between them and before he knew what he was doing Savian was lowering himself over her until her breasts rubbed against his chest and her legs wrapped around his waist. Her arms were tight around him, as his arms framed her head. He stared down at her as he continued to move inside her, unable or unwilling—he wasn't quite sure which—to take his eyes off her.

On and on, slow and sweet, they continued to move, until he'd had no choice but to kiss her again, to stroke his tongue over hers the way his dick was stroking along the walls of her sweet pussy. As the kiss deepened her hold on him tightened, until he could feel her clenching and throbbing around him. Knowing that she was yet again finding her release with him, pushed Savian over the edge and he followed her with quick thrusts of his hips until his own release poured inside of her, his lips still on hers.

He'd smiled at her so many times tonight. He'd listened to the baggage from her past and hadn't reprimanded or judged her. He'd thought of everything he possibly could to make her happy. And he'd stayed on top of her as they'd made love, his gaze had been locked on hers, his lips kissing her tenderly. Jenise was in deep.

There was no doubt in her mind now and probably no turning back. Shockingly, she wasn't interested in turning back at all. As she lay wrapped in Savian's arms, her head resting on his chest, eyes closed as she listened to his steady breathing, she decided that this was where she wanted to be. Savian Donovan had been another curve ball in her life and damn if she wasn't going to take her grandfather's advice once again, and this time catch that ball. The smile that spread across her face was slow and genuine as she let the scent of the mistletoe and the magic of this moment lull her into the first stages of sleep.

It was there, right on the precipice of reality and deep slumber when she heard it.

"Please, don't let me fall in love with her," Savian whispered into the silence of the room. "Please. Please. Please."

CHAPTER 11

Miami, one week later.

"Al wants to pay her the money. He wants her out of our lives for good this time," Reginald told Bruce as they sat in the private back room of their favorite cigar bar.

"That's his guilt talking," Bruce said. "You know he's never gotten over the fact that she has those pictures of him and he can't remember if he slept with her or not."

"She threatened to tell Darla that they had slept together. Those pictures of him lying naked in his bed were her proof," Reginald replied. "But, like I've said before, I think it might be time for us to take some real action this time."

When his younger brother sighed, Reginald took a drag on his favored Don Arturo Destino Al Siglo, exhaling the smoke in slow, measured puffs.

"This has been going on for far too long, Bruce. For more than thirty years now we've all be living under this secret, praying it would never come to light. I'm tired of this charade. I need peace," he told his brother honestly.

Savian and Parker were both suspicious, coming to him with their questions and doubts. Reginald hated the look in his sons' eyes as of late. He hated the lie that he knew they were beginning to suspect.

"Aren't you tired of lying to your family?" he pressed.

Bruce sat back in his chair, his cigar sitting lame in the ashtray as he stared across the room. "Dion and Sean are asking questions."

Reginald nodded. "So are Savian and Parker."

"That email has got everyone up in arms. Henry called me last night to say he thinks Trent might be investigating the message," Bruce added.

Reginald shook his head then. He knew his nephew well even though Trent had grown up across the country from him. He was a no nonsense, find the answers type of guy. If there was something Trent wanted to know, he found out. And if what he found out wasn't what he wanted to hear, then there would be hell to pay. The Senior Donovans had always teased Henry that he'd managed to have a son that was just like their brother Bernard. In his prime, Bernard had been the Donovan brother not to be messed with. He had a short temper and a low tolerance for bullshit and if someone were crazy enough to cross him, well, they'd better find a good place to hide.

Roslyn Ausby had hidden, and she'd done it well, for more than fifteen years since they'd given in to her payment demands the first time. Now, she was back, and Reginald didn't know what had gotten into her, but the woman was on a mission. Thinking back on it now, he figured this had always been her mission in the first place—to get as much of the Donovan money as she could. Reginald didn't want to pay her again.

"I don't think we should pay her either, but I'm not sure how else we can handle this without causing a scandal," Bruce was saying.

"We're stronger now," Reginald replied. "We've all put our blood, sweat and tears into building this name. I think we can counter whatever she does. But we have to face it head on, we can't keep hiding from it. That's making us too vulnerable."

Bruce nodded in agreement. "Bernard said he had a plan."

Reginald shook his head. "Bernard's plans are dangerous. Remember he was the one that wanted to go shake some sense into her from the start."

"He was also the one that slept with her in a hotel without knowing who the hell she was," Bruce spat.

"Yeah, he did do that," Reginald admitted. "She was good, that Roslyn. She had a plan and she carried it out, trapping our brothers in a snare that could potentially destroy them."

"That could now destroy us all," Bruce added.

"Not if we don't let it," Reginald told him. "We've got to get ahead of this thing."

"What are you saying?" Bruce asked as he looked over to Reginald.

"I'm saying we should be the ones to break the news. Tell our families and hell, maybe even make a public announcement. If we take away her ammunition she has no choice but to slink her conniving ass back under the rock where she came from."

He'd been thinking about this for the last few weeks, ever since Savian had stood in his house and called him a liar. His son had stared him down like the man Reginald had raised him to be and confronted him with the confidence of a Donovan. And Reginald hadn't known what to do. The last thing he wanted was to stare into Savian's eyes and lie to him. But he'd been doing that all their lives. Lying to all of his children and most painfully, to his wife. He didn't want to do any of that anymore.

"That's what I think we should do," he reiterated. "We should come out and tell the truth."

Bruce picked up his cigar then. He smoked Don Arturo as well, but preferred the Siglo de Amistad. He took a deep puff and released the smoke slowly before saying. "The problem with telling the truth, Reggie, is that we—you and I—don't even really know that for ourselves. Actually, none of us do, thanks to Roslyn's manipulating ways."

He was right, Reginald thought contemplatively. They didn't know who the father of Roslyn's baby was. Hell, they didn't even know for certain if the child actually existed. But if it did, and if they called Roslyn's bluff…he took another puff of cigar and sat back in his chair. Bruce did the same.

Dion was the last one to enter Savian's office, closing and locking the door behind him. Savian, Parker, Regan and Sean—who hadn't gone away to visit Tate's family as planned—were already there, each of them waiting until Dion came in and pulled another guest chair closer to Savian's desk.

"Trent traced that license plate from the SUV that Jaydon climbed into at Morelli's house," Dion began immediately.

He was wearing black slacks today and as it was nearing five o'clock, he'd already taken off his suit jacket and his tie was loose around his neck.

"So who is it registered to?" Savian asked first.

He'd thought when Dion had sent the text message telling all of them to meet in Savian's office ten minutes ago, that he'd found out something about what their fathers were hiding. While this information was valuable too, Savian couldn't help but feel a little disappointed.

"That's the kicker," Dion told them. "The Yukon XL Denali registered in the state of New York belongs to Dane Henry Ausby."

After this statement Dion stared at each one of them with raised brows.

"You know how Trent is," Dion continued. "He took that name and proceeded to dig even further, but the only thing he came up with was a birth certificate for Dane Ausby. His mother is listed as Roslyn Ausby."

"You're looking at us as if we should know who that is," Regan said, with a frown. "But I don't think I've ever heard that name before."

"I have," Sean spoke up. "At the Mother's Day cook-out. Dad and Uncle Reggie had walked away from the rest of the family, going to stand closer to the dock. I was playing with Briana and that huge pink ball mom bought for her. The ball rolled down the hill bouncing close to where they were standing and when I went to retrieve it, I heard them saying the name 'Roslyn'. Both of them said it."

Dion nodded. "And the moment Trent gave me this news I remembered you telling me that a few days after the cook-out when we were discussing what the Seniors might be hiding."

"Wait a minute," Savian said, shaking his head because things were clicking into place, but he didn't like the picture it was creating. No, he certainly did not like how all this was playing out.

"You're saying that the SUV that Jaydon was riding in belonged to a man that may be connected to whatever is going on between our fathers? So our fathers are somehow connected to Morelli's murder?"

"And if that's true," Parker added. "Then the idea to expose those fake pictures of Adriana and I also has something to do with our parents?"

"No way," Regan said. "There's no way our fathers would let your name be dragged through the mud, or you be charged with murder. Not to mention the hit the company has taken with these last months of negative publicity. I don't believe that."

"Morelli said somebody was going to bring us to our knees," Savian recalled as he sat back into his chair heavily. "He said he couldn't wait to see it happen as if he knew it was coming."

"Dammit!" Sean cursed and shook his head. "They're connected to all this."

"More like all this may be because of something they did," Parker added.

Dion nodded. "That's what I'm thinking. When we were talking about the window breaking at their homes, the first thing Sam Desdune asked about was enemies. Anyone in our pasts that we'd pissed off that might want revenge."

"Wait. Just wait," Regan said sliding to the edge of her seat, her hands shaking as she lifted them to push her hair back from her face.

In that second, Savian remembered that his sister was pregnant and that maybe talking about all this in front of her might not be such a good idea. He looked at Parker, who must have been thinking along the same lines and had already stood to move close to Regan.

"My father and your father," she said pointing at Dion and Sean. "You think they did something to someone in their past and now that person is back and trying to make us pay for our parents' mistakes?"

Dion looked at Parker before he replied, "Considering all that we know now, it fits. But we're not certain, so don't get all upset. Trent's going to look into a few more things. We're going to try and find more information before we tell Miami PD that we know who the truck was registered to. It would be great if we could find Jaydon before the cops do as well, so you know Trent's also working on that. He doesn't want Bailey to know just yet, so he hasn't pulled D&D into this at all."

Regan was already shaking her head and Parker reached down to touch her shoulders. "Listen, how about you call Gavin to come pick you up. Savian and I can fill you in on the rest later."

"No," she said shaking her head immediately. "I'm not leaving and you're not going to cut me out of this. And if either of you try, I swear I'll make your life a living hell."

"Moreso than you already have," Sean quipped and received a quick and heated look from Regan.

"We won't keep you in the dark, Regan," Savian said in his calming voice. "But you have to promise to take care of yourself. There's no telling what we may uncover, but you have to know that my little niece or nephew's health comes first."

He couldn't believe he was saying that. Sure, Savian loved his younger sister, more than he thought Regan would ever know. Finding out she was pregnant had been a shock and until this moment he hadn't been sure how he'd felt about that revelation.

"I'll be fine," Regan shot back.

The comment was no surprise to any of them in that room.

"So what's the plan where our fathers are concerned?" Parker asked.

"I say we keep this between us for the moment and see what else Trent comes up with," Dion told them.

"He's right," Savian added. "Because if we're right and they did make an enemy that's back to seek revenge, then this is far from over."

An hour later, thoughts of his father, the murder and the possibility of what might be coming for all of them had Savian about to lose his mind. He needed some relief and immediately thought of her.

"Gwen let me in," Savian said as he walked into Jenise's office unannounced.

She looked up, surprised to see him.

It had been a week since they'd returned from New York and he hadn't seen her since then. He'd called and tried to make dates with her, but her answer had been that she was busy working on another case. Every time he'd called. Today, he'd decided not to call.

"She should have told me," Jenise said. She set her pen down but only looked at him for a second before she glanced at her computer screen again. "I'm really busy today."

Savian continued to walk, until he was standing right at the end of her desk. "You've been really busy since we came back."

"Yeah," she said, still not looking at him. "That's true. I told you I was thinking of hiring an associate. Well, things have really picked up, so I may have to do that sooner than I thought."

He nodded. "I think that's a good idea."

When it seemed she didn't know what else to do with herself, she let her hands fall flat on the desk and sighed. "I'm going to take care of that. But right now, I really need to—"

"Stop it," he said in a voice that was more controlled than he was feeling. "Tell me what's going on."

"What do you mean?" she asked, still not looking at him.

Savian was not in the mood for this right now. He'd wanted to share a nice meal with her and then maybe watch one of those holiday movies she loved so much. She was obviously not on the same page with him. He leaned over the desk, taking her chin in his palm and turning her head until they were staring eye-to-eye. "Tell me why you've been dodging my calls and turning down my suggestions to meet up for the last week."

"Savian," she began with a sigh.

"No," he said shaking his head. "We don't do pretenses, you and I. We put our cards on the table and play the hand we're dealt. So just say what you have to say. Did I do something wrong?"

She looked as if she definitely had something to say and Savian took that to mean that somewhere along the line he'd messed up. Well, that was fine. All she needed to do was tell him and he'd fix it. That was simple enough. But instead of doing that, Jenise pulled back from him. She stood from her seat and walked around him to close her office door. When it was closed she said simply, "I can't do this anymore."

He heard the words. No, he'd actually felt them like tiny spiky darts flying into his back. He turned to face her then. "What can't you do?"

"I can't be just your lover," she stated plainly, calmly, like she'd just given him her lunch order.

"Why?" he asked, folding his arms over his chest.

"It's not enough, Savian." She took a couple of steps away from the door but didn't get too close to him.

Thank god, she didn't get too close because Savian wanted nothing more than to take her in his arms and kiss away the words she was saying. He wanted to touch and feel her until everything bad and painful melted away.

"It was fine in the beginning. You were my client so I shouldn't have been sleeping with you in the first place. Besides that, I'd told myself these last seven years that I was better off with the minimal amount of contact with men. Just have sex, have fun, keep it moving, that was my motto. It was my therapy and it worked for a really long time. But just like I'm over what Wes did to me, I'm over trying to rehabilitate myself for something I didn't do in the first place," she told him.

"Okay," he said with a slow nod. "I get all of that. What I don't get is why you think hiding from me is the best answer."

"It's the best answer because for whatever reason you subscribe to the no-strings attached relationships, you're not ready to move past it. Case in point, you haven't even shared with me the reason why you hold yourself so distant in relationships. Why do you not want to be committed to a woman, Savian? Why don't you want to fall in love?"

Again with those words that felt like weapons. He felt like he was being ambushed and he hadn't come here prepared for that. With everything he'd just learned about the people Savian was sure he loved, he couldn't imagine feeling that way about someone else. It just wasn't worth it, was what he'd always thought before. Now, he didn't know what the hell to think.

"I like you, Jenise. I like you a lot," he admitted, and knew instinctively that would not be good enough.

"I said 'love', Savian. Not 'like'," she snapped.

He sighed. "New York was a big thing for me," he told her. "I knew it would be special for you and so I did it. I've never planned a trip for another woman before. I've never slept in bed all night with another woman."

She was nodding as he spoke. "I won't thank you for the trip again. We've been there, and done that. And I'm not going to thank you for making me the first woman you slept with, although I'm sure some would consider that a magnificent feat."

"Why are you doing this?" he asked her solemnly because Savian really did not understand. He couldn't, for the life of him, figure out why it was suddenly harder to breathe.

He'd thought things were changing between them and he'd decided that he was comfortable with that. He wasn't going to keep questioning what was happening, but instead had planned to embrace it, for as much time as he could. Now, she was changing the rules and he wasn't sure he could keep up.

"Because I have to," she told him. "I have to be better and demand better for myself. What Wes did to me was totally messed up, but I didn't know he was married. If I had, I would have never started sleeping with him. I didn't have any control over that relationship and instead of actually asserting control over what I wanted from the next guy in my life, I allowed myself to find a safe spot and I hid there. Well, I'm tired of hiding now. I know what I want and if a guy is not willing to give it to me, then he's not worth my time."

"So I'm not worth your time?" he asked, the words like lumps in his throat.

"You're worth so much more than you think you are, Savian. And that's the problem for us. I'm ready to move forward and you're not."

"I have moved forward," he insisted. "I just told you that New York was a first for me."

She nodded. "It was a first and it was a step in the right direction, but then you turned yourself right back around."

He dragged his hands down his face, helplessness not a good feeling for him. "I don't know what you're talking about."

"You begged not to fall in love with me," she said abruptly. "Like you were wishing on that mistletoe you so romantically had tacked up along that bed. You enjoyed New York. You enjoyed having sex with me. But you don't want to love me."

Jenise was shaking her head now, folding her arms over her chest in a move that warned him to stay far away. "I cannot continue to give myself to someone who has no intention of giving me anything in return."

He did not know what to say, or how he felt about what she'd just said. He'd had no idea that she'd heard him that night because he'd thought she'd been sleep. He had wished he wasn't falling in love, had been wishing it with every fiber of his being, because he knew that it just wasn't possible. It could never be. But how did he say that to her? How did he tell her that now without sounding like a complete jerk? Everything she'd just said made absolute sense. She did need to do what was best for her and Savian wasn't sure he was it.

"I understand," he said finally.

"Good," she said with a nod. "I'm glad you do. Now, if you'll excuse me. I really have to get back to work, Savian."

"Yeah, I guess you should," he said because really, there was nothing else to say. There was nothing else for him to do. Not this time.

CHAPTER 12

By Saturday night Savian was in a crappy mood. How he made it through the rest of the work week he had no idea, but this was the third weekend that he'd disregarded his routine of going into the office for a few hours. Instead, he'd spent hours this morning working out. He'd run on the treadmill and done so many sets of leg and arm weights that his muscles had all but screamed for mercy.

Eventually, he'd showered and walked into his kitchen dressed only in basketball shorts in an attempt to find something to eat. The shopping service had dropped off his weekly order yesterday, so the refrigerator was fully stocked. Still, his stomach growled as his mind thought of cheesesteak eggrolls with spicy chili sauce, instead. With a huff, he slammed the refrigerator door, grabbing an apple from the fruit bowl in the center of the island. After finishing the fruit he'd gone into the living room where he sat until falling asleep. He had no idea how long he'd been sleeping when the persistent ringing of his cell phone woke him.

"Yeah, hello?" he answered groggily after rolling to the other end of the couch to grab his phone from the end table.

"This is Devlin. I've got some news."

Savian sat straight up on the couch, his eyes now opened completely, his mind instantly awake. "What is it?"

"Part of running a background check includes looking into financials. I ran bank statements on each of the Senior Donovans. General consensus—they're all rich," Devlin said dryly.

Savian did not respond.

"When I didn't come up with anything I decided to go back a little further. The Seniors have been reputable citizens for years. If there was some dirt to be found, it would have been well before this last generation of Donovans began to make their mark on the world," he reported.

"Right," Savian agreed. Whatever the Seniors had done, it had to be a long time ago. But who would hold a grudge that long? And what could have possibly happened to make someone that angry that they would bide their time like this before striking?

"Fifteen years ago," Devlin said. "There was a wire transfer from Bernard Donovan's account in the amount of $83,333. That's an odd amount, don't you think?"

"An odd amount indeed," Savian replied.

"On the same date, Henry Donovan also did a wire transfer from his personal account. It was for the same amount," Devlin told him.

"And the others?" Savian asked when a sickening feeling began to swirl in the pit of his stomach.

"I had to use my contacts at the Federal Reserve to go deeper into all of their accounts. Each one of the Senior Donovans made a wire transfer for the same amount, on the same date. And that's not all," Devlin stated. "One day after the wire transfer, Reginald Donovan opened a safe deposit box. It's the only one he has and it's only in his name. His wife Carolyn's name is on two of his accounts at the same bank, but not on the safe deposit box."

Holding the phone in one hand, Savian used his other to squeeze the bridge of his nose, hoping the pressure would stop the quickly developing headache.

"My father has an account at Sunbright Limited National Bank here in Miami. It's in his name only. My mother has her own account there too. I didn't know about the safe deposit box."

"I figured as much," Devlin said. "That's why I contacted one of my old Navy buddies that happens to work at the bank's headquarters down there. I flew in yesterday and we went into the bank after hours to open the safe deposit box. I'm emailing you a copy of the only thing found in that box now."

"What was it?" Savian asked Devlin.

"It's an agreement," he replied. "Between the Senior Donovans and someone named Roslyn Joyce Ausby."

Savian cursed. He thanked Devlin for his help and then he threw his phone across the room and cursed again.

Before he could think better of his actions, Savian was up and going into his bedroom. He dressed quickly then came back into the living room to figure out where he'd thrown his phone and just how much damage had been done to it. The screen was cracked, of course. He was frowning as he stuffed it into his pocket, not even thinking about how much he'd paid for the phone for its screen to shatter as if it were only worth about twenty dollars. Now, cell phones probably weren't built to withstand being thrown against a wall, but that wasn't the point.

As he left his apartment and rode down on the elevator, he thought, there were much more pressing things going on than his broken phone. Pressing, as in, like a vice that was slowly being tightened at his temples, squeezing until he wanted to scream in agony.

His father was definitely connected to this Roslyn Ausby person. And she was the mother of Dane Ausby. And Dane owned the SUV that carried Jaydon away from Morelli's house. And all this meant his father was in big trouble. His father, and the rest of the Senior Donovans, he might add.

Savian drove so fast he was certain he would be pulled over by a cop at any moment, and wouldn't that just be grand. He'd have a speeding ticket to add to all the other stressful events in his life. The heavens must have been shining down upon him because he made it to Jenise's apartment building without incident. He hadn't even noticed that he'd parked on the same floor as her apartment and stepped off the elevator heading directly down the hall without a moment's hesitation. The second he was at her door, he knocked.

He needed to talk to someone about this, to get a fresh and non-emotional reaction to the facts. Jenise was the only other person, outside of his siblings and cousins that he trusted. So when she opened the door he only said, "Hi. I need to talk to you about something," before walking straight into her apartment.

That wasn't the smartest thing he could have done. Then again, he hadn't expected what he saw when he came to an immediate stop in her living room.

"Hello?" the tall, dark-skinned man said as he stood from the couch where he'd been sitting with a drink in his hand.

"Hello," Savian replied slowly, before turning around to look at Jenise in question.

"You should have called first," she told him.

That's when Savian noticed she was wearing a robe. The white silk robe he'd purchased for her when he'd taken her to New York. He'd bought her lots of things to prepare for that trip. Negligees, underwear, two outfits including shoes, and a coat. He'd been at her place so much in the weeks before they'd left that he'd had an opportunity to see what sizes she wore. But it had never occurred to him that anyone besides him would see her in that robe, or in the sexy little nightie that had come with it.

"I should have called?" he asked, feeling now like one of the weights he'd been lifting earlier was sitting in the center of his chest. He couldn't breathe and he could barely see straight.

That's what it was, he wasn't seeing things correctly. There wasn't a man sitting in Jenise's apartment as if he were ready to take her to bed and peel that robe from her delectable body. No, that man was definitely not sitting in her living room, enjoying a drink after having peeled that robe from her delectable body and made sweet love to her. No! No! No!

"Savian," she said.

"No!" he yelled in response. "Just...no!"

He was moving again, heading to the door.

She called his name one more time, but he ignored it, slamming that door so hard behind him he could have sworn he heard the wood cracking.

The next time Savian was behind the wheel of his truck he said a prayer. He did not want to get into an accident, or cause anyone else harm, but he was sure he shouldn't be driving in the state he was currently in. His breath was still coming in jagged puffs as he pulled out of the parking garage and headed back to his apartment. After a while of trying to keep his hands from shaking on the steering wheel, he'd switched on the radio, hoping the music would help to calm him down.

When the Christmas music blared through the speakers, he gritted his teeth and slapped his palm against the knob to hurriedly turn it off. He wanted to punch something. No, he

wanted to punch someone. That guy with the drink in his hand
would do. And so would Wesley Boyer. And Dane Ausby. He
couldn't hit a woman so thinking about Roslyn Ausby only made
him curse again.

What the hell was happening to him! To his life and his
family?

He slammed his truck's door and went back to his apartment,
into the dark living room he'd just left, and dropped down onto
the couch once again. Dragging his hands over his face, Savian
searched for calm. He reached deep inside for a quiet and
soothing place, just as the therapist had taught him to do all those
years ago. He groaned when he couldn't find it, realizing with a
start that the quiet and soothing place he'd recently come to rely
on was with Jenise.

Standing quickly then, he paced the length of his living room,
going from the floor-to-ceiling windows to the wall where family
pictures hung in a circular pattern. His mind whirled with words
and events, faces and places. For a moment he felt as if he wasn't
sure if he was coming or going. His chest hurt. He struggled for
air and fought for clarity.

He could see her smile and hear her laughter. The Christmas
tree lighting had made her happy. She'd sniffed that mistletoe
before they'd made love on the bed and after they'd come out of
the shower. When they'd watched the holiday cartoons on the jet,
she'd sang along with those songs as well. She said she deserved
better than him. And she did. Was it the man in her apartment?
Was he the better man for her?

Savian was just steps away from the wall at that point and
when he yelled with exasperation he pulled back a fist and
slammed it into the wall just beneath the family portrait taken
about ten years ago.

❧

"You're going after him," Tucker asked when Jenise came out
of her bedroom fully dressed.

"He misunderstood," she told her brother.

He'd come down to Miami under the guise of checking on
her, but really Tucker was running away. His confession that he
was tired of practicing law came as a shock to Jenise, but she'd
listened attentively as he explained that he just wanted to travel

for a while, to see where he landed and what type of life he really wanted to live. She'd encouraged him, unlike their parents, because she understood what it felt like to want something and not be able to have it.

"He could have simply introduced himself," Tucker continued from the spot where he still lounged on her couch. He'd turned on the television while she was gone and now flicked between the many cable channels.

"You could have introduced yourself," she replied grabbing her purse, jacket and keys.

Tucker laughed. "Nah, it was too much fun watching him get jealous."

"He was not jealous," she said. "He was upset about something."

"Yeah, about seeing you in a robe, with a man sitting on your couch," Tucker continued. "If I were in love with you I would have been jealous too."

Jenise was at the door by that point and she turned to look back at her brother. "Savian's not in love with me," she told him.

Tucker laughed again, this time foregoing his words of wisdom and concentrating his energy on flicking those channels. Jenise left him there because it was obvious that he was finished with their conversation. Tucker had always had a very short attention span.

It was late and the last thing she wanted was to drive to a place she'd never been before. She'd had Savian's home address in her files so she'd entered that into her GPS. Why she was even going over there, Jenise couldn't figure out. It was over between them. She'd told him so a few days ago when he'd come to her office, and she'd meant it. Sort of. There was a part of her that wanted to give Savian all the time he needed to see if he could ever return her feelings. Then there was another part, the independent and self-sufficient part of her that—as she'd told Ms. Carolyn—did not need a man to define her, which said she was doing the right thing by walking away. If Savian wanted her, he would do the right thing as well.

Only Jenise wasn't totally sure what the right thing was now, especially after seeing how strained and out of control Savian had appeared standing in her living room. Now she was driving to his condo, hoping he was there and not out somewhere driving in the condition he was in. She was worried for his safety and concerned with how he was going to take her coming over to his house unannounced.

On the flip side, she was pissed that he'd come over to her place without calling or texting first and then had the audacity to—as Tucker had so bluntly put it—get jealous. If he'd waited a few more seconds instead of getting angry and storming out, she would have introduced him to Tucker and none of this would be happening right now.

She parked on the street because she wasn't sure of the policy in this tall, fancy building. Besides, it was almost eleven at night and the last thing she wanted to do was get into an argument with some garage attendant over whether or not she belonged here or was invited. She went through the revolving doors and saw the front desk attendant that she probably needed to visit before being allowed upstairs to the apartments. Jenise didn't feel like that nonsense either, so while the attendant was busily texting or playing a game on his phone, she eased her way down the hall on tiptoe so he wouldn't be made aware of her entrance. Clearly, since he hadn't bothered to look up when she'd come through the door, he wasn't that intent on doing his job tonight.

The elevator was slow, the bright blue of the lighted numbers ticking off as she rode all the way up to the twenty-eighth floor. Moving off the elevator she found herself taking measured steps, wondering if she had made the right decision. She hadn't really thought about it once Savian had slammed her door shut, she'd just turned around and went into her room to get dressed. Now that she was here, she had to figure out what she was going to say to him.

At the door she heard yelling and Jenise was instantly worried. With a fist she banged on the door, calling his name over and over again. When it swung open she was taken off guard and stumbled inside. Savian caught her before she fell flat on her face, asking with every ounce of anger he was apparently still feeling, "What are you doing here?"

"I came to make sure you were alright," she said, her flats clicking on the brightly shined black marble floors as she moved further inside the foyer of his condo.

Savian closed the door and turned to face her. He looked just as he had when he'd been at her place, but the scowl on his face was deeper—if that was even possible—and his hand…

"What happened to your hand?" she asked, immediately going to him and lifting his hand in hers.

"Nothing," he said and attempted to pull away.

Jenise held tighter. "This isn't nothing. Your knuckles are bleeding and they're swelling. What did you do?"

"I said nothing. You can go now," he told her before abruptly yanking his hand away.

Jenise frowned and thought for just a second about leaving. Then she pulled off her jacket and walked past him. "Where's your kitchen?"

She kept walking until the narrow foyer gave way to a larger living room. Luckily for her, this place boasted a stunning open concept, so she could see a set of sleek metal and glass stairs, the huge dining room table and just beyond that, the marble-top island of the kitchen. Without asking, she continued through his personal space, which was elegantly decorated from what she could see without too much light. Had he been sitting in the dark?

There was staggered recessed lighting partially illuminating what appeared to be the path through the house without having someone bump into the furniture. She was certain he had more lights in here, he'd just chosen not to use them at the moment. In the kitchen, she went to the sub-zero stainless steel refrigerator and opened the freezer door. She didn't see any ice trays. When she closed the door she felt like saying, 'Duh', since there was an ice machine right on the side door. Looking around she found paper towels that she grabbed and carried with her back to the refrigerator. Layering a few towels she filled them with ice and then turned to go back out to find Savian.

He was in the kitchen, leaning against the island.

"I'm not going to ask what you're doing since you didn't bother to answer my first question," he said, arms folded solemnly over his chest.

Jenise looked around the room once more, elated when she finally spotted a light switch. She hurriedly moved to turn it on and was grateful for the immediate illumination.

"First, I'm here because you acted like an ass at my apartment and second, I'm going to put some ice on your hand before it gets so big you won't be able to hold it up anymore," she told him.

"I'm fine," he said as she approached him.

"Yes, I'll just bet you are," she snapped.

Standing in front of him she noticed he kept his arms tightly folded against his chest. With a sigh she pulled on his wrist, knowing he'd rather let his arms loose than to have her actions continue to cause physical pain.

"That's what I thought," she said triumphantly as she placed the ice gingerly on his hand. "Now, tell me how this happened."

"I don't need first aid and I'm not telling you what happened," he said tightly.

"Fine," Jenise replied. "Then I'll just say what I have to say and leave. That was my brother, Tucker, at my apartment. He's staying the night and has a flight out to the Bahamas in the morning. If you had remained there a moment longer I would have told you that."

Savian sighed heavily. "It doesn't even matter. I don't know why I came over there in the first place."

Jenise nodded. "Right. It doesn't matter. Look, Savian, just because we're not seeing each other anymore, doesn't mean I don't care about you. If there's something going on you can tell me."

"How can I tell you anything when you're convinced that I'm not good enough for you?" he asked while frowning down at her.

Jenise wanted to reach up and touch his forehead, to smooth away the lines of worry that had developed there. She wanted to touch his cheek as he often did hers, offering silent comfort. She did nothing but stare at him.

"You're a piece of work," she told him. "One minute you want to keep your distance. The next, you're taking me on a whirlwind trip and giving me everything I could ever imagine. You flow hot and cold like you were a human faucet. And you know what, Savian? I'm sick of it!"

Again, he pulled away from her. "I didn't ask you to come here."

The ice fell to the floor, scattering over Jenise's feet. She was sick and tired of this bullshit with him!

"You didn't and I don't have to stay here and take this treatment from you," she said before turning and walking the same way she had before. Only this time, Jenise paused before coming to the foyer. As she stood in the living room she looked to the wall where the pictures were hanging and saw the gaping hole. Had he punched the wall?

"Savian," she said his name quietly. She should stay because there was obviously something going on with him.

No, she couldn't. Whatever it was, Savian needed to deal with it on his own. It wasn't her problem. Jenise headed for the door.

"When I was sixteen years old I was charged with attempted murder and assault."

Jenise heard the words and stopped immediately. She did not turn around but she knew he was close.

"I was too quiet. I thought I was better than them. They hated my clothes, the lunch my mother packed for me, the car that brought me to school each day. I was a Donovan but my money couldn't keep them from bullying me every chance they could," Savian continued.

"I could have told my parents or the teachers or whoever, but I didn't. I let it go on for most of the school year because they were just saying things. Running off at the mouth because they hadn't the guts to do anything else. I wondered why all of the girls in school were dying to be with a Donovan—any one of us, considering Parker, Dion and Sean had all gone to the same private school as I did. When I was fourteen, a senior asked me if I was a Donovan. I said yes and she showed me her tits in the stairwell. She said I could suck them right there if I wanted to and then later she'd let me do more. I turned her down and two days later I heard Parker telling Dion she'd made him the same offer, which he'd immediately taken her up on. They were like that, Parker and Dion. They liked the girls and the attention. I didn't."

Jenise's hands had begun to shake and she quickly clasped them in front of her, still refusing to turn around. His voice sounded so strained and tortured, she couldn't bear to look at him.

"I played basketball when I was sixteen, mainly because I was tall, not necessarily skilled and I knew it would look good on my college applications. Even though, I was certain my parents' money could get me into any school I wanted to attend. They waited for me after the game, all three of them. Jay, Miguel and Stewart."

Savian paused then, as if saying the names had caused some type of inner pain. Jenise thought about turning to him, but she refrained. There was more and he needed to get it all out.

"Stewart pushed me first. He was the smallest of the bunch and Jay said that even he could beat my ass. Miguel thought that was hilarious, so he pushed me next. Jay was the leader of their pack, he gave the orders. When he told Stewart to punch me in the face, Stewart attempted to do what he was told. I caught his wrist before he could land the punch, and I broke it."

He continued, "Miguel cursed when Stewart howled in pain. He said I'd be sorry for doing that and he came at me. I bent forward, catching him at the knees and scooped him up into the air, before slamming him down on the floor. I guess Jay had no choice but to show his crew how it should be done. When he walked up to me, I broke his nose. He flailed back, yelling and screaming like I'd sliced off a finger instead, and he fell, hitting his head on the corner of the bleachers. The janitor heard the noise and when he came in to see what was going on he told me to stay right there. I was in cuffs twenty minutes later, charged by the end of the night and released into my parents' custody."

"Savian," she whispered, spinning around to look at him then.

He'd been leaning against the wall, his hands at his sides, head tilted back to rest against the wall. "The charges were dropped once I admitted how long they'd been bullying me and my father threatened to charge them in return. I didn't want him to do that, but he did. That was the first time he told me that sometimes I had to fight fire, with fire." He shook his head. "I couldn't believe when he'd said that because my father was always a non-violent man. But my mother was hysterical about the charges. She wanted to shut the school down by suing them for letting the bullying go on for so long. I didn't want that either. I just wanted to be left alone. I never wanted the attention of being a Donovan, yet it followed me everywhere I went."

"As I grew older, I learned to accept who I was and my place in life. Well, the therapist my mother insisted I visit, taught me that's what I needed to do to survive. She also taught me about managing my anger." Savian looked down at his hand and then over to the wall where the hole was. "Guess I'm not doing so well in that regard."

"You're doing the best you can," Jenise said as she moved slowly toward him. "And that's good enough, Savian. Who and what you are is good enough even without the name, don't you understand that?"

He shook his head. "I broke Morelli's nose too," he told her. "That night I went to his house, I punched the bastard because he was threatening my family. I would have punched him again if he hadn't fallen to the floor. In that moment I saw Jay falling and hitting his head all over again. Jay had received seventeen stitches for the gash in his head. What if Morelli's gash caused his death? Would my parents and their money be able to get me out of that mess? And at this stage in my life, did I have the right to put that type of stress on them? The answer was no, on both counts, so I walked out."

"And you were still charged with his murder," Jenise said feeling a sharp pang in her chest at the words. "I knew from the very beginning that you weren't a killer, Savian. That's why I didn't ask you if you'd seen Morelli. I knew it right here," she said reaching for his bruised hand and placing it on her chest. "In my heart I've always known that you were a good man. A decent and strong man."

"I'm a mess," he said with a frown.

"You're human and we all make mistakes," she insisted.

He used his other hand to touch her chin. "I'm tired of making them with you."

Jenise leaned in to kiss him then. A soft kiss. A healing kiss.

Savian immediately joined in, moving his hand to cup the back of her neck, the other going around her back to pull her close.

This kiss was different from any they'd shared because it had meaning. Jenise could feel it pouring from him into her, surrounding them in a warm embrace. Now she knew why she'd really come here, it was for him, for this. There was no walking away, she knew that now. They were two battered souls, two people bound and determined to sacrifice any bit of happiness for the one moment of mistakes in their lives. Savian didn't think he could be loved, not for real, because since he was a young boy, women had wanted him for his name and his money. Guys had despised him for the same reason. Thus he didn't want either— friends or girlfriends. It was heartbreaking.

Yet, the kiss was rejuvenating. The feel of being wrapped in his arms once more, of tasting his tongue on hers, sent warmth spearing throughout her entire body. So when he pulled away, she moaned with resistance.

"I don't know, Jenise. I just don't know," he whispered, his lips moving over her jawline, up to her cheeks.

"It's okay, baby. We'll figure it out together," she told him, rubbing her hands up and down his arms.

"I don't know what's happening," he continued, resting his forehead against hers. "I can't remember how to live without you."

Jenise smiled up at him then. "Now, you don't have to."

CHAPTER 13

Reginald reluctantly sat in a chair, dropping his head as he cried.

"I can't do this anymore," he said. "Not again, Bruce, I just can't."

Bruce clapped a hand on his brother's shoulder. "She's going to be alright, Reggie. The doctors are just running all the tests to be sure. But she's going to be alright."

Reginald shook his head. "It could have been like Darla," he said. "Just like Darla, dammit. Why did I let her go to that meeting alone? I always go to the church stuff with her when it's close to the holidays because you know crazies come out trying to rob everybody during this time of year. I should have been there."

"And then you would be lying in a hospital bed as well," Janean told him. "You would be worthless to Carolyn at that point."

"What the hell happened?" Parker said as he came rushing into the emergency waiting room, Adriana right behind him.

Savian and Jenise had just rounded the corner, right in time for Savian to look at his father expectantly. Reginald raised his head when he heard his oldest son's voice. Now, he looked up at both of them.

"She's going to be alright," Janean said looking up from where she sat next to Reginald.

"What happened?" Savian asked. "Tell us right now what happened to our mother."

He was looking directly at Reginald, accusing him without the words. "Where's your sister?"

"We didn't call her until we were almost here because we wanted to hear it first, just in case it's too much for Regan to bear right now. What's going on, dad?" Parker had taken a step towards his father. Adriana immediately grasped his arm to hold him back.

"Now, let's just stay calm," Bruce said, standing so that he could be a barrier between his brother and his nephew.

"Let's just tell the truth for a change," Savian replied instead.

Bruce opened his mouth to speak but Reginald was already standing. "He's right," Reginald said moving around his brother. "I'm going to tell you both the truth. Your mother was driving home from the church holiday bazaar and her car swerved off the road. You know where that curve is just before you get to the stretch of road near the house."

"The road that drops down to the ocean," Parker said incredulously.

Adriana gasped as Jenise moved closer to Savian.

"Sonofabitch!" Savian roared. "What do you mean she swerved? Mom's been driving for more than forty years and she's been coming around that curve for just as long. How could she have swerved?"

"Now hold on, son. We're still you're elders," Bruce stated sternly.

"Then it'd be nice if you started acting like it," Dion said as he made his way into the waiting room.

Sean came in with his brother. Their wives were not with them.

"Did my mother swerve off the road or did someone try to drive her off the road? Someone that has it out for you and your brothers?" Savian asked.

Reginald didn't know what to say. That very thought had been coursing through his mind from the moment the paramedics called his cell phone to tell him that Carolyn had been in an accident. He'd remembered the exact moment years ago when Al had called him to say that Darla had driven her car off the road and she'd died. They'd all wanted to believe it was suicide because Darla had been diagnosed with cancer months earlier. But Al had known better. He'd known that it had something to do with Roslyn Ausby. Now, Reginald was facing the same theory.

"I don't know that what you're saying is true," Reginald stated, because he didn't know. No matter how much he suspected, he didn't know for sure.

"Liar!" Parker spat.

"Stop it!" Janean yelled and came to her feet. "What is the matter with you? All of you? That's no way to talk to your father, and you know your mother would not have you being disrespectful. Now, I'm going to assume that emotions are running raw here because we're all upset. But I'm going to warn each of you right now, to cut it out before I really get angry."

The boys went silent. All of them.

Then a nurse came out to tell Reginald he could see Carolyn now.

"We should go in together," Reginald said to his sons. "She'll want to see all of us."

Savian nor Parker moved. Dion and Sean glared at him. Bruce was the only one to step beside him.

"I'll go with you," Bruce said. "Janean you stay with them so you can be here for Regan when they tell her."

Janean nodded and Bruce led Reginald away.

"They know," Reginald said.

Bruce nodded. "I agree. They're not looking at us like we've just committed treason for nothing. So what are we going to do about it?"

"We're going to tell our family the truth," Reginald said. "No more lies, no more trying to work this out without them knowing. We're going to tell our families and then we're going to tell the world. Nobody else is going to die because of this secret. I mean it, Bruce. I won't let it happen again."

They were at the hospital room door when Bruce touched Reginald's arm. "You're right. It's time. We'll give the brothers a call as soon as you get Carolyn home and settled, and then we'll tell them what we plan to do."

Reginald nodded and went into the room to see his wife.

⟨≻⟩

"I'm going to the house," Savian said as he and Jenise climbed into his truck at the hospital's parking garage. "I want to be there if she needs something or if her condition changes. I can drop you off at your apartment."

They'd spent the night together last night and then the entire day, together today decorating his condo because Jenise said it was pitiful that he did not have any holiday decorations. This was after she'd made him flex his hand numerous times to assure her he did not need to go to the emergency room. He did need to get his wall fixed and soon because that hole was going to be a constant reminder of how he'd lost his temper yet again.

"I want to stay with you," she said reaching over the console to gently take his still sore hand. "If that's alright."

Yesterday at this time, Savian would have said no, it wasn't okay. He would have probably wanted to be alone with his feelings and his thoughts. Today, he did not.

"Sure. Thank you," he told her.

They pulled up just behind his father's car and Savian stepped out of the truck quickly so that he could offer his mother assistance.

"Savian, what are you doing here?" Carolyn asked when he was there to open her door. "I know you have better things to do with your Sunday evening than watching after me."

"I want to watch after you," he said, taking her by the arm and helping her out of the car.

"Oh nonsense, I'm fine. Just a bit sore," she told him.

By that time Reginald had come around to the side of the car and Savian could see Jenise coming over as well.

"You were just in a car accident," Savian reminded her, not that he thought any of them needed reminding.

Carolyn waved a hand. "It was nothing big. I wasn't thinking. I tell you kids all the time about being so worried about those cell phones. But your father's been after me about keeping mine on and near me. I heard it beep and looked down to see a message from him. That's when I swerved and thank god for that big 'ole rock that stopped me from tumbling over the cliff."

Thank all the gods for that big 'ole rock, Savian said to himself.

"I'll get your purse, Ms. Carolyn," Jenise said and Savian knew it was because she didn't want him to say anything else about the accident.

Last night, after they'd showered and lay comfortably in his bed, Savian had told Jenise about what he thought was going on with his family. She'd been shocked, but supportive, telling him that he should wait before judging anyone. They were both proof that there was more to a person's past than anyone could sometimes imagine. He'd agreed with her on that stance, until they'd received the call about his mother's accident.

"Thank you, Jenise. You're so sweet to be here, too," Carolyn said.

"You should come inside and lay down, Carolyn," Reginald told her.

"Yes, I think you're right," she replied, moving slowly with Reginald on one side of her and Savian on the other.

When they came to the front door, Reginald used his key to let them in, while Savian hurried to the security pad to punch in the applicable code. Once inside, Carolyn stopped and looked around.

"Thank you, Lord," she said over and over again, tears welling in her eyes.

Savian watched her, feeling a wave of gratitude wash over him as well. He did not know what he would have done if she had not walked away from that accident. If she had di…he shook his head because he didn't even want to think about it.

"I may need one of those pain pills," Carolyn said when she was finally ready to move again.

"Then you'll need something to eat," Jenise stated. "I can fix you something while you go up to bed."

"Really? Someone's going to cook for me for a change. You two hear that?" she joked with Reginald and Savian. "You keep this one here."

The last was said as she leaned in toward Savian. He met her halfway and she kissed his cheek. "I mean it," she whispered. "Keep her."

Five minutes later, Savian was leading Jenise into his mother's massive country inspired kitchen. The walls were canary yellow, the cabinets and counter tops bright white. More color accents came in everything from the fruit inside numerous bowls Carolyn had placed throughout the kitchen and breakfast space, to the artsy color knobs on the cabinets and the lively floral squares that were a part of the backsplash pattern.

"This space is a cheerful," Jenise said. "Just like your mother."

"Yeah, my mother loves color and anything that makes her feel at home. When I moved out and told her I didn't need her to hire a designer for me she said to just be sure I picked furnishings that made me feel like I was home," he told her.

"And did you do that?" Jenise asked as she looked in the refrigerator.

Savian managed a light chuckle. "Of course not. I picked stuff that matched and that I could order online."

"Yeah, I could tell," she replied.

"Oh, I didn't hear you complaining about my furnishings at all today," Savian said.

"That's because I was hoping the Christmas decorations would help it out. But not even that gorgeous nine foot high Scotch Pine tree you bought makes it look better," she said.

He watched as she moved easily through this kitchen she was in for the first time. It looked as if she were going to fix his mother a sandwich as she'd found the bread and the container which held the lunch meats and sliced cheeses.

"What type of condiments does she like?" Jenise asked when she'd headed for the refrigerator once more.

"Deli mustard," he said and moved to the cabinet where the plates were, to get one down.

"So you don't like any of my furniture?" he asked her when they were side-by-side making the sandwich together.

"It's a bit stiff. You could use some color and some softer touches," she said as she spread the mustard onto each slice.

Savian slapped honey ham onto the bread and then a couple slices of Swiss cheese. His mother loved Swiss cheese.

"You mean like flowers and those statue things you have in your home office?" The frown on his face probably gave away the fact that he did not like that idea at all.

"Yeah," Jenise said laughing. "Something like that."

She cut the sandwich—on the diagonal because Savian told her that's the way his mother always cut their sandwiches. He poured her a glass of ice water while Jenise cut the lemon and added slices to the glass.

"If I told her I was having a sandwich for Sunday dinner my mother would have a fit," Savian said looking down at the plate.

"I could cook something but I don't want her to have to wait to take the pain meds," she told him.

Savian nodded. "Right, I get it. Well, I'll take it up to her."

Jenise nodded and smiled at him. "I'll wait down here and look around for more ideas that we can steal for your place."

He was smiling as he walked away. As he took the steps he realized that he could have been crying at this moment instead, so he enjoyed the smile even more.

Jenise couldn't believe what Savian had just said.

"Are you serious?" she asked. "You want to make-out on your childhood bed? Like you want me to believe that you never made out with a girl in here before?"

The sobering look he gave her said, 1) that he was serious and 2) that he really had never made out with a girl in his room before.

"Who said anything about making out?" he asked. "I asked you to take off your clothes so I could see you naked in my bedroom."

When he'd come down from taking his mother the food, Savian had surprised Jenise by asking her to spend the night at his parents' house with him. He didn't want to leave his mother and he didn't want to spend the night without Jenise. Saying 'no' had never crossed her mind. Now, she was in the room he'd occupied for the first seventeen years of his life. He assured her that it was still in the exact same condition as it was the day he'd left for college.

That meant, navy blue walls with stark white baseboards, two huge windows on one wall, a long desk on another. There were four bookshelves overflowing with books and magazines. Reading was one of Savian's favorite hobbies. His full-sized bed stood in the middle of the room, two lanyards—one from Disney World and the other from Disney Land—hanging on either side of his headboard.

"And what are you going to do while I'm getting naked?" she asked playfully.

"Get naked too, of course," he replied with a fake look of surprise on his face. "Come on," he said, pulling the gray t-shirt he was wearing up and over his head.

"I feel like we're playing truth or dare or some other teenage game," she said.

He shook his head. "Nah, you're just stalling. Besides, it's getting late, we'd be undressing to go to bed soon anyway."

It was nearing ten-thirty. The time she'd been with Savian had seemed to go so fast. Spending the night at his place last night had been a beautiful surprise. He'd driven her back to her apartment early this morning because she'd wanted to see Tucker off, and then they were going to buy him a tree. The formal introduction between Tucker and Savian had gone well and when Savian had suggested she pack an overnight bag, she'd happily done so. Now, that bag was sitting in the corner next to Savian's basketball themed trash can because they'd done so much shopping they'd forgotten to take her bag out of his truck.

"That's true, but I have a very nice nightgown over there in that bag to put on," she told him as she was removing the belt from her waist.

Savian shook his head again, just before tossing the undershirt he'd taken off across the room to land like a professional shot into the clothes' hamper on that side of the room. "I should tell you that I'm not really a fan of nightgowns."

Jenise had taken off her flats and was now unbuttoning her jeans. "Really? Because in the last few weeks you've given me six of them. I counted."

He untied and removed his boots. "That seemed like the polite thing to do. I wasn't sure telling you to sleep naked was going to go over too well."

"Hmm," she said with a nod. "But you seem mighty comfortable asking me to strip now."

He was pushing his pants down, his boxer briefs too, and stepped out of them before replying, "I'm stripping with you. That's gotta count for something."

She grinned and then sighed. He had the best body. Muscles everywhere and his erection always ready and waiting for her.

"I'm on top," she said when she was naked. He'd been staring at her breasts, a glazed look coming into his eyes, his penis twitching and causing her mouth to water.

"I'm not complaining," he replied before jumping onto the bed.

Jenise couldn't help but giggle because she'd never seen Savian like this before. He'd been absolutely distraught when he received the call about his mother's accident. She figured it had been a good idea that they stayed here for the night. He probably wouldn't have been this relaxed if they hadn't.

He lay on the bed, taking his length in his hand and stroked from the base to the tip. "We're waiting," he told her.

"Is that for me?" she asked coyly.

"Oh yeah," he replied.

She was over him in seconds, positioning herself so that he was immediately pressing his length into her. They both moaned with that action. He felt so good, every last inch of him going deep inside, felt so damn wonderful she closed her eyes to let the pleasure settle through her. He clasped her hips immediately, telling her to, "Ride me. Now," in a gruff voice.

Jenise did as he said, riding him hard and fast until they were both out of breath, trying their best to hold in the groans and moans of pleasure, especially when they climaxed simultaneously.

She'd been grateful for the private bathroom connecting to Savian's bedroom. If she'd had to walk out into the hallway to get to the main bathroom and bumped into Mr. Reginald or Ms. Carolyn, she would have been so embarrassed. Instead, she and Savian shared a wonderfully hot bath, in the tub that wasn't quite made to accommodate two adults. They'd gotten more water on the floor than they should have and used a bunch of towels to clean it up. Laughing, they came out to the bedroom and, at Savian's request, slipped into bed naked.

Now, they lay there, Jenise resting on his chest with Savian's arm around her.

"It's been a long day," she said sleepily.

"Too long," he replied.

"We have work tomorrow," she stated, hating the thought of having to go into the office and spend hours away from him.

"We do," he replied.

She took a chance and asked, "Dinner tomorrow night? I know this great Mediterranean inspired place. I think you may know the owner."

He'd chuckled. "Sure. I bet I could get us a discount, too."

Jenise smiled, happy with the easy rapport they now had and even happier with the feeling of being in his arms one more time.

"That sounds terrific," she chimed in.

There were a few moments of silence where Jenise had been just about to fall asleep. Then he said, "Let's get married on Christmas Day."

She stopped breathing. Really, her eyes shot open and Jenise was certain she didn't breathe for a few seconds before the air whooshed out of her as Savian adjusted himself so that he could look down at her.

"I mean it, Jenise," he said seriously. "Last night and today has shown me that life is too short. If you want something you have to reach out and take it before it's too late. I want you. I need you. I love you."

Just like that, she thought. The words were so Savian. The moment, she thought was much more her style because it was romantic as hell without any planning or trying involved. He said he loved her. The words replayed in her mind, warming her heart. She'd never told him those words, but she'd felt them every day since they'd been in New York.

"I love you," she said wanting to give him something in return.

He smiled, bringing a hand around and touching his finger to the tip of her nose, then to tap on her chin.

"So marry me on Christmas Day. I promise you it will be magic."

Jenise smiled. If she hadn't known her answer before that moment, she definitely knew it now.

"You said the magic word," was her reply. "Yes, I'll marry you on Christmas Day."

CHAPTER 14

The next week and a half went by with a whirlwind of activity. His mother was elated the morning after her accident when Savian announced he and Jenise were getting married while they sat in the courtyard having coffee. The look on her face was worth every painful and stressful moment he had gone through in all of his life.

"I don't know what to say," Carolyn had immediately exclaimed. Her shaking hand finally managing to put her coffee cup on the glass-topped table without it, or the table, cracking. "A Christmas wedding. How wonderful! Oh, it's going to be beautiful. Just beautiful!"

"Congratulations, son," Reginald had said.

Savian could see the genuine joy in his father's face. He heard the pride in his voice and because he loved Jenise and his mother with every fiber of his being, he did not bring up what was going on between the younger and the Senior Donovans at the moment. Instead, he'd given his father a nod and a, "Thanks, Dad."

"Have you thought about where you'd like to have it? Christmas is only a week or so away. So we have to get moving fast on the planning," Carolyn said, effectively ending those few moments of tension between Savian and his father.

Jenise chimed right in. "So, I haven't even talked to Savian about this yet. But I've been thinking about it all night," she added with a smile so bright it lit up every dark space in Savian's mind.

"I really love this space right here. I had a chance to see a little bit of it last night and then again morning when we came down to get breakfast started, Savian said this was your favorite spot. The moment I came out here I knew why. I'd love to get married right here. If that's okay with you."

The tears came quickly and Jenise had immediately begun apologizing. Waving a hand to silence them. his mother shook her head until she was able to speak.

"That's perfect," she said, her voice cracking. "Just perfect."

So, the date and the location were set, and by the time Savian had finally arrived in the office—after driving Jenise back to his place to get her car and changing his clothes—Dion, Sean and Parker were waiting for him in his office. He'd walked in, closing the door behind him and could only grin at the message they'd scribbled on the dry erase board that normally sat in the corner.

What took you so long? Welcome to the Married Donovans Society!

"Ha, very funny," he'd said as he passed the board and went to stand behind his desk. "You're not married yet, Parker."

Still grinning, but leaning over the desk with his arm outstretched, Parker shook his younger brother's hand and said, "Yeah, well that's just a technicality. Adriana's talking about a destination wedding so that may take a little longer than a week and a half to plan."

"True," Savian added as he also shook Dion and Sean's hands. "I hope Jenise has enough time to do this the way she wants."

"Never fear," Dion said. "As I was leaving my office I ran into Regan and Lyra. They were on their way downstairs to grab Tate and then were heading over to Jenise's office. I overheard my beautifully pregnant wife asking, 'How could she possibly work on a day like today?' To which your adoring sister replied, 'I know. We have way too much shopping to do for any work to get done today.'"

Savian had to laugh with the guys on that one, and not just because of what was said, but moreso because of Dion's dead-on impersonations of the women. They'd spent another half hour talking about the wedding and before his cousins and brother had left, they'd made Savian promise to meet them after work today to go shopping for Jenise's ring.

"Who proposes without a ring?" Dion had asked.

"I did and it cost me dearly," Parker chimed in.

Sean nodded his agreement. "Yes. Believe me, you want to pick out the ring for her, not have her pick it out for you. Your bank account will thank you later."

Savian had leaned back in his chair with a grin that was becoming more natural than he ever thought it would. "But I want to make sure I get something she'll really like."

"That's why you're going to take us with you," Dion added.

"But you don't know her like I do," Savian objected.

"No," Sean told him. "But we know we're Donovans. There's nothing we won't do for the women we love. We'll just be there to remind you of that fact."

Savian had spent the rest of the day thinking about his wife-to-be and that soon, she would become a Donovan.

He wondered if that would be a good or bad thing for her.

"We called you all here because there's something we want to tell you," Bruce began.

It was the night before Christmas Eve and they'd each received a text message to meet in the conference room at Excalibur at six o'clock. Savian, Parker, Dion, Sean and Regan each sat in the spot they normally occupied at the table that was normally reserved for business matters. Savian had a sinking suspicion, however, that this meeting was about something else entirely. It was also the only place that they could meet that wasn't full of wedding preparations.

"You've each been asking questions about the vandalism at our homes and that cryptic email message, and lately Carolyn's accident," Bruce continued. "We want to clear the air."

Regan spoke first. "We appreciate that. We're all family here, we have to stick together, always, and that's not possible if we don't all know what's going on with each other. You taught us that, daddy. When we were just little kids you taught us to always look out for each other, remember?"

Regan had captured their father's gaze and held it, adoringly, just as she had when she was a little girl. Reginald nodded.

"You're right, baby girl. That's why we're going to tell you that there is something going on. Something that happened a long time ago. At the time," Reginald said, clearing his throat, "we thought we were making the right decision for everyone involved. We never wanted to hurt the ones we loved in any way. But people make mistakes. The good thing is that eventually, hopefully, they figure out the error of their ways and do whatever they can to make it better."

The last was said as Reginald looked to Savian.

This was the man that he'd looked up to all his life, so Savian did not turn away from him. Instead, he gave a quick nod, signaling he was ready to hear the rest.

"As you all know there's a wedding coming up very soon," Bruce interjected. "Your mothers have been running around these past days buying up everything they can and getting with the other women and planning. It's been a lot of activity going on. And we're all excited," he said. "Congratulations to you again, Savian."

"Thanks, Uncle Bruce," Savian said tightly.

"The family's coming in tomorrow. Since the wedding is on Christmas Day, your mothers thought it would be a good idea to have the family holiday dinner on Christmas Eve. Henry, Bernard, Everett and Al are all coming. Their kids are too," Reginald said. "So we'd like to wait until the day after the wedding to talk to everyone together. Carolyn mentioned last night that you and Jenise aren't leaving for your honeymoon to Australia until Monday morning."

Savian wanted to know right now and he was certain his siblings and cousins did as well. Still, he recognized their dilemma. Telling whatever this secret was before the holiday could quite possibly destroy the celebration for all of them. Of course that depended on what the secret was. Considering his father and uncle were standing in front of them now, suggesting they wait, it must be something big. After all, it did involve the murder of at least one person. He'd begun to wonder what else had happened during the time they'd kept this secret, things that hadn't yet reached out to touch the family.

"I think that's a good idea," Sean said. "I don't want anything to affect Briana's Christmas. She's too excited and so is Tate."

Dion nodded. "I don't want Lyra upset right now at all. We're trying to do all we can to keep her off bed rest for as long as possible. Too much stress is not going to be good for her."

"Or for you," Savian said to Regan.

She was already shaking her head. "Not knowing is going to worry me more. But I agree, let's wait until after Christmas. If it involves the entire family, then we should all be together when the secret is finally revealed."

Parker sighed. "I agree. Let's wait until Saturday," he said. "But not a second after that. Because whatever happened all those years ago has come back to haunt, not only you guys, but all of us as well. Somebody out there definitely believes that revenge is a dish best served cold. I'd rather we be prepared to fight fire with fire, if we have to than to continue to wait around like sitting ducks."

Savian looked at his father as Parker spoke those words. Apparently, Reginald had said that to both of them.

"We'll tell you all everything on Saturday. Not a day later," Bruce said solemnly.

Christmas Eve

Jenise stood beside her husband-to-be at the head of a huge dining room table in Carolyn and Reginald Donovan's house on Thursday evening.

The house was already beautifully decorated and Jenise had been fighting back tears since she'd arrived there two hours ago. In the past week and half she'd shopped for a dress, explained her vision for the perfect Christmas wedding, selected a reception venue, talked about food and cakes and wedding favors, bands, DJs and yes, mistletoe. There was going to be lots of mistletoe throughout the entire wedding. She was exhausted and excited and overwhelmed with the love she could feel in this room.

Her family had arrived this morning. Morgan was staying with her at her apartment, while her mother, father, grandparents and brothers were all situated at a hotel. Sure, it was last minute during the holiday season, but the Donovans seemed to know everyone and Savian had called a man named Jason Carrington that he'd met when he'd been in Monterey last summer for an industry conference. Jason Carrington owned Carrington Resorts and had just opened his first east coast hotel in Miami six months ago. Jason had happily given Jenise's family the top two penthouse suites for the holiday weekend and the following week as a wedding gift.

All of Savian's uncles were here. Jenise had been introduced to every one of them and their wives personally. They were scattered around the room at the moment, but she could look up and see each one: Henry and Beverly, Bernard and Jocelyn, Everette and Alma, and Albert. Their children had also come, and while she was eventually going to need a chart to keep them all straight, she was certain she had them mostly together right now. There was Linc and Jade, Adam and Camille, Trent and Tia, all three of Henry's sons. Max and Deena and Ben and Victoria were Everette's sons. Keysa and her husband Ian and Brynne, who had a beautiful smile and bubbly personality, were Bernard's daughters. Brock and his wife, Noelle, Brandon and Bailey were Albert's children. Of course the children had children and so the house was now full of giggles and child-chatter that filled Jenise with such a spirit of home and love that she'd felt even more blessed than she had the day before.

Six months ago she was working ten to twelve hours a day, going home and falling face-first into her bed. If she had a date every other month that was good, a bout of satisfying sex was even better. But there'd been nothing like this. She'd never imagined this was where she'd be and this man would be all she could think about. Her gaze fell to her mother at that moment. Marianne practically beamed. She'd been elated when Jenise had called that morning when she'd finally arrived at work, to tell her that she was getting married. She hadn't asked who Savian was because she'd heard the name Donovan before, which made her even happier. A half hour later when Gwen had buzzed into her office to say that Lyra, Tate and Regan were there to see her, Jenise had thanked the heavens for the reprieve. Of course, she'd had no idea that reprieve would lead to hours and hours of shopping and planning with the women, but that had been a good thing also.

"We want to thank all of you for being here on such short notice," she began when the room had finally started to quiet down, courtesy of Savian taping his fork on his champagne glass until Jenise thought it might break.

"Savian and I are extremely blessed to have such a wonderful and supportive family."

There'd been a little clapping at that point and then Savian said, "We wanted to let you all know that we don't need anything as a wedding gift. We talked about it and we're going to start looking for a house when we return from our honeymoon. But we do not want any of you to spend your money on us."

Jenise nodded. "What we would appreciate much more, is if you would instead make donations to charities that are near and dear to us."

Savian moved from beside her to set his glass down and pull out the cards she'd made earlier that day. He began passing them around the room as she spoke.

"Stand for the Silent is a national non-profit agency that currently reaches over a million students in more than a thousand schools. We'd like to reach more, to assist by providing counselors and support teams to help every victim of bullying across the country," she said.

Carolyn shed silent tears as she looked down at the card.

"We'd also like to support the My Big Is Beautiful Forever Foundation which is a relatively new start-up that also supports children, young adults and adults who struggle with their weight and the stigma the world puts on them. The national spokesperson that was just named a few months ago for this organization is a good friend of mine that I went to college with, her name is Amber McNair and she's a beautiful person inside and out, regardless of her dress size," Jenise said.

Morgan was the first to begin clapping when she finished, followed by Regan and Adriana, and then Ms. Carolyn. Before long the entire room was clapping and everyone was standing.

"I'd like to make a toast," Reginald said over the noise.

Everyone picked up their glasses, holding them high. "To my son and the beautiful and intelligent woman who has agreed to marry him. May each of your days be filled with love, loyalty and trust. God bless you."

"God bless you," Carolyn chimed in, clinking her glass to her husband's.

Savian touched his glass to Jenise's, then leaned in to do the same with his father's. They sat down to eat after that. There was so much food and wine and a Christmas punch that Jenise almost choked on after sipping, that she wondered how tomorrow would compare to this.

After dinner, the family moved to the living room where there was a twelve foot tree decorated in heirloom ornaments, handmade pieces by Carolyn's children and some she'd collected over the years. The gold and white themed tree stood tall and majestic in the corner of the large space. The kids happily milled about on a hunt to find the gift boxes with their names on them as the adults exchanged a few boxes of their own. When one had been given to Savian he'd leaned over to show Jenise that it had both their names on it.

"Oh, didn't we say no gifts," she'd whispered to him.

"Guess that announcement came too late, besides, we said no wedding gifts, not Christmas gifts," he told her.

She'd nodded and decided to simply go with the flow.

It took Savian a few moments to get through the lovely dark red paper and the gorgeous gold bow that had been expertly tied on top. When he finally got past through the wrapping paper and wadded through all the tissue paper inside, he pulled out a miniature grandfather clock. It was gorgeous with its dark wood color and bright gold face and pendulum.

"Oh that's a lovely clock," Carolyn remarked.

"It is. Who is it from?" Beverly Donovan asked.

Savian continued to dig through the paper. "There's a card down here. I just saw it."

Jenise reached into the box as well and finally pulled out the card. She opened it and read, "Time is ticking by."

In her mind she immediately heard ticking, like that of a clock or a bomb, or…her heart began to beat faster.

"Let me see that," Trent Donovan said seriously as he appeared beside her and reached for the card.

Jenise handed it to him and heard his brother Linc curse.

"Not in front of the children," Linc's wife, Jade scolded.

"Not tonight," Carolyn added. "And not tomorrow."

Carolyn had stood then, coming over to them and taking the box and the clock from Savian. "Give me that," she told Trent, taking the card.

"I'm not having anything or anyone spoil our family time. I just won't. We're getting ready to sing Christmas carols and drink that spiked egg nog that Bernard made that I'm sure will knock us all out until tomorrow morning. We do not have time for foolishness," Carolyn continued, taking that box and going to one of the many closets in this house and dropping it on the floor inside. She slammed the door and was brushing her hands as if she was through with that as Alma Donovan stood, brushing down the front of her cashmere sweater.

"She's right, let's get this Christmas cheer going," Alma announced.

There was a huge white piano that sat as impressively in its corner of the room as the tree did. Everette made his way over to it and began to play. It sounded like "Silent Night", but Jocelyn suddenly stood and declared, "Something more cheerful!"

Her words were a little slurred as she'd been on her second glass of her husband's spiked egg nog.

"Here, here!" Janean chimed in.

"Dashing through the snow, in a one horse open sleigh," Carolyn began acapella.

The Senior women joined in immediately, while Jenise noted the Senior men still had a serious look on their faces. When her mother stood and began singing while helping Carolyn pour and pass out glasses of egg nog and Christmas punch to those who preferred it, Jenise began to sing along as well. It was Christmas Eve and tomorrow she was getting married. Nothing was going to put a damper on that, not if she could help it. Before long they were all singing and drinking, one song after another and another, until they finally went to bed.

They were completely unaware of the black SUV parked at the end of the driveway.

CHAPTER 15

Christmas Day

Jenise slipped her feet into red satin shoes with glittering silver four-inch heels. She let the white princess cut A-line skirt of her dress fall to the floor, covering the shoes. The dress had a corset front and in the back, through the laces of the corset, was rich red satin that cascaded down the back of the gown and spread outward to the three-foot train.

"You look gorgeous," Morgan said as she stood in front of her.

They were in Carolyn's bedroom, across from a wall of mirrors that was in the walk-in closet. Her mother stood on one side of her and Morgan on the other.

"In my day women were married in all white, from their veil to their underwear," Marianne said as she lifted the tiara and veil combination that Jenise had selected.

Rolling her eyes, Morgan took the tiara from her mother. "That was almost forty years ago, mama. Women have evolved since that time and this red and white is lovely for the holiday."

Her sister talked as Jenise leaned forward and let her position the tiara. After the ceremony she would trade the tiara and veil for a lovely red flower and feather that she'd found in a second-hand store at an after-Christmas sale last year.

Morgan was her maid of honor and she looked lovely in the white slip dress and red velvet choker. She knew well the saying that only the bride should wear white, but Jenise wanted her entire bridal party dressed in white with red accents today. Adriana and Regan were bridesmaids, their dresses just a little different design in than Morgan's. They all wore the red chokers and white shoes with red bows on the back. Savian and his guys—Parker as his best man, Sean and Dion as groomsmen— would be dressed in white tuxedoes, red straight ties and white suede wingtips. Savian would be the only one dressed in all white, except for the red rose with holy berry accents in his boutonniere. She couldn't wait to see him.

"It's time ladies," Regan said as she came into the room.

Her hair was raven black this time, pulled away from her face and to the side in a neat chignon. Adriana came in behind her with her hair in the same style, her smile bright as she looked at Jenise through the mirror.

"Thank you all so much," Jenise said as she looked at these women who each meant something special to her.

"Don't you dare cry," Regan warned and stepped forward to fan her hand in front of Jenise's face. "If you start, we'll all begin boo-hooing and that is simply not acceptable."

"She's right," Morgan added and pulled the veil over Jenise's face after she'd given the okay.

"It's time to get married," Marianne said from behind Jenise, a wide smile on her face.

"Yes ma'am," Jenise said to her mother. "It is time to get married."

She'd never thought she would be saying those words to her mother and with as much anticipation as she was feeling. But here she was, on a sunny Christmas afternoon about to go downstairs and marry the best man she'd ever met.

Jenise almost teared up again as she walked down the stairs. Along the railings the real pine garland that had been hung yesterday, was now lit with white twinkle lights that glittered off the marble floors. There was more garland draped over all the entryways, shining with light. In the center of each entryway was also a fresh sprig of mistletoe. As she walked through the house Jenise marveled at all the Christmas touches and the sweet smell of pine wafting throughout the air.

"We're ready for you now," Tate said from where she stood by the French doors that would lead out to the courtyard.

White silk drapes had been hung at the doors so that the guests—only the members of the Donovan and Langley families because she and Savian had wanted the ceremony to be private—could not see her as she stood inside. In about two hours they would head out to Briza on the Bay for the reception. Tate was acting as their coordinator while Jenise stood by the tree, posing for a picture that Lyra, their photographer had motioned for her to take.

Music began playing, an instrumental version of "Silent Night" with the gorgeous sound of the harp for emphasis. Tate motioned for Marianne to come forward and when she opened the doors, Adam Donovan was waiting on the other side to usher her mother down the aisle. Next up was Adriana, red and white rose bouquet in hand. Regan followed her moments later. And then it was time for Briana. She was the absolute cutest flower girl that Jenise had ever seen wearing a white dress with a huge red satin sash and back-tied bow at her waist, and red rose petal appliques around the hem. On her mother's command she stepped up to the door, curly tendrils of hair framing her face, mistletoe tucked into the tight bun on top of her head.

Tate bent down to kiss her daughter's forehead and whisper something in her ear. Briana looked up at her mother with nothing but love in her eyes and smiled. She stepped through that door with her white basket in the shape of Santa's sleigh, filled to the brim with red rose petals and holly berries. She would drop them both down the white runner as she walked. Jenise felt herself getting misty-eyed as she imagined it, since Tate had closed the doors again.

"It's almost your turn," her father said as he came to her side. "You ready?"

Jenise looked into Bradford Langley's stern dark eyes. His thick mustache and beard covered most of his face, but his high cheekbones rose as he slowly smiled. She nodded at him. "I'm ready."

"Then let's do this," he was saying just as they looked up and Lyra snapped another picture.

The music changed to a slower version of Mariah Carey's "All I Want For Christmas". Her father chuckled at first, then he threw his head back and laughed. Jenise didn't know when the last time she'd heard her father so genuinely happy. It made her smile as he tucked her hand between his arm.

"Only my child would select this for her wedding march," Bradford said in his booming voice. "Only my child indeed."

"I like it," Lyra said, humming along with the music.

They approached the door and that was the first time Jenise felt a flutter in the pit of her stomach. She was about to become a married woman.

The doors opened and her father began to move. Jenise did not.

"Jenise?" Bradford called to her as he looked back.

She took a deep breath, letting the music play in her mind and remembered the first time she'd heard this song with Savian. They'd been in her apartment and he was placing the angel on top of her tree. She'd been staring at how delightful his ass looked in the jeans he was wearing while Mariah was shouting 'baby, all I want for Christmas is you'. The thought made her smile.

She looked up to her father and said, "Let's do this."

The walk was short, the smiling faces staring at her were not only friendly, but familiar and comforting. It was lovely out here with the pergola draped in white twinkle lights and bouquets of mistletoe all around. Beneath it stood the minister from Ms. Carolyn's church, and lined up neatly in front of him were her friends and family…and her husband-to-be.

Savian was gorgeous in his white tuxedo, shirt and tie. The red holly berries on his lapel made her giggle and when his lips spread into a huge grin in response, her heart melted. She was doing the right thing, marrying this man on this day was definitely magic.

It seemed like only moments later when Savian had finished reciting his vows to her that he slipped the gorgeous diamond encrusted band onto her finger. It glittered against the marquis cut chocolate diamond engagement ring he'd given her. His band was platinum with only two diamonds in the center. One for him and one for her, together, always.

The kiss was also magical as the band they'd hired had begun to play "I Saw Mommy Kissing Santa Claus" and everyone clapped.

"I now present to you, Mr. and Mrs. Savian Omar Donovan!"

More applause and smiles and Jenise was officially the happiest woman alive.

Three hours later, Savian danced with his wife again. This time, he'd selected Charlie Wilson's "You Are".

"You are beautiful," he whispered as he'd taken her in his arms in the center of the dance floor.

He'd had to admit the place looked magnificent with all the white satin and lights, red tablecloths and different sized vases filled with red berries, rose petals and white floating candles.

"I love you," she replied.

"Today has been truly magical," he told her.

She closed her eyes when he touched his forehead to hers. "Thank you so much," she said.

"No," he responded with a slight shake of his head "Thank you for loving a battered and confused man like me."

She'd looked up at him then. "You're my man now," she whispered. "All mine Savian Donovan."

"And you're all mine, Jenise Donovan."

He'd kissed her lightly on the lips then because anything more and he'd want to leave for their honeymoon immediately. Thankfully, the song ended soon and they were able to return to the head table where they'd been seated.

"Let me get another picture of you two," Bailey said coming up to the table using her cell phone camera. "I cannot believe you're finally married. You'd better take really good care of her because we don't want her giving you back." She joked.

Jenise had leaned in, wrapping her arms around him. "Don't worry I'm never letting him go."

"So there," Savian said with a quick lick of his tongue before Bailey snapped the picture.

She went away laughing and Briana appeared with Linc's twin daughters, Torian and Tamala.

"Uncle Sabe," she'd called to him.

When he'd first met Briana she hadn't been able to pronounce his name, which wasn't a shock. Savian couldn't remember how many times his name had been mispronounced when he was in school. She'd shortened it to Sabe and the name had stuck. In fact, he never wanted to hear her call him anything else.

"Yes ma'am," he replied as he looked down into her pretty face.

"We want more cake," Briana told him without preamble.

"We can get it ourselves, but we had to ask a grown up first," Tamala, the taller of the seven-year-old twins announced.

"Well, then I guess I have to be the grown up that tells you to eat as much cake as you like," he told them with a smile. Savian reached out to tweak each of their noses and loved the sound of their responding giggles before they ran off.

"They're going to be sick to their stomachs tonight and Trent is going to have your head," Jenise said from beside him.

"I'm not afraid of Trent," Savian said. "He's not walking around with a machine gun on his hip anymore."

Jenise had just begun to chuckle when the room suddenly went dark. Savian stiffened beside her.

A light came on soon enough but it was in the center of the floor. A weird sound signaled a projector screen that had begun being lowered. Everyone around them went quiet, looking expectantly at the screen as if it were a part of the reception. Savian knew it was not.

There was a flash on the screen and then a picture appeared. It looked like some type of party with young people mulling about and music playing in the background. In just a few seconds a familiar face appeared on the screen. It was Uncle Bernard, at least thirty years earlier. Uncle Henry and Uncle Al appeared right after, the three of them sharing a drink and congratulating Uncle Henry. Uncle Bruce, Uncle Everette and a much younger Reginald joined them for the toast and then a cake was wheeled over. Uncle Henry was graduating from college.

Savian did not like this. He looked further down the table to where Parker was sitting. His brother was frowning at the screen as well.

The party scene faded out and the front entrance of a hotel appeared. Going into the hotel was Uncle Henry. Another scene change and the sound of airplanes taking off echoed throughout the room. That scene switched to what looked like another hotel where an empty glass and a wig were on the nightstand, next to a watch that had a name engraved in it—Bernard Donovan. There was another scene, this time of the front of the Donovan Oilwell building in Houston which was quickly replaced by a close-up shot of Uncle's Al's house in Houston, Aunt Darla's favored black Camaro parked in front, signaling the picture must have been taken before she died.

By this time Henry and Bernard had stood. Trent did as well, looking around the room for Devlin, Savian suspected. Devlin had sent him a text message saying he'd decided to stay in Miami once he heard all of the Senior Donovans were coming in for the wedding and Savian had invited him to join in the festivities. However, he couldn't say he remembered seeing Devlin at all today.

When the final scene appeared on the screen, Jenise reached for Savian's hand. It was of a baby lying in a hospital bassinet. The card at the end of the bed read 'Dane Henry Ausby', but 'Ausby' had been scratched through and above it 'Donovan' had been written in. There were audible gasps and Savian was about to stand up and to go find out who the hell was running this little slide show. But then the screen went totally black, read letters appearing one, by one until it read, MERRY CHRISTMAS, DAD, and the letters began to run and fade like blood.

...meanwhile

THE FIRST TIME

Bailey was unusually edgy tonight. She'd felt that way since Savian had opened that box with the clock in it last night. Sleep hadn't come quickly and so, in the morning she'd awakened groggy and out of sorts. Nothing had changed throughout the course of the day, except that her father was acting strangely and her brothers were eyeing her much more intently than usual when they were together.

She did not address the situation with them because she knew that both Brock and Brandon wanted her to return to Houston to look after their father, instead of 'playing cops and robbers' with Trent and his company, as they'd so rudely referred to the job she was doing at D&D Investigations. Bailey did not want to return to Houston and she certainly did not want to babysit her father. There was nothing wrong with Al, she'd continued to tell herself. Nothing at all.

He certainly was not getting sick as her mother had.

That, Bailey would not take into consideration at all. And what Bailey did not want to consider, she ignored.

Savian and Jenise's wedding had been gorgeous. It had also been somewhat eye-opening for her in that if Savian could find love, she wondered why the hell she couldn't. It could possibly be because she was too stubborn, too opinionated and too picky to find a man.

No, she thought with a shake of her head as she'd walked out of the reception hall, looking down at the picture she'd just snapped of Savian and Jenise, that was definitely *not* the reason.

When she was pulled quickly away, a hand slapping hard over her mouth, she immediately went on alert. Until he spoke into her ear.

"Turn around and look at me. Look real closely and tell me you don't want it," Devlin said slowly, seductively.

"I want it," she replied without a moment's hesitation. "I definitely want it."

"I'm tired of resisting you," he said, his gaze intent on hers in the dim coat closet, as his hands quickly worked the buckle of his pants free.

She'd reached under her dress, pulling her panties off and tucking them in the bodice of her dress. "I'm tired of playing this game."

"This means nothing," he said as she heard him tear open a condom package.

"Absolutely nothing," she said, taking the package from him and removing the latex. She looked down, taking his hard, hot length in her hands—yes, she needed both—and smoothing the latex over him.

He grabbed her at the waist then, lifting her up off the floor. Bailey eagerly wrapped her legs around his waist. He thrust inside her immediately, "Not a damn thing. I swear it doesn't mean a thing," he murmured.

Devlin had pressed her back against the wall, his length stretching and filling her until she was momentarily speechless. She shook her head. "Let's just do it and get it over with," she whispered.

"Yeah," he said, his mouth close to her ear. "Let me scratch that itch you've had for so long and then we'll go our separate ways."

He pulled out and thrust back in with even more force as the first time. Bailey gasped, clasping her hands behind his neck and rotating her hips around him.

"And we'll never speak of this. Not ever," she told him, before her head fell back against the wall, her eyes closed in ecstasy.

"Never," he said and began to pump faster. "Never. Ever."

ALWAYS
IN MY HEART

A.C. Arthur

Dear Reader,

I had not intended to write Rico Bennett's story just yet, but after WRAPPED IN A DONOVAN, I began thinking about him and how and when he would find love. I'll warn you upfront that his story is short—a novella—as will be all of the Donovan Friends books. These will be complete stories, with no cliffhangers and there is no definite schedule of which friends will receive a story and when.

Each time I've written about Rico in previous books I've always felt that he was struggling with something. I imagine there would be a certain amount of pressure on a person born the son of a Brazilian princess and a communications mogul. While the other Bennett siblings, aside from Gabriella, seem to know their direction and follow it regardless of the repercussions, Rico never struck me as the same type of person. Sure, he's working at the family company and doing everything that is expected of him, but there's so much more to him than just his job and his family, so much more that he's kept carefully hidden throughout the years.

Evangeline "Eva" Romaine Miller had a perfect life. Then tragedy struck and in the blink of an eye she was tasked with not only surviving on her own, but taking care of her younger brother as well. Every choice she's made since her parents' death has been with Makai's best interest in mind. She's given up her own dreams and walked a path she never imagined she would, just to ensure her brother's education, something she knew her parents would have done for both of them had they lived.

This is the story of two people coming to terms with who and what they are and learning to love themselves on the inside and outside, regardless of what anyone else thinks. For Rico, this journey is challenging. For Eva, it's eye-opening. For them, together, it is the love of a lifetime.

I hope you enjoy going on this journey with them. As always,
Happy Reading,
AC

CHAPTER 1

"You're just going through a mid-life crisis. Go have a few drinks, get yourself some smokin' hot sex and chill out for a week or two and you'll be just fine," Gabriella said as she continued to move.

Rico's shock and dismay must have appeared clearly on his face as his youngest sister stared back at him through the mirrored wall of the in-home gym of their parents' mansion.

"Don't look at me like that, I'm dead serious," she continued, stepping furiously on the elliptical machine. "For the last few weeks you've been a brooding irritable mess. And don't think I'm the only one that notices your condition. Bree said something the other night when you walked out of the room because the triplets were crying."

"I didn't walk out because they were crying," Rico replied, immediately defensive. "I had an important phone call to take."

Gabriella's lips twisted upward in her 'tell me another one' facial expression. "I didn't hear your phone ring."

"Ever heard of vibrate?" he snapped back, thrusting his hands forcefully into the front pockets of his slacks. "Besides, I came right back and when I did, I held Daniel until he fell asleep clutching my tie."

"And that may have been the most relaxed I've seen you in months," she said when the machine beeped and she slowly stepped off.

"Relaxation is overrated," he replied.

"It should be a priority, especially to someone your age."

"What? My age?" Rico was frowning again as Gabriella casually walked past him leaving the gym.

He was walking right behind her as he argued, "I'm only thirty-nine. You're the one who just had a birthday, not me."

Her hair was pulled up, a long ebony tail bobbing back and forth as she moved.

"I turned twenty-seven, you're about to be forty. There's a difference, big brother. Deal with it."

She continued down the hallway until she came to the break in the wall. She could either go down the three steps taking her into the sunken family room, or to the right and up more stairs to where the bedrooms the Bennett children used to occupy were housed. At this point, Gabriella was the only one of them left living in this house. All of the others—Alex: lived with his girlfriend, Monica Lakefield, Renny: lived with his wife Bree Desdune and their triplets, and Adriana: lived with her fiancé, Parker Donovan.

Rico had an apartment closer to the city because he was far too impatient to sit in traffic. Driving from the part of Greenwich where his parents and Renny lived, into the office everyday was a thirty minute ride, one filled with unpredictable traffic from all the other weekly commuters. Alex usually worked remotely as the condo he shared with Monica was in Manhattan, just a few blocks away from the Lakefield Art Gallery that Monica, along with her sister, Karena, managed. Since Bree had the triplets and Karena was married to Bree's brother, Sam Desdune, most weekends Alex and Monica were in Greenwich spending time with their nephews and nieces. That made Rico wonder when his older brother would finally marry Monica and start a family of his own.

Adriana was in Miami, happily planning her wedding to Parker Donovan, so Rico had no doubt she'd be pregnant and glowing soon after that big day. He wasn't terribly thrilled by that thought as Parker Donovan and his family seemed to have a dark cloud looming over them. There had been one incident after another lately with the Donovans, from the lunatic that had attacked Adriana, to the same idiot guy getting himself killed and Savian Donovan being accused—but eventually cleared—of murdering him. Just a couple of months ago Adriana had told them about another disturbance at Savian and Jenise Langley's wedding. Rico had a feeling this was only the beginning and he hated that Adriana might get caught in the cross fire of whatever storm was brewing within the Donovan family.

Then there was Gabriella, the energetic and sometimes flighty youngest child of Marvin and Beatriz Bennett. It had taken her almost twice as long to finish college as any of the other children because she couldn't figure out what she wanted to do with her life. Just a year after her graduation when Marvin had finally decided that she would work at Bennett Industries, the family's communications and technology company, she'd surprised them once again by announcing instead that she wanted to pursue a career in interior design. Nobody was certain whether or not that would stick, or how good at designing Gabriella would be, but for now they'd all decided to support her.

At the moment, however, his youngest sister was doing a pretty good job of annoying the hell out of Rico.

"Look," she said calling his attention immediately back to her smirking face, only slightly damp with sweat. "I know you're the big brother and you like to think you have all the answers, but what I'm telling you is true. Look it up on the Internet if you don't believe me."

"I'm past the midlife crisis age," he said through clenched teeth.

Gabriella shrugged. "Late bloomer."

"You're ridiculous," Rico said and moved past her to go down into the family room. As she was on the steps, he figured she was going up to her room to shower and change, or to find some other way to irritate someone else. He didn't care, so long as she got away from him for a while.

"I'm right and you're pissed off about it," she shot back. "You're pissed off about everything lately. If the sun shines too bright. If a baby cries too loud. When Adriana announced she's getting married. Even when mom went back to Pirata to visit her family. You're in a constant crappy mood and we're getting tired of it. So like I said, have a drink, get some sex, go on a vacation. Do something and get over it already."

With that she was gone. As if her words were that heavy and truthful that all she needed to do was speak them and drop the damn mic. Rico grit his teeth remembering that it was perfectly natural for little sisters to be a pain in the ass.

What wasn't natural was for them to be right. At least partially anyway.

That conversation had taken place on a Wednesday afternoon. On Friday night, Rico had driven up to New York and was now sitting in the classically decorated lounge area of The Corporation.

The Corporation was an elite private sex club. There were facilities located all over the world, its clientele reaching as high up as the White House staff, to as low as everyday businessmen committing to pay the exorbitant membership fees. It was all for the pleasure of having any and everything they desired sexually without any recriminations or judgments.

That's how the club had been pitched to Rico when he'd been offered a year's free membership. The offer had come last summer when Rico had traveled to Los Angeles for Jackson Carrington, his college friend's, wedding. It was during the wedding reception that Jackson's brother, Jerald, spoke to Rico about the club. The black pamphlet with THE CORPORATION printed in gold block letters across the front had been in Rico's top left desk drawer for months, before he'd finally picked it up again. That had been around nine hours ago, Rico recalled as he now stood staring out the floor-to-ceiling windows of the high-rise building. There had been pictures in the brochure of a few of the more popular Corporation locations—New York, Beverly Hills, Turks and Caicos—so he had noticed the different themed décor in each one. New York was definitely the hip and trendy locale as evidenced by the black painted walls, white tiled floors and contemporary gray and black furniture.

For about the hundredth time Rico wondered what the hell he was doing here. It had been an impulsive act as he'd shut down his computer for the day and pulled open the drawer to see the brochure staring up at him. At first he'd thought he couldn't go. There had to be a meeting of some sort taking place over the weekend, because Rico worked seven days a week unless there was a federal holiday or a family catastrophe. But no, his calendar was empty. That had been the first sign.

Surely the family—either the Bennetts or the Desdunes— were doing something this weekend. An anniversary party at Lucien's, the Desdune family creole restaurant, or perhaps his mother was watching the triplets again and subsequently wanted all her children at the house. There had to be something to do in Greenwich, something he was used to doing and that didn't take him totally out of his comfort zone. But after a call to Alex and Renny, he was assured there was nothing. Sign number two.

With nothing keeping him in town, Rico had grabbed the brochure and went to his apartment to pack a bag. He'd spend the weekend in New York, see some sights he hadn't seen in a while, and maybe catch a show. He didn't have to actually go to The Corporation. Yet, here he was, at almost ten thirty on a Friday night, wearing navy blue slacks, a white shirt and a Tom Ford suede blazer. The floor attendant who had greeted him with a gorgeous smile when he'd stepped off the elevator and walked up to the white marble desk, had taken some very personal information from him about fifteen minutes ago. Shortly after he'd walked away, another staff member, dressed in all white— pants that were so tight there was no way she could be wearing anything beneath them and a shirt that was basically the same fit, her jacket not as snug, added a touch of class to the otherwise blatantly sexual look—had approached him with a drink in hand. A Ketel One martini with a twist, exactly what he'd informed the floor attendant was his preferred drink.

Now, as he sat there enjoying the perfectly mixed beverage, he wondered again about the decision to come here. Rico had plenty of women he could call if "smokin' hot sex" as Gabrielle had referred to it, was all he desired. It wasn't as if he never dated. He just did so sparingly because work was a priority. Spending time with his family was a priority. Just about anything came before long-term dating in the priority department for Rico. Still, there were some pretty memorable women he'd slept with that he knew for certain would be game for another tumble. Only Rico wasn't game, not for them, not tonight.

He wanted autonomy tonight. A mind blowing sexual connection—actually mind clearing—was what he was aiming for. Rico wanted the sex to be so good that it would clear Gabriella's words of a mid-life crisis from his mind. So great, that the worry about Adriana's safety would vanish, at least temporarily. So damn fantastic, that he could have just one weekend without thinking about work, getting back to work, or finishing work. All he would manage to do after the sex would be get up, get dressed, get something to eat, get some sleep, get up the next day and repeat. He'd set aside three whole days and hoped like hell it could be achieved.

Then he saw her and everything he wanted, the way he'd anticipated feeling, the pleasure he'd envisioned, all of it, vanished.

She was the third sign.

∞

This was a bad idea.

Eva knew it the moment she'd finally caved in to Kenya's request.

"Come on, Eva. I just don't want to go alone," her best friend insisted.

They were in Eva's studio—or rather, the second bedroom of the apartment she rented on Banner Avenue in Brooklyn. Makai, her twenty-year-old brother stayed in the other bedroom while Eva used a pull-out bed in the living/dining room area. It was a small sacrifice to have the two open windows and space to paint using the natural light. The room also gave her privacy to work when Makai had company or she just wanted to tune everything else out and focus on her craft.

Right now, with one of the bulbs from the ceiling fan light unit flickering and Kenya's persistent chattering, focus wasn't a possibility.

Dropping the brush she had been using into the jar of water sitting on the windowsill, Eva sighed. "I wasn't planning on going out tonight," she replied as she looked over to where Kenya was standing. "Besides, isn't this your first night working there? Why would I tag along with you when you go to work?"

"Because," Kenya said tossing Eva an exasperated look over her shoulder. "You're my friend and I need you."

Kenya DuMont a.k.a. Starshine, the most popular dancer at the TEASE nightclub, did not *need* anyone or anything. She was a thirty-seven-year-old bartender turned manager, turned dancer and now...companion. Yes, Kenya had accepted a job which she insisted was going to pay her a minimum of one thousand dollars per night, as a paid companion to rich and famous men. In Eva's mind that was a lot of fancy talk for being a prostitute, and while she would be forever thankful to Kenya for suggesting she try her hand at erotic dancing, Eva was firm on drawing the line long before she was ever paid to have sex with any man.

"I can't go into the room with you and hold your hand while you have sex with a stranger," Eva told her. "And seriously, I don't know why you accepted this job in the first place. You make so much more at TEASE with all the tips and personal service you provide to your regulars, *without* having sex with them."

They'd had this conversation before where Eva felt like she was the older sister, giving out advice. When in actuality Kenya was ten years older than Eva's twenty-seven. Eva had begun working at the sport's bar where Kenya was a bartender and manager when she was eighteen. In the first two years they'd grown so close—with Kenya doing whatever she could to help Eva get custody of Makai and to make sure Eva got the lion's share of the tips that were to be split between all of the wait staff—that when Kenya landed the dancing gig at TEASE in Manhattan, she'd insisted Eva join her. Five years of professional dance classes when she was a teenager added to Kenya's vouching for Eva to the manager at the strip club, but their friendship had kept them close through the thick and thin times that came afterwards. They were as tight as blood sisters and that's why Eva felt it her duty to try, one more time. to steer Kenya in what Eva thought was a better direction.

"Yeah, after I let them grope and grab on me all night long. They pay very well for that," Kenya said, her lips already upturned, neck swiveling with attitude. "This place is so much more upscale. Hell, it looks like a regular business building from the outside. And once you get all the way to the top floors where they're actually located, you still don't know that you're in an establishment where people pay for sex."

Picking up a towel and wiping her hands thoroughly, Eva shook her head adamantly. "That doesn't change a thing. All that means is that now you'll be groped and grabbed by rich men, who probably have rich wives and spoiled kids at home."

Kenya waved a hand. "You know I don't give a damn about what happens once they leave the club. I taught you that a long time ago. This is business, not personal."

Eva smiled blandly as she slipped off the stool. "Right. It's never personal. Get your money and get going. I remember and that's why I'm still confused about why you're doing this."

Kenya sighed this time, lifting both hands to tuck her thick straight hair behind her ears. "I'm not getting any younger, Evie," she began.

She'd always called her Evie, even after Eva had stated her real name was Evangeline Miller. Kenya hadn't thought that was sexy enough, especially once they'd decided to work at TEASE. They'd come up with Eva Romaine – the nickname that her parents had given her when she was born combined with her middle name. Still, Kenya kept on calling her Evie.

"You're gorgeous," Eva told her. "You look better than half these twenty-year-old girls we see down at the club."

This was the honest truth. Kenya still had butter smooth skin and no wrinkles in sight. As a result of her weekly standing appointment at one of the top salons in Brooklyn, her hair was always on point. And she dressed like a sophisticated socialite, not the stripper that Eva knew she was.

"You don't understand because you're still so young," Kenya continued. "But I want something a little more settled. I'd only have to work two or three nights a week at this place. I say which days and I say which clients. These aren't ignorant, drunk men looking for a quick lay. They're businessmen—doctors, lawyers, politicians—guys that have good heads on their shoulders."

"Yeah, but those are not the 'heads' you'll be dealing with," Eva quipped. "At the end of the day they're still men paying for sex. They won't respect you any more than they do when you shake your ass and collect the dollar bills they throw at you."

Kenya sighed. "Since when did you become so cynical?"

Eva breezed past her as she headed out to the living room. "Since my parents died when I was seventeen, leaving me and my brother who had celebrated his tenth birthday two months earlier, to fend for ourselves."

"You mean leaving you to become a stripper just like me?" Kenya added as she followed Eva into the kitchen.

Eva yanked open the refrigerator, grabbing a bottle of water and opening it. She took a long gulp before looking at Kenya again. "I did what I had to do to make sure Makai was taken care of. You know that greedy Ruby wasn't about to let him go as long as she was still receiving that check from the state."

Kenya nodded. "That's right, I do know. I was there. I saw how easily you made the decision to work at TEASE and make triple what you were ever going to make at that sport's bar. You did what was best for your situation and I supported you all the way. That money you made financed this apartment, put Makai through private school and it paid the first two year's college tuition for him. You go to work just like any other person in this world. And when I go to The Corporation tonight, I'll be doing the same thing."

Kenya was absolutely right. Eva had told herself this same thing since the day her parents died. Everything that she'd done, each time she'd stepped on that stage as the illusive Eva Romaine, dancing and swaying to the music, while removing her clothes, she knew exactly why she was doing it. First, it was to save herself and her brother from their mean and greedy neighbor turned foster mother, and then it was to give Makai the life and advantages that she knew their parents had planned for him. So how could she stand here being so hypocritical with Kenya?

"I just want you to be safe," Eva said. "You have other options now."

"Like what? Get a nine to five? I'm too young to collect social security and they don't usually pay out to strippers anyway. What else can I do besides shake my ass? Answer phones and get coffee for minimum wage? No, thank you. I enjoy my lifestyle and since there's no man I deem good enough to allow him to put a ring on this finger and kids are not my cup of tea, this is the perfect life for me," Kenya told her with a definite nod.

Eva could only sigh. "I hear you," she told her friend. "I hear everything you're saying."

"Good," Kenya snapped her fingers quickly. "Now, you've got one hour to get dressed. I'll pick you up and we'll head into the city. It'll be fine. You'll be there for support only and when I'm set for the night, you can leave."

"How am I supposed to get back if you pick me up?" Eva asked, hating that she was even remotely considering this.

Kenya was already walking out of the kitchen and heading towards the door in the living room. "I'll pay for your cab ride, just be ready in an hour."

CHAPTER 2

Eva's first thought upon walking through the glass doors was that there should be music. Something light and classical like Bach or Chopin would add to the sleek mix of contemporary furnishings and crisp, bold colors.

The receptionist—no, Eva was almost positive the woman with the wide expressive gray eyes and pouty mouth could not be described as just a receptionist. She looked professional enough wearing a black pant suit. The jacket had a single button that closed the material around her rib cage. Beneath it she wore a red lace bra and around her neck a leather collar with a diamond at her throat. She was chic and sexy and polite as she spoke with a faint British accent.

The walls were painted black, which could have either made the room too dreary or—the look that they'd actually managed to pull off—become a bold statement. The spherical shaped white marble desk was meant to be the focal point of the room, with two large red rose arrangements in crystal cylinder vases. There was nothing else, no phone, no computer, nothing but the beautiful woman and her alluring gaze. She held a tablet in one hand and there was a slim clear earpiece at her ear. It all gave Eva the impression of something out of a James Bond movie.

"This is for you," the woman said to Eva as she handed her a red rose pin. "This should be clearly visible to all the members and staff. It will let them know that you are a guest for the evening."

Kenya had not been given a pin. Instead she had passed her leather jacket to the woman and slid a black card through a side slit on the woman's tablet. That was a far cry from the old ragged time clock on the back wall at TEASE.

"Thank you," Eva managed to say as she took the pin from the woman. Tucking the small clutch purse she carried under her arm, Eva slipped the pin onto the lapel of the black hipster jacket she'd worn.

She noted that Kenya wore all black tonight, a form-fitting dress that fell to her ankles, a dangerously sexy slit up her left leg that ended high on her thigh. Her shoes were black, with straps going up her bare legs. The dress dipped low in the back and hugged her ample breasts in front. Eva, who hadn't been sure what to wear to such an establishment—considering she wasn't one of the working women here—had opted for a royal blue wrap dress that accentuated her best parts—the round firm bottom that came courtesy of a deadly amount of squats on a daily basis and her pert, if small, breasts. She'd thrown on the jacket because it was chilly out this evening, but she'd matched it with leather ankle boots with four-inch heels. Her hair fell in a curly tail over her right shoulder.

"Let's go to the lounge," Kenya said reaching for Eva's hand and pulling her along. "Since I'm new I don't have any special requests yet."

"So, the men just get to pick you out of the other women in the room? Is that how it works?" Eva asked as they walked through a long hallway of more black walls, but with small white spotlights shooting up from the floor.

"The available 'hostesses', that's what we're called, are wearing all black. If the members have not already made an appointment with someone for the night, they'll know where to look to find a partner. Once they make a selection they'll let the floor attendant—the gorgeous British woman we just met—know. She'll compare the member's requests and assure that the hostess that has been selected is suitable to his needs. Then, the evening proceeds," Kenya explained.

"Wow," Eva replied with a nod. "Sounds so organized. What if you don't like him?"

They'd come to a larger room now, this time the dour black walls were highlighted by crisp white tiled floors, and black leather chairs. There were straight backed contemporary seats, some single and double, and chaise lounges placed throughout the space. The entire back wall was comprised of windows, floor to ceiling giving a skyline view of Manhattan lit up in all its glory. Again, Eva listened for music, something classy and elegant would fit nicely here. It would also take her mind off the fact that there were more than twenty men in this room at the moment and just a handful of women. That shouldn't have been alarming to her considering she was used to a similar ratio when she worked at TEASE, but then she was up on a stage performing. Tonight, she had no idea what she was doing.

"It's not my job to 'like' him," Kenya informed her.

Eva nodded. "Right. Just like dancing. Get through the performance and get done." She recalled another bit of advice Kenya had given her years ago.

"Exactly. Now, let's get a drink and mingle," Kenya continued, leading them toward one of the far walls where three women wearing all white stood.

"Where's the bar?" Eva asked.

"Right here," Kenya said as they approached the women.

"Good evening, Kenya," the tallest of the women with platinum blond hair that added an unmistakable pop to her all-white attire, said, "I'll get your drink. And what will your guest have this evening?"

Kenya looked at Eva giving her a huge grin. "Tell her what you want and she'll get it."

"I'll have white wine, please," Eva said before clearing her throat.

There was no bar in sight so she wondered if these women were magical and that's why they were dressed in all white. Would they pull a glass and bottle of Chardonnay from the air?

The woman nodded and stepped away from the line of the others. Kenya turned away also. "Come on, she'll bring the drinks to us."

"How do you know all this if tonight's you're first night on the job? This place seems like a covert world that we're trespassing in," Eva said while looking around at the men dressed in business suits.

Expensive suits, she might add. Each of them were wearing expensive suits and shoes. They didn't get this clientele at

TEASE often, but every now and then they'd been known to host a bachelor party or some other type of get together for a celebrity. Over the years, Eva had come to notice the quality in clothes, shoes and cars. Not that any of this meant the customers she dealt with during these special events were any less crude or misguided as the regulars.

"They told me everything when I came for orientation. I had two interviews, a background check, a physical that checked for things I didn't even know existed and even a credit check," Kenya informed her.

They'd come to a stop near the edge of the windows. Eva sat because the cute booties she wore were hell on her toes.

"All that to sleep with men you don't know?" Eva asked. She was immediately sorry for the question and looked up to Kenya offering a slow smile.

She was there for support, not to criticize the decision Kenya had made for herself. Eva, of all people, knew exactly how it felt to have her back against the wall and to make a decision that would probably be frowned upon by others. She'd spent the last seven years of her life ignoring anyone else's thoughts about her and what she did for a living, because that's what she needed to do to survive. Kenya was her best friend and had been a very instrumental part in getting Eva to where she was in her life. She owed her much love and respect and vowed to give it to her, no matter what critical thoughts she might be having.

"He looks nice," Eva suggested.

"Which one?" Kenya asked.

Kenya wore her hair longer tonight, sparing no expense for the extensions she often used, and it swayed behind her as she turned her head quickly in the direction Eva was looking. As they both danced at TEASE, they'd learned long ago that appearance was everything. So from their sexy costumes, to the expensive monthly spa treatments—manicures, pedicures, waxing and massages—to the careful way in which their natural hair, and the hair they purchased, was styled. They'd made money off this package, so it stood to reason that they would invest a lot of time and money into it.

"Both of them, really," Eva replied in reference to the two guys that were not too far away from them.

One wore a modern fit suit that accented his slim frame and the other a suit that may have been tweed or wool that gave him a mature and debonair look. The tall, slim guy was white with piercing blue eyes that brightened as he lifted his glass and nodded towards Eva and Kenya. The other was of Latino descent with his dark eyes and even darker hair. They were both really handsome and Kenya smiled her reply to Eva's comment instead of actually speaking.

"I'm going to say hello," Kenya said a few seconds after the blonde lady arrived with their drinks.

Eva took a sip of her wine. "Is that what you're supposed to do?" she asked while still sitting. The wine was excellent. Eva thought if she had to sit here for the duration of the night having free drinks, she'd be just fine with that.

Kenya smoothed down the front of her dress and squared her shoulders, an act which made her generous breasts even more appealing. She was a butter-complexioned bombshell. Her waist looked extra small in the black material, spanning out to curvy hips and ass, which were her signature when she danced. As for Eva, her waist could be considered small, but that was because she was only five feet four inches and worked out religiously because her eating habits were in direct contrast to the life of a dancer. Kenya hated the gym and preferred her waist trainer, juicer and salads for breakfast, lunch and dinner instead. The word 'bombshell' would never be used to describe her, but she had the moves and flexibility that made even her 'B' cup breasts and size twelve body look sexy as hell as she worked that pole on stage.

"You know I don't have the patience to sit and wait for anything," Kenya said tossing Eva a wicked smile over her shoulder.

Eva chuckled as she brought her glass to her lips once more. Kenya definitely lacked patience. Unlike Eva who was perfectly content sitting here, at least until Kenya had found her beau for the night. Then Eva was heading out of the posh sex den, and going back to her apartment where she could top her night off from work with a good chick flick and some mint chocolate chip ice cream. Makai would most likely be out with his friends. Friday was the one night of the week that Eva didn't raise hell about him going out. At twenty, Makai definitely felt like he was grown, but until he had that college degree and a good job, Eva still felt every bit as responsible for him as she did the day after her parents had died.

"Good evening. Could you come with me?"

Eva's head snapped up at the sound of the female voice. It was the blonde again, but this time she wasn't bringing drinks, which was a pity because Eva had almost finished her wine.

"Excuse me?" Eva asked.

The woman simply smiled, her hands folded neatly in front of her and asked again, "Could you come with me?"

Eva frowned. "Where?"

Kenya had assured her all she had to do was stay there until she was done, nothing more.

"To a more comfortable room in the back," was the woman's response.

She also lifted an arm as if to guide Eva in the direction which she wanted her to go. Eva didn't move. Instead she looked around the woman to see if she could spot Kenya. When she didn't see her or the men that Kenya had gone over to speak to, Eva's frown grew. On a huff she came to a stand, extending her hand with the just about empty wine glass toward the blonde.

"Actually, I'll be leaving now," she said.

"Please, miss. There is someone who would like to see you in the other room," the woman replied, taking the glass from Eva who immediately began shaking her head.

"Oh no, you're mistaken. I don't work here. I'm just a guest."

When the woman only continued to hold that smile—which Eva was now convinced had to be painted on her face—Eva touched the lapel of her jacket, lifting it higher so the woman could see the red rose pin that signified her as guest.

The woman nodded and this time touched a hand to Eva's elbow. She was still smiling as she began to guide Eva across the room.

"I know who you are, Ms. Eva Romaine," she said as they walked.

"How do you know my name?"

"At The Corporation we make sure we know as much as possible about everyone."

"But I don't work here," Eva said again, more insistently than she figured she had before. "I just came with my friend. She's the employee. This was her first night and she was feeling a bit nervous."

Funny enough, Eva thought she was the one sounding nervous as they left the lounge area and headed down a dark hallway. It was in the opposite direction from where she'd come in, which Eva figured wasn't a good sign. The vibe had immediately shifted from having a carefree drink in a luxurious establishment to feeling as if she were walking into something she would not be able to get out of. With that thought in mind, Eva stopped walking and turned to the blonde, who was, yes, still smiling at her.

"I didn't come here for this. I'm not...I'm...this is not what I do," she said in an attempt to say as nicely as she could that she was not a piece of ass for sale.

"Going into this room does not commit you to anything, Ms. Romaine. It's just a meeting. When you're ready to go, you leave," she said, more seriously than she had said anything else tonight.

Eva didn't know why but she believed her. This place was nothing like TEASE, where the back rooms meant lap dances and much more depending on how much the customer had to spend. In all the years she'd worked at the club, Eva had never been in one of the back rooms. She showed up for her shift, took the stage, danced, grabbed her tips and left. Staying later to have a drink at the bar was only something she'd done once or twice. Dancing in the sex industry was her job, it did not define her life. She was sure to tell herself that every day. It was what got her through.

A black door opened in front of her and Eva walked through. She heard it click shut behind her only seconds before she heard the music. It wasn't loud but the effortless sound of the bow against violin strings echoed throughout the room, pulling her immediately inside, regardless of her previous hesitation. There was a soft scent in the air as she inhaled deeply. Something light and floral maybe. Soothing. Her first steps led her deeper into the dimly lit room. These rooms weren't black, but covered in a cream colored wall paper that glowed like soft gold in the light.

The furniture, two couches and a high-backed chair were dark brown leather. The rug was plush, with a geometrical design. The light came from lamps on either side of the room. There was a doorway to what she assumed would be a bedroom. She quickly turned her attention in the other direction.

It was warmer in here than it had been out there and as she stood, still looking around, Eva removed her jacket. She draped it over the back of a chair and dropped her purse onto its seat.

"Hello?" she called out when she still hadn't seen anyone after a few more moments.

There was no answer, but the music continued to play. She was swaying before she could stop herself. The memory of the classical dance class her mother had insisted she take the summer she was ten years old, as fresh in her mind as if it were yesterday. This had been her introduction to classical music and to the flexibility of her body. Sure, she'd taken ballet two years before, but she'd felt totally different when her movements had been choreographed to the illustrious and ingenious sounds of Mozart and Brahms. Her favorite, however had been, the clever and insanely exciting numbers she'd performed to music by Chanda Dancy. For Eva, dancing to music composed and performed by an artist that looked like her, gave her a tremendous boost in confidence. Three years later, after more dance classes, thirteen-year-old Eva believed that she could dance professionally and that even though she was on the short and curvy side, she would still be successful. Then her mother lost her job as a legal secretary and their household income rested on her father's postal worker shoulders. Dance classes, as well as other extra-curricular activities stopped, and Eva's venture into the cheaper and more solitary craft of art began.

"I like the way your body moves."

His voice was smooth, hushed and came from behind her. Eva turned quickly not sure when she'd actually begun to dance to the music that was playing, and certainly unaware that she was being watched. Not that she had a problem with people watching her dance, it was her job, of course. But here, in this place, where she was just a guest, it had thrown her off a bit.

"I…ah, I didn't know anyone was here," she said, wrapping her arms defensively around herself. "I called out but nobody answered."

He was sitting in a chair that was tucked into a corner that wasn't near either of the lamps she'd seen. That meant he was draped in darkness until, he leaned forward, elbows resting on his knees, head lifted, gaze directly on her. And that's why she did not make a move to leave. His gaze, the way it held her perfectly still even though she had no idea who this guy was or what he wanted from her.

CHAPTER 3

This was happening very fast. The decision to come to The Corporation, seeing this woman walk into the room, requesting her for the night and watching her sway seductively to music that was by all rights soothing, but in no way sexy. Until now.

Rico knew without a doubt, that from this moment on, whenever he heard classical music, he would think of her.

"What's your name?" he asked as she continued to stare at him.

Her lashes were long, he noted each time she blinked, and wondered if they were real or fake.

"Eva," she replied, bringing her hands together.

They were now clasped in front of her as her feet shifted slightly. She had great legs, toned and covered in black nylon.

"I'm Rico," he told her because he wasn't sure how this episode should play out. He'd never been in this situation before—the one where he paid for sex with a gorgeous woman.

"You have great taste in music, Rico," she told him, her voice clear in the otherwise awkward silence between them.

"You like to dance to classical music?" he asked. "That's not what I expected."

None of this was what Rico had expected. Was it really this easy? Did a membership card actually allow him his pick of any woman, and was this particular woman really going to have sex with him for money? Rico realized at that moment that he had no idea how much he would be paying to be with her, and he was certain that she wasn't the one he should be asking. This wasn't a motel and he hadn't picked her...he hadn't picked *Eva* up on some corner.

"I can dance to almost any music," she answered. "But, yes, I like classical music. It's always been a favorite of mine."

"So you're a dancer?"

She blinked and then shrugged. "Yes. I am a dancer."

"Then dance for me," Rico told her.

When neither of them moved or said a word, he sat back in the chair, letting his palms rest on his thighs. "Dance for me, Eva."

Her look was one of uncertainty, which, again wasn't what Rico expected.

"I didn't really come here tonight to dance," she replied finally.

Her hands were moving then, twisting so that her fingers were twined together in one moment and then flexing apart in the next. The dress she wore fit her perfectly, accentuating the blatant curve of her backside. She was also on the short side, something he hadn't originally noticed from a far because of the high heels she wore. Upon further assessment—his gaze having rested momentarily on her pert breasts and the long tresses of hair draped sexily over one shoulder—he realized that she did not possess the traditional dancer's body.

Tall, lithe, almost of a boyish quality is what he generally pictured when he thought of a woman dancing to classical music. Yet, Eva had swayed so seductively to the music, like it was second nature to her. Her calves were thick, but toned. Her waist curved inward, but not skinny. That dress hugged her body, cupping her neat little breasts the way his palms ached to do.

"I'd really like to see you dance," Rico stated. "Can you do that for me? Please."

The music was still playing, even though he'd stopped listening to it the moment she'd walked into the room.

She did not respond verbally, but let her arms fall to her sides. With a shake of her head, as if she weren't sure why she was doing this, Eva closed her eyes. Then, she began to move.

Rico was mesmerized. His gaze followed every movement, every step and sway that seemed as if she knew this particular song very well. He imagined her in a leotard and tights, instead of the form fitting dress that allowed for much more movement than he would have thought possible. Her feet would be bare, her hair flowing free. She would move across a stage gracefully, enigmatically. And he would grow just as hard and aroused as he was becoming at this very moment.

He had no idea when his legs had gapped open, or when one of his hands had moved to lightly grip his growing arousal. Yet, when she'd come closer, standing right between his knees, turning her back and moving her hips and ass to the high-pitched violin solo, he definitely heard the low moan that escaped from his throat. Her hand toyed with the hem of her dress, pulling it up slightly so that more of her thigh was visible. So much of her thigh that the lacy edge of the nylons, held by a black satin garter peeked at him alluringly.

Rico undid his belt and the button of his pants. He kept his gaze focused on the straight line of her back, the dip of her hips and the plumpness of her ass. The zipper moved slowly as he took deep breaths, in an effort to slow this surprising pleasure down a bit. Then she lowered herself, dipping down until she was almost sitting on his lap. His fingers itched to touch her, but he refrained. His breath came quicker, his tongue licking over his lips as he waited.

When she turned around abruptly, resting her hands on her hips and stared down at him, Rico was still trying to hold on to his control.

"Is that why you called me back here?" she asked. "How did you know—"

Her words were cut off when her gaze dropped down to see his hand cupping his rigid arousal. He hadn't taken it out, so he felt safe that he didn't look like a horny teenager about to rub one off at the sight of her. Still, the way she was looking at him, did make him feel like he was doing something immoral, which again, caused him to question why he was here in the first place.

She began backing up at that moment.

"I've got to go," she was saying as she turned away from him. "I think you have the wrong idea. I'm not..."

Rico didn't give her a chance to finish. In the seconds that she'd moved and declared she was leaving, he'd stood, wrapping an arm around her waist and turning her quickly to face him. Her mouth opened to protest and he plunged, his tongue diving fast and furiously into her mouth, taking, devouring, enjoying much more than he'd ever anticipated.

She kissed him back.

There wasn't really another choice.

Okay, maybe she could have pulled away. But, Eva admitted as her arms wrapped around his neck, she didn't want to.

She liked how his hands felt around her waist, his mouth on hers. His tongue was warm and thorough as it stroked deep inside her mouth, coaxing her tongue to mimic its motions. Her eyes had closed involuntarily, her body following that same unscripted plan, pressing closer to his.

His name was Rico. That's all she knew.

No, that wasn't true. She knew without any doubt that he was kissing the hell out of her. Whatever that meant. She didn't know, nor did she care. All that mattered was that he didn't stop.

His hands pressed flat against the small of her back, holding her firmly against him as he continued the delicious assault on her mouth. She'd come up on tiptoe, her arms clasping behind his neck, locking him to her, almost as if she owned him. That must have suited him just fine, because in seconds Rico was walking her back, keeping her in his tight embrace, but definitely moving her deeper into the room.

Eva had no idea where she was going. She couldn't recall what the room looked like because behind her closed lids was only his face, his eyes, so intently staring at her as he'd spoken. There was nothing significant about his dark brown eyes, just that they'd looked at her as if she were not just the only person in the room, but in the entire world instead. He was pouring that look into the hottest kiss she'd ever had, coupling that with his touch and succeeding in driving her absolutely crazy with need.

She hadn't come here for sex. In fact, she had been against Kenya coming here for that purpose. Yet, now, all she could think about was Rico tossing her back onto a bed, pushing her skirt up and taking her. Yes, she wanted him to take her right here and now. The man she'd just met and only knew his name.

When her back hit the wall Eva gasped, breaking the contact of the kiss. Her eyes opened in that moment and so did his. Their gazes locked, bodies still pressed together they simply stared at each other. She was breathing heavily and so was he. She loosened her arms just enough so that her hands flattened on the back of his shoulders. Gripping her fingers she marveled in how taut and strong he felt. He didn't look big, not like some of the muscled guys she'd seen at TEASE, but there was definitely strength here. That quiet kind that emanated throughout the air surrounding his slim frame. It was echoed in the twitch in his jaw as he continued to watch her and nothing else. He wanted to do more. Rip her clothes off and have his way with her, maybe? Hell yes, would have been her instant reply to such an action.

Instead, she stood still, wondering, waiting, and anticipating.

"I've never done this before," he said softly.

"Neither have I," she replied without a thought.

"I want you," he admitted.

She sighed. "I want you, too."

"Is that all that matters?" he asked, a brow lifting as if to punctuate the question.

"I believe so," she told him. Again, there was no hesitation on her part. Later, most likely when she lay in her bed tonight, Eva would wonder what the hell had come over her. But not now.

Now, was for them.

Letting her hands slide slowly from his shoulders, she pushed his dark jacket from his arms, until it fell to the floor. She touched the first button on his shirt while holding his gaze. He didn't speak, but didn't stop her from unbuttoning the first and then the next button. When she slipped the shirt from his shoulders watching as it fell to the floor, his fingers found the hem of her dress, lifting it up until he could touch the snaps of the garter she wore. His lips parted then, a whoosh of breath coming from him as his fingers moved up and down her thighs, over the garter and the lacy tops of the stockings she wore. When he touched the bare skin of her thigh, Eva sucked in a breath, her eyes fluttering until finally they closed as his hand moved up her inner thigh.

The music still played in the background. A different song this time. Something slower, with the addition of a harp. It was an odd song, yet it seemed as if Rico's every move was perfectly choreographed to the music. This was the beginning of the song so it was slow, as if just starting to pick up pace. Rico's hand traced a heated path up her inner thigh and when he finally cupped her juncture, the music's tempo went just a little higher. His other hand cupped her chin as he leaned in, thrusting his tongue inside her mouth for one quick stroke. Between her legs his fingers pressed against the thin material of her panties. Her heart beat faster.

With the fingers of his other hand still gripping her chin, his thumb touched her lower lip and Eva licked it. He jerked at the touch, his lips going thin as his fingers worked quicker, rubbing back and forth over her clit through that damn material. She sucked his thumb into her mouth, her fingernails digging into the bare skin of his shoulders. His fingers were magical, they had to be. Eva had never recalled feeling this hot and hungry by a simple touch of a man's hand. There had to be more to this, more to explain what she was feeling.

He ripped her panties, yanking again to pull the material away from her skin. Strings and a patch of silk, that's all they were, no wonder they'd given up so freely. Eva had no excuse for why she planned to do the same. Except that she didn't think any woman alive would have been able to resist him, especially not the second his fingers touched her hot flesh. Pushing past her swollen vulva lips, sliding effortlessly through the moistened folds he found the nub he'd been in search of and pressed against it hard.

She yelled out the moment the harp solo grew louder, the strings more constrained in their melody, her heart about to pound right through her rib cage. He didn't wait, but immediately thrust a finger deep inside her, while the other stayed pressed against her clit. She bucked and he pushed her further into the wall. His hand slipped from her face, and went instead between them to where he simply pushed his already unfastened pants down.

The sound of the pants hitting the floor had them both going still. Eva bit her bottom lip, trying like hell not to circle her hips to produce movement of his finger inside her again. Rico looked as if he were thinking, trying to decide whether to keep going or to stop.

"I'm going to take my hands off you," he said slowly, as if each word were causing him a measure of pain.

"I don't want you to move," he continued. "Not. One. Fucking. Muscle."

She didn't. Well, she did scrunch her toes in her shoes, not only because they still hurt, but because she wanted...no, she needed him to hurry up and put his hands on her again.

He moved quickly, bending down to dig into his slacks and pull out his wallet. The hunt for the condom packet was mercifully short and in the next instant Eva could hear the foil ripping. She'd let her head fall back against the wall and closed her eyes, hoping that if she didn't see him she could remain still without begging and pleading for him to continue. He must have been feeling the same way because in the next instant he'd grabbed one of her thighs, hiking it up high on his waist and tucking her leg behind his back.

"Hold on," he whispered against her mouth as he thrust his sheathed length deep inside of her.

She held on. Tight. And damn, she was glad she did. He filled her so fast and so thoroughly she'd blinked several times and gulped a couple of breaths before dropping her forehead to his shoulder. He licked along her neck, as if this was the exact position he'd wanted her in, while pumping in and out of her with erotic efficiency. Eva could barely breathe, let alone wrap her mind around what was going on. He felt so good inside of her, and so right. They should slow down, move to the bed possibly. At the very least pause so that she could take off those damn shoes. But no, that would mean he would have to stop moving inside of her and she would have to cease rotating her hips to meet his every thrust.

That, she had no intention of doing. Instead she continued to hold on tight, loving the slap and slide of him inside of her. She'd never had sex like this before, not in this position, not while still mostly dressed and certainly not in a sex club. That might be hard for some to believe considering her occupation, but it was the simple truth. Her personal life was nowhere near as enticing as her work persona. Maybe that was the reason she was actually here, doing what she was doing.

Rico's hands gripping her ass, holding her hard and fast as he continued to move had her mind once again blurring with desire. It was her turn to lick his neck, inhaling deeply of his scent—

cologne mixed with man, equaling a truly intoxicating aroma. He made a sound at the contact and Eva was encouraged, so she licked him again, this time sucking the spot gently when she finished. He ground deeper into her, his fingers digging into her cheeks fiercely. She circled her tongue over his skin this time, suckled again, and enjoyed the guttural moan that escaped from him. When he moved slightly, a hand snaking between them so that he could once again touch the hardened nub of her clit, Eva hissed in pleasure. Her teeth clamped together and she breathed in and out, hard and fast. He worked her clit as he pumped in and out of her and there was just nothing else. She could not see, could not think, and could barely breathe through the thick waves of pleasure soaring through her. Her entire body convulsed as her release took hold, one leg shaking as it was still locked around his waist, while the other barely managed to hold her up.

Rico's release wasn't far behind as he thrust hard inside her, then went completely still, his one-handed grip on her ass growing tighter, until there was almost pain. When he was finished, when they were both still heaving and reveling in the remnants of their release, the music stopped completely, and the room suddenly grew cold.

Eva didn't know what to do or to say. It seemed, that Rico didn't either.

Eventually, he moved first, which made more sense because she wasn't exactly sure how to get out of this position without his cooperation. He backed up slightly, not so much that he was completely free of her, but enough so that he could look down on her. That intensity in his glare was still there, only this time it was joined by a sheen of confusion. Eva could relate. She was confused as hell too.

What had they just done? Well, the answer to that, literally, was simple. Still, there were unanswered questions floating in the air. Ones that had embarrassment and doubt swirling around in her mind. She pushed him until their connection was broken and she could stand on her own two feet. That wasn't such a success since her legs were still a bit wobbly, but Eva hurriedly pulled down her dress and moved from the wall to cross the room. She was grabbing her purse and jacket before he spoke.

"I'm not really sure how the payment thing works," he said.

She could hear that he was rustling with his clothes and when she turned back to stare at him, he was thankfully buttoning his pants.

"What did you say?" she asked, blinking and forcing her gaze to meet his face, instead of his crotch.

He cleared his throat. "I told you this was my first time. I only have a guest membership here and I wasn't certain I was going to actually use the services tonight. So I didn't get a chance to ask how the payment process works."

Eva blinked again, about two seconds before her cheeks heated and her hands began to shake. "You think…I'm not…wait a minute," she said trying to catch her breath and keep a semblance of pride. Finally, she squared her shoulders and looked him in the eye, praying her words would be as clear as they needed to be and that afterwards the good Lord would grant her one last prayer and get her the hell out of this place as quickly as possible.

"I'm not a prostitute," she told him. "Tonight was my first time here too. But I came as a favor to a friend, not as a working staff member. So you, Rico, can keep your damn money."

CHAPTER 4

Eva almost cursed the sun that was shining way too brightly this morning, and then when she cracked the second egg and watched the shells fall into the bowl alongside the yolk, she was really pissed. Correction, she told herself, she was irritated. Had been all night long.

What had she been thinking? What the hell did she do? Exactly what she'd told Kenya she shouldn't. Especially, since in the end Eva had even turned down the money.

"I didn't get a chance to ask how the payment process works," he'd said as she'd been trying to leave.

He'd thought she was a prostitute, and really, she couldn't blame him at all. She'd acted just like one.

The loud whir of the garbage disposal sounded as she dumped the destroyed egg down the drain. She wished what had happened last night could be disposed of as easily. As it was she'd been carrying this guilt all through the night. Getting up later than usual, just a little past ten, she'd noticed that Makai was still asleep and had decided to make breakfast with the hope that doing something normal would make her feel better. She was just like any other woman in the world who worked five days a week, paid her bills on time and lived the single life. She wasn't different, no matter how many times she'd recalled Ruby telling her so.

Third time was the charm because she managed to get four eggs into the bowl without shells and scrambled them until they were nice and fluffy. She'd been just dividing and putting them onto two plates, when Makai came into the kitchen.

He was fully dressed, his five-foot, eleven-inch frame easing into the room with wide eyes just like when he was a little boy. Breakfast was his favorite meal.

"Good morning to you too," Eva said when he'd reached over the counter to snag a piece of bacon before she could put it onto his plate.

"Mornin', sis," he said while chewing. "What's the occasion? You haven't cooked breakfast on a Saturday morning in a while."

She'd shrugged, determined to keep her mind focused in the present—minus last night. "Just felt like having some bacon and eggs," she told him.

"You were out late last night. I thought it was your night off," Makai continued, as he remained standing but had taken the fork that she'd set beside his plate and already begun to eat.

He was so handsome now, Eva thought as she decided not to chastise him for eating in a hurry. His root beer brown skin now accentuated by bulging muscles in his arms and chest. He was wearing a basketball jersey which told her exactly where he was heading—to the gym to play ball with some of his high school friends. It was nice the way they'd kept in touch. Eva hadn't been able to enjoy that luxury since just two years after she'd graduated from high school, they'd moved from Hartford to Brooklyn. Besides, she'd doubted that any of her friends had been thrust into adulthood as quickly as she had and thus, they probably now had absolutely nothing in common.

"I went out with Kenya," she replied, not willing to go any further with that.

"Yeah? Where'd you two go?" he asked.

She shook her head. "Just to dinner."

"Not with any of those lame ass dudes that come see y'all at the club, I hope," he said with a frown.

Part of their deal was to always be honest with each other, so when Makai was thirteen and he'd asked what Eva did for a living, she'd told him. In the time since then, he'd never approved or judged, but he'd accepted.

"No. You know I don't mix business with pleasure," she said, taking a long drink of the orange juice she'd fixed for herself.

Those words didn't go down as smoothly as she'd liked as memories of last night flashed in her mind.

"Good," he said. "Still, you know I'm making a little bit of paper now, down at music store. I can start taking on some of the bills and you can dedicate more time to your art."

Eva was already shaking her head in opposition. "I thought we talked about this, Makai. You were going to quit that job at the store so you can take that internship at Leef & Jenner."

Makai forked the last bit of his eggs into his mouth and chewed quickly, before emptying his glass of orange juice. "I don't work for free, sis," he told her simply.

"It's an internship, Makai. That's not exactly working for free."

"Are they giving me a paycheck every week like they do at the store?" he asked arching his thick, dark brows and looking more like their father every day.

She frowned. "Don't play with me, you know how it works. You were on the Dean's List the last five semesters so they enrolled you in the business and technology internship program. Getting the offer from Leef & Jenner was a blessing and you know we don't walk away from blessings."

"We also don't always know what a blessing is really. The devil knows how to give us what we want too, remember?" he countered.

Eva couldn't argue that. As children they'd grown up in the Baptist church their parents had attended in Hartford. Just a week before his death, their father had been ordained a deacon and their mother was the president of the Women's Auxiliary. The night their parents were killed they'd gone out to celebrate that and her father's promotion at work, while Eva and Makai stayed home. Their family had seen her father's elevation in the church and on his job as blessings. And then their parents were gone. So, yes, Eva and Makai had become very leery of what was truly a blessing and what was not.

"Look, it's an opportunity," she told him. "One I really think you should take. Think about your future, Makai."

Makai had been accepted to Columbia, Fordham, Medgar Evers and Brooklyn College. He'd received a five thousand dollar scholarship through the Future Leaders Association he was a member of and Eva insisted that he use that to go to Columbia. That's when she'd changed from working three nights a week at TEASE, to working five nights. The tuition was expensive, but she was convinced that Makai's future was worth the sacrifice. The first year he'd stayed on campus, then when he'd learned that she had taken on more hours at the club—much to her chagrin—he'd decided he would come home and commute. Now, he stayed with a friend who lived about ten minutes from campus during the week, and came home on weekends.

"I've been thinking about my future a lot lately, Eva. Don't worry. I'm not going to let you down," he promised.

"Don't worry about me. I mean, I'm just trying to make sure you are afforded all the opportunities that you would have had if mama and daddy were alive. They would be so proud to see you going to Columbia right now," she said, happy at least that he was thinking about what he would do when he graduated from college.

"They would also want me to do something to get you out of that strip joint," he snapped back.

"That is none of your concern," was her reply. She inhaled deeply and let out a slow breath. Talking about the club and what she did for a living was never a subject she liked discussing with her little brother. "So, you weren't home last night, either. Were you at study hall or the library?"

"Nah. Went out with the fellas," he replied. "Found this new spot we wanted to check out."

"And what about finals?" she asked immediately after she'd swallowed her last bite of food. "Spring semester's going to be wrapping up soon. How are your grades looking?"

Makai, who had finished his food well before her, as usual, only shrugged. "I got this," was what he told her before tossing his backpack over his shoulder.

The kitchen opened directly into the living room, so Eva watched as he walked a few steps, bent down near the sofa and picked up his basketball.

"What time will you be back?" she asked out of habit.

He tossed her a strange look, but then shrugged and replied. "I might be out a while. Going to meet up with some peeps after the game. You working tonight?"

She nodded her response.

Makai frowned.

"Be careful. Text me when you get there and when you get home," he said.

For a second Eva thought about giving him that same look he'd just given her a few seconds ago, the one that said "I'm grown, stop clocking me", but she refrained. "I will."

Shaking her head, Eva got up and began to clear the dishes. She thought about how far she and Makai had come since she'd been awakened late that fateful night, to police banging at their door. Hours later Makai sat crying in her arms. Eva had been so shocked and afraid she hadn't been able to shed a tear. Her mind had instantly begun running through questions that no seventeen-year-old should ever have to consider—where will we live? How will we eat? Who will send Makai to school? She hadn't had the answers then. They wouldn't come until days later, and even that hadn't worked out the way she'd planned. As she closed the door to the dishwasher Eva stood totally still, trying to push back those painful memories of the past.

A loud knock on the door had her jumping, her hand going quickly to her chest. Then she sighed, smiling as she moved toward the door.

"Ha! You're grown but you still forget your house key, every time," she was saying as she walked through the living room toward the front door.

Makai had been famous for leaving his key in the house in the mornings when he'd left for school. It was one of those times that Eva was thankful for the fact that she worked nights and was able to be there every morning to get him ready. It was funny to her that even though he would soon be a college graduate, in some ways, Makai was still the little boy she'd watched grow up.

So, Eva was smiling when she turned the knob and opened the door. That smile

slipped slowly and definitely from her face the moment she saw who stood on the other side.

"Good morning, Eva," Rico said.

"What are you doing here? How did you know where I lived?" Eva asked, immediately on edge.

The main reason for using a different name in her profession was to keep her personal life separate. She lived a good distance from the club and never took a cab directly to her apartment building from work. The name on her lease was Evangeline Miller. On all her paperwork at the club, her address was a post office box in the name of E. Romaine LLC. She never wanted any of the customers from the club to know where she lived or to get close to Makai.

"Can I come in?" he asked.

"No," was her immediate reply, her hand shaking slightly as she gripped the knob of the door tighter. "You shouldn't have come here. I don't know how you found out where I lived, but you shouldn't be here."

Eva attempted to close the door on him. In return, he made a simple move, grasping the door and holding it open, his strength easily topping hers. Eva looked at the door then, saw his hand—the lighter complexioned skin and the gold ring on his last finger—and frowned. Her skin was darker, her hand smaller, with no rings on any of her fingers.

"I don't want to make a scene, Eva. I just want to talk to you for a few minutes. Then, I'll leave," he said, his voice almost gentle.

Eva didn't want to give in. Not the way she had last night.

"There's nothing to talk about, Rico. What happened last night, just happened. Today is a new day," she told him.

He pushed a little and Eva had to take a step back while still trying to keep him out. He'd come closer, staring at her through the opening of the door. Today, he was wearing dark shades so she couldn't see his eyes, even though she could still feel their intense gaze through the lenses.

"This is ridiculous. I'm not here to hurt you. I just want to talk and I'd rather not have your neighbors hear our entire conversation. Now, can you please, let me in?"

She didn't want to. At the same time she didn't want to feel like an idiot trying to hold the door when it was apparent that Rico was not only bigger than her, but stronger too. And he was right, she did not want her neighbors to hear them. Taking a deep breath she stepped back again, opening the door wider so that he could come in.

He smelled good, she thought as he walked past her. Really, really good and she hated herself for noticing. In the light of day, she noticed even more about him. Like the fact that he was much taller than her, probably somewhere around six feet, four inches tall, or something like that. He had an easy and confident gait as he stopped in the center of her living room and turned back to face her. Eva closed the door and then leaned against it, folding her arms over her chest. She'd let him in, but she didn't have to get close to him, because truth be told she didn't know if she could continue to resist him if she did.

He wore tan slacks today, with a matching shirt that again buttoned down the front. His shades and the camel colored tie-ups he wore made him look like he might possibly belong in an expensive black convertible, driving around South Beach, instead of standing in the middle of her Brooklyn apartment.

"Why didn't you tell me you didn't work for The Corporation?" he asked, slipping his glasses off slowly.

There were those eyes, zeroing in on her in seconds. Eva wished the floor would suddenly open up and suck her in at that moment, because while he was dressed and smelling good, she was wearing old gray sweatpants and an even older yellow t-shirt covered in multi-colored paint splotches. Her feet were bare, and so was her face. And her hair, she almost groaned. Eva Romaine wore wigs, very expensive and professionally styled wigs. While Eva Miller wore her hair natural, usually in a short curly afro. This morning, as she hadn't taken the time to do anything with it, her hair was probably more of a matted mess.

"You didn't ask," she replied tightly. "And actually, I did tell you that I'd never done that before."

He eased his hands into the front pockets of his pants, standing with his legs slightly spread as if he owned the damn world.

"It was my first time, too," he told her. "At The Corporation, I mean. I'm not an official member. I was just there on a guest pass."

"So was I," she replied.

He nodded. "I know. When I asked the floor attendant about you, she told me you were there as a guest of one of the hostesses. When I found that hostess in one of the other rooms, I asked her who you were and where you lived."

"You talked to Kenya? She gave you my address?" Eva could not believe that. Kenya was the one that had drilled into her head the importance of privacy. Never strip where you sleep, she'd told Eva.

"No," Rico said, shaking his head. "She pretty much told me to go to hell." He chuckled. "She's a good friend."

"Yes, she is," Eva added. She had a feeling that Rico wasn't used to being talked to the way Kenya had probably spoken to him. A part of her wished she'd been there to see it.

"Look, we both got the wrong idea," he said. "So let's just start over."

Then he pulled a hand out of his pocket and walked over to her, with it extended. "Hi, my name is Rico Bennett."

Eva looked at his outstretched hand and then up to his face. He was serious and she was...uncomfortable. But she wasn't rude.

She sighed. "Hello Rico, I'm Eva," she said, taking his hand.

He held it tightly as he moved even closer to her. "You're Evangeline Romaine Miller and no, you're not a prostitute. But you do work at the TEASE nightclub. What exactly do you do there, Eva?"

She yanked her hand from his so hard, Eva thought she might have dislocated her shoulder. "Who the hell do you think you are? How dare you come in here after, what...did you have me investigated? How do you know all of my business?"

"Whoa," he said, turning as she'd begun walking away from him. "It's nothing like that. When your friend wouldn't tell me where you lived, I called someone that I knew who could get me the information."

"Why?" she asked. "Why did you need to find me so badly? And I swear if you say because you wanted to pay me for last night I may just lose all my good upbringing and hit you."

Rico shook his head and looked as if he might be actually trying to hide a smile. "There's no need for violence. I said we were going to start over so I was just trying to get the preliminary stuff out in the open."

"Everything like who I am and where I work? I haven't asked you those types of questions," she quipped.

"No, you haven't," he said. "But you can."

When Eva remained silent, he continued, because that was the type of person he was. She could see that, even though she'd barely known him for twenty-four hours. If he had questions, he would get the answers. Whatever he wanted to know, he would find out. What he did after that, well, Eva assumed he did exactly what he wanted to do, each and every time.

"I'm an executive at Bennett Industries. I'm thirty-nine years old and I live in Greenwich. What else would you like to know?"

She blinked and digested that information. "Why are you here?" she asked.

"Because I couldn't stop thinking about you," he replied as simply as if he'd just given her his date of birth.

"I told you I wasn't a prostitute," she insisted. "And I don't sleep around, despite how last night may have appeared."

He looked at her seriously. "And I've never paid a prostitute to have sex with me. Despite how last night may have appeared."

"This is crazy," Eva said, sighing again and running her fingers through her short curls.

"I'll admit this is a different type of situation for me too," Rico added with a shrug. "But I'm not adverse to change."

"Well, I am," she told him. "I've had enough upheaval in my life. I was doing good here for a while, until last night."

"You liked dancing," he said, still watching her. "Do you dance at TEASE?"

"Are you asking me if I'm a stripper?"

She was standing in her house, dressed in old ratty clothes and probably looking like she'd just rolled out from under the bed, and he was asking her if she took her clothes off for money. If this scenario didn't agitate her so much, she might have thought it was funny.

Rico only lifted a brow, a dark brow amidst his light hued skin. His hair was dark too, like a raven's wing, and wavy. He had an exotic look to him, like maybe he was of a mixed race. And he was gorgeous. His strong jaw, aristocratic nose and those eyes, damn, he was just a really good looking man. And he'd gone through a lot to stand in her living room and ask her questions. Well, she figured, maybe he should get the answers he wanted. Maybe the truth would shut down his curiosity once and for all.

"Yes, Rico Bennett. I'm a stripper. I go by the name of Eva Romaine. However, I don't do private shows, so if that's what you're looking for, you'll have to show up at the club tonight at nine fifteen. And I only take cash."

❧

Rico didn't know what he wanted.

Truth be told he was still reeling from last night. From going to a sex club, to having the best sex he'd ever had in his life, with a woman, who, as it turned out, didn't even work there. He'd been beyond shocked at her words when she'd left him standing in that room, his dick still hard for her. Minutes later, after a trip to the bathroom and a couple of splashes of cold water on his face, he'd set out to find out who the hell she was.

"She doesn't work here, Mr. Bennett?" the floor attendant had told him.

"What the hell do you mean she doesn't work here? Why did you bring her to the room if she's not an employee?"

The woman raised a very elaborately arched brow at him before replying, "She was a guest here, just as you are. You requested her and we accommodated your request."

"How can I request a person that doesn't work for you? You advertise a satisfying experience here and I'm telling you right now that I am not satisfied." No, he was confused and working up to being enraged.

If she wasn't a staff member then why the hell did she let him…why did she agree to…? He didn't even know how to put it into words. This was definitely not the type of evening he'd bargained for, and yet, to a certain extent, it was.

"What's her name?" he asked through clenched teeth, his hands fisting at his sides.

"Eva Romaine," she replied.

"What's her address? How can I get in contact with her?"

"I don't have that information," she answered, shaking her head.

"Why don't you have that information? Look on your little tablet and tell me what I want to know." He was losing it, he could feel it.

This wasn't like him. Renny was the hot head of the family. Rico was normally the voice of reason. Alex was the know-it-all so he would never find himself in this predicament in the first place.

"As a guest, we only have her name and the name of the person who invited her," she told him.

"Well, who is the member? Tell me and I'll take my questions to him," he said, trying like hell to sound more reasonable.

"It's a she and she's not a member. She's a hostess. Starshine."

What the hell kind of name was that? Rico rolled his neck on his shoulders, still making the effort to calm down. He was in a sex club where women were paid to show men a good time. No matter how professional and sophisticated an outfit this place was, the type of business that took place here was still pretty simple. Which is why he was convinced that the information he sought shouldn't be this hard to ascertain.

"Where can I find Starshine?" he asked.

The floor attendant tapped on the tablet for a moment too long, and Rico walked around the desk to look over her shoulder.

"She's upstairs," he said after reading the color coded chart on the screen. "Thank you, I'll just go up there and speak to her."

"You can't do that, Mr. Bennett. She's with members right now."

"Are the members she's with shareholders in this company?" Rico asked. He was speaking of Jerald Carrington, not himself, which she probably knew. Either way, the threat was still clear.

"Sir, please. I ask that you remain courteous to all members and staff," she implored.

Rico bristled at the fact that she'd had to tell him that in the first place. His mother would have been livid if she knew that he was being anything but polite. Beatriz Bennett was a stickler for manners and respect, at all times.

"I will," he told her with a nod and walked towards the elevators.

The upper level of The Corporation was similar to the first in that there was a floor attendant waiting as soon as he stepped off the elevator. A statuesque redhead, holding the same type of tablet as the woman downstairs and sporting an ear piece that he knew meant she was aware of who he was and where he was going.

"The Aloha Room is this way, Mr. Bennett. I'll walk you down," she said coming from around the desk and leading the way down the hall.

Rico followed, asking himself over and over again why the hell he was doing this. He really needed to stop questioning himself since the answers he desired weren't coming anyway.

She paused at a black door. There were no numbers or letters or anything to delineate it from the others, but he presumed she would know the difference. When a gentleman—still dressed in his pants and dress shirt, to Rico's relief—answered, the woman asked politely to speak to Starshine. Rico had to admit he didn't know what to expect at that name. Was this woman going to be as bright as a star? So gorgeous that she shined? Or, perhaps the name represented her talents. He frowned because that was not what he wanted to think about at this moment.

When the attractive woman—who, while pretty also struck him as if she could be any woman on the street—stepped into the hallway, Rico was momentarily speechless. Nothing about tonight was as he'd thought it would be.

"I'm not telling you where she lives," had been Starshine's response after he'd asked for Eva's address. "She doesn't work here so she doesn't want to hear from any of the members."

"We had an, ah…conversation, this evening," Rico told her. "I'd just like to continue speaking with her."

Starshine shook her head adamantly. "Then you should have asked for her phone number. Or maybe you did and you struck out. Either way, I don't have to divulge her personal information. So you can find yourself another way to have a good night."

With that she was gone and Rico was left with no more information than he had before coming up here. That irritated him to no end.

So the late night call to Sam Desdune had taken place in Rico's hotel room. Rico and Sam went way back to the time when the Bennetts were receiving death threats. Sam and his private investigating firm had proven to be well worth the money they'd been paid. In minutes, the request had been made and Sam, even though he was wary, agreed to get Rico the information. By six a.m. the next morning there was a complete report on official D&D Investigations' letterhead waiting in Rico's inbox.

Standing in her apartment now, staring at a woman that looked so drastically different than she had last night, and knowing what he now knew about her was definitely surprising. And intriguing. Which was why he was still here.

"I liked watching you dance last night," he said, looking away from her.

He made her uncomfortable. He could tell by the way she fidgeted whenever he stared at her and how she kept folding and releasing her arms.

"That was a freebie," she told him.

Rico nodded and continued to move around her small living room. The furniture in here was basic, a sofa and a love seat. A recliner off to one corner, a big screen television mounted on the wall opposite the sofa. The colors were soft, beige and peach, a few knickknacks on the coffee table, framed pictures on the end tables. What really caught his eye was a large painting. It was hanging over the sofa and stretched the entire length of the wall.

It was of a dancer, that part he could see clearly. She wore a white dress that at first appeared bright against the stark black background, but then drifted away with the swaying and fluid motions of the brush. In the back of his mind he could hear the music, similar to the classical notes that were playing last night. She would be on the stage alone, moving as if the music played only for her. The uplifting of her arms, the way her head was tossed back, the effortless stretch of her body, it was absolutely perfect and the sexiest thing he'd ever seen.

Then he turned and saw Eva.

She was watching him as he looked at that painting and something in the way she was standing, the expectancy in her gaze as she waited silently, had his heart beating just a little faster.

"Did you paint this?" he asked, pointing back to the painting.

She blinked as if she wasn't yet certain if she were going to answer him.

Then she shrugged and replied, "Yes."

"You're a dancer that also paints," he said. "Why is everything about you so unexpected to me?"

He hadn't meant to speak the question out loud, but now that he did, Rico wanted that answer more desperately than any of the other questions he'd been asking himself since he'd arrived in New York.

"What else have you painted? Can I see your work?"

"No," she replied quickly. "I mean, why? I don't understand why you're here, Rico or why you want to know so much about me."

"Because I do," was the only response he could manage. "I liked watching you dance last night and I really enjoyed touching and feeling you."

She moved again, this time clasping her hands behind her back. Rico wondered if she knew how innocent and enticing that stance made her appear.

"I'm starting to think that I must like you, Eva. And since I'm not really the type of guy to mince words I figure I should tell you right now that I'm looking forward to touching and feeling you again."

She shook her head this time. "Stop it," she said, sighing and then inhaling deeply. "I can't keep up with you. First, you show up here when this is the last place in the world you should be and then you're asking why I'm a stripper and an artist. You had someone look into my background and now you're telling me you want to have sex with me again. I don't understand any of this, and to tell you the truth Mr. Bennett, I think it might just be better if you leave."

Rico did not want to leave. In fact, he could think of nothing else he'd rather do than stay here with her. Some would believe he was a man used to getting what he wanted, but they'd be sadly mistaken. Rico was a man used to doing what was expected of him. He walked the straight line and was sometimes tasked with making sure others did the same. The right thing to do here would be to respect Eva's wishes and leave. She was absolutely correct in saying that he was confusing her. Hell, Rico was confusing himself. None of what had happened from the moment he'd seen her at that club, to this very second, was something he would normally do. Yet, he couldn't find it in himself to feel any regret, or to consider backing away.

"You're right," he told her. "I apologize. This must seem really bizarre to you. I can see how it would, but believe me, I'm not here to cause you any harm. As a matter of fact, I'd like to invite you to a gallery showing. It's today at four. I can come back and pick you up."

This time she folded her arms and eyed him cautiously. "You didn't know I was an artist until just a few minutes ago and now there's suddenly a gallery showing you want to take me to. Look, I don't know what type of women you're used to dealing with, but trust me when I say, I am not the one." She stopped talking before she made it to the door, her hand poised over the knob when Rico spoke again.

"It's at the Lakefield Gallery. Lorenzo Bennett is featuring his "Love In The Springtime" collection," he told her. "And again, you are right. I didn't know you were an artist when I came here, but Lorenzo is my brother and I did have plans to stop by the gallery today to support him."

His words hit the exact mark he'd been aiming for, rendering her completely still, her back towards him.

"So, what do you say, Eva? I can come back around three to pick you up?"

CHAPTER 5

From the outside, the building looked much like other buildings in Manhattan—red brick, black iron fire escape stretching up the length of its front, large black framed windows and the address and name of whichever business it housed on a square sign.

Large slim letters, black against a platinum background, announced the Lakefield Galleries. The first floor boasted sparkling clean store-front windows and double doors, all framed in shining silver metal. Above the doors were the building's street numbers in the same contemporary font that was on the sign.

"You ready?" Rico asked.

It took Eva a moment to realize she'd been sitting in the now parked smoke gray Range Rover, not saying a word and not making any attempt to get out.

"Yes," she replied quickly. "I'm…ah, I'm ready."

He gave her a small smile before stepping out of the driver's side door. She was reaching for the passenger door handle, when it opened for her. A man dressed in black pants and a red jacket held the door wide for her to get out. Rico came up quickly, passing the man the keys to the truck. He reached for Eva's hand. She took it and let him lead her out of the truck, even though she was quite capable of getting out on her own.

"Nervous?" he asked as they stepped up onto the sidewalk.

"Not really," she lied. "I've been to an art gallery before."

He nodded, continuing to walk toward the doors. "You're extremely talented, so I'm sure you've been to more than your share of art galleries. I only asked because you're biting your bottom lip. That's normally a sign of someone being nervous."

She hadn't realized she'd been doing that and immediately ceased as they stopped in front of the double doors.

"I've never met an artist whose exhibit I'm seeing," she told him.

"Then that's another reason I'm glad I came to New York for the weekend," he said, this time, smiling as he opened the door.

He had a great smile. It formed slowly, but grabbed every bit of her attention as it grew, displaying straight white teeth and the expertly shaped mustache. Walking inside ahead of him, Eva tried not to let how handsome he was go to her head. Hell, she'd been trying all afternoon to get over how rich and successful he and his family were, as well.

Kenya had given her that information the moment they'd stepped into the dress shop on 25th Street earlier today. They'd spent a few hours shopping because Kenya was convinced Eva needed something new to wear to the gallery. Telling Kenya about the gallery invitation also meant Eva had to come clean about what she'd done last night. Kenya's reaction had been quick.

"You do know he's Ricardo Bennett, second son of three fine ass men born to Marvin Bennett, the communications mogul and Beatriz Bennett, formerly Beatriz de Carriero, the crown princess of Pirata," she'd said, all in one breath.

"Where in the world is Pirata and why do you know all of this?" Eva asked as they walked to the back of the store.

Eva very rarely shopped in the city for her clothes. The skimpy outfits she wore at work were handmade by a woman named Peaches who she and Kenya were introduced to about a week after working at the club. As for her casual wear, Eva preferred to shop online. Her size twelve, short, pants were always available online, whereas in stores they seemed to cater to the "regular" sized people of the world.

"It's a small village in Brazil and I know this because you know I'm a tech geek and a few years ago Bennett Industries merged with Coastal Technologies—which were, at the time, the bane of my existence because their accounting software sucked big time! Anyway, once Coastal merged with Bennett Industries the products they produced were of a much better quality. So I did a little research on the Bennetts and even once toyed with the idea of applying for a position there."

"You applied for a position at a multi-national company? What type of position?" Eva asked, trying not to sound so surprised.

Kenya was already pushing jackets over a rack, her attention divided between looking for something for Eva to wear, and on the conversation.

"Bennett Industries was in communications before it added the technology division, so they have this social networking department where reps tell clients how to better use social networking to benefit their businesses. You know I can tell you anything about Snapchat, Kik, Twitter, any of those sites, you name it, I've got an account and I've mastered them. How do you think so many men know about Starshine?" With that she'd given Eva a smile and a wiggle of her prettily arched brows.

Eva grinned in return.

"Okay, so Rico's a rich guy. I suspected that since he was at The Corporation," she said shaking her head at a red jacket with rhinestone lapels that Kenya held up.

"I wish I had known who he was when he'd barged in on me asking all those questions about you," Kenya continued.

Eva stopped looking at the jackets. "Would you have given him more information if you knew?"

Kenya looked up, pursing her lips as if she were really thinking about the question. "Nah, but if I'd known he was rich I would have at least called you to find out why you'd walked out on him," she said. "Which, by the way I'm still wondering. I mean, damn girl, he is super fine! Even if you didn't know about the money, how could you ignore those eyes and that body? He's built like an NBA player, tall, lean and yummy!"

Eva recalled that body, his strong arms in particular as they'd held her up against that wall and thrust deep into her. She also remembered his face very clearly and agreed wholeheartedly with Kenya, Rico Bennett was fine. He was also way out of her league, or at the very least, in a league she didn't want to get involved with.

"I was embarrassed I told you. I didn't go there to have sex with anyone," she admitted.

Kenya shook her head. "But of all the men to pick to have sex with, he was absolutely the right one."

No, Eva had thought. He wasn't. What he was now, was an opportunity.

"I'm not filling my head with any romantic notions. I just accepted his offer to go to the gallery so I can meet his brother. I've never met a real life artist before."

"Hmph, that's because you act like painting is a hobby of yours instead of pursuing it as a career," Kenya quipped. "If you got out of that apartment and tried to network at all, you'd have your paintings in a gallery and would be rubbing elbows with even more artsy folk."

Eva frowned. "That's not in the plan, you know that."

"Look, Eva, you know I love you and I love Makai, too. What you did for him is commendable and I'm sure your parents would be proud. But that boy is a grown man now. He's out here doing his own thing, so it's about time you started doing yours."

Eva hadn't wanted to have that discussion with Kenya so she'd begun talking about clothes. They'd eventually decided on the understated charcoal gray pencil skirt and crisp white blouse. A wide black belt cinched her waist in tighter, while black platform heels gave her the height that an adult woman should have, instead of the child's height she'd been cursed with.

As Rico walked his tall and fine-self beside her into the gallery, she was even more grateful for the four inch heels.

"I'm sure Renny will enjoy meeting you, especially when I tell him how talented you are," he said.

On second thought, Eva frowned as her heels clicked loudly over the glossed tile floors. The walls were white, the floor was white and there was black modular seating in a straight line down the center of the room. Behind a clear glass counter to the right were two women, one, an Asian beauty and the other a black woman with shocking lavender eyes. Both women looked at Rico and smiled. The Asian woman even waved at him. Eva tried her best not to frown.

"Look, Rico. I hope you don't think I have any high ideas about coming here. I wasn't even aware that Lorenzo had a showing today and I certainly did not know that you were his brother," she was saying, her hands tightening over the black suede clutch she carried. "I don't need, or I mean, I don't want you to tell your brother or anyone else about my work. That's my business and I'd like to keep it that way."

He'd been looking at one of the large abstracts on the left wall. It was a colorful piece, and a little busy for Eva's tastes. When he turned to her he was frowning, his thick brows creasing, dark eyes assessing. She willed her arms down to her sides, even though her fingers wanted to knead that poor clutch even more. It was hell trying not to bite on her lip, but since he'd already commented on that, Eva didn't want to give him any other reasons to think she was nervous about being here.

"I'm no art buff, but I know good work when I see it. That picture in your living room is fantastic. It had movement and emotion. The moment I saw it I felt like that woman was going to dance right over to me and wrap her long fingers around my heart," he said, then clapped his lips closed tightly.

"I mean, it was a very good portrait. Now, I haven't seen anything else you've done, but by that one alone, I would say you have a tremendous amount of talent. Which is why I've been trying to figure out all afternoon, why you would be dancing in a club instead of painting for a living."

His frown had grown, even though he was looking at her as if he could see the true answer before Eva could think to speak it. No, she thought. Her personal reasons and feelings were none of his business. That's not why she was here.

"There's a reason I do everything in my life. I'm not some daft female looking for attention or to get rich. Painting has always been a hobby for me and I'm not trying to change—"her words were cut off by a woman's voice.

"Rico!" the woman called, and now there were another pair of heels clicking across the floor. "Oh my goodness, Renny didn't tell me you were coming."

The woman, who looked to be only a bit taller than Eva, if both of them stepped out of their heels, was smiling broadly as she wrapped her arms exuberantly around Rico's neck. He hugged her close, smiling in a way that Eva hadn't seen him do so far. It was a genuine smile, just as the hug was tight and very familiar. Again, she mentally scolded herself for having any type of feeling—even though she refused to give it a name—where another woman was concerned with Rico. He wasn't her man so there was really no need for her to feel…whatever it was she felt.

"He didn't tell me about the showing," Rico said as they broke apart. "I had to read about it in the morning paper."

The woman shook her head, loose curls scraping over her cheeks with the motion. She was almost the same dark brown complexion as Eva, with larger, more expression-filled eyes and full lips. Her dress was deep red and hung perfectly over her petite frame. Eva sucked in a breath, hoping her stomach wasn't protruding from beneath the wide leather belt she wore. She had a tendency to bloat in the week or so before her cycle.

"I swear he's become so absent-minded since we had the babies," she continued.

Rico nodded. "He's always been absent-minded."

They both chuckled and then, as if finally remembering that she was standing there, Rico turned his attention to her. He reached out, touching his fingers to her elbow, and pulling her closer to him.

"This is Eva Miller," he said. "She's my guest today. Eva, this is my sister-in-law, Sabrina."

Eva smiled immediately. "It's nice to meet you, Sabrina," she said sincerely. It was really nice to meet Rico's sister-in-law, she thought, chastising herself for the assumption she'd made a few seconds ago.

"Oh, no," she said with a wave of her hand as she looked at Eva. "Just call me, Bree. Rico's never brought a guest to an event before."

"I think this was an impromptu decision for both of us," Eva replied.

"Well, whatever. Come on up. Renny's exhibit is on the second floor this time. He told Monica he would need the whole floor with all the lights out," Bree said.

She'd already taken the arm that Rico was holding of Eva's into her own hand, and was pulling Eva along as she talked.

"I'm sure Monica took that bit of direction very well," Rico said from behind them.

Bree looked over her shoulder and nodded. "You know how those two clash whenever it comes to his sculptures being on display. Actually, Renny acts like that anytime his sculptures are shown outside of his own gallery."

Then Bree looked at Eva and said, "Monica Lakefield owns and runs this gallery. She's Alex's girlfriend. You know, Alex, the oldest Bennett brother."

Eva simply nodded because she did recall Kenya saying there were three Bennett brothers.

"Well, Monica can be a bit of a pill, but Renny's pretty stubborn too. Karena, she's married to my brother Sam, and she's Monica's sister. She usually handles the exhibit but she and Sam have been trying to have another baby so she's been a little busy. If you know what I mean."

Bree laughed and Eva found the sound infectious. She grinned too and nodded. "Ah, yes, I think I know exactly what that means."

In the next few minutes they were taking an elevator up a floor, then exiting to a very dim space with golden lights shooting up from the floor to highlight every stand holding a Lorenzo Bennett sculpture.

Eva was immediately on the move, going to the first sculpture of a woman lying back on a chair, her legs spread wide, one hand between them. She wasn't a huge fan of sculptures, but Lorenzo's work had always pulled her in. Maybe because of her job, or it could be because of the emotion she always felt radiating from his pieces. It matched what she felt when she picked up her brush to paint. It started in the pit of her stomach and circled like a brewing storm, until her hands were moving, the picture in her mind coming to life on canvas.

"It's breathtaking isn't it?" Rico asked from behind her.

"Yes," she said in a small whisper. "It is."

"It's funny that I've never thought of his work using that particular term until this very moment."

He was standing close behind her now, so close his breath fanned over her neck, which was bare since she hadn't worn one of her wigs today.

"I think it's because I can so easily see you in this position," he continued and Eva shifted.

"I'll just bet you can," she replied, because there had been many nights when her pleasure was her own to find. She continued walking the floor, noting that more people were arriving and milling about.

Rico followed her, remaining silent most of the time while she looked at the pieces, her mind whirling with inspiration, fingers eager to get back to her place and paint. That's how art had always made her feel, rejuvenated. She'd turned to it after the dream of dancing had been tampered by the lack of finances, and it had always soothed her in a way that nothing else had ever been able to. Even now, after particularly hard nights at the club, Eva could come home, take a shower and go right to the canvas. There she could pour out all of her frustrations—the ones that she'd never dare let anyone see. As she'd stated to Rico, her decisions were her own to make, just as her disappointment and sadness were her own burdens to carry.

"Look what the wind blew in," she heard a male voice say.

As she turned, it was to see Rico reaching out and clasping another guy's hand and being pulled in for a hug. The other guy was an inch or so taller than Rico, and much broader in the chest and shoulder area. He was also handsome, his skin just a shade darker than Rico's.

"When I called you and Renny you both said nothing was going on this weekend," Rico was saying to the guy when they'd stepped away from each other.

"Yeah, that's because we know the art gallery isn't really the place you like to hang out," the guy said. "There's no boardroom here."

Rico smirked, but laughed anyway.

"Alex, I'd like you to meet Eva Miller. Eva, this is my older brother, Alex," Rico said.

Eva shook his hand and smiled, seeing the resemblance in their dark eyes and brows, the wavy hair and the strong jaw. "Hello, Alex. It's nice to meet you."

It was nice meeting Rico's family, even though it shouldn't have mattered to her at all.

"No, Eva. I can assure you that the pleasure is all mine," Alex said after shaking her hand. "This is the first time Rico has ever introduced me to one of his female friends. I feel like it's a holiday or something."

Rico did frown at that, but Eva held her smile in place. "We just met and decided to come here today."

Why had she said that?

"I told her I could introduce her to Renny," Rico said before she had a chance to try and correct herself.

"Trying to score some brownie points by saying you know the guy that creates these sexy pieces. I hear you, little brother," Alex joked.

"Hey, you guys look to be having way too much fun over here," another woman—who Eva was glad to see was curvy like her—said.

She was accompanied by another man who had immediately stared at Eva. His intense gaze made her just a little uncomfortable and she found herself taking a step closer to where Rico was standing.

"It's good to see you," the woman said to Rico as they met for a hug. "Sam didn't mention you were in town."

"We just decided to come to the exhibit this morning," Eva blurted out. "It wasn't planned."

Everyone stared at her and she wished there was someplace she could hide, she was so embarrassed. What the hell was she doing? Why were these people making her nervous?

"Ah, this is Eva Miller. Eva, this is Sam and Karena Desdune," Rico said by way of introduction.

"And this," Bree said coming to join them, with her husband in tow. "Is the love of my life and the creator of these magnificent pieces, Mr. Lorenzo Bennett."

He was the first to come toward her, his arm outstretched. "Hi, you can call me Renny. I'm glad to see my brother has such great taste in women."

Eva's heart was thumping wildly as she extended her hand to his. "It's such a pleasure to meet you, Mr. Bennett. I really enjoy your work. It's so dramatic and sexy, but that's not all, there's so much depth and emotion in every piece. They just reach out and grab you the moment you see them."

"Wow, okay," Renny said, looking over his shoulder to Rico. "Not only is she pretty as a picture, but she has some art knowledge as well. Good job, bro."

"She's also a very talented painter. Talk about emotional and sexy," Rico said.

He had the good sense to look sorry and shrug when she pinned him with a heated glare.

"Oh, you paint?" Karena asked. "Do you have an agent? Are you showing anywhere now?"

"It's not abstract is it?" Bree asked. "I keep trying but I just cannot get into all those lines and shapes and things."

Everyone was staring at her and again Eva was uncomfortable. She shouldn't be, but she was. She didn't know these people and nobody, besides Kenya and Makai, knew that she painted. Now there were six sets of eyes on her, expecting her to say something, to tell them whatever they wanted to hear she guessed. Nervously, Eva licked her lips and clutched her purse again.

"I'm not a professional by any means. I just do a little painting here and there in my spare time," was her response.

"I'd love to see your work," Karena said. "We're always on the hunt for new and undiscovered talent."

"New and undiscovered talent? Where?" a tall, punch-in-the-gut sexy woman said as she joined the group.

Alex slipped an arm around her waist and Eva assumed this was Monica Lakefield, the manager of this gallery.

"Rico's girlfriend paints and he says she's really good," Karena told her.

"I'm not his girlfriend."

"We're just friends."

Eva and Rico spoke simultaneously.

"Uh huh, sure," Bree said sharing knowing glares with the rest of the group. "We're going to go work the room."

"Right," Karena added. "We are working here. But I meant what I said, Eva. I'd like to see your work. Here's my card. Maybe we can schedule something this week."

"How about tomorrow for brunch?" Monica asked. "If she's good I don't want to wait for someone else to snap her up. We can meet at your parents' restaurant." Monica nodded towards Sam.

Karena touched her husband's arm. "That's great. Then I can get your mom to watch Elijah since you have that conference call with Trent Donovan," she told him.

Sam nodded. "I can call them now and make a reservation."

"Wonderful," Monica said. She pulled out her own business card and slipped a pen from Alex's inside jacket pocket to write on the back of it. "Here's the address to Lucien's. They have wonderful beignets. We'll have some with coffee and look at your work. Tomorrow at eleven thirty. Does that work for you?"

No. Yes. Well, what the hell?

"Sure," Eva ended up saying. "But I don't really think you'll be interested."

"Nonsense," Karena said. "Let us be the judge of that. And even if we aren't impressed, we can still have those delicious beignets."

Alex nodded his head with a grin toward Rico. "The beignets are delicious."

Rico, who looked as surprised and she'd venture to say, as worried as Eva was, only frowned at his brother in response. "Yeah. They're delicious alright."

This weekend was truly a time for firsts in Rico's book. Hours after being at the art gallery, watching in quiet amazement as Eva surveyed each one of Renny's pieces, he was dropping her off at a night club where she worked. As a stripper.

For a while today, he'd been able to forget what her profession was and concentrate solely on the woman. He found himself really enjoying that woman. The way she smiled, the tone of her voice as she spoke knowledgeably about the art surrounding them to other patrons. She'd even suggested a portrait for an older woman to purchase after a fifteen minute discussion on the colors and the tone of the work. The woman had thanked Eva profusely, telling her she'd be sure to tell the gallery managers how well their staff was trained. Rico had been offended that the woman would have automatically assumed that she was a staff member as opposed to a buyer, or artist herself. But when he said something, Eva had just shrugged and said,

"People always see what they want to see when they look at someone. I can't help if they get it wrong and it's not my job to convince them otherwise."

He'd thought about those words moments after the woman was long gone. Maybe he was a bit naïve, but Rico always presumed people were thinking the right things about him. Especially since he'd made it a point to do the right thing much more often than not. As a young boy he'd quickly learned exactly what his parents had expected of him—to get an education, to work for the family company, to possess integrity and therefore demand respect from his peers. Rico had done just that. He'd gone to the right school—receiving his MBA in Business from Harvard—worked for his father's company as the chief financial officer, and maintained an impeccable professional and social reputation. Not once, in all his years had he ever veered from the path that he'd known was set before him. He was, he believed, exactly what people thought he was.

Eva, he could now see, was not.

"Thank you for today," she'd said as she reached for the door handle to get out of the truck. "I really appreciate you introducing me to your brother, and your family." She said the last with a little chuckle.

He'd smiled too. "I wasn't really counting on all of them being there. But I guess I should have figured they would be. Actually, the only ones missing were Bree's older sister, Lynn and her husband, Brice. Their son, Jeremy, had a soccer tournament this weekend. Still, they can be a lot to digest all at once, so I'll apologize if they made you uncomfortable."

"Oh no," she'd replied, shaking her head. "I had a good time with them. I didn't know how today would turn out, but I'm actually glad I accepted your invitation."

"I was happy to extend it," he said, not wanting her to get out of the truck. "How about you call-in sick and we go somewhere for a late dinner?"

"No," she replied immediately. "I can't do that."

"Why? I haven't been such a bad host today, have I? I mean, I think I only hit on you once considering we spent over an hour standing in a room full of naked sculptures."

She laughed again and Rico thought he'd never heard anything as endearing. She was very pretty, a small dimple appearing in her left cheek when she really laughed. Her skin looked so smooth, he barely resisted the urge to rub his fingers along the line of her jaw, or to pull her close and kiss her mouth softly.

"I'm a working woman, Rico. I need my paycheck and my tips. Calling out is very rarely an option for me," she told him.

"I heard you telling Bree that it's been you and your brother for a long time now. Is he much younger than you? Do you support him financially too? Is that why you work here?"

Because, for the life of him, he could not figure her out. She was beautiful and smart, a talented dancer and painter. So why wasn't she doing one of those things professionally? Why this club and why be a stripper?

"I have a responsibility," she said. "To myself and to my brother. I know you may not understand it, since I'm sure I'm not the type of woman you're used to meeting, but it is what it is. This is my life."

Her words had been said so simply and matter-of-factly as if there was no reason to ever question them. Yet, Rico did. She was so much more than what she thought she was and he hated that she couldn't or wouldn't see that.

She'd stepped down out of the truck and ran—as it had begun to drizzle—into the side entrance of the club, while he'd sat behind the wheel watching her go.

This was it, he thought. She was gone and now he could leave as well. Sure, the weekend wasn't technically over, but he'd had the terrific sex he'd planned for last night, and he'd assuaged his guilty conscience for not paying her by taking her to the gallery to meet Renny. They were now even and he could just drive back to the hotel, order room service and check his emails. In the morning he would check-out and head home to his normal life.

So why was he driving further up the street to where he'd glimpsed a parking spot?

Rico had never been in a strip club before. Sure, he'd attended a few bachelor parties where strippers were the main attraction, but those had been in hotels or rented venues, never in an actual strip club. He'd shaken his head as he paid the cover charge and walked inside, listing another "first" for this trip.

It didn't take long, he thought, about fifteen minutes after he'd arrived and had found a booth seat way in the back of the place. Her name was announced by a woman dressed in a long black silk robe with more sparkling things on it than a Christmas tree. The room was pretty dark, with most of the light coming from the small purple holders in the center of each table and the spotlights that surrounded the stage. It was a simple introduction, one that resulted in immediate applause from the just about full house of men and, to Rico's surprise, women.

When the curtain opened the applause was still going as the eerie intro to The Weeknd's "The Hills" began to play. It wasn't a song that Rico listened to frequently, but Gabriella loved to blast anything by The Weekend while she was working out, so he'd just heard this song a few days ago. But never, not in all his dreams, would he have imagined watching someone dance to this song, the way Eva was now doing.

The first thing he noticed was that her hair had changed. She'd put on a wig, with long curly hair that moved over her skin, brushing the heavy mounds of her breasts the way he figured each man in this room wished his fingers could. Her outfit was simple, and yet jaw-dropping at the same time—a red thong, with rhinestones marching down the back disappearing between the plump globes of her otherwise bare ass. The top was red also, with more rhinestones, this time lining the top edge of the bra so that it almost made the generous cleavage she displayed appear highlighted by the sparkling. The shoes she wore were silver, with dangerously high heels that she moved in as easily as if she were barefoot.

The crowd was captivated by her.

Rico was captivated by her.

It seemed like much longer—a lifetime perhaps—but was most likely only seconds later when she ripped the bra away, tossing it across the stage, her breasts jiggling with the motion, as something like glittering stickers covered her nipples. The crowd went wild, people immediately jumped out of their seats and headed for the stage. Rico's dick had grown so hard, his eyes so glazed as he'd been watching that he couldn't move. Forget about moving, right about now, breathing was a task.

She dominated that stage and the attention of every one in that room as she moved. He couldn't take his eyes off her, even though he wanted to when he saw the men rushing up to tuck the dollar bills in the ban of her thong. More money was tossed on the stage as she danced from one end to the other, giving the crowd exactly what they wanted. A part of him, the very primal part, wanted to pull her off that stage and sink his length deep inside of her once more. Especially when she lifted one leg, stretching it straight up while her hand gripped the heel of her shoe, to keep the leg upright. Rico had immediately recalled holding that same leg up while thrusting in and out of her last night. He recalled it and damn, he wanted to do it again.

All of these thoughts were in immediate contrast to the possessive part of him, the part that hated the fact that her breasts, and just about every other inch of her body was bared for these strangers to ogle and fantasize about. That part wanted to run up there and carry her away from this madness. But he couldn't. This was her job. Eva Romaine was a stripper. It was her life, as she'd told him not too long ago. There wasn't anything he could do about that. Nothing, he should want to do. He shouldn't have come inside. Going back to the hotel and checking his email now seemed like a much better idea.

Yet, Rico still did not move.

He couldn't.

Not until the song was over and Eva was taking a bow. She bent low at the waist before coming back up to smile at the crowd. That's when she saw him. Rico felt her gaze as it locked with his, through that dark room and over all those people. He stared and so did she. Until the curtain began to close and she hurriedly backed up behind it before the material was caught around her body.

He was up and out of his seat in seconds, heading back toward the bar, and the walkway he'd seen other staff members using.

"Whoa, there, handsome. Just where do you think you're going?"

A woman—wait, Rico did a double-take—yes, it was a woman, dressed in jeans that sagged just a bit below her waist and a black t-shirt that didn't quite hide the curve of her breasts, and black Doc Martin boots. She'd stepped into the doorway he wanted to walk through to get to Eva, and now she had a hand flat on his chest as if that were going to be enough to keep him there. Actually, for the sake of not making a scene, it was enough. Still, he frowned as he looked down at her hand, then back up to her face. She'd cut off all her hair, until the barbered style was closer to her scalp than Rico usually received.

"I need to see someone," he told her, again looking down at the hand that was still pressed against his chest.

A slow smile began to spread across her light-skinned face.

"You wanna go back there and see Eva Romaine, I bet," she said, before shaking her head.

"That's big bucks, my man. And you've got to wait over there in one of the booths for her to come out," she continued.

"Now you know Eva don't do no booth work," the bartender, who for some reason had come all the way to the end of the bar to enter the conversation, announced.

"I don't want her in any booth," Rico told them. "Look, if its money you want. I'll pay whatever the fee is, I just have to get back there to see her."

He'd already pulled out his wallet and was getting to the bills when one of his business cards almost fell from its slot. The woman finally moved her hand then, to reach down and scoop it up before Rico could be shocked that she'd done that in the first place.

"Ricardo Bennett," she said as if tasting the name to see if it satisfied her. "You some fancy pants corporate guy, huh, Ricardo?"

She was waving the card back and forth in front of her face like a fan. "A fine ass fancy pants," she added, looking him up and down. "How much you willing to pay?"

"What's the regular fee?" Rico asked.

"There ain't none for Eva, 'cause she don't do no booth time. I said that already," the bartender, with the long rusty colored beard stated.

"How much you willing to pay for that ass?" the woman continued. "I can set it up so you have a real good time, Ricardo." She moved closer to him, this time rubbing the edge of the card along Rico's jaw. "A really good time. What you think about having two along for the ride?"

"He thinks that's gross," Eva said as she pushed through the black curtain that served as a door. "One man, one woman, and one, whatever you're trying to be. No thanks, Nadja."

Eva now wore a short gray trench that was belted tightly at her waist. She still wore the silver shoes she'd had on while dancing and the curly wig was still affixed. Grabbing Rico's arm she pulled him away from the woman he now knew was named Nadja.

"Let's go," she told him.

He followed her out of the club without another word and without looking back.

They weren't outside two seconds before she released his arm and whirled around to face him.

"What the hell do you think you're doing? That's where I work, Rico. Where I dance and nothing else. I told you before, I'm not a prostitute."

The wind had picked up since they'd been inside, blowing her curls until they were partially covering her face and she used her fingers to push the hair back behind her ear.

"I know you're not a prostitute," he replied. "I wasn't implying that you were."

"You were going to pay Nadja to let you come back and see me," she insisted.

"To 'see' you, Eva. That's all I was going to pay her for."

"Well, she obviously got another impression."

"I don't give a damn what impression she got. I wanted to see you. If it meant paying off that petty bouncer, then so be it," he stated.

She was shaking her head. "I just don't understand you. I don't get why you're still here. Why you came to see me? Why any of this is happening?"

"That makes two of us," he told her. "Look, let me just take you for a drink. We can talk some more and see if either of us can figure out this connection between us."

When she opened her mouth to speak, Rico raised a hand and shook his head this time.

"Please don't insult us both by denying it. There's something that keeps pulling us together. I don't know why and neither do you. Don't you think we at least owe it to ourselves to try and figure it out?"

She looked like she wanted to tell him no, but she didn't.

"Fine. One drink," she said with a pointed look.

Rico nodded in agreement. "One drink."

CHAPTER 6

She never said where they had to go to have that 'one' drink, Rico thought as he let her into his hotel room.

A few minutes later he'd fixed them both a glass of wine at the mini-bar in his suite. She'd put the duffel bag she'd carried out of the club down by the couch and walked to stand near the patio doors, arms folded over her chest, still wearing her coat.

"Tell me how you came to be responsible for taking care of your brother," he said as he approached, arm outstretched offering her the glass.

The look she gave him said that was the last thing she wanted to talk about. Still, she took the drink and sipped from it slowly as her gaze returned once more to the outside. He'd used the company's directory to find a hotel for the weekend, but had called to book the penthouse suite himself. The glass doors opened to a rooftop patio that he hadn't had time to go out and explore. The way Eva was staring through those doors, he couldn't help but offer.

"We can go outside if you'd like."

She took another sip and then nodded. "I would like some air."

With a nod Rico flipped the latch on the door and slid it to the side. "After you," he said and watched her walk out before him.

He followed, closing the door behind them. She walked immediately to where the lounge chairs and tables were set.

"I guess people have lots of parties out here," she said, her back turned to him.

"I guess," he said. "I'm not really a party person."

"Neither am I," she said as she turned to face him. "I guess that's something we have in common."

"I guess so."

They fell quiet again as Rico gave her time to decide whether or not she was going to answer his request.

She moved further away from him, going to stand near a potted plant. Her gaze fell to her glass, her fingers gripping the stem much too tightly. It was obvious this wasn't an easy topic for her and he was just about to tell her it was okay, that they could talk about something else, when she looked up at him.

"My parents died when I was seventeen years old," she began. "A man—Theodore Tremill—had a heart attack while driving his eighteen-wheeler. He was traveling from Daytona to Maine, driving along the highway on that rainy night in April, when they said the pain radiated up his left arm so fast and so strong that he let go of the steering wheel to grab it. As he opened his mouth to yell his chest seized and the truck, going more than eighty-five miles an hour, crossed two lanes and jumped the median strip to crash head-on into my father's Ford Taurus."

Rico gulped the rest of his wine, then set the glass down on the small table closest to him.

"They were dead instantly. No suffering," she continued. "That's what the doctor told us, but I've never really believed that. I mean, there was an instant where they had to see that truck barreling toward them. Just a few seconds when they knew they would never see their children again. That, would have been suffering for them. It would have been heartbreaking."

"Just as it was for that seventeen-year-old girl," Rico said.

She inhaled deeply, dumping what was left of her wine into the plant soil. "For the first few hours I was too stunned to really feel anything. I heard people around me talking but I couldn't understand anything they were saying. Nothing except that my parents were never coming back."

Still twisting that glass between her fingers she shook her head in an attempt to keep the hair out of her face.

"Makai had just turned ten two months before. When the police officer and the social worker had showed up at our house that night with the news, he'd been in bed. I let him sleep until the morning. Since it was close to four a.m. when they'd arrived, the social worker agreed to stay a couple more hours until I could wake him and tell him at a decent hour. We spent the first week in a foster home. The woman, Mrs. Fields, she didn't want a seventeen-year-old girl, but she was willing to keep Makai. He screamed like he was in pain at the thought of us being separated and I thought of the first thing I could to keep us together.

"We had a neighbor named Ms. Ruby. She'd babysat for us a few times when I wasn't old enough to stay at home with Makai by myself. I figured she'd been okay then, so why not ask her if she could let us stay with her a few more months. My birthday is July first. I was going to turn eighteen then and I could legally take care of Makai on my own. Ms. Ruby didn't like the idea at first, not until the social worker told her how much money she would receive from the state, per child. So she agreed and Makai and I stayed together."

"When you turned eighteen you took him?" Rico asked when she'd gone quiet again, this time looking up at the starless sky.

"I was so naïve back then," she said with a sigh. "I didn't have anything when I was eighteen. Our parents had life insurance policies, but they were both small and they'd borrowed against them so many times that there was hardly any value left. On my eighteenth birthday I received a check from the insurance company for seventeen hundred dollars. I knew that wasn't enough to find a place and pay bills, so I looked for a job instead of leaving Ms. Ruby's immediately.

"The state check for me stopped coming, so my seventeen hundred dollars went to Ms. Ruby as my room and board for two more months. Ms. Ruby didn't like us being there and she didn't even try keeping that a secret. One day she slapped Makai because he'd spilled the milk from his bowl of cereal. Makai hated milk, but Ms. Ruby was insistent that he eat and or drink whatever she put in front of him. I hit her with the broom and told her if she touched him again I'd kill her. From that moment on I was every ungodly name in the book. Ms. Ruby did nothing else for Makai, except let him eat and sleep there. I cooked for him, cleaned up after him, washed his clothes and got him ready for school."

Eva took a deep breath and released it slowly.

"I was so excited when I found a job at a sport's bar, waiting tables. The tips were good and the best part was that the manager had an apartment on the upper level of the building. She let me move in there with Makai. Two years later, Kenya, she was the manager at the sport's bar, got an offer for the job at TEASE. She told me it was in Manhattan and how much money she would be making and she asked me to come with her. Even though we'd long since moved out of Ms. Ruby's place, she was still making noises about possibly trying to get Makai back in her custody. I knew it was just so that she could get that state check once more, but I didn't feel like trying to fight her. So, since I had two mouths to feed and every time I heard from Ms. Ruby I became nervous about being able to keep my freedom, we moved."

"Where did you live before?" Rico asked her, feeling as if he wanted to either shake Ms. Ruby, or have her ass arrested himself.

"Hartford, Connecticut," she replied.

He nodded. "Not that far from me. I live in Greenwich."

That meant that for a while she'd lived very close to him. He wondered what would have happened if he'd met her before now, under different circumstances. Eva didn't look like that information made any difference to her.

She let out a breath and shrugged. "So that's how I got Makai and that's how I started working at TEASE."

"You wanted to take care of your little brother, I get it," he said.

Eva shook her head. "I *had* to take care of my little brother. It's the way my parents would have wanted it. Getting a good education and good jobs was important to them. They always taught us to study hard. So I made sure Makai studied hard and had everything he needed to get a good education. I was making so much at TEASE that I was able to send him to a private school for the middle and high school years. And then when it was time for college, he received a partial scholarship, but he didn't have to worry because I made enough money to pay for the rest. He's a junior now at Columbia, majoring in business. He's already getting offers for internships at big companies, so he's going to graduate and make something of himself."

"While you continue to show strangers your tits and pick up dollar bills from the floor," he said quietly. "I'm almost positive that's not the life your parents had planned for you."

"You don't know that, Rico. You don't know anything about them, or me for that matter. Just because I told you all this about my past doesn't mean squat. You're still who you are and I'm still me. You come from a rich and fancy house in Greenwich while there were days I wondered where our next meal would come from and if or when the power company was going to realize I'd given them a bad check."

There was a moment of silence, when the wind blew around them and the years of their pasts between them. Rico admired her in that moment. He respected the young girl who had taken a tremendous responsibility on her shoulders and made it work. He also valued the woman that stood before him with absolutely no shame in the decisions she'd made. Just as he'd always been certain that everything he'd done in his life was the right choice, Eva had no doubts or recriminations about her life and with her fierce confidence, dared anyone else to feel any for her.

"You wanna know something, Eva? I don't think any of that matters," Rico told her honestly. "I know people say you should get to know someone, date a person, and find out who they really are before you make any commitments or any long term plans. And at another time I'm sure I would have believed that wholeheartedly. But not here, not now. And not with you."

She sighed.

"There's nothing here for us, Rico. You live in your world and I live in mine. It's that simple," she told him.

"I want you, Eva," he replied, taking a step closer to her. "I know that right at this very moment, I want you more than I want air. The tips of my fingers are tingling with the urge to run them across your silken smooth skin. My tongue is moist and ready to lick along the inside of your thigh and that thin string of the fire engine red thong you're wearing. That's what I know, Eva and dammit, that's simple too."

He was standing right in front of her, the cool pelting of the first raindrops splattering against his face as they began to fall. Rico ignored them, reaching out to yank the belt of her coat free.

He pushed the lapels open, his bare hands touching the searing skin of her waist as he pulled her closer to him.

She came into his arms willingly, her lips parted as she blinked against the rain. "I watched you while I danced," she told him.

Rico's body hardened, his erection pressing painfully against the zipper of his pants. He lowered his head to kiss her, but she avoided the contact.

"When I first started working at TEASE, Kenya told me to find one person in the room and imagine I was dancing for that person alone, instead of an entire room of horny men."

Her words were a whisper against the damp air, her lips so close to his he groaned as they moved.

"I never did that. Instead I danced for myself. In my mind there was only me and the music and I danced until the music stopped, not looking at any one person, or even caring that they were there. But tonight," she said and took a breath. "Tonight, it was all for you. I don't know why."

"I don't care why," he said, touching his lips urgently to hers. He sucked the bottom one into his mouth, then licked the top one, alternating, until she wrapped her arms around his neck and pulled him closer.

She took over from there, kissing him with unfettered hunger, working his mouth as expertly as she'd worked that pole. Rico's hands went to her ass, gripping each globe as his eyes closed and he remembered the way they'd bounced as she'd moved on stage. The strip of rhinestone-covered red silk glistened through her cheeks and his mouth had watered at the thought of licking her there. For now he sucked her tongue into his mouth, loving the moan this act solicited from her.

The rain was coming down harder now, but Rico barely felt it. He was burning for her, his hands moving over as much of her flesh as he could manage to touch, until pushing the coat over her shoulders was a necessity. She wore only the bra and thong she'd had on when they'd left the club, the long curly tresses, now straight and hanging down the center of her back as Rico arched over her so that he could lick and suckle her neck.

It was Eva who pulled herself upright, pushing him back as she walked. "You said you want me, now," she told him as they moved. "I want you, too."

"Here I am," he replied. "Take what you want."

He hadn't expected her to push him until he fell back onto one of the two cushioned couches that decorated the rooftop deck.

"That's exactly what I plan to do," she said before reaching around him and into his back pocket for his wallet.

She removed the foil packet then tossed the leather pouch to the side as she ripped it open. Rico was already working the buckle and zipper of his pants, releasing his rigid length, hissing as the cool drops of rain fell onto his heated flesh. Her hands moved quickly, efficiently, grasping him at the base, holding him as she deftly slid the latex down and over his length. Then she was straddling him, reaching up to grab the wet strands of her hair and toss them back over her shoulders once more.

Rico gripped her hips, loving the sight of water running in seductive rivulets between her breasts and down her torso. Leaning forward he licked them, the salty and sweet taste sending punches of lust straight to his dick. She came over him then, her legs open wide as he guided her down slowly. She'd gripped his shoulders, her nails digging into his skin. The second his tip touched the warm opening of her center, Rico's gaze jerked up to find hers. She was staring directly at him, biting her bottom lip as she lowered inch by delicious inch, down his shaft.

He groaned, holding her still when he was completely impaled. Kissing the rise of her breasts over the bra she wore Rico began to suck the skin. There would be a mark when he was finished and he didn't give a damn. Actually, that's what he wanted. To mark her. Claim her. Make her his forever.

She moved then, rising up until he was almost completely out of her, then slamming down again. Up and down, up and down, she rotated her hips and moved over him, while the rain poured down around them. It was chilly and then it was scorching. His hands held her tightly as she bounced over him. Hers held him tightly as if she couldn't bear to let go. Somewhere in the distance there may have been thunder, but all Rico could hear was the blood pounding through his veins.

He'd told her that he wanted her and she was giving him her all. She arched backward, her head falling back. Rain slapped against her skin leaving her heaving flesh saturated as she continued to work him. Rico held her tightly, thrusting upward to meet her rhythmic strokes. With his hold firm on her, he came to his feet and she instinctively wrapped her legs around his back. His thrusts came faster, in and out he slammed into her, holding her as she continued to arch, moaning and writhing with his every stroke.

The slapping sound of their skin meeting was almost drowned out by the persistent patter of the rain. Rico didn't care. He had no thoughts about being outside while at the same time buried deep inside of her. All he could think of was how good her hot walls felt clamping around his dick. How wonderful her warm skin felt beneath his hands. She was beautiful as she rode him, like some warrior goddess on a mission to conquer.

Well she could have him, she could wield her powers around him and wrap him in the delicious passion that enveloped them now. Anything, that's what he would give her at this moment, any damn thing she wanted.

"Rico!" she yelled his name as her thighs tightened around him.

"Yes, baby, yes," he murmured, his fingers digging into her hips the same way hers were holding onto his shoulders.

They came together, on the rooftop deck, in the rain.

He'd carried her into the room when they were done, stopping at the bathroom where he watched her walk in. She went straight to the mirror, stripping off her coat, the bra and the thong that had been twisted with their previous actions. Without looking over to him, she reached up her hands and pulled out pins that he figured held the now wet and stringy wig in place. After removing it, her blunt-tipped fingers ran through the short curls of her natural hair and then she turned on the water at the sink.

"You're beautiful without the wigs," he told her.

She'd taken one of the cloths from the basket on the side of the sink and used it to wipe the rain and some of the make-up from her face. Turning to look at him, she smiled. "Thanks. Eva Romaine needs the hair. It adds to the show."

Rico nodded. He could see that. It was sexy as hell to see those long strands of hair rubbing over her breasts, then scraping over her bare back as he watched her ass gyrating. "I like Eva Miller much better."

She didn't look at him that time, but kicked her shoes off and headed for the shower. After she'd stepped beneath the spray of water and didn't close the stall door, Rico figured she was inviting him in.

They didn't speak while she lathered another cloth and ran it slowly over his chest. Eva had never bathed a man before, but she wanted her hands on Rico, there was no more denying that. Kenya had been right, he was lean and tall and yummy! And he was standing naked in a shower with her. Never in a million years would she have ever imagined being with a man this way. She'd never even allowed herself to think along the lines of a relationship and now…well, this wasn't exactly a relationship. But it felt damn good, just the same.

She rubbed over his shoulders, down his arms, over abs that she swore looked like they should be on the cover of a fitness magazine. That's when she saw it, the small tattoo just beneath his right arm. It was a heart with a skull in its center. Curious now, she lifted his other arm and saw another tat, this one was of a snake, winding its way around a bulging bicep. He didn't say a word as she assessed his body art, even when she turned him around so that she could see his back. There, a little larger than the other two, but not so big that it would ever be seen if he wore a tank top, was another one. Her soapy fingers ran along the letter "B" with all the vines moving in and out of it, twirling together, until just beneath the design it read "Family. Love. Forever."

"A few years ago my family was threatened by a lunatic that not only wanted to take down our company, but also tried to hurt us physically," he said, his hands planted flat on the clear glass wall of the shower.

Eva continued to rub her hands over his back, down to his taut buttocks, and then back up the sides where she knew the other two tats were.

He answered, without her even having to ask.

"Other execs at the company weren't happy when I waltzed in, fresh out of grad school to take the top financial position in the company. Never mind that my father had built the company or that I'd graduated in the top five percent of my class in undergrad and grad school. I wasn't good enough. Until I had to show them just how good I was for the position. They tried lots of things behind my back, but in the end, I was able to weed out the snakes and rise as the victor," he told her, his voice calm, level.

He took a deep breath and she watched as his muscles contracted, the strength in his body on full display even as it rippled through her fingers.

"I dated this girl in college. I thought she was really nice. I trusted her. She was also dating a guy on the basketball team. Trying to weigh her options, I suppose. When he announced he was heading into the NBA draft, she was right beside him, declaring him the love of her life." He shrugged. "The rest is history I guess."

"These aren't the normal spots for a tattoo," she said when he'd turned to face her again.

"Doesn't look good for an executive to walk into the office with tats showing. Nobody in my family even knows I have them. It's just my thing."

Eva nodded, figuring out something she wasn't sure Rico would have ever said to her, or to anyone else for that matter. "You don't want anyone to know that you've ever had a weakness, do you?"

"I wouldn't say that," he replied.

"You wouldn't because that's not the right thing to say. Do you always do the right thing, Rico? Are you so perfect that having a broken heart, or needing to prove yourself to someone, or even being afraid of losing your family has to be kept a secret?"

"I don't keep secrets," he told her, moving so that she had no choice but to back up against the shower wall.

"But you don't share your feelings with anyone either," she said, her hands still moving along his warm skin.

"You want to know what I'm feeling right now?" he asked, pressing closer so that his rigid length tapped her lower belly.

The reaction was instant and potent, desire shooting through her like a burst of fireworks.

"I think I can figure it out," she whispered, her fingers already kneading his muscled biceps.

It didn't take long, maybe a second or two for him to cup her ass, lifting her until her legs were wrapping around his waist. He slipped into her so surely and deeply that she gasped and then she simply held on. The feel of him so deep and thick inside of her was intense and never failed to make Eva forget any and everything else that was going on around them. Hell, she'd just had sex with him outside in the rain, for crying out loud. And now, here they were again, and he felt just as good—no, better— than he had before.

How could he know just how to move, just which angle to drive to make her heart beat faster and her thighs quiver? She was so wet and slick for him, each and every time. The feel of him going in and out, slow and then fast and then slow again, she could barely catch her breath. Then he was moaning, his face buried in the nape of her neck as he held her close. She held him tightly, loving the feel of holding this complex man in her arms. It didn't matter if he never admitted any feelings for her, or if she ever saw him again, right now was all that counted. That's what she tried to tell herself, even when she climaxed, whispering his name and then feeling his deeper thrusts when he joined her in release.

It didn't matter.

And yet, it did.

"Don't tell me you didn't enjoy that," Rico said.

They'd managed to finish their shower and made it all the way to the bedroom before reality kicked in. Eva was now, walking out of the bedroom, wearing the skirt and blouse she'd had on yesterday at the gallery. Rico followed her.

"That would be lying and like you Rico, that's not really my thing," she replied.

"Then I don't get it. What's the problem? Why can't you spend the night with me?"

She'd picked up her jacket and was now pushing her arms into it. "And then what? What happens in the morning?"

"Well, for starters, you go to the meeting with Monica and Karena to see about getting your paintings out to the public," he told her.

"I've already thanked you for taking me to the gallery. If something comes of that meeting, I'll thank you for that as well," she quipped and grabbed her purse. "But that's it, Rico. There's nothing else for us. You don't even live in this state."

"I don't live in another country," he countered. "Location is something we can work with. I can come here for weekends. Once you start selling your paintings, you could even move to Greenwich. You said Makai's majoring in business, I'm sure I could find him a job at my company if you're worried about leaving him. We can make this work, Eva."

She looked at him incredulously.

"I feel like I have to keep telling you that I'm not a prostitute," she said in a quiet voice.

"And I feel like I have to continuously remind you that I've never called you, or treated you like one," he said, anger bubbling in his gut as she moved closer to the door, that duffle bag now on her shoulder. "You're the one that keeps bringing that up. I'm trying to tell you that we can do this. We can find time to spend with each other if it's what we really want. Hell, I'll pay for the apartment for you and for Makai. I'll give you whatever you want."

She had opened the door by that point and turned partially so that she could look at him. Rico's hands fisted at his sides as he noticed, as if for the first time, how sad she actually looked.

"Can you hear yourself? You may not be saying the word 'prostitute', but what you're suggesting would sure as hell make me feel like one. Goodbye, Rico."

The door closed and she was gone before Rico took his next breath.

CHAPTER 7

Eva didn't touch the beignets even though they looked and smelled delicious. She was afraid her topsy-turvy stomach would reject the doughy treats the moment she chewed and swallowed. She sipped her mimosa instead, slowly, but surely.

Monica Lakefield had already unzipped Eva's portfolio. The portfolio she'd hastily put together this morning. Years ago Makai had given her a leather carrier for Eva to transport her paintings, but she'd never taken them anywhere. They all sat in her room, propped against the wall in stacks she'd organized by theme. Or rather moods—because painting had always served a therapeutic purpose for her, she categorized them by whichever mood she was in when she painted them. The pictures of her paintings she'd chosen to show the Lakefield sisters were a mixture of happy, sad and content.

The older Lakefield sister had perfectly manicured nails and one gorgeous diamond ring sparkling from a finger on her right hand. So Monica and Alex were dating, but not engaged. That was something to know, Eva thought as she waited, less than impatiently, for her to speak.

"How long have you been painting?" Karena asked.

Eva cleared her throat and scooted closer to the table. "I'd always enjoyed art class in school and after my parents could no longer pay for the formal dance classes, I went back to painting with my water colors and looking at the art magazines I checked out of the library. I was thirteen then. I began painting seriously—I mean every day—when I turned fifteen." Because she didn't have a boyfriend like the rest of the girls in her class. Painting, once again, filled a void.

"So you've had no formal training in art? No classes, no mentors. Nothing," Karena continued.

She was looking at two pictures, one of a man and woman in the midst of a dance routine. The woman was arching backward while the man held her arms, the soft pastel colors blended together like a muted rainbow. Eva had painted this one when she was feeling content.

"Nothing," Eva said. "I know they're not polished or professional. That's why I hadn't bothered to show them to anyone. That and I just never had the time to sit and research who I should be showing them to." She clapped her lips shut as she felt like she might be babbling.

Monica held up a picture, staring long and hard at it. When she slipped it back into the portfolio she looked candidly at Eva.

"I can give you the name of an art agent because you should not be negotiating your own contracts and sales," she said.

Her hair was cut in a sleek asymmetric bob that fit her cool and aloof demeanor as well as the pale gray pantsuit and Stuart Weitzman pumps. Karena had a more subdued look. While just as pretty and intelligent as her sister, she wore a navy blue sweater pencil skirt and a white turtleneck, but her shoes were a fun and whimsical denim material platform that matched the bangle bracelet on her arm. For the first few seconds of their meeting Eva had felt a little under-dressed in her black leggings, coral tank top and thigh length black jacket. She wore red patent leather sandals and carried a red clutch with her portfolio.

"An agent?" Eva asked, bringing herself back to the conversation. "I've never thought of getting an agent."

Karena smiled at her. "You're gonna need one," she said. "Because we love these paintings.

"I really like this one," Monica said tapping the portfolio that leaned against the wall their table was near.

Eva knew exactly which painting Monica was referring to. It was one that Eva had painted after a night at the club. She hadn't been able to sleep, still revved up from dancing three sets in one night. She'd collected twenty-seven hundred dollars in tips that night and was feeling pleased with herself, even though some drunken idiot had reached out and grabbed her tit during the third set. Nadja and her crew of bouncers had not only tossed his ass out of the club, but Eva heard that they'd given him a pretty good beating as a warning for the next time he tried to get touchy-feely.

"I had a lot of energy that night," Eva told her.

"You paint with your emotions," Monica said nodding her head. "It shows. No, it practically screams through every one of your paintings. Whatever you were feeling is right there on paper for all to see, without really seeing you."

Eva felt uncomfortable at the quick and acutely accurate assessment.

"We'd like to show your paintings at the gallery," Karena said. "The sooner you get in touch with the agent Monica's going to refer you to, the sooner we can work on dates and look through all of your paintings to select which ones will be best for the show."

"What? Wait a minute," Eva said her hands shaking as she set them flat on the table. "You want to show my work? You're serious?"

"Yes, we are," Monica answered as she was reaching into her purse to pull out her wallet.

After a few seconds of searching Monica retrieved a card and handed it to Eva. "Her name's Marsha Madigan and she's superb. She's so good I don't like dealing with her sometimes, but you need the very best in your corner."

Eva took the card, still not believing what they'd just said.

"You're very talented, Eva. And now we owe Rico a dinner or something in thanks for bringing you to us," Karena was saying as she wiped her fingers and chewed the last of her beignet.

She'd put the pictures she was looking at back in the portfolio while Eva had been staring like an idiot at Monica giving her the agent's business card.

"We're just friends. I didn't ask him to bring me there to meet you. Actually, he didn't even tell me he knew the owners of the gallery. Just that Lorenzo was his brother," she said, again fearing she was talking too much.

"Really?" Karena asked. She lifted a brow as she glanced at her sister who simply shook her head and pulled out her phone to begin looking at her calendar. "So you and Rico aren't dating?

Because I could have sworn I caught some type of vibe between you two. Definitely a romantic connection."

Eva shook her head immediately. "No romance. No, ah, nothing. I just met him on Friday, which is another reason I'm finding it hard to digest all this. It's happening so quickly."

"Well," Karena said as she picked up her glass. "I believe in love at first sight."

Monica cut in with, "What's your availability this week, Eva? I'd like to look at all of your work on canvas to see if we can formulate a theme for the showing. If you call Marsha today—I just sent her an email telling her that I'm referring a new client, so she's waiting for your call. Once you talk to her, I know Marsha will be calling me first thing tomorrow morning, so I want to have some dates and ideas ready. She'll want to see your work in person, but I'm betting she'll try to meet with you today also. I hope you're available."

Her tone was efficient and no nonsense. This was what she did for a living and it impressed the hell out of Eva.

"Ah, I'm ah, I work at night. I have a real job, I mean. Painting has been a hobby all these years. So yes, I'm available during the day, any day this week," Eva replied.

"Oh you work at night," Karena said. "I could never do that. Especially now that I have Elijah. I'd miss his midnight bathroom runs and questions. What do you do, Eva? In your real job, I mean."

Eva paused. It seemed that everyone in the restaurant went silent, as if they too wanted to hear the answer to that question. Monica had even stopped typing on her phone to look at Eva expectantly for a response. What was she supposed to say? Should she lie? Would they care? How was she supposed to handle this?

Was this the real reason why she'd never tried to be a full-time artist? Was she afraid that the two worlds she'd immersed herself in would mix like oil and water?

"I'm a dancer at the TEASE nightclub," Eva replied before she could ask herself another question, or make another excuse.

It was the truth and it was out there for these two sisters to deal with in whatever way they saw fit.

"You're a—"

"A dancer," Karena said cutting her sister off while her smile spread. "That's why you paint dancers. There's our exhibit theme, Monica. We can call it 'Shall We Dance'."

Monica's lips pursed and after a few heart stopping seconds, she smiled as well. "I like it. What do you say, Eva? Shall we dance?"

Monica lifted her mimosa for a toast. Karena immediately followed suit. Eva, who was still trying to figure out if all of this was real, picked up her glass and moved it to the center of the table until it clinked with the other two.

"I think we shall," was her response, and then she sipped her mimosa and laughed. A giddy and excited laugh that she'd never heard from herself before.

"Since when do you pay for company?" Alex asked about two seconds after he and Renny walked through the door of Rico's hotel room.

"What?" Rico asked, when he'd managed to open both his eyes and realize that his brothers were there and he was standing at the door in his boxers and t-shirt.

"Close the door before you catch a cold," Renny said with a chuckle. "You never were a morning person."

He wasn't. For as ambitious and studious as Rico could be, he had always hated getting up early in the morning, especially on weekends. During the week he had his alarm clock by his nightstand and the alarm on his cell phone to wake him. Last night, or rather sometime in the early morning hours he'd been so pissed off that he didn't want any contact with anyone, so he'd turned off his cell phone. He'd fallen onto the hotel's king-sized bed and lay there until sleep had finally claimed him. After closing the door and walking over to the couch where he plopped down with a groan, he figured that couldn't have been more than two hours ago.

"What time is it?" he asked.

"It's two in the afternoon," Alex told him. "I hope you requested a late check-out."

He hadn't, Rico thought with another sigh. He was certain the hotel had already happily charged him for another night's stay.

"Damn. I was supposed to be home by now," he grumbled.

"Long night with Eva?" Renny asked.

That was the last name he wanted to hear. Especially since it was the only name he'd heard all night.

"Is that what you came all the way over here to ask me? If I got laid last night?" Rico asked, unable and pretty much unwilling to hide the fact that he was groggy as hell.

"No. We're here to find out why our esteemed brother hired a stripper to spend the weekend with him," Alex announced.

Rico was instantly awake, sitting up and staring over to where his older brother stood. Renny was lounged in one of the other chairs in the room, while Alex had a hand thrust into one pocket of his pants glaring down at Rico.

"Who told you that?" he asked, trying like hell to keep his voice even.

"Monica called me the minute she and Karena wrapped up their meeting with Eva," Alex said.

"They loved her work, by the way," Renny said as he used his finger to swipe over his cell phone. "Bree just texted me a few pictures that Karena took during the meeting. She's really talented. Her paintings just about speak to you through every movement."

Rico sighed. "I know."

"You know she's a stripper and you paid her to spend the weekend with you, or you know that she paints with good movement?" Alex pressed.

Rico stood then, dragging a hand down his face. "I'm not having this conversation in my underwear," he told them before walking out of the room.

"Thank goodness," Renny quipped.

Alex still stood brooding. He walked over to the bar and fixed himself a glass of water. When Rico returned he was sitting down across from Renny, glass half emptied.

"You ready to talk now?" Alex asked.

"First," Rico began as he finished pulling a second shirt over the tank he'd slept in, "I didn't pay her to do anything."

He'd put on a pair of sweatpants as well and now sat back down on the couch. "And I didn't know she was a stripper when I met her."

"Where'd you meet her?" Renny asked.

Rico frowned, knowing this wasn't going to go over well, but not bothering to lie in any case. "At a sex club."

"You went to a sex club?" Alex asked, the look on his face saying he didn't believe it.

Rico nodded. "Your friend was the one that invited me. Well, Jackson's brother gave me the complimentary pass. Apparently he owns stock in this place. It's called The Corporation and they cater to any and every need you could have. I went there with the hope of relieving some stress."

Renny chuckled. "I'll bet you did."

Alex gave his younger brother an irritated glare. "So you went to a sex club and you found a stripper. I guess that makes sense."

No, it didn't, Rico thought. Nothing between him and Eva made any sense at all.

"Look, she's a nice woman and a great artist. That's all that matters," Rico told them. "I'm gonna get a shower and head out in the next hour."

"And what about Eva?" Renny asked. "Any plans to see her again?"

"No," Rico replied immediately. "This was just a weekend thing. Tomorrow I'll be back to work and your entertainment will be over."

CHAPTER 8

One Week Later

"You said this wasn't a big deal," Alex stated when he marched into Rico's office late on a Thursday afternoon. "You said you'd just met her and had no plans to see her again. That it didn't matter that she was a damn stripper!"

Rico had looked up from his computer to see his brother enter his office and heard him slam the door behind him. Now, Alex was standing on the other side of his desk, slapping a piece of paper stapled to an envelope and enclosed in a plastic bag down on his desk.

"What the hell are you talking about now, Alex? And what's this?" Rico asked picking up the plastic bag.

"That's what I want you to tell me. What the hell happened in New York last week?"

It was well after seven and truth be told Rico probably should have left the office hours ago. Every night this week he'd been here until at least nine. He'd go home, shower, heat something in the microwave for dinner and fall into bed. The next day he would start all over again. It had become a purposeful routine. Only now his eyes were feeling grainy he was so tired of reading ledgers and reports and staring at his computer. The last thing he felt like doing was trying to read through a plastic bag. Yet, something caught his eye immediately—her name.

Eva.

Rico read the entire note.

"Turn it over," Alex directed as he finally dropped into one of the guest chairs.

There were two pictures, one of Eva dancing in that red outfit and the other of him and Eva standing outside the club that same night.

Rico cursed. He tossed the plastic bag across his desk and rubbed his hands down his face.

"We're not paying her a dime. She's pissed off because I didn't accept her proposition for a threesome that night," Rico told Alex. "It's all bullshit!"

Alex was rubbing a finger over his chin, as he stared at his brother.

"The letter sounds like you did take her up on her offer," he said.

"Oh come on, Alex! Do you really believe I'd agree to a threesome? What the hell type of person do you think I am?" Rico exploded.

"I don't know, man. Why don't you tell me?" Alex shook his head. "Because the brother I know would never have paid for female companionship. Hell, my little brother changed women about as often as he changed the battery in his smoke detector. I can't tell you when the last time I've even heard of you going out on a date, let alone seeing a woman you were with. But I did see this Eva person with you on Saturday and I've gotta say you two looked pretty cozy to have just met."

Scrubbing his hands over his face gave Rico the few seconds he needed to rein in the heated words he wanted to say. How could Alex sit here and essentially say he had no idea what to expect from him? He was his brother and Rico had never given anyone in his family cause to question him. Ever.

"I didn't pay for her," he said slowly, letting his hands fall down to rest on the desk blotter once again.

"But you went to a sex club looking for someone to pay for," Alex stated in a tone that matched the way he brokered a business deal. "So why didn't you pay for her? If that's what both of you were clearly there for?"

"That's not how it was," Rico insisted.

He knew he wasn't explaining himself and hell, he shouldn't have to. Alex should have trusted what he said, regardless of the fact that he'd admitted Eva was a stripper.

"Look, I'm a grown man, Alex. I can do whatever I want, when I want. Especially with my own money."

When it looked like Alex was about to say something in rebuttal, Rico simply shook his head.

"There's never been a day that I haven't taken this family into account. Everything I do, everything I've ever done has been with the company and our family in mind," he continued, telling the absolute truth. Rico had thought so much about his family that there were times he barely considered his own wants or feelings.

"I'm not disputing any of those facts. I'm just trying to figure out why someone would send a blackmail note to my office, with pictures of my brother who may or may not have been involved in some type of orgy," Alex replied.

Rico shook his head. "If I wanted to participate in an orgy, I think I'm old enough to do so without needing anyone's approval."

"That you are. But when your behavior comes back on us, then it becomes my business. Hell, Rico, it wasn't that long ago that we were dealing with that bastard Roland Summerfield and his dangerous plans of revenge. Not only did he try to kill some of us, he tried to destroy Bennett Industries."

"That was years ago Alex and I remember that time clearly. I was the one to call Sam in to help us, remember?"

"Then who's going to help us this time? She's demanding half a million dollars to keep this secret. And you know that once we pay her, she'll want more and more. It'll never stop and eventually, the pictures will surface anyway," Alex continued.

Rico slammed his hands on the desk as he stood. "No pictures will surface because there are no pictures. There are no pictures because I didn't participate in a threesome with this crazy broad!"

"Fine. But something happened this weekend and it's better if you just tell me now so we can face this head on."

Alex was probably right, but Rico didn't feel like answering any more questions or bearing his soul just to keep his big brother happy.

"I went out and enjoyed myself for a change, that's what happened this weekend. Now, if you'll excuse me, I'm going home," he stated.

Rico grabbed his briefcase and stuffed the plastic bag with the letter inside.

"What happens if she sends that letter to dad, or worse, mom?" Alex asked.

Rico was already on his way out of the office. He didn't even bother to turn around before yelling, "I'll handle it!"

"Rico," Alex called to him and Rico heaved a sigh.

He didn't want to turn around, didn't want to see the questioning gaze in his brother's eyes again. Alex didn't understand what he'd done and that was fine, Rico thought. It wasn't for him to understand. But he certainly wasn't going to stand here and be reprimanded.

"What Alex?" Rico said as he turned to face him.

"I'm not judging you, if that's what you think," his older brother said. "I don't like receiving blackmail letters and I don't like not knowing when something is going on with a member of my family."

"Nothing is going on with me," Rico told him.

"Are you sure about that?" Alex asked. "You were in a mood before last weekend occurred. Then when I saw you on Saturday you looked as if you were enjoying yourself for the first time in your life. I even told mom and Gabs that they should have seen you laughing and looking at artwork. They couldn't believe you were spending time in a museum in the first place, let alone laughing about it."

"You told them about Eva?" Rico asked, immediately alarmed.

Alex shook his head. "No. I mean, I told them you were with a very pretty woman who was also an artist."

Rico let out a breath he hadn't realized he'd been holding.

"That's what she is to you, right, since you're not paying her? A woman and an artist?" Alex asked looking at Rico pointedly.

He shrugged, this time because he wasn't totally certain how to answer Alex's question.

"She's a very nice woman who was dealt a bad hand in life. I respect her for how far she's come and I wish her the very best in her future," he said, the words leaving a strange sensation in his chest after he'd spoken them.

"That's all," he continued because the silence was posing too many questions in his mind. "We met and now we're moving on. And like I said I'll take care of the rest."

Alex nodded. "I trust your judgment," he told him. "Always have. But I think we should at least give dad and Renny a head's up about this."

Rico sucked in a breath, letting it out slowly, his fingers gripping the handle of his briefcase. "I guess you're right. Let's take care of that this weekend at mom's dinner party."

"Sounds good. What are you going to do about that letter?" Alex asked, coming to stand by Rico near the door.

"I'm going to find out exactly who I'm dealing with and then I'm going to put that misguided chick in her place," he said before turning and walking out of the office.

It was another forty minutes before Rico walked into his home office. He'd stopped during the ride home to buy himself some dinner because he'd eaten his last microwave meal last night. Tonight's meal did require a real oven, but it wasn't home cooked, a fact that would have made his mother very angry. The thing was, Rico could cook, and he usually did at least two or three times a week. But not this week. He hadn't been able to do much besides work this week. And now, he had this to deal with.

While his food baked in the oven, Rico sat behind his desk and started his computer. While he waited for it to boot, he dialed Sam's number and put the call on speakerphone. He opened his briefcase and pulled out the plastic bag, looking at the note and then flipping it over to view the pictures once again.

"Sam Desdune?" he answered.

"Hey, Sam. It's Rico. You got a minute to talk?"

"Sure. Just getting back from walking Romeo and Juliet. Is everything alright?" Sam asked.

Despite all that was going on Rico caught himself smiling at the mention of Sam's two Great Danes. They were huge and friendly dogs that Rico enjoyed visiting with anytime he was at Sam's place.

"We've got a situation I need your help with," Rico said, typing in his password and pulling up his email.

In addition to giving his father and brother a head's up about what was going on, Rico felt like he needed to tell Eva. Just in case Nadja tried to approach her as well. When they were at the art gallery Eva had added her name to the mailing list to receive the gallery's monthly newsletter. Rico had done the same, and in the process memorized her email address.

"Sounds serious," Sam was saying on the other end of the phone. "Hold on for a second, let me go to my office."

As Rico waited for Sam to get situated he typed in Eva's email address and then stopped, unsure of how to start this message to her.

"What's going on?" Sam asked moments later.

"Alex received a blackmail letter today from a woman that I met last weekend," Rico began.

He pulled his cell phone out of his pocket and snapped a picture of the letter, then emailed it to himself.

"I'm going to email you the letter if your computer is on you can pull it up in a few seconds," Rico told him.

"Are you talking about Eva?" Sam asked. "She's trying to blackmail you?"

"No," Rico replied quickly with a shake of his head. "Not Eva. Another woman."

"Okay," Sam said slowly. "So you met two women last weekend?"

"Can you just pull up your email, please," Rico stated as calmly as he possibly could.

Instead of calming down since he'd been at the office, Rico's mood was just as irritated as it had been before. He couldn't believe Nadja was pulling this stunt and couldn't wait to sit her down for good.

"What the hell?" was Sam's next question? "Who is this woman?"

"After we left the gallery I dropped Eva off at work. I went inside to watch the show and then tried to go in the back to speak to her. This woman, she's like a bouncer there and she tried to swindle money from me as payment to simply see Eva. I was willing to pay that, but then she made another offer—a threesome. Eva came out then and turned her down flat. Eva and I left together and I didn't care that I'd never see or hear from

Nadja again," Rico said, resting his elbows on his desk. "I just don't know why she'd try a stunt like this."

Sam was quiet a moment. "You said she sent this to Alex? Why? How did she even know who or where Alex was?"

Rico paused contemplating that question, then he cursed. "Dammit! She took my business card out of my wallet."

"Uh huh, and she googled your name the first chance she got, found out you were loaded and started planning," Sam deduced.

"Sonofabitch!" Rico cursed again.

"Yeah, I'd call her that myself. But look, don't get too excited about this. Let me do some digging and then we'll put our heads together to see how we'll deal with this."

"I don't want my family hurt because of me, Sam. This can't get out to the press," Rico told him. One of the things that worried him most in his life was letting his parents down. This would be an embarrassment to the entire family and in Rico's mind, more than disrespectful to the people that meant the most to him. He couldn't let that happen.

"That's not an option, man, you know that. We'll handle this woman and we'll do it quietly. Just let me get to work and I'll give you a call back," Sam insisted.

Rico nodded, squeezing the bridge of his nose as he took another deep breath. "Yeah. Okay."

"Don't talk to her, Rico. Don't call her. Don't write to her. No contact until you hear from me. You got that?" Sam asked.

"Yeah," Rico replied again. "I got it."

"And one more thing," Sam said. "I've gotta ask you this."

"Go ahead," Rico said sitting back in his chair.

"Do you think Eva could be involved?"

"No," was Rico's instant response. "When I left her she made it perfectly clear that she didn't want to have anything to do with me. And she's not the type to do this. She's been stripping at that club for all these years to take care of her brother and to put him through college. She's not about to jeopardize her own freedom now. If she was willing to go that far for money, she would have done it well before meeting me. No, definitely no," he stated with finality.

"Okay," Sam said after another quick silence. "Then let me ask you this, do you think this Nadja person would contact Eva about this?"

"No," Rico stated adamantly despite his previous concerns and the email to Eva that he still hadn't composed. "This is about me and my money. It has nothing to do with Eva. I doubt Nadja gives a rat's ass about Eva."

~

"Nadja?" Eva said her name in complete surprise. "What are you doing here?"

"I'm here to see you," Nadja said as she moved past Eva and waltzed into her apartment.

Dressed in slacks, a blouse and boots, the outfit she'd chosen for her second meeting with Monica, Karena and now, her new agent, Marsha, Eva closed her door and stared questioningly at Nadja. She was wearing, as she most often did, jeans, Timberland boots, t-shirt and a denim jacket. When she turned around, still perusing Eva's place, her diamond earrings sparkled in the fading sunlight.

"I didn't invite you here," Eva said. "And I know I've never given you or anyone else at the club my address."

Nadja shrugged. "Doesn't matter. I've known where you lived for a while now. Just never had a reason to drop by."

Eva did not like her answer, but she wasn't in the mood to argue. In fact, she was going to be late for the meeting if Nadja didn't get on with this little visit.

"I don't like unannounced guests," she told her. "Don't make that mistake again. Now, what do you want?"

Nadja smiled. "You got a hot date? Maybe with that sexy ass guy you brought up in the club the other night."

Folding her arms over her chest now, Eva cocked her hip and glared at Nadja. "I didn't bring anyone into the club."

"Oh yeah you did. That rich dude with his fancy clothes and exotic looks. He's what...half Brazilian, huh? Fine as hell that's what I'd say he is."

Eva frowned. "I didn't know you were looking in that direction anymore."

Again, Nadja simply laughed. She lifted a hand and scratched the back of her head too, but still found this situation much funnier than Eva did.

"He's worth looking at," Nadja told her. "In fact, he's worth a hell of a lot more. Which is why I'm here."

"Can you please just get to it? I have somewhere to go," Eva told her with a weary sigh.

"Alright, alright," Nadja said moving closer to Eva as she nodded. "What do you say about getting some of that money the Bennetts have?"

"What?" Eva asked, hoping she did not hear what she thought she'd just heard.

"You know he's loaded. His family's loaded. So they won't miss a few hundred thousand," Nadja said. "So I propose we hit him up for just a little bit of their fortune."

"Are you crazy?" Eva asked. "You are, aren't you? You're out of your damn mind. Look here Nadja, I'm going to tell you this one time only so make sure you're listening. I am not interested in getting anything from Rico Bennett and if you know what's good for you, you'll leave him and his family alone too."

"Oooohhh, is that a threat?"

Nadja was walking closer, until she was standing directly in front of Eva now.

"What are you going to do if I don't leave him alone?"

Eva simply shook her head. "I'm not afraid of you and neither is Rico. So be smart and walk away from this nonsense."

"You don't even know the details," Nadja told her. "Well, let me tell you how this works. Pretty boy Rico's got an older brother that runs the business. Big brother gets a letter with a few pics of little brother hanging out at a strip club, with guess what? A stripper."

Eva frowned.

"Now what happens when there are also pictures of little brother, the stripper and a very sexy female that knows how to please a man *and* a woman? Yeah, I see you're listening now."

Eva was listening. In fact, her heart was beating so fast and loud she thought Nadja and the people next door may have been able to hear it.

"What have you done?" she asked quietly, her voice unable to go any higher because her mind was screaming "no!" so loudly.

"Oh, I'm not finished yet. See, that's why I came to see you," Nadja continued. "I put the ball in motion. Big brother knows little brother was at the strip club. But I'm thinking to really sweeten the pot, you and I should take some pics together. Joe down at the club is on board to help us. He's tall and lanky like pretty boy Rico, so all we have to do is get it on with Joe, together, and then have some pictures snapped. We can easily photoshop them with Rico's face. Then we'll get the big bucks."

"You're an asshole," Eva spat.

Nadja only smiled, lifting a hand to rub the back of her fingers over Eva's jaw. "And you're sexier when you're angry. I've been watching you on that stage for weeks now." She moved closer as she talked, pressing up against Eva, using her other hand to grab Eva's breast.

It happened so fast. If Eva had paused to think about it she may or may not have stopped. But as it was, she was acting on adrenaline alone, feeling embarrassment and anger spewing through her like a brewing storm. Without the space to really pull her arm back, Eva lifted her fist and caught Nadja's jaw with a quick punch. When Nadja stumbled back Eva followed up with another punch to her gut, before she pushed her and watched her fall to the floor.

"You stupid bitch!" Nadja yelled as she scrambled across the floor trying to get up.

"No, you're the stupid one, bitch!" Eva spat, anger clear in every word she spoke. "In addition to admitting to me that you're trying to blackmail Rico and his family with false allegations, the moment you put your grimy hands on me, you committed assault."

Nadja had gotten to her feet and was rubbing the back of her hand over her lip that was bleeding just a bit in the corner.

"Sexual assault, Nadja, that's what you just did is called. If you don't get out of my house right now and drop this bullshit claim with Rico's family, I'll call the police and press charges against you for the assault and I'll tell them everything I know about your little blackmail scheme. Not only will you not get a dime of his money, but you'll be locked in a cage where you belong."

Nadja pushed past Eva as she headed for the door. "Like I said," she told Eva. "You're a stupid bitch."

Eva watched her walk out the door before giving a sigh of relief and shaking the hand that she'd hit her with. Damn it was throbbing now, and so was her heart as she thought about Rico getting that blackmail letter.

CHAPTER 9

Another Week Later

The next week passed in a whirlwind of activity. Rico and Alex had met with their parents and Renny on Saturday night. Beatriz had planned a dinner party to celebrate the day she and Marvin had met. All of the family was present, even Adriana and her fiancé, Parker.

"It seems pretty thin to me," Renny said as he'd sat on the arm of the chair near the fireplace in Marvin's private study.

Rico always loved coming into this room. As a young boy he would sneak in when Alex and Renny were playing with a toy or a video game. The oak desk and the reclining burgundy leather business chair had been humungous to the tiny built Rico. He would climb up into the chair and sit there for endless moments, staring at the papers on his father's desk, wondering what the words said or meant, eager for the day when he would sit behind his own desk and know exactly what to do with those papers and any other business issues that might arise. His future was already mapped out and he'd only been six years old.

As an adult, he still enjoyed the office with its woodsy and all male scent. The masculine furniture made of heavy wood and selected in dark, warm colors was familiar and comforting. There were four large windows on one side of the office with wooden blinds to let the sun in when Marvin felt up to it, and to keep it out when he didn't. Tonight, the blinds were closed and the mood was somber.

"The press won't care how thin it is," Alex offered. "It's a story. The last single Bennett brother spending his time and money in a sex club."

Marvin frowned. "I could think of a worse way to spend your time and money."

The brothers looked at him in surprise. Marvin had always been a straight forward and stern type of father. He told his children what he expected of them and then he sat back to wait until they did it. When they didn't, as Renny, Adriana and now Gabriella could attest to, it could get a little tense. Rico had never wanted to walk that path. Now, it appeared he was not only walking it, but skidding down the road to destruction as if it were actually a race.

"It was a one-time thing and I didn't spend any money," Rico offered. The moment the words were out of his mouth he regretted them.

No, actually, he was tired of saying them, tired of having to give an excuse for making a decision. He was a grown man after all. If he wanted to have sex with a prostitute, he could, he was rich enough. If he'd met a stripper instead and ended up spending the weekend with her, well, that was his prerogative also. He wasn't going to feel guilty and he wasn't going to cower, no matter how he'd handled things in the past.

"Then you got free services," Renny said with a grin. "That proves you're even luckier than I thought."

Rico wished that were true.

"Have we heard from this person since the letter was received?" Marvin asked.

"No, sir," Rico replied. "And I've already contacted Sam Desdune to look into her background to see what type of person we're dealing with."

"Good," Marvin said with a nod. "Desdune is a good guy. I trust his work. We'll wait to hear what he suggests."

Sitting behind his desk, with the rotund stomach he seemed to be proud of as a sixty-three-year-old man, Marvin looked over to Rico. "Tell me about this woman in the picture."

Marvin had a dark tree bark complexion to go with his booming deep voice and southern upbringing. The Bennett children, mixed with Beatriz's golden Brazilian skin tone, all had a distinctive bi-racial look, from their dark eyes and wavy hair, to the lighter toned skin. Their father always said they were a beautiful mix of two cultures and destined to do great things. Rico didn't feel like he was doing so great at the moment, but there was no time for a pity party, no tolerance for one either.

"We met. We clicked and spent some time together on Friday evening. There was a misunderstanding and I had to find her on Saturday. That's when I found out she was an artist and I invited her to Renny's showing," Rico told his father.

"She's extremely talented," Renny added.

Alex, who had been looking pretty stressed by this conversation, nodded his agreement to Renny's comments. "Monica is very excited about working with her. I think they're planning a show for early summer."

That was news to Rico as he hadn't spoken to Eva since she'd walked out of his hotel room two weeks ago. He'd started to email her the night after Alex had given him the blackmail letter, but the draft message still sat in a folder on his computer, never having been sent. He hadn't known what to say to her or how to say it, so he'd typed some words and then declined to send them.

"An artist," Marvin said. He picked up the plastic with the pictures inside and looked at them again. "A very pretty artist who is working as a stripper. That's quite a choice. Do you know why she made it?"

Rico had been sitting on the chocolate brown leather couch, one ankle crossed over his knee. He rubbed his hands over his thighs as he prepared to answer his father.

"She's taking care of her brother. Her parents died when she was seventeen," he replied.

"Really? I don't think she told Karena and Monica that much," Alex said. "How old is her brother?"

"He's twenty. A business student at Columbia," Rico said. "His grades are good and he was offered an internship at Leef & Jenner. He has a lot of potential."

"Hmmm, you sound like you've been doing a little investigating on your own. Or did you learn all of this in the two days you spent with this woman?" Marvin asked him.

His father had leaned back in his chair, folding his beefy hands over his girth, watching his middle son through slightly lowered lids.

This was something else Rico hadn't planned to tell anyone until it was absolutely necessary. He hadn't even decided if that time would ever come.

"No, I looked him up when I came home, called the school and talked to a few of his professors," he said.

Marvin nodded. "You're about offering him a job—a good paying job—so his sister won't have to work as a stripper any longer."

Rico only shrugged because he hadn't been totally sure what his intentions were towards Makai Miller. He'd just made the calls and let the information he gathered sit in a folder on his desk, similar to the way that email to Eva was sitting in his DRAFT box.

"That's what I'd do if I were interested in this woman. And before you tell me you're not interested, let me remind you that this picture is telling a different story," Marvin said with a grin. He held the picture up and flashed it at Rico. "The interest seems mutual."

Renny snapped his fingers and grinned. "I thought the same thing when I saw it, and when I mentioned it to Bree, she was certain there was interest. In fact, she said she saw it at the gallery."

"Karena and Monica have had questions about that too. I've heard them talking, but I'm trying to stay out of it especially since I don't have any information to offer," Alex said.

"There is no information because there is no interest," Rico told them. The moment the words were out he knew they were a lie and he hated the thought of lying to his family.

"Okay," he said after a few seconds of his father and brothers staring knowingly at him. "There might be an interest, but it can't go anywhere. We're from two different worlds and that's that."

He stood then, rubbing a hand down the back of his head. "I'll get a report from Sam and we can talk again about the blackmail situation. The rest...well, there's nothing else."

He'd walked out of the room without waiting for another word from anyone. It was better that way, Rico thought. Getting through the rest of the dinner while avoiding the knowing looks of the Bennett men had taken all the energy he'd had that night. And now, days later, Rico still felt worn out.

Bennett Industries was about to roll out an updated cell phone and tablet duo so marketing and production were in a tizzy, budgets were being ignored and there was general chaos at the office. Today's meeting at the Manhattan office of the marketing firm they'd hired was hopefully going to stem some of this anxiety. It was a late afternoon meeting that Rico wished he'd scheduled for early morning instead. To top that off, Sam had sent him a text at lunchtime, scheduling a conference call. Rico was going to take the call in his car while he drove to New York.

As if on cue, his cell phone rang at that moment. He adjusted the Bluetooth in his ear and answered, "Bennett."

"Hey, it's Sam."

"Hi Sam. How's Karena?" Rico asked.

Another issue that had come up was Karena having to be rushed to the hospital a few days ago. Bree hadn't been able to give Renny too many details about what was going on and so Rico had only received a message that Sam would get back to him when things had calmed down.

"She's doing good. Getting some rest on doctor's orders. You know she's hating that especially since they're working on Eva's new show," Sam said.

Eva was having a show. Rico had learned that information at the dinner party and he was excited for her. He was proud of her. And he still hadn't gotten the nerve to tell her.

"Was it something serious?" he asked.

Sam sighed. "It seems that having a second baby isn't as easy as it was with the first. So we've been doing some different things and she was taking some type of supplement that didn't agree with her."

Oh wow. Rico sort of wished he hadn't asked. The last thing he wanted to talk about was having babies and trying to have babies. But that was probably what happened with married couples. Rico wondered if he would ever be in this position with a woman, or rather his wife. He wasn't getting any younger, but he'd never really thought about having a Rico, Jr. Eva was still young, she should be healthy enough to have babies and…wait, what the hell? He was not driving in this car thinking about having babies with a woman he couldn't even get up the nerve to send an email to.

"Well, I hope she's feeling better," he said to Sam, pulling himself back into the here and now. The realistic and the practical.

"Yeah, she is. I've just been juggling things with her and Elijah. Bree has been coming over to the house to help because Karena doesn't want our parents to know what's going on. To top that off, Lynn and Brice are out of town, so Jeremy's staying with us. It's been stressful to say the least."

Sam chuckled, so Rico joined in. He had no idea what Sam was going through, but a part of him, a very small part that Rico felt like he'd done a damn good job of ignoring all these years, wanted to know.

"But that's not the purpose of this call," Sam added. "I wanted to tell you what I found out about Ms. Nadja Carter."

"Okay," Rico said, feeling mildly better by the change in conversation.

"She has a couple of misdemeanor charges, mostly shop lifting. Born in the Bronx, twenty-four years old. Has been working at TEASE for three years," Sam began.

"What about her finances? Is she desperate for money? A gambler?" Rico asked, frowning, but not surprised by what he was hearing.

"None of the above," Sam said. "Two years of community college, no degree, no certificate, paid via financial aid. Student loan payments are made every month and on time. As well as her car payment and credit cards."

Rico didn't understand.

"Now, here's where it gets interesting. Nadja's current address is on Duane Street in a fourteen million dollar Tribeca loft townhouse."

"What? How does she afford that? Who else has she blackmailed?" Rico asked.

"That's what I'm about to tell you. The house is in the name of Renee Lorminsky," Sam said and then waited a beat. "As in Councilman Bill Lorminsky."

Rico let the names roll around in his mind for a moment before replying, "Wait. What? You're telling me that Nadja lives with Renee Lorminsky. Bill Lorminsky's daughter is gay?"

"Exactly," Sam replied. "And after I went over a few past press conferences and appearances, the last campaign footage and the personal history of Renee Lorminsky, I figured it out. The councilman doesn't know his daughter is gay. Nobody knows."

"Except Nadja Carter. So she's blackmailing Renee too. Take care of me and my bills or I'll tell your father and the world," Rico said, shaking his head.

This should not be an issue in this day and age. With same sex marriages being approved by the higher courts, celebrities, athletes and even preachers coming out of the closet, how could Nadja have created a complete lifestyle by threatening these people?

"I think they're actually in a relationship, so some of the taking care of her, may be coming as a result of that connection and not necessarily a blackmail plot. At any rate, I'm sure this is a situation that Nadja does not want interrupted. Which means—"

"That we threaten her trifling ass the same way she tried to threaten us."

"Bingo!"

The call with Sam and the meeting that had taken two hours, too long, but had been very successful, had Rico in a good mood. This mood had him calling Lucien's and placing a to-go order of jalapeno-crawfish dirty rice, shrimp and grits and Mrs. Marie Desdune's to-die-for bread pudding. The pick-up was quick, and soon he was back in his truck, driving down the familiar streets that would take him to an apartment building in Brooklyn.

He was taking a chance, Rico knew that as he parked his truck and retrieved the insulated bags that the manager at Lucien's had insisted he carry his food in. Rico was certain other carry out customers did not get these type of bags, but the moment he'd given his name for the order and then showed up to swipe his credit card to pay, they'd known who he was. Since Sam and Bree had worked that first case for them, ending in Renny and Bree's marriage, the Desdunes and Bennetts had been family.

It was with the complete confidence he'd been born and bred with that Rico took the elevator and walked down the hallway of the floor where he knew Eva lived. He knocked on the door and waited, expecting her to be there even though he had not called first. He assumed she would share this meal with him and couldn't wait to hold her in his arms one more time.

"Hello," Rico was forced to say with a measure of shock as a guy answered her door.

"Hey. We didn't order anything," the man said.

He was dressed in dark jeans and a plaid shirt, and wore black rimmed glasses that brought Rico's attention to the diamond stud earring in his left ear.

"Makai?" he asked, taking a guess, and praying he was right.

Because if he'd come all the way over here just to interrupt Eva on a date with some dude, Rico didn't know what the hell he was going to do.

"Yeah. Who are you?" Makai asked in return.

"My name's Rico Bennett. I'm here to see your sister, Eva," Rico said wanting to breathe a sigh of relief, but refraining.

Makai stepped aside to let Rico in, and once he closed the door said, "She didn't tell me she was expecting anyone."

"She didn't know I was coming. I wanted to surprise her," Rico said, as he set the food down on the coffee table across from the couch.

"Oh. Well, she's working," Makai said. Then he immediately corrected himself. "She's in the other room painting."

He apparently knew the kind of work his sister did and was guessing that Rico had met her at the club. Well, he had but, he wanted to make sure Makai knew he was not some type of pervert or jerk that had been hanging out at the club waiting to see Eva.

"She told me about you," Rico said. "You're a student at Columbia, right?"

Makai, who had continued to assess Rico with his dark brown eyes and that air of brotherly protection, nodded. "I do."

"And you study business," Rico continued, knowing exactly what this young man was thinking. "I work at a communications and tech company. We're based in Connecticut, but I come into Manhattan from time-to-time for meetings."

Rico had retrieved his wallet from his jacket pocket and was pulling out a business card. "You should give me a call so we can meet and discuss your goals. We may have a place for you at Bennett Industries when you graduate."

Makai took his card and looked it over. "You're the CFO of the company?"

"Yeah," Rico nodded. "I'm really interested in sitting down and talking to you. I think you have a lot of potential."

There was another moment of questioning before Makai was the one to nod. "I'll definitely give you a call," he told Rico.

"Okay, cool," Rico replied, hoping he'd made some leeway with the young man.

He wasn't lying to him, he did think Makai Miller had potential. His grades were good and his professors spoke highly of him. If internships were already coming in from other reputable companies, by the end of the next school year, there would be even more businesses hungry to hire new and young energetic minds. Rico wanted to get first dibs on Makai.

"I'll go get Eva," he said and Rico let out a small sigh of relief at knowing he had passed the brother's test.

It made sense that they were protective of each other, they'd been on their own for so long. They depended solely on each other. Rico couldn't relate to that as he'd always had his family. What he knew without a doubt was that both of them were too young and had too much going for them, for all this pressure and expectancy to be dropped on their shoulders. If giving Makai a job would take some of that pressure away from him and from Eva, Rico was glad to help. And if having one night where she didn't have to prepare a meal could be a step toward assisting Eva, he'd do that too.

Turning to look at the painting above her couch once more, he realized that he was willing to do just about anything for her.

⸎

Why was he here?
She looked a mess.

It didn't matter. She didn't want to see him.

Yet, she didn't tell Makai to make him go away.

"Hi," Eva said eventually.

She'd been standing in the doorway watching him stare at that painting. He looked so damn good dressed in a dark brown suit, his beige tie slightly askew. She'd missed seeing him, which was stupid, since she'd only seen him two days in a row, two weeks ago. Before that she'd never known of Rico Bennett. She wondered now whether she'd been better off that way.

"Hello, Eva," Rico said as he turned slowly to face her. "I was in New York for a meeting that ran late. Got hungry and decided I didn't want to eat alone."

He nodded towards the bags on her table and Eva shook her head.

"You brought me dinner?"

"Yeah, I never bought you dinner when I was here before. My mother would have a fit if she knew that. She's a staunch supporter of taking a pretty girl out for a good meal," he told her.

He was already moving, unpacking containers from the bags. There were paper plates and cutlery, napkins and bottled sodas. The smell was mouth-watering and her stomach churned in response.

"You two have a good meal. I'm gonna head out now," Makai said.

He'd gone back into his room and put on a jacket. "Oh, I'm sure there's enough for all of us. Right, Rico, there's enough?"

Rico paused, then looked over to Makai. "Sure, man. Sit down and join us. I bought a ton of food."

Makai shook his head and winked at Rico. "Nah, I'm cool. You two enjoy. And Eva, you be good."

He had smiled at that statement as he made his way out the door. When Eva turned back to him, Rico was smiling too. "You two aren't funny," she said.

"No. Of course not. But we do want you to eat. So come on over here before the food cools all the way down. They packed it in these insulated bags but in another couple of minutes we'll need to throw it in the microwave," he said.

There was no way to get out of this without being "good" as Makai had instructed. So Eva moved over to the couch and took a seat.

"What did you get?"

He pulled off the plastic lids to show her and Eva moaned. "I love shrimp and grits."

"Good. I wasn't sure, but I decided to go with something I liked and something my mother always enjoys when she goes to Lucien's," Rico told her.

"I hope she enjoys the grits because they're perfect," she said after accepting the container and fork he gave her and taking the first bite.

He took a forkful, chewed, swallowed and agreed. "You're right, they are. I'll be sure to tell her that Lucien's is still keeping up the tradition."

For the next few minutes they ate in total silence. Rico taking a seat in the recliner next to the couch, and Eva keeping her distance. He was thinking and so was she. He didn't know what to say. Neither did she. It was all so ridiculous. They were adults. They'd had sex and now they were having a meal. They could damn sure have a conversation.

"Why did you come here tonight?" she asked him, because there was no sense ignoring the elephant in the room.

He'd just finished his grits and the last of the dirty rice. Using a napkin he wiped his hands and mouth. He put it down and then sat back in the chair, raising his gaze to her.

"There was no place else I wanted to go," he replied.

Eva didn't know what to say to that.

"I wanted to call you to congratulate you on booking the show," he continued. "Actually, I typed an email and I was going to send it to you, but I didn't. It's still in my DRAFT folder."

He chuckled at that, but she didn't find it funny.

Probably because she had a draft text message still on her phone that she'd been about to send him the day Nadja had come to visit her.

"I wanted to contact you too," she admitted. Finished with her food she put the container on the table and folded her legs under her on the couch. "When, ah, Nadja, she came to see me and—"

"Wait a minute," Rico said sitting up in the chair. "She told you what she tried to do?"

Eva nodded. "Yeah, she told me and I told her I'd go to the police and charge her with assault and tell them what she was attempting if she didn't call it off."

He looked like he was thinking about something. No, he looked angry as a muscle twitched in his jaw before he spoke tightly. "Assault? What did she do to you?"

With a wave of her hand Eva said quickly, "She grabbed my tit and I busted her lip."

"You punched her?"

"What? You're surprised I know how to defend myself? I take my clothes off in front of hundreds of men a night, the last thing I need is someone following me out of the club and getting too touchy-feely or worse, violent. So I took self-defense classes right after I started dancing and I carry a blade in my purse. Since she was in my apartment and I was dressed for a meeting I figured simple hand-to-hand was the best form of attack."

This time when he laughed, Eva couldn't help but smile. She liked the sound of his laughter. He looked so relax in that moment, his eyes even twinkling a bit as the smile had spread across his face.

"I'll bet she didn't figure that would happen," he told her when he'd finally regained his composure.

Eva couldn't help it, she was smiling too. "No. She was pretty surprised when I knocked her on her ass. Even more shocked when I told her I'd press charges. But she left and when I didn't hear anymore from her or see her at the club I figured she'd changed her mind." She took a deep breath and sobered a bit. "I'm really sorry that she was going to try and do that to you and your family."

Rico was already shaking his head. "It wasn't your fault."

"If you hadn't met me—" she started saying, but he interrupted.

"If I hadn't met you then I wouldn't be here now. I wouldn't want to kiss you more than I wanted to take my next breath. And you wouldn't have to try and figure out a reason to stop me," he said.

Before Eva could come up with that reason Rico was out of his chair and walking towards her. She clasped her fingers, then pulled them apart, letting them fall beside her on the couch. Should she get up? Run? Call for help?

"Rico," she said.

"Uh huh," he replied as he grabbed her by the shoulders and pulled her up against him. "Your answer is taking too long."

When his lips touched hers Eva knew she was in trouble. How many nights had she dreamed of this kiss? She could close her eyes and remember the soft swipe of the beginning of his kisses. Soft, but confident, persistent and intoxicating. The quick touch of his tongue against hers would come next. She would hold her breath then, like jumping off a diving board and expecting to smack cleanly into the water. But then he would open his mouth, slanting over hers, taking her tongue on a wild and sensual ride of pure bliss. That's when she began to drown, falling and falling deeper and deeper into him, without any hope of breaking free.

The memory frightened her, but this kiss, right here and now, scared the living daylights out of her.

Rico moved quickly, cutting the kiss short only so he could sit her back down on the couch. He knelt in front of her then, cupping her face in his hands.

"Every day," he said, his voice gruff. "Every second of every day, I think about you. I hear your name. I see your smile. I want your touch. Every. Damn. Day."

Eva could do nothing but breathe. Quick and shallow breaths as her body hummed with growing desire, her heart beating a painful rhythm because she knew that no matter how good this felt, it had to be a mistake.

He was already pulling at the hem of her shirt. The extra-large white t-shirt that used to be Makai's before she spilled paint on it and then claimed it as her own. He lifted it over her head, his hands immediately grasping her breasts through the neutral colored cups of her bra. Eva wanted to tell him to stop but damn, it felt so good. His thumbs rubbing over her taut nipples, just before he reached behind her and unsnapped the bra. When her breasts were free he kneaded them both as if they were some type of precious jewel. He stared down at her like he'd been thinking about her as much as she'd been thinking about him.

"Rico," she said his name again. In her mind she could hear it over and over and over again. In the moments that he made her come, the time she felt like she was flying, soaring through the air with pleasure, she would call out his name. "Please."

"Oh yes," he said, leaning in closer. "Every bit of pleasure, my sweet. I'm going to give you every, single bit."

His tongue licked over the first nipple and Eva thought she would spontaneously combust at that very moment. Heat spread through her body like a ravage disease and she grabbed the back of his head to hold him right there. While one hand worked one breast, his mouth sucked the other, until she heard herself whimper uncontrollably. With his mouth still on her breast, his other hand moved to dig below the rim of her sweatpants. She felt like her panties had voluntarily slipped out of his way, leaving the path open for him, waiting for his touch. His fingers were swift and strong as he pushed through the plump lips, sliding easily in the cream her instant arousal had produced. When those fingers delved into her center, pressing gently against her slickened walls, Eva let her head fall back and moaned loudly.

This was so good. In a few minutes he would strip her of all her clothes. He would climb on top of her and take her to a place where only he'd been able to take her before. It would feel so good and so right. She would love it.

And then, it would be over. Again.

She shook her head, but Rico did not stop. His mouth had moved from her breast and was tracing a very heated path down her torso. He'd pulled his fingers from her then, lifting them to his mouth as he looked up at her. He suckled his damp digits while keeping his eyes on her and Eva shifted uncomfortably. She wanted him more than she'd ever wanted anyone in her life. Wanted him inside of her once more. She could ride him again, or maybe he'd ride her this time. Would he take her from the back or put her legs up on his shoulders while he pumped into her? Did it matter? As long as she came. As long as he came. As long as they came together.

"Rico," she said grasping his shoulders.

"I've got you, sweetie. Just relax, I've got you," he whispered, his hands already pushing her pants over her hips, his mouth dropping clever little kisses over her mound.

"No," she whispered and knew he hadn't heard her. "No."

It was louder and more adamant and Rico definitely heard her this time because he stopped immediately, pulled back and looked up to her.

"We can't keep doing this," she replied, pulling her pants back up immediately. "It's not fair to either of us."

"What are you saying?" he asked, his facial expression as surprised as she was that she'd said this.

Eva reached over the chair to find the shirt he'd taken off her. She hurriedly pulled it over her head and stood. "We know this is an impossible situation. So what's the point in us continuing to go over the same issue?"

"I don't care that you're a stripper, Eva," he replied when he'd finally come to his feet. "I just don't give a damn."

Eva nodded. "Because you're now hoping that I'll be a successful artist and I can stop working at the club," she said.

"I didn't say that," he replied.

"But you're thinking it," she told him. "I know you are. I could see it in your eyes when you congratulated me. You think that's the answer to everything."

"I think that's another option for you, yes," Rico said. "But the choice is yours. The choice has always been yours."

"And my choice is to live my life in the way that I have to. Do I hope that people love my paintings? Sure, I do. I'm nervous as hell about the entire show, but I'm also excited and ready to take this next step. But I'm not quitting the club. I made a promise," she said.

"Makai is an adult now. He's doing well in school and he's looking forward to his future. How much more do you think you owe him?" Rico asked her.

"I owe him everything," she said. "I stood between the caskets of my mother and my father, my arms stretched out so that I could touch both of them at the same time and I promised them. Nothing," Eva continued, even when her lip began to quiver, "nothing is going to stop me from doing that. Not even you."

CHAPTER 10

Three Weeks Later

6:30 a.m.
Rico:GM
Eva:Morning to you.
1:00 p.m.
Eva:How's your day going?
Rico:The rollout went well. Sales should be good. How about yours?
Eva:Finished the painting. Took me forever. Thinking about calling it 'All Night Long'
Rico:Can't wait to see it.
6:00 p.m.
Eva:Cooking spaghetti and garlic bread. Kenya coming over.
Rico:Sounds good. Stopping by my parents' house tonight. Hope mom cooked.
Eva:Freeloader. LOL
Rico:No shame in my game.

"Who are you texting and smiling at?" Gabriella asked.

Rico looked up to see that she'd walked into the kitchen where he'd been sitting at the island enjoying a glass of lemonade.

Most times when Rico came to his parents' house, this was the first place he'd stop. It was habit since while he was growing up this room was the hub of the Bennett household. His parents' had a large house on thirty acres of lush grassy land. It had been custom built thirty-five years ago with eight bedrooms, two offices, a home gym and theatre, a pool and his mother's precious gardens. The estate was impressive and Beatriz had spared no expense on decorating it way back then, and whenever she deemed it was appropriate for what she called a 'fresh look'. Still, the kitchen and family room combo was the heart of the home.

The space was warm and welcoming with its wide planked light wood floors, pale gray walls and stark white cabinets. There was a ten foot long quartz island with wrought iron stools on one side. Across from the island were the state-of-the-art stainless steel appliances his mother absolutely needed to prepare all the delicious meals she fed her family, while along one entire wall were floor-to-ceiling windows with a view of the pool. Behind the island was a custom-made oak table that easily seated twelve. They'd shared many family meals here, using the formal dining room for holidays or parties only. On the other side of the table were two couches and two recliners, all centered around the massive rock framed fireplace.

That's where Gabriella was headed after she'd taken a bottled water from the refrigerator. Putting his phone into his pocket, Rico slipped off the stool and followed his sister across the room. He watched her sit on one of the comfortable couches and cross her legs before taking a seat across from her.

"What have you been up to?" he asked when she reached for a book that had been right next to where she'd sat.

The book was now on her lap as she opened her water and took a long drink. Capping the bottle and setting it on the end table she flattened a hand on the book.

"Studying," she told him.

"Studying what this time?" Rico asked.

Gabriella was not only the youngest Bennett child, she was the only one that had taken longer than the four, and in Rico's instance, six years, to graduate college. This was due to her indecisive nature. A factor that also contributed to the 'flighty' reputation she'd earned in the Bennett household.

"You know I'm studying interior design now," she told him, with a roll of her eyes.

Rico nodded. "I recall hearing something about that. So when are you going to be finished with those classes?"

She'd been drumming her fingers over the book, watching him in a way that Rico wished she wouldn't. The last time he'd been in a room with Gabriella she'd told him he was going through a mid-life crisis. He certainly did not want to have that conversation with her again.

"Don't change the subject," she said without hesitation.

"What subject? I thought I was making pleasant conversation. Isn't that what you do while you're waiting for dinner?"

Gabriella narrowed her eyes at him and shook her head. "Mom's not even finished cooking yet."

Rico knew that. He'd peaked into the oven when he'd come into the kitchen and saw the homemade chicken pot pie crust just turning a golden brown.

"I know. That's why I was relaxing until she finished. Then you came in and I figured it would be rude to ignore you," he continued, knowing he was irritating her by evading what she obviously wanted to talk about.

"You can ignore me all you want," she said, "but I'll bet you have no intention of ignoring whoever you were texting."

Rico didn't reply, instead he looked out the window to the early evening sky.

"Was it Eva?"

He frowned because he couldn't help it.

"That's right, I know all about Eva. Bree told me, since you obviously weren't going to open your mouth about her," Gabriella continued. "When really, you should be thanking me for sending you out to find some fun that weekend. If I hadn't given you the kick in the butt you needed, you would have never gone to New York and thus, would not have met her."

She had a point there, but Rico wasn't ready to concede.

"I meet women all the time," he told her.

Gabriella nodded. "Right. You meet women and take them to art galleries and interview their brother for a job at the company, all the time."

"Damn, how did you know about the interview?" Rico asked, then regretted the fact that he was even admitting what she'd said had been correct.

She smiled knowingly. "There are no secrets in this family, Rico. Especially not when it comes to someone's love life.

Hence the reason I don't have one because you all would drive me crazy staying in my business."

"If you don't want us in your personal business, maybe you should take note and stay out of ours," he quipped.

"Oh no you don't," she told him. "That is not even going to work with me. Now, are you going to hire her brother or not? He'll probably do a good job."

"You don't even work at Bennett Industries. So how would you know who would do a good job there or not?" he asked.

She was wearing black sandals with her pink tipped toes on full display. Her foot dangled in the air as she bobbed the leg that was crossed over the other. "Alex told Monica he'd been coming to your office to speak to you and he saw, what's his name? Makai, that's it. He saw him coming out of your office, so he assumed you were interviewing him."

Rico sighed. He had interviewed Makai last week. Eva's brother had called him one afternoon and they'd talked about his future aspirations briefly over the phone. Makai had driven to the office and they'd spent another hour and a half talking about his qualifications and education. Rico had suggested Makai continue with school to get his master's degree and even hinted that there may be some tuition reimbursement available through the company, if he worked there. Makai had seemed genuinely interested, even if he was a bit leery about why Rico was offering in the first place. That meant the conversation had inevitably gone to Rico and his intentions towards Eva. He told the young man exactly what he was about to tell his sister.

"Look, Eva Miller and I are just friends," he said, looking pointedly at Gabriella.

She immediately arched a brow and pursed her lips. "Friends?"

"That's what I said. And before you go on, I'm sure if I went through your phone right now I'd see strands of text messages between you and your 'friends'."

"True," she said. "But I'm almost positive none of my friends have me smiling the way you were when I walked in."

Rico couldn't speak to that. He hadn't seen how he was smiling. He could imagine however, because he did laugh a lot when he was corresponding with Eva. The emails and text messages had started the day after he'd gone to New York for that meeting and ended up having dinner with her. She'd pushed him away again, citing the fact that she believed he was waiting for her to quit her job as a stripper. He'd lied and said he wasn't and then felt like crap the next day because she'd seen through that lie. The first email he'd sent to her was to say he was sorry. Later that same day, after she'd accepted his apology, Rico sent another message asking what she was watching on television. Thus, their daily conversations had begun.

"We're just friends, Gabs. You can leave it alone now," he insisted.

"Are you just friends because she lives in another state or because she's a stripper?" she asked seriously.

Rico wasn't surprised that she knew. Hell, she seemed to know every damn thing else.

"I'm not going to talk about this with you," he told her.

"Why the hell not? I'm a grown woman and believe me I've seen my share of strippers."

Rico closed his eyes, willing himself not to visualize his little sister sitting in a chair with some beefed up male stripper shaking himself in front of her. No, he shook his head as he looked at her again, he definitely did not want to go there.

"Look, I'm just saying that if you're ashamed of her in some way, then that's just stupid. So what, she dances on a pole for a living. If guys like you weren't paying to see her dance on that pole, she wouldn't do it. The way I see it, you're being mighty hypocritical for holding that against her."

"I'm not holding anything against her. It's just not going to work for us," he said.

"Because she's a stripper."

"No!" Rico yelled and then clenched his teeth. "It's not going to work because I said it's not. She also says it's not. We both know our limitations. My world doesn't mix with hers and neither of us are thinking of changing our lives. So we'll just be friends."

It had taken him a while, but Rico had finally accepted that fact.

Gabriella shook her head. She stood and grabbed her book and water. "You disappoint me, big brother. I thought you, of all people, had your head on straight enough to not be so damn stupid."

She'd walked away before Rico could wrap his mind around the shock that she'd spoken to him in that way. He was still sitting on the couch, shaking his head when his mother came in.

"People aren't always what you plan for them to be, Ricardo," Beatriz said as she moved around in the kitchen.

Rico could hear her just fine from where he sat, still he returned to where he'd originally been sitting at the island. He stood there watching his mother move around. Beatriz was still a beautiful woman and looked just as good as any thirty-year-old, even though she would be celebrating her sixtieth birthday later this year.

"I've learned not to expect anything from people," he replied. "It's simpler that way."

He had adopted that stance after the relationship debacle in college, but when he'd met Eva, he'd forgotten. Just for a moment.

"I've never met this young woman but I heard she's a delight," Beatriz continued.

Rico looked at her in question.

His mother shrugged. "Karena was at the house when I visited Bree and the babies. She said this Eva is a very talented artist."

He simply nodded. "She is."

"And yet you're still hung up on her being a stripper?"

"I'm hung up on the fact that she's taking her clothes off in front of strange men every night. How am I supposed to pursue a relationship with someone who does that?" he asked, then ran his hand down the back of his head. He hadn't meant to blurt that out.

"The same way she would have a relationship with someone who went to a sex club with the intention of paying some stranger to have sex with him."

Beatriz said that as casually as if she were telling him what flavor of ice cream they were having for dessert. She hadn't even looked at him while she was talking, but continued taking out the large, piping hot pot pie from the oven.

Rico hated that his mother knew about him going to the club. He was also embarrassed as hell. "That was just one time. I'd never done that before," he said.

"And what's her reason for stripping?"

Rico sighed, knowing exactly what point his mother was trying to make. "Because she was young and she needed to take care of her brother."

"Couldn't she have found another job?" Beatriz continue.

"She did, but it wasn't enough money. She needed to get away from the woman that used to be their foster parent, and she was trying to keep custody of Makai. She moved to New York and you know it's expensive to live there. Then she wanted Makai to have the best schooling, so the money helped them along a lot," Rico told her.

Beatriz came to a stop in front of the island. She lifted both hands, palms up and said, "No strings sex versus working to take care of her brother. Which one would I choose?"

She'd been moving her hands up and down like scales, as if she were really weighing those two options. Rico got her drift and frowned.

Beatriz smiled, then came closer until she could reach up and touch her palm to her son's cheek.

"If you like this girl, then you go for it, son. None of us are perfect, no matter how hard we try to be. You've been so busy doing every little thing you thought your father and I wanted you to do all your life, you've never once done what your heart desired. I'm telling you now because I'm your mother and neither of us are getting any younger," Beatriz said with a little chuckle. "If this is the woman for you, don't let her get away, and don't judge her the way you've always thought everyone was going to judge you."

Rico shook his head. "Mama, you don't understand."

Beatriz touched a finger to his lips. "Oh, I understand, Ricardo. I know my child and I've watched you all these years poking your chest out because you weren't making the same mistakes Renny or Gabriella was. You went toe-to-toe with Alex and even took responsibility for watching out for Adriana. But you never stopped to just be Ricardo. You never trusted that being that man would be enough for us, and for yourself.

"Now, I'm telling you to end this foolishness. If that woman is as nice as I've heard she is, I don't care if she's taking her clothes off. You know how much confidence and pride that takes for a woman to do? She's probably a better woman than some of these college graduates or high-strung business types you usually meet. One thing you can be certain of is that she's loyal and she's independent and damn smart to have achieved all that she has with her brother before she's even thirty years old."

She's independent.

She's smart.

She's loyal.

Rico replayed his mother's words the rest of the evening, until he was home late that night lying in his bed, staring up at the ceiling.

Eva was a good woman. So good that she'd been able to push aside their attraction and just be his friend for these past few weeks. He'd enjoyed that friendship because it was the first real one he'd had in all his life. He looked forward to waking up each morning and hearing from her. He liked knowing how things were going with her and how she was feeling about those things. Rico had shared stuff with her that he'd never shared with anyone else and he thought that she was doing the same with him. Only all of this was being done via email or text message. He hadn't seen her. He hadn't touched her in weeks. What did that mean?

His phone vibrated on the nightstand beside his bed. When he reached over to look at the screen, Rico sighed.

Eva:How did dinner go? My spaghetti was the bomb!

Rico didn't respond to her message. Instead, he closed his eyes, gripping the phone in his hand as he asked himself again.

What did all of this mean?

∞

Rico leaned over, resting his hands on his knees as his chest heaved.

"Get your head in the game!" Renny yelled as he walked by, smacking Rico on the ass.

He cursed.

They were losing and it was his fault.

Whenever they could squeeze in the time, the Bennett brothers met at the local gym to play basketball. Since Renny had married Bree, Sam and his older brother Cole Desdune had been added to the mix. The last couple of months had been filled with schedule conflicts on all of their ends, so this time, their game was more of a twilight activity since they'd waited until everyone was home from work. Tonight, Rico, Alex and Cole were on a team. Sam and Renny declared early on that they could beat the threesome easily. So far, they'd been right, and Rico hated that fact.

Standing up straight, Rico ran back out onto the floor, ready to focus. If they lost this game Renny was never going to let him live it down and Alex was going to be a brooding pain in the ass. So Rico stood near the rim, waiting for Sam to take his free throw, watching that ball and waiting for his opportunity to run it down to the other side of the court.

His head hadn't been in the game, he thought. Renny was absolutely right. Rico hadn't responded to Eva's text last night, or the one she'd sent this morning and he felt like a colossal ass for not doing so. Gabriella and his mother's words kept circling in his mind, while his own concerns continued to rise. He didn't know what to do, or to say and until he did, Rico didn't want to take one more step where Eva was concerned.

"Heads up!" Alex yelled when the ball slammed into the floor right beside where Rico was standing.

"Shit!" Rico yelled and ran to get the ball.

In the next fifteen minutes he ran and dribbled, shot the ball and missed. He cursed and ran some more, got the ball again and missed another shot. Alex gave him a look, while Cole simply took over, scoring a few more points for them. Sam and Renny still held the lead as was clear by their triumphant high-fives and crude taunts. It was just after Sam had bumped into Rico calling him something along the lines of an inexperienced college boy— in much more offensive terms—that a phone started to ring from the bench.

"I think that's me," Sam yelled. His ringtone for calls from Karena was "Fire and Desire" by Rick James. They'd all heard it and had teased him about already.

"You okay?" Alex came over to ask while they had a break.

"I'm fine," Rico replied tightly.

"You don't look fine and you're playing like shit," his brother continued.

"Whatever, I'm not getting paid for this you know," Rico said and was about to walk away, when Sam called his name.

"What?" Rico answered turning around to see Sam running toward him.

He wasn't in the mood for anymore jibes or concerned looks. He just wanted to finish this game and get home to the solitude of his own house. He could sulk much easier there.

"That was Karena on the phone," Sam said.

Rico nodded. "We all knew that."

Sam shook his head. "She just got a call from Eva's agent. Apparently her agent called to check on Eva's progress. Eva answered the phone and was very upset. She told her agent she couldn't talk because her brother had just been shot."

"What?" Rico asked, instantly on alert now.

"Makai was shot," Sam replied. "By a cop."

CHAPTER 11

Chaotic did not seem to be the best word to describe what was going on. Rico and the others had immediately left the gym after Karena's call. He'd begun dialing Eva's cell number the moment he was behind the wheel of his truck. There was no answer. By the time he'd pulled up to his apartment building he was an angry mess, running into the building and slamming his palm on the button for the elevator.

Keys were hastily dropped on the table by his door as he moved through his apartment quickly, heading directly for the bathroom. He turned on the water in the shower, then moved away without getting in. He dialed Eva's number again. He waited until the voice mail switched on this time, but could not find the words to leave a message. Instead he placed the phone on the edge of the sink, turning up his ringtone so that he'd hear if she called back while he was in the shower. She didn't and the shower had been quick. He'd dressed even faster and was just about to head out when his phone jingled from the back pocket of his jeans where he'd placed it.

"Eva? Hello?" he said the moment the phone was at his ear.

"It's Sam. Karena wants to be there for Eva as well. So we're on our way to the city," he told Rico.

"I'm leaving my apartment now."

"Okay. Drive safely, man. You can't help her if you get into a wreck on your way there," Sam told him.

Rico disconnected the call and made his way back down to where his truck was still parked in front of the building. He hadn't even bothered to drive it into the garage. He was on the road in minutes, his mind whirling with all types of scenarios.

Sam said Makai had been shot by a cop. Rico cursed, slamming his hands on the steering wheel before turning onto the highway.

Police brutality was a hot topic these days, with killings of African American men and women happening more and more frequently. The debate over justice and police reform was widely discussed, but so far nothing substantial had changed. Like many Americans, Rico hated any type of injustice and had watched local and national news coverage of such events with as open a mind as he could muster. Sure, there were people on the streets committing crimes, a good number of them African Americans, but did that mean they deserved to die? By the same token, Rico knew from stories that Cole had told them, how the disrespect and distrust of police by citizens, was affecting the cops trying to do a good job. This, Rico felt, put him and no doubt other family and friends of cops in the middle of a growing crisis.

Makai was an intelligent young man, with a bright future ahead of him. Rico prayed for him in those moments and he prayed for Eva. His chest was heavy with worry over how she was dealing with this situation. Makai was everything to her so this was bound to hit her hard. With that thought in mind Rico drove faster, understanding that he may get pulled over and thus have his own confrontation with a police officer, but not giving a damn at this moment.

Less than forty-five minutes later Rico was pulling into the hospital's emergency room entrance. Finding a place to park wasn't easy and finally he ended up in a space that Rico wasn't totally sure wouldn't get him towed. That didn't matter right now. He jumped out of the truck, almost forgetting to grab his keys and ran towards the entrance. If anyone he knew saw him at this moment they would be nothing short of astonished because Rico hated hospitals. He always had. There was no great trauma that he'd endured, simply the fact that he knew people either lived or died here. As he passed through the electronic doors he held on to the fact that the last time he'd entered a hospital, his nieces and nephew had been born.

At the first information desk he found, Rico immediately asked for help.

"I don't have anyone listed by that name," the nurse told him without looking up from her computer.

There were people everywhere, some sitting in the seats lined along one wall and others standing in small groups. Outside an ambulance siren buzzed and two men, who he assumed were doctors in white coats and blue bootie covered feet ran through a set of double doors.

"What do you mean you don't have anyone listed by that name? He's here. I know he is," Rico argued.

He pulled out his phone and checked the text that Sam had sent him while he was driving. Cole was a detective with the Greenwich Police, so he'd reached out to an officer he knew at the NYPD. He'd found out which hospital Makai had been transported to and told Sam where to go.

"Sir," the nurse said again. She was staring at her computer screen and managed to look up once to take a file that was being pushed at her by another nurse. "I told you we do not have a patient listed under the name of Makai Miller. Try another hospital."

Rico cursed. His fists clenched and he was just about to ask for her supervisor when a hand on his arm had him turning.

"Hey," Sam said.

Karena was standing right beside him.

"Come on outside and let me talk to you," Sam continued.

"What? We don't have time to talk. They're telling me that he's not here. Are you sure Cole got the right hospital?" Rico asked.

"Just come on out here where it's a little quieter," Sam insisted and pulled on Rico's arm to get him to move.

At Sam's side Karena clutched a tissue in one hand and used the other to rake her fingers through her hair.

Rico sighed and walked out through the doors he'd just entered, whirling to face Sam the moment they were outside.

"What the hell is going on? Is Makai here or not?" Rico asked.

That's when Rico noticed how somber Sam looked.

"Cole called me back about twenty minutes ago," Sam began. "I'm sorry, man. Makai died on the operating table."

Karena used that tissue to wipe the tears that fell slowly from her eyes as Rico looked from Sam to her and back to Sam again.

"He died," Rico said slowly. "That bright twenty-year-old young man that was going to come and work for Bennett Industries this summer is gone? Just like that."

"I know. It's terrible," Karena said. "I met him only once when he came to the gallery with Eva. It was so obvious how much he loved his sister and wanted her to succeed. Their dedication to each other was just...it was inspiring," she finished.

"What the hell happened?" Rico asked, his temples throbbing as he struggled with his own emotions at the moment.

Sam sighed. "Cole said the officers pulled over a SUV that they'd been on the look-out for when the driver got out and started shooting. The officers returned fire. Makai was the passenger. They were both killed, as was one of the officers."

"Three people," Rico said, shaking his head. "Three deaths because of a traffic stop. Are you kidding me?"

"That's all we know for now. More details are bound to come out once the cops really get into their investigation," Sam said.

Rico nodded. He took a few steps away from Sam and Karena, closing his eyes as he came to a stop. Eva. Her face was all he could see when he closed his eyes.

He turned back to Sam. "Is Eva still here? Do you know where she is?"

Sam nodded. "When we got here one of the nurses told us that the family had gone to the chapel. That's where we were coming from when we saw you. They'd already left."

"I'm going to her apartment," Rico said and was walking away without waiting for Sam's response.

He had to get to Eva now. Nothing else mattered but her. He'd think about the rest later. He'd find out exactly what happened to Makai and decide then what he wanted to do about it, but for now, it was just about her.

✦

It was over.

Eva went into Makai's bedroom and slammed the door. She fell onto his bed face-first and sobbed brokenly into the pillows. They smelled just like him which only made her tears come faster and her chest heave more painfully. If she had bothered to turn on a light and looked around she would see him everywhere in this room. From the posters of NBA and NFL players to the desk in the corner with every bobblehead character from the newest Star Wars movie lined across the edge as if they were ready for some futuristic battle. It was all Makai.

He loved sports, playing and watching them. Movies were his next favorite, sci-fi or action. He read a lot, but listened to music even more. He loved eating collard greens and creamed spinach, but hated brussel sprouts with a passion. When he was twelve, he'd come home from school crying because he was short and stocky and the boys talked about him in gym class. That next summer, as if the Almighty had heard his plea, Makai had gone through a growth spurt and by the time he returned to school in the fall he'd grown four inches and had slimmed out considerably. He'd kept that tall and slim physique by playing ball or running. He hadn't had a girlfriend since Patricia, almost seven months ago. He wanted…

Eva shook her head, because it was no longer what Makai liked, had gone through or what he wanted out of his life. He was gone now.

The call had come just as she'd stepped out of the shower. She'd been painting all day long, trying like hell not to think of the fact that Rico seemed to be ignoring her. Over the last few weeks she'd grown accustomed to talking to him via text or email. Kenya had even inquired that she'd never known Eva to check her email on her phone as much as she was doing now. Of course, she'd told Kenya that was due to the upcoming show and needing to correspond with her agent on a daily basis. That hadn't been a total lie, but each time she opened that inbox she'd looked specifically for his name. Who would have ever thought she would become friends with a man like Ricardo Bennett? Things had happened so fast with them and yet, they hadn't seemed to happen at all. There would be no romance between her and Rico and she'd accepted that, taking the friendship as the best they would get. He hadn't answered her text last night or her 'good morning' text from this morning.

She'd had to move on, going into her room to paint a new picture, letting her mood guide the moment. A break for lunch sometime in the afternoon and then she'd remained in that room until almost nine that night. Her dinner had been a slice of bread smothered in peanut butter that she'd finished as she'd gone into the bathroom to take a shower. She'd felt relaxed and ready for bed as she dried off. Then she'd slipped into her pajamas and went out into the living room to get her bed ready. That's when her cell phone rang.

Her heart had skipped a beat at the thought of it being Rico. But he never called her and she never called him. She'd answered, not in a million years thinking that it would be an emergency room nurse calling to tell her that her brother had been shot.

It was a traffic stop, that's what one officer said when she arrived in the emergency room. She'd barely managed to get the words out when she'd dialed Kenya's number, but her friend had immediately responded that she would meet her there. They'd demanded to see Makai immediately. Instead, a man in a suit had come over and ushered them into a smaller room, down the hall from the main waiting room. That's where they were seated when the first nurse came to see them.

"He's being taken into surgery," she said to Eva when Kenya had all but pounced on the poor woman. "He sustained three bullet wounds, one to the shoulder, one in the thigh and one in the abdomen. He's lost a lot of blood, but the surgeons are working on him now and I'll come back with an update as soon as I know something."

Her name was Gwen and she'd walked over to Eva, taking her hand in hers as she spoke softly. Eva had only been able to nod as worry and fear had clogged her throat. Kenya, on the other hand, was not nearly as calm and made sure everyone in the emergency room knew that. Eva had sat in that chair for almost an hour, rubbing her hands together, lowering her head and whispering the same prayer over and over again.

"Not him, Lord, please, not him. Not tonight. Not this night. Please."

Over and over she said the same words as she began to rock back and forth. It was chilly in the room and she'd only worn a short sleeved shirt. It had taken all her coherent thought to put on a bra and shoes before grabbing her purse and leaving the house, so her outfit was actually her pajamas. Eva didn't care, all that mattered was Makai. He had to walk out of the hospital, he simply had to.

But he hadn't.

Her eyes were puffy and irritated from all the crying, but she couldn't stop. Makai was dead. He would not come home again. He was gone because the shot to his thigh had ripped through his femoral artery and he'd bled to death on the operating table.

They'd let her go into another room to see him because when Gwen had returned to deliver the news Eva had fallen to the floor, screaming that it wasn't true. This room was super quiet and warm, as if it were made comfortable just for Makai. Kenya had stood to Eva's right, while Gwen stayed near the door. Makai lay there with blood on his neck and face. She couldn't see anything else because of the light blue sheet they'd used to cover him. His eyes were closed and he looked as if he were sleeping, but Eva knew that he'd never wake up again.

"Not tonight," she whispered, turning her face to the side so that she could suck in air and exhale.

Rolling onto her side Eva pulled her legs up into a fetal position and continued rocking. Makai was gone.

Tonight. He'd died tonight.

She couldn't think of anything else.

So when the door opened she didn't hear it. When it closed quietly she didn't bother to move. And when his strong arms wrapped around her, picking her up from the bed and sitting her in his lap, she didn't speak.

Rico held her tight, kissing her forehead as he whispered, "I'm so sorry, baby. So very, very sorry."

She grabbed his shirt, clenching the material in her hand as she looked up at him through tear-blurred eyes.

"He died tonight," she said, her voice sounding weaker than she'd ever heard it before. "Ma…Makai died tonight."

Rico nodded. "I know, sweetie. I'm sorry. I know he's gone."

He was kissing her forehead again, his arms going tighter around her now. Eva shook her head. She pulled on his shirt and made him look at her again.

"My parents died tonight. All those years ago on this night, they were taken from me and from Makai. And now…"

She couldn't speak another word, the tears came too quickly, the pain pulsed too deeply.

Six days later.

"Did you see Nadja in the church? Now she knows that's the last place her trifling ass belongs," Kenya said.

She was lighting a cigarette as she talked, and took a puff, breathing out the first streams of smoke as her statement echoed throughout the room.

Eva had a headache. She'd had one every day since that night at the hospital. However, in the days following that Rico had been there with a glass of water and aspirin. He'd stood next to her, holding her hand at the funeral home and when the funeral director had asked for a check Rico had written one. She had life insurance and she'd been sure to say that immediately, but the funeral director was not going to wait until the policy had been processed and for the insurance company to issue her a check. So Rico had paid for it, and she'd let him because her meager savings account was not prepared for a hit like that.

He'd stayed at her apartment every night, holding her in his arms and letting her know that it was alright for her to sleep. That he wasn't going to leave her.

To their credit, Kenya had been there every day as well, as were Sam and Karena. Monica and Alex had stopped by too.

"After that stunt she tried to pull, I can't believe she had the nerve to show her face. Did she say anything to you?" Kenya asked.

Eva had been sitting by the window, staring out at the traffic on the street, her thoughts on their own track. Kenya was still talking. It seemed she'd been talking non-stop this week. After a second of trying to figure out what her friend had said, Eva replied, "Yes. She expressed her condolences."

"The nerve!" Kenya continued. "I still don't trust her. You know she saw Rico there. What if she tries that blackmail stunt again?"

"She won't," Rico said.

He'd been in the kitchen with Sam and Karena unpacking all the food that had come from Sam's parents' restaurant. She would have to remember to send them a card, Eva thought. She had lots of cards to send out.

"How do you know that for sure? People like that don't change their stripes," Kenya quipped.

"I paid her a little visit explaining that it would be in her best interest to drop any ideas she had of getting money from the Bennetts or bothering Eva again," Sam said, coming into the living room to take a seat on the couch.

"But you never know," Kenya insisted.

Sam shook his head. "I think she'll think twice before trying again. Her home life will be at stake if she doesn't."

"It's done, Kenya. I'm not worried about her anymore," Eva stated.

Kenya took another puff from her cigarette. Eva watched her. Kenya had given up smoking five years ago.

"Well, I'm going to change and go downtown to join the protests. You should think about showing up, Eva. They've been out there since the shooting and a statement from you would be good," Kenya told her.

"I don't know," Eva said.

"What do you mean you don't know?" Kenya asked. She'd already stood and was going to retrieve her purse from the table where she'd put it down.

"I just left my brother's funeral, Kenya. The last thing I want to do is be around a lot of people," Eva replied.

Kenya held the cigarette between her fingers now, pointing toward Eva. "Those 'people' are out there to show their support of you and all that you're going through."

"Maybe we should talk about this tomorrow," Rico suggested as he'd come to stand by Eva.

"Tomorrow won't change what happened," Kenya continued. "That cop shot and killed Makai and I don't care that he did have the nerve to bring his sorry ass up in here yesterday!"

Eva had known that would come up. She'd been dreading talking about what had happened just moments before she'd left the house to go to the viewing.

"I agree with Rico, Kenya. Why don't we all talk about this tomorrow?" Karena suggested. "Today has been such a trying day already."

Kenya apparently was not trying to hear that and Eva watched with growing concern.

"Nobody cares what his guilty conscience has to say. He killed Makai and that's the bottom line. I hope they toss him in jail for the rest of his life!" Kenya yelled.

Everyone in the room looked at her, but no one spoke again. Eva figured nobody knew what to say. Kenya had been there for Eva, always. Since the day they'd met there had been nothing that Eva had gone through that Kenya wasn't there to support her with. And through the years Kenya had come to love Makai as if he were her own younger brother. All of this meant that Eva could definitely relate to how Kenya was feeling. She was hurt and grieving, and for that reason, Eva decided to keep her voice level and calm as she spoke.

"I don't want to join the protests, Kenya. I was actually thinking of pleading with the public to go home and get on with their lives," she spoke slowly, her hands shaking just a little.

"Are you crazy? Was I at that hospital by myself? Did you not see what that cop did to Makai?" Kenya asked, shaking her head in disbelief.

Eva remembered. She doubted that in a million years she would ever forget the sight of her brother lying dead with blood on his neck and face on that bed. She also hadn't forgotten the night she'd learned of her parents' death. The hollow burning in the center of her chest was identical. Still, she couldn't forget the sound of Officer Alfred Peterson's voice as he'd spoken to her yesterday afternoon right here in her living room.

"I want to extend to you my deepest sympathies," he'd said, holding the flat cap he'd snatched from his head the moment he entered the apartment in both his hands.

"I know that I'm probably the last person you want to see or hear from right now, but I had to come," he'd continued.

Eva had looked to Rico in question, wondering why he'd opened the door and let this man into her home. The officer's picture and bio had been splashed over every news channel, local and international, since the night of the shooting. He'd been hailed a good cop, giving twelve years of service to the NYPD. He was a father and a husband and a devoted member of his

Baptist church. In other words, he was not a killer. Yet, Makai was still dead.

Rico had held her hand while Sam and—who Eva would later learn was Sam's brother Detective Cole Desdune—had stood near the door.

"I don't understand," she'd said with a shake of her head.

"I know," Officer Peterson replied instantly. His hands continued to twist that cap, ringing it tightly. "I don't either. I mean, I was there and I know I shouldn't be here. My union reps and my lawyer advised against it and so did my captain."

He was shaking his head too. "But I couldn't stay away. I couldn't not tell you how sorry I am that things turned out the way they did."

"That you killed my brother," she said slowly as if they all needed to remember that fact.

Peterson nodded. "You're right. I fired the shots that killed your brother and if I could take it back, I want you to know that I would. Things just happened so quickly. There were so many shots and—"

His shoulders heaved then and the man that stood more than six feet tall with slightly graying hair and thick lips, dropped his head and cried. Cole had stepped up behind him, placing a hand on his shoulder.

"I'm just sorry," was the last thing Officer Peterson had said to her.

He'd walked out of the apartment with Cole going behind him.

"I don't understand," Eva had said again, her eyes filling with tears as she looked to Rico.

"The police department's investigation is complete," he told her. "They're having a press conference in a couple of hours. Cole's friend on the force thought you should know what they're going to say first."

Eva hadn't wanted to know, and then she knew she had to hear it, for Makai's sake. She let Rico lead her to the couch where she sat down. Rico sat beside her, still holding her hand, while Sam came over to kneel in front of her.

"On a Thursday afternoon a police report was filed stating that the record store where Makai worked was robbed by three males," Sam said. "Early Friday morning, three dead men were found in an alley, two blocks away from the music store. Responding to a tip that the murders were related to the robbery, Officers Benile and Peterson pulled over the truck registered to the manager of the record store. Other officers had tried contacting the manager by phone and had gone to his apartment earlier in the day. An APB was put out on the manager and his vehicle. Benile and Peterson were heading back to the station when they pulled up behind the truck and ran the tags. They initiated the stop, watched the truck pull over and then that's when all hell broke loose."

Eva had been openly crying by then.

Sam continued, "The store manager was driving the truck. As soon as he stopped, he jumped out and began shooting. The officers fired back. At some point Makai, who was the passenger in the store manager's truck, stepped out. Peterson saw the gun in Makai's hand and continued firing."

"No," Eva had said. "Makai does not have a gun. Why would he need a gun? He was a good student, a good man. He wouldn't need a gun."

Sam nodded. "The gun didn't have any bullets in it," he told her. "But it was seen in Makai's hand and found near his body at the scene. Bullets from that gun had also killed one of the men they'd found in the alley. The other bullets from that murder were from the gun the store manager had."

"Wait a minute," Eva said, lifting a shaking hand to wipe her face. "Just wait a damn minute. You're trying to tell me that my brother and his store manager killed the guys that broke into their store and then the police killed them?"

Sam sighed. "I'm telling you that the official report is going to state that the officers were justified in returning fire. Officer Benile was killed in the line of duty."

"So was Makai!" Eva yelled.

"I know that, Eva. I know," Sam continued. "The statement is going to be that the shooting was justified and the police department has officially ended their investigation. The district attorney may look into it to see if Officer Peterson should be charged."

"He shouldn't have come here," Eva began saying. "He should not have come here."

"No, he shouldn't have," Sam said. "He resigned from his job and may still be criminally charged. Coming here wasn't a good idea at all. But Cole said he was insistent."

"He wants me to forgive him," she said.

Rico gripped her hand tighter. "You don't have to do anything you don't want to, Eva. You let him say his piece and that was very kind and brave of you."

"I don't want to forgive him," she told Rico. "I don't want to and I don't have to."

Still, Eva had tossed and turned all night hearing Officer Peterson's words and thinking about what the police said had happened. They could be lying, she wasn't naïve enough to believe otherwise. But what if they were telling the truth? Would Peterson have come to her house if that wasn't the way things had happened? She didn't know and her head had been pounding by the time she'd awakened this morning. Hours later, she was still feeling awful and really was not in the mood to go back and forth with Kenya.

"To answer your question," Eva said to Kenya. "I'm not crazy. I'm just tired. I'm hurt and I don't know what really happened that night. But I'm at least willing to admit that at this point, we don't know enough to go out on those streets and shout that this was an unjustified shooting."

An instant chill came over the room and Eva stood because she knew this was about to get ugly.

The cigarette still burned between Kenya's fingers. "Justice needs to be served whether or not it's a cop or a junkie on the street that did the shooting," she said. "Cops aren't above the law and it's time we stopped acting like they were."

"I'm not saying they are," Eva replied. "But justice goes both ways. What about that guy that was killed in the alley with the gun that Makai was holding? Doesn't his mother deserve justice for her son's death? You're so ready to go out and kill a cop or have him thrown in jail for the rest of his life, what if Makai being killed was justice for that woman's child?"

"You're being ridiculous and irrational. He was *your* brother. Ever since the first day I met you all you've ever talked about was taking care of him and making sure he had a bright future. Now, you're ready to sell him down the river just because of what some cop tells you. That's bullshit, Eva and you know it!"

"It's not bullshit. It, unfortunately, is our reality. Nobody deserves to die, not by another's hand. If Makai was involved in something illegal that included murder, then how do I go out there and protest with all those other people that he was unjustly killed? How do I defend the circumstances that led to his murder and stand on moral ground that he should still be alive? If you can do that, Kenya, that's fine. But I don't know if I can. And that doesn't mean I didn't love my brother. I loved him with everything I am. I gave him every opportunity. He didn't have to work at that record store and he didn't have to be carrying that gun."

"He should be alive," Kenya said, shaking her head. Tears streaming down her face.

Eva shook her head, her shoulders trembling as her own tears had quietly begun to fall again. "I wish he was," she whispered. "I wish to God he was alive, and that my parents were still alive. There's a huge hole in my heart and my life now. I don't know what to do now that none of them are here. But I can't bring them back and I can't make excuses for whatever Makai might have been doing. I can't and I won't."

CHAPTER 12

Four Weeks Later

Rico had been in back-to-back meetings all day. A result of rescheduling everything for the time he'd spent with Eva last month. It was where he wanted to be, where he *needed* to be. Now, he was paying the price.

Exhausted did not accurately describe how he was feeling, which was why he'd declined his mother's offer of meatloaf and mashed potatoes—one of his favorites—for dinner. Instead he'd come straight home after his last meeting had wrapped up at close to eight at night. Sometimes when he came home in the evenings Rico would enjoy a glass of wine while he prepared his dinner. Tonight, it was a cold beer while he stood staring into the refrigerator attempting to find the quickest meal he possibly could. He'd removed his suit jacket and his tie was hanging in some awkward fashion around the collar of his partially unbuttoned shirt.

The doorbell rang before he was able to find a suitable meal and Rico let the stainless steel door of the refrigerator close with a muted clap. He took another gulp of his beer as he walked through the living room and across the short foyer to answer it.

"Hello," she said, a smile spreading slowly across her face.

Rico's smile came much quicker and was probably broader as he replied, "Eva, what are you doing here?"

She was gorgeous in a grid print black and white dress that flirted seductively over her mid-thigh and thick heeled black shoes with straps that winded up and around her ankle. Her natural hair—the hair he loved to see—was twisted in some fashion on one side. The rest was a medium sized afro of full springy curls, a lighter shade of brown than he had seen her with before.

"I figured it was my turn to find your home address and show up unannounced," she answered.

It was good to see her smiling, he thought as he continued to stare at her. Correction, it was good just to see her.

"Is it okay? I'm not disturbing you am I? Oh, I'm sorry do you already have company?" she asked looking down at the beer bottle in his hand.

Rico shook his head. "Come on in," he told her, moving aside so she could do so.

When she walked past him she smelled like fresh soap and berries. It wasn't a scent he was used to picking up from women, but when the woman was Eva, it simply worked. He closed the door and turned to see her standing in the foyer, her small yellow purse hanging on one shoulder, dangly banana earrings catching his gaze. She seemed so bright against the sterile background of his stark white walls.

"I was just...I mean, I came because...wait a minute," she said holding up a hand and shaking her head. "Let me start again."

She shifted her feet and unnecessarily adjusted the purse strap on her shoulder. Clearing her throat she began, "I came back to Hartford yesterday to see the headstone that was just placed on Makai's grave. I wanted the funeral in New York because that's where Makai had spent the majority of his life. But he needed to be laid to rest with my parents. They're all together now." She took a shaky breath and sighed.

"I'd planned to drive back to New York today, but then I wanted to thank Karena and her family for all their support, so I ended up here in Greenwich."

Rico nodded. "And Sam gave you my address."

"Yes, he did. I didn't ask for it. Even though I have a check for you in my purse. The insurance company finally paid on the policy, so I can reimburse you for the money you put up for me."

"You don't have to do that," he told her. "I was happy to help."

"No," she said. "That's what I paid all those premiums for. I want to pay you back, but I'll admit I was just going to mail the check. That was before Sam pulled me aside today when I was about to leave and told me I should stop by since I was this close. Karena chimed in that it would be rude of me not to at least come over and offer to buy you a drink. But I see you've already started on that."

She tilted her head toward his hand and Rico looked down at the almost empty bottle. "Why don't you join me for another?" he asked with a suddenly dry mouth.

Why did she look so naturally pretty as she stood there not exactly telling him that she wanted to see him, but being only feet from him anyway? He wanted to hug her, to hold her against his chest and feel her warmth spreading throughout him the way he had when he'd stayed with her in New York. Each time he'd seen she was about to break down as she made arrangements for her brother and at night when she cried herself to sleep. He'd enjoyed that feeling, had even been getting used to it. Then, it had been time for him to leave. She didn't ask him to stay once the funeral was over and after her confrontation with Kenya she'd wanted to be alone. Now, four weeks later, he ached to touch her again.

She followed him into the kitchen, setting her purse on the black granite counter as he went to the refrigerator.

"Would you like a glass of wine?" he asked her.

She shook her head. "I'd like the same thing you're drinking, if you don't mind. It's been a pretty rough day, or days," she told him.

Her smile was there, but it wavered a bit as her eyes clouded over slightly. Rico took the beer from the refrigerator and opened it for her. He came around to the side of the counter where she stood and handed it to her.

"I won't say that it'll get easier," Rico told her. "I've heard so many people say that during times like this, but I don't actually know that it does, so I won't say it."

Eva took the beer from him and drank. Her eyes closed as she swallowed and when she finished she set the bottle down on the counter. "I don't know that it will either," she said softly. "I hope it does, but," she paused and shrugged. "I don't know."

"I want to help it become easier," Rico said without knowing why or how he would do such a thing.

When she didn't speak, he set his bottle on the counter too and put his hands on her shoulders. The material of her dress was so cool, but the heat from her body filtered through and he swallowed hard.

"Every day I want to be there, to hold you when you cry, get you a beer when you're thirsty, rub your back when you're tired."

The words simply flowed from his mouth. He'd never said them before, not in his mind or in the emails and text messages he'd sent her. This was the first time they'd surfaced and they sounded so natural. They felt so right.

She looked down briefly, then lifted her gaze back to him. Licking her lips she shook her head and then gave a nervous smile.

"I'm not the type of woman that dates a man like you," she said.

"Don't be ridiculous," Rico replied immediately. "I mean, look, I know how things started out with us and I was an ass. I know that now. No, I knew it then but I wasn't willing to accept that you...you are the exact type of woman a man like me needs."

"I was going to say that I'm not the type of woman that dates a man like you but who gives a damn about types," she told him with a chuckle. "I like what you said better."

He smiled. "We're always hit or miss, aren't we?"

"It seems that way."

"I don't want it to be that way anymore," he said. "I want candlelight dinners in fancy restaurants, quiet evenings at home in front of the fire, calls in the middle of the day just to say, 'I love you'."

Tears filled her eyes but when Rico attempted to hug her she flattened her hands against his chest. She blew out a breath and tried to keep those tears from falling.

"I never thought about any of that. Not in all my adult years," she said. "I went from high school student to surrogate mother in a matter of months. But every day I believed that God had a plan for me. I believed that by dancing for money and not having sex for money, I was walking the path that was laid out for me. I did everything I could for Makai, everything but save him when he needed to be saved."

She took another breath, this time releasing it slowly, her fingers rubbing softly over his chest.

"When that nurse told me he'd died, one of my first thoughts was 'what do I do now?'"

She touched Rico's tie, holding it in one hand, rubbing her fingers over the small white polka dots.

"You live, Eva," Rico said. "You go on and you live."

She nodded. "I know. Just like I did before."

She smoothed his tie down and looked up at him, touching her fingers lightly to the line of his jaw.

"But no, not like before, Rico," she whispered. "I didn't know you before. I didn't know that I could paint a picture and people—art professionals—would like them. I didn't know that there could be another plan for me."

"You are so much more than I ever thought," Rico said, his heart more full than he'd ever felt before.

He was in love with her. It seemed so simple to admit that now, but in the weeks since he'd known her, he never entertained the thought.

"You didn't think you could be with a woman like me, a stripper," she told him.

"I was a fool," he admitted.

"No," she said with a shake of her head. "You were honest. I think you've spent all your life being honest and up front with people, so much so, that you do the same with yourself. Only this time, you had to realize the same thing that I did, that there could be another plan."

She looked at him tentatively then, as if she knew what she'd said was right, but she was wondering if he were going to be smart enough to agree. Rico had never considered himself unintelligent.

"Let me make you happy, Eva. Let me make up for the weeks we lost," he said pulling her closer to him. "Please."

She shook her head, but reached up to wrap her arms around his neck. "How about we both try to make each other happy?"

He smiled. "I think I can handle that."

Rico hugged her close and tight, loving the feel of her in his arms once more. He rubbed his hands up and down her back, while hers smoothed over the back of his head. They stood there for what seemed like endless moments, holding each other, silently committing to something neither of them had planned for when they met that first night at The Corporation.

"Spend the night," he said on impulse. "I want to hold you all night and wake up with you in the morning."

Eva pulled away from him then and Rico was alarmed to see the fresh tears streaming down her face. Using his thumbs he wiped them away.

"I'll spend the night," she said when he had opened his mouth to speak. "But I want you to make love to me until the morning. Can you do that for me, Rico?"

He could and he did.

It began right at that moment in his kitchen when he'd kissed her. A long, slow, seductive kiss that had her weak in the knees. She'd kept her arms around his neck, holding on not only for her life, but for his too. They'd both been so lost in who they thought they were, that when the time came they'd been terrified of letting those two people become who they were meant to be. She wanted that now, desperately, hungrily, she wanted to be with Rico.

When his hands had brushed at the hem of her dress, moving it upward so that he could grip her ass, she'd moaned against him.

"I want you," he'd growled against her ear.

"I want you, too," she'd replied, stroking her tongue over his lobe.

"Right here, right now," he continued and pushed her panties over her hips.

"Yes," she whispered, moving her legs so that he could push her panties down and then stepping out of them.

He lifted her up at that point and Eva wrapped her legs around him. She loved clasping her legs around him, holding him securely to her, knowing that in these moments he could not get away. He set her on the counter and her legs fell away from him. The granite was cool to her bare skin, but when he undid his pants and released his thick erection, she warmed all over. Reaching down she touched him, taking his full length in her hands.

"I've wanted you since that first night. It was the music," she told him. "I remembered thinking that any man that could sit and listen to classical music and let me dance to that music was going to be pretty fantastic in bed."

He chuckled then, dragging his hands up her thighs, his thumbs finding her clit and rubbing slowly over the tightened bud. Eva sucked in a breath as she opened her legs even wider to his assault.

"I loved watching you dance that night. I'd seen you in the lounge and liked the way you smiled, the way that short dress wrapped around your body," Rico said.

He licked his lips after speaking and Eva moaned, wanting that tongue on her right now. Her hips arched in response to her thoughts and he smiled knowingly.

"Tell me what you want, baby," he said. "Tell me exactly what you want me to do and I'll do it."

Eva had worked in the industry where there could be an 'anything' goes type of mentality about sex, but she'd never actually experienced it. So talking dirty, or even asking candidly for what she wanted from a lover had never crossed her mind. Today, however, with the heat of his thick length in her hand and his fingers slipping seductively between her wet folds, she felt totally uninhibited. The fact that it was Rico, the guy she hadn't wanted all these weeks, the one that had acted as if he couldn't offer her anything but sex, but had continuously shown up to support her in her personal life, made it feel natural to tell him what she needed.

"Your mouth," she whispered. "I want your mouth on me, Rico. Now!"

He obliged and her hands slipped from his sex without warning as he bent down and licked the nub his finger had so expertly stroked. She bucked instantly, her head falling back as she flattened her palms on the counter behind her and lifted up to him. He cupped her buttocks, bringing her closer to his mouth like he had a bowl of delicious cream he was about to drink. He was an expert, or his tongue was perfection, she couldn't figure out which, but when her thighs trembled, her release ripping through her like a hurricane, Eva realized she didn't care. Whatever he was she wanted all of it.

Rico pulled away from her quickly, lifting her off the counter and lowering them to the floor. He lifted her legs, dropping her ankles on his shoulders and thrust his complete length into her. Eva screamed. She was full and wet and eager for another release. Rico, apparently was too. His thrusts came fast, his hands flattening on the floor behind her head as he leaned down over her. Harder and faster, deeper and deeper still, he plunged into her and Eva could swear the room was spinning. Or was it her? Had she been whipped into a funnel, twirling around with each stroke he made, riding the exhilarating wave of pleasure? She had no idea and dammit, she didn't care. It was just so good she did not want him to stop. Ever.

He did stop however, but only when her body had convulsed, his going tight and still as they climaxed together. It took a while for them to catch their breath and to finally get up off that kitchen floor, but they did. They showered and then lay in his bed after Rico had fixed them ham and cheese sandwiches.

"I resigned from TEASE," she said when they lay in the darkness of the room.

Rico was quiet for a moment, a few very long moments, and then he asked, "Are you sure that's what you wanted to do?"

"Yes," she replied instantly. "It is."

He did not speak.

"Makai never wanted me to work there. He wanted me to paint full-time, to make something out of my art. He said that's what my parents would have wanted me to do," she told him.

"Is that true?" he asked.

Eva took a breath. "My mother loved to watch me dance. She said I had a natural talent. When I started painting, her and my dad said the same thing, that I was a natural. They never doubted that I would do one or the other, or even both when I grew up. In a sense, I did. I danced at TEASE and I painted at home. I didn't let them down," she said, her voice shaking.

"No," Rico said turning over so that he could look down on her. "You didn't. You should believe that with all that you have become. You did not let your parents or Makai down. They loved you very much."

She nodded. "And I loved them. I lost them," she said sadly. Then she reached up to cup Rico's face in her hands. "I love you and I'm going to hold on to you for as long as I can."

He leaned in then, kissing her softly. "I love you, too, Eva. And I'm going to hold on to you even longer."

Rico wasn't in as good a mood as he'd expected after having spent the night with Eva. They'd awakened together early the next morning and she'd fixed them omelets overflowing with all the vegetables she could find in his refrigerator and the Swiss cheese they'd had left over from their sandwiches the night before.

"You need to go grocery shopping," she told him when she'd opened the freezer and saw all the microwave meals he had in there.

"They're just for back-up," he said defensively. "I normally cook."

"Good," she'd quipped. "Because I like home-cooked meals. I can do my share, but taking turns would be nice too."

He'd warmed instantly at her words and their implication. "Does that mean you're moving in?"

She'd paused then, finishing her glass of orange juice. "It means that I'm not as sad as I thought I would be returning to Connecticut and now that I'm committing to my painting, I can actually work from anywhere. So, I guess I'm saying that I think I may start looking for a house to buy. A place where I can have a formal studio to work in and maybe a room big enough to dance sometimes. I don't know, I've just really started thinking about this new direction I'm going in."

He'd kissed her on the forehead, not wanting to push, but more than eager to start looking for a house with her. With the dawn, had come more realizations for Rico. He was ready to spend his life with her. Was he crazy for that? He didn't think so. Had this all happened pretty fast? Hell yeah, but then not fast enough. He'd wasted enough time second-guessing and denying in this relationship. He wasn't about to waste any more.

"That sounds like a good plan," he told her. "And since today's Saturday, we can drive around and see what might be on the market."

She'd frowned then. "Not today. I have to get back to New York."

"What?"

"I hadn't planned all this when I left, Rico. I have to go back and get things situated there. I have to find a real estate agent, pack and make-up with Kenya," she said.

"She's still angry with you, huh?"

"She's still grieving," Eva said. "I know how that feels."

"Sam said the district attorney won't have an answer until the end of the month. How will you feel if they don't press charges against Officer Peterson?"

"I don't know," she'd replied honestly. "I can only take this one day at a time and those days will be much easier if I'm not holding grudges and praying for some sort of revenge. I want the truth of what happened to be revealed, whatever that truth may be."

Rico nodded. "I agree with you."

She hadn't been very optimistic about Kenya feeling the same way, but she was certain that their friendship would survive. Rico, on the other hand, wasn't sure he wanted to go another day or two without seeing her. And he certainly did not want to meet his parents at the country club to talk about possibly having Adriana and Parker's wedding there. He'd agreed to that weeks ago, when he was still in denial about what he really felt for Eva, and try as he might all day long, he couldn't come up with a good enough reason to cancel.

Gabriella couldn't make it because she had some type of conference to attend this weekend. Alex and Monica were out of town. Renny and Bree were busy with the triplets and Adriana was in L.A. auditioning for a part in a movie.

"You're the only one left that Adriana will even partially listen to," his mother had said over the phone. "Just meet us there at seven and we'll do a quick walk through to see if it fits her vision."

"How am I supposed to know what her vision is?" Rico had asked.

"You know what she doesn't like," his mother said. "All you have to do is tell her if you think she'll like it or not. She'll never just take me and your father's advice."

Rico had to admit his mother was right about that. Adriana would want a younger view of the wedding venue, so he'd agreed. Now, he was driving to the old stately country club. He'd dressed in slacks, a button front shirt and a navy blue blazer because the club had a policy of men wearing jackets any time they visited during the evening hours. He parked his truck and walked around to the front entrance where his mother said she would meet him. When she wasn't there, a staff member greeted him instead. The woman, dressed in a dark skirt suit with a gold pin bearing the club's crest on her right lapel, escorted him further back into the building and down a long hall. Finally she opened a door and Rico stepped inside.

"Surprise!"

A room full of people yelled and Rico thought he'd lost a couple years off his life they'd startled him so badly.

"Happy Birthday!" Gabriella said coming up and hugging him tightly. "You're officially an old man now!"

Rico hugged his sister, accepting her sloppy kiss on his cheek as he declared, "Forty is not old."

His birthday was on Monday, but that didn't stop what looked like over a hundred people from coming out to celebrate tonight. He couldn't believe it as he was ushered further into the room.

"Welcome to the forty and over club," Alex had said when he hugged him.

Monica had hugged and kissed him, wishing him a happy birthday just as Karena, Bree and Marie Desdune. Lucien and Cole had hugged him, giving their wishes and Renny clapped him on the back making some silly remark, also about Rico being over the hill. Finally, his parents approached him.

"Happy Birthday, son," his father had said after a tight hug. "You're gonna love this stage of your life."

Rico wasn't so sure. Already he'd almost lost the woman he loved and stood by her as her brother, someone Rico had met and admired, had been killed.

"Happy Birthday, Ricardo," his mother said when she hugged him.

"I'm not speaking to you," Rico joked with her.

She looked beautiful as always in a beige pantsuit, her hair pulled back from her face so the diamonds at her ears could sparkle.

"Oh nonsense," she said, making a playful swat to his arm. "I only did what Gabriella told me to do."

"What? This was her idea?" Rico shook his head as he looked across the room to see his baby sister smiling and chatting with people. He couldn't help but love her, even though later he'd vowed to wring her neck.

Almost two hours had passed where Rico enjoyed a delicious meal and more well wishes from people at the office, guys from the gym and of course, more of his family. His father's brother Charles and his wife Joanna, had come from Baltimore for the party, along with his mother's aunt Olivia and a man that looked young enough to be her son Leonardo's age. He hadn't seen these family members often so it was good to catch up and humbling that they'd all thought enough of him to come out tonight.

There was just one person missing from this enjoyable celebration.

"We're going to sing happy birthday and have cake in a few minutes," Gabriella had come by his table to tell him, before disappearing again.

As hostesses go, Gabriella was one of the best. She hadn't sat down for one moment, but was busily moving about the room making sure everything went smoothly. Rico had to give it to her, the black and white decorations and the southern cuisine were his favorites. She'd known him well enough to plan a party that fit his personality. Yet, she'd had no idea that all he'd really wanted to do to celebrate his birthday this year, was to spend it with Eva.

He'd texted her twice since arriving at the party, but she hadn't responded. He'd been trying not to worry, but he wanted desperately to hear from her. Now, he was going to have to smile through the happy birthday singing and the cutting of the cake before he could step outside and call her.

A DJ had been playing music that people were sporadically dancing to, so when that music stopped, Rico and a few of the other guests looked up to the front of the room. A spotlight had appeared in the center of the dance floor and all the other lights went dim. When a huge cake was rolled into the middle of the floor Rico smiled because he knew the retro Mickey and Minnie Mouse cake design was all Gabriella's idea. She loved going to Disney World and had even made Rico take her there last year for her birthday because she'd been depressed about her lack of career choice and he'd made the mistake of offering to cheer her up. It was sort of a private joke between them and he'd looked around the room for her to acknowledge her thoughtfulness. He'd have to get her something pretty special for her next birthday.

Rico had been so busy looking for Gabriella that he hadn't immediately noticed the woman that came to stand in the spotlight. The one that was dressed in all white, a big white rose adorning her short curly hairstyle. He noticed her the moment the music started again. The slow, blues-like notes of an instrumental song. When she began to dance his smile spread wide, his heart so full he thought he would burst.

Eva danced to the music as if it were composed just for her. She moved across the entire dance floor keeping everyone in the room mesmerized by her fluid movements. She reminded him of the painting in her living room, the one of the dancer that had reached out and touched his heart. His gaze followed Eva's bare feet as they touched the shiny wood floor, her strong legs as they lifted and carried her back and forth, her arms as she held them high, and let them sway to the rhythm. The voluminous white skirt moved around her like the wind and when she did a run and jump into the air, stretching her legs and arms out fully, in perfectly symmetrical lines, he stood up and clapped loud and long.

She turned to him then, as if she'd waited for that moment. The dance continued, but she moved from the dance floor, skirting around each table until she came to his. For a minute he felt like that first night when he'd met her as he'd sat in that chair and she'd danced between his legs. She was just a little further away from him this time, but she danced, just for him. He knew that with every move, every turn and when the song finally came to an end and she did a move that landed her on her knees directly in front of him, the room erupted in applause.

Rico grabbed her up in his arms then, standing and spinning her around, smiling up at her feeling happier than he had in his entire life.

"I love you, Eva Romaine Miller," he said before kissing her. "I love you."

She'd wrapped her arms around his neck. "I love you, Rico. You and this moment, I love so very much." She kissed him then and moved to whisper in his ear, "Always, Rico. You will always be in my heart."

The Rumors Series
Rumors
Revealed

Sexy Paranormal

The Shadow Shifters
Temptation Rising
Shifter's Claim
Seduction's Shift
Hunger's Mate
Passion's Prey
Primal Heat

Wolf Mates
The Alpha's Woman
Her Perfect Mates (coming Sept. 2016)

61161196R00190

Made in the USA
Charleston, SC
17 September 2016